PRAISE FO

The Belly

"The characters in this novel will dance r imagination! Cameron's representation …neteenth-century Chicago is rich and evocative, and the whispered echoes of old New Orleans in Dora's fragmented memory left me hoping this author goes there with her next novel."

—Brenda Rickman Vantrease, author of *The Heretic's Wife* and *The Mercy Seller*

"A beautifully written page-turner with characters that leap off the page, *The Belly Dancer* transports readers into an exotic and sensual world within a world, as plucky but initially naïve Dora Chambers fights Chicago society's conventions and her husband's indifference to discover, in the thrall of the Egyptian Theatre, a passion beyond her wildest dreams. Will she risk security and society's approval to live what many would think a dissolute life? Cameron keeps us guessing until the end. I loved it . . . (and picked up a few useful tips about seduction in the process!)."

—Lynette Brasfield, author of *Nature Lessons: A Novel*

"*The Belly Dancer* is a must read for everyone who was ever tempted to peek under the tent when the dancing girls came to town. Cameron brings the Chicago World's Fair to life in a richly woven tale of scandal, seduction, and the dance that has captivated audiences for centuries."

—Anne Thomas Soffee, author of *Snake Hips: Belly Dancing and How I Found True Love*

continued . . .

"I just finished reading DeAnna Cameron's *The Belly Dancer.* What a fantastic read! Cameron's protagonist, Dora Chambers, must perform a tension-filled balancing act between the two very different worlds in which she finds herself. The socially restrictive sphere of Chicago high society and the wondrously sensuous environment of Cairo Street and the Egyptian Theatre at the Chicago World's Fair of 1893 are brought to vivid life here. This is a cleverly plotted story in which the worlds of belly dancers and Lady Managers collide, forever altering the way Dora defines herself. *The Belly Dancer* kept me riveted, turning the pages right to the climactic close."

—Natasha Bauman, author of *The Disorder of Longing*

"A terrific historical tale that proudly salutes the nineteenth-century suffragette movement leaders and their everyday troops while also affirming society is so much stronger when barriers of specifically group aimed restraints are limited." —*Midwest Book Review*

"The 1893 World's Fair was a marvel, and in her debut, Cameron uses this backdrop to demonstrate one woman's view of herself. Society is forever altered because of what she learns in the lush, sensual, and exotic world of belly dancers. With a strong and vibrant picture of the era and a feminist approach to history, Cameron makes statements about women's rights and society's constraints." —*RT Book Reviews* (★★★★)

Titles by DeAnna Cameron

THE BELLY DANCER

DANCING AT THE CHANCE

BERKLEY BOOKS, NEW YORK

THE BERKLEY PUBLISHING GROUP
Published by the Penguin Group
Penguin Group (USA) Inc.
375 Hudson Street, New York, New York 10014, USA
Penguin Group (Canada), 90 Eglinton Avenue East, Suite 700, Toronto, Ontario M4P 2Y3, Canada (a division of Pearson Penguin Canada Inc.) • Penguin Books Ltd., 80 Strand, London WC2R 0RL, England • Penguin Group Ireland, 25 St. Stephen's Green, Dublin 2, Ireland (a division of Penguin Books Ltd.) • Penguin Group (Australia), 250 Camberwell Road, Camberwell, Victoria 3124, Australia (a division of Pearson Australia Group Pty. Ltd.) • Penguin Books India Pvt. Ltd., 11 Community Centre, Panchsheel Park, New Delhi—110 017, India • Penguin Group (NZ), 67 Apollo Drive, Rosedale, Auckland 0632, New Zealand (a division of Pearson New Zealand Ltd.) • Penguin Books (South Africa) (Pty.) Ltd., 24 Sturdee Avenue, Rosebank, Johannesburg 2196, South Africa

Penguin Books Ltd., Registered Offices: 80 Strand, London WC2R 0RL, England

This book is an original publication of The Berkley Publishing Group.

Cover design by Judith Lagerman.
Interior text design by Kristin del Rosario.

PUBLISHING HISTORY
Berkley trade paperback edition / April 2012

Library of Congress Cataloging-in-Publication Data

Cameron, DeAnna.
Dancing at The Chance / DeAnna Cameron.
p. cm.
ISBN 978-0-425-24559-0
1. Women dancers—Fiction. 2. Ambition—Fiction. 3. Theater—New York (State)—New York—Fiction. 4. Triangles (Interpersonal relations)—Fiction. 5. Success—Fiction. 6. Broadway (New York, N.Y.)—Fiction. I. Title.
PS3603.A4495D36 2012
813'.6—dc22
2011023859

PRINTED IN THE UNITED STATES OF AMERICA

10 9 8 7 6 5 4 3 2 1

ACKNOWLEDGMENTS

To everyone who helped make this novel possible, I am deeply grateful for the support and encouragement. I am especially indebted to my agent, Ellen Pepus, for her invaluable advice and guidance, and to my editor, Jackie Cantor, for her tireless enthusiasm and hard work.

I also offer special thanks to Trav S.D., a vaudeville expert and author of *No Applause—Just Throw Money: The Book That Made Vaudeville Famous,* for reading early portions of the manuscript for accuracy.

Other early readers who offered comments and thoughtful questions that contributed to the final manuscript include Kas Sartori, Claudia Alexander, Jenny Brown, Michele Stegman, Sue Swift, Diane Beaumont-Rice, Margaret Batschelet, Bella Street, Bronwyn Stuart, Meg Benjamin, Susanne Dunlap, and Susan and Harry Squires.

I am also thankful for the community and assistance of the writer networks associated with the Romance Writers of America and the Historical Novel Society.

ACKNOWLEDGMENTS

With sincere appreciation for their help and support, I offer my thanks to the caring staff at Laguna Beach Books, especially owner Jane Hanauer, Lisa Childers, and Danielle Bauter. And to the always inspiring Merry and Dallas Colvin, I thank you for your generous encouragement and friendship—and for hosting so many wonderful belly dance parties at your exotic oasis of a shop in Long Beach.

To the kind and attentive staff at the Foothill Ranch branch of the Orange County Public Library, I thank you for the Silent Room. It was a wonderful discovery during the writing of this novel, and a much appreciated resource.

To my friends and family, I cannot express how fortunate I feel to have you in my corner. Your constant encouragement means so much to me.

To my baby girl, Chloe, thank you for all the gummy smiles and long naps. And most importantly, thank you to my amazing husband, Austin. I couldn't accomplish any of this without you.

One

NEW YORK, 1907

FOR A FULL HALF HOUR THE STAGE MANAGER SAT on a stool near the footlights, his fingers curled on the hooked head of his cane, silently watching the vaudeville players at morning rehearsal. Not a single word of correction or praise passed his lips, not even the typical complaint that a minute be cut from one bit or added to another. Harland Stanley was biding his time.

But now, as Pepper MacClair hunched against a white gazebo set piece with her knees pulled to her chest and the hem of her black cotton frock skimming the top edge of her boots, she watched the man pummel the heel of his steel-braced foot into the boards, not once, but three times in a brutal call for quiet.

In an instant, the music stopped, the voices fell away. This was why they were here, the reason the scrawled note had been tacked to the call board telling performers and stagehands alike they were expected on the stage. No exceptions, no excuses. Even the wardrobe mistress was sitting upon a crate, tugging her needle and thread through a ripped seam on an extra-large pair of green plaid trousers.

Jimmy, the opening-act juggler, roused himself from beside the piano, the brim of his bowler clenched between his fidgety fingers. "Mr. Stanley, before you say anything about that *Variety* notice, I'd like to say in my defense that it was hardly raining plates upon the stage. It was one plate, sir, only one."

The stage manager raised his palm. "I am not concerned with your dropped plate, Mr. Jack." He turned to Marvani, the magician. "Nor am I concerned with the dove that seemed to disappear beneath your cape until it escaped by way of your sleeve." He turned to the Shorty Shakespeareans, a troupe of thespians measuring between three and four feet tall. "Neither will I remark upon certain forgotten lines from the *Midsummer* scene, except to say it was most unfortunate that these events—and others—were witnessed by the only critic to visit The Chance Theatre in well over a year. Shall we leave it at that?"

The stage filled with murmurs of shame and sheepish agreement.

Pepper watched her fellow players in disbelief before scrambling to her feet. "No," she declared. "We should not leave it at that."

She searched for a supportive nod from any quarter, but no one met her gaze.

Except Stanley, who stared back with a hateful glare. "I suppose you would prefer I make light of these errors? Or lie and say such mistakes don't matter?"

"No, but what you might say . . . You could say . . ." She did not know what he should say, only that what he had said was frightfully unfair. The day the critic appeared had been an awful day at the theater. Another stagehand had quit, the third that month, and a ventriloquist with two weeks left to his contract had gotten himself arrested for disorderly conduct during the dinner break. The shuffling backstage had taken a toll, as Stanley was very much aware.

He smiled and watched her fluster.

"You could say the notice was undeserved," she blurted at last.

"Undeserved, Miss MacClair?"

"Yes, very much undeserved." Fresh conviction swelled within her. "You could say it was untrue. That we are not a 'band of vaudeville fools, misfits and deviants.'" She was quoting the portion of the notice where the critic had poked fun with the phrase, alleging it to be more apt than *Vaudeville Stars, Marvels and Delights*, the show's title since The Chance Theatre had opened its doors sixteen years before.

Stanley pounded his cane like a gavel. "I will not be lectured to, Miss MacClair. Not by anyone, and certainly not by a seamstress."

His words cut, though not as deeply as did the muffled laughter behind her. She shot a look over her shoulder and saw Beatrice Pennington's froth of white-blond curls at the edge of the crimson curtain. Her dance partner was already dressed in their Dancing Dolls costume—the snug black bodice that covered little more than a corset and the black tulle skirt that dropped to the knee. Beside her, Trixie Small, the third and youngest member of their trio—a girl of a mere sixteen years—stared in horror at the stage beneath her feet.

Pepper ignored them. "I am a dancer now, Mr. Stanley, and have been since the start of the season, as you well know."

"Seamstress, chorus girl, it hardly makes a difference. May we move on to the business at hand?"

She would have pressed him, forced him to admit the wrong, if she had not seen the message implicit in the expressions of those around her. The others wanted her to stop. Jimmy and Marvani. The dog trainer and the wardrobe mistress. Even the stagehands. She read the meaning in their dodged and downcast glances: If Stanley preferred to ignore the notice, they did as well.

She plopped down against the fake gazebo's step and crossed her arms over her chest.

"Thank you," he said with false sincerity and turned to the others. "I have called you together to say that Mr. DeGraaf will not return this week as planned, and it is with deepest regrets that he has advised me his convalescence will extend indefinitely."

Disappointment tinged the air. The sickness that had kept the theater's owner away had seemed a blessing at first. A welcome reprieve from the old man's booming Dutch curses and nightly rants. But now that The Chance had been left solely in Stanley's tight-fisted charge, even Pepper was eager for DeGraaf's return.

The marquee and playbills still read *James P. DeGraaf Presents*, but for the past five months it had been the stage manager filling the show's slots, and he was doing it with one embarrassment after another.

Last week's headliner had been the worst yet. The man sang Irish ballads so maudlin and morose that more than one patron fled mid-act with a hanky pressed to her nose. The singer had taken it as a source of pride, even crowed backstage about his "keen ability to stir the soul." Pepper had to clasp her hands to keep from smacking him silly. Only a simpleton called a bit that sent the audience fleeing from the seats a success, but if he did not know that yet, he likely never would. He was a lost cause, and as far as she was concerned, so was Stanley.

"So you are still in charge," she said. "That is the big announcement?"

"No, Miss MacClair. Mr. DeGraaf's son will be stepping in during his father's recovery."

Robert DeGraaf was returning to The Chance? The old man had sent his son off to a Cambridge college on a sweltering September morning more than three years ago, and the younger DeGraaf had not stepped foot in the theater, even once, in all that time.

The boy had never spent much time at The Chance, but the veterans knew him well enough. "How can a young man reared in classrooms and drawing rooms know anything about running a theater?" "When has he ever showed an interest in his father's business?" "What good can he possibly do?"

Pepper held her tongue. The complaints about Robert were not new, and they had never been fair. He could certainly do no worse than Stanley. She, for one, welcomed the change, and it had nothing to do with her feelings for the younger DeGraaf. Absolutely nothing at all. Robert had promised he would come back for her. No matter what anyone said, he was keeping his word.

"When is he expected?" She could see instantly that Stanley saw through her casual tone.

"Soon, Miss MacClair. I am sure it will be soon. Mrs. Basaraba, there is one more matter concerning Wardrobe."

The woman looked up from the trousers in her lap and peered over the rim of her spectacles.

"The new headliner will need a gown for today's performances." He paused and pulled a watch from his vest pocket. "She should arrive within the hour."

The wardrobe mistress's eyes widened. "Impossible! I have three pairs of breeches to finish, and the trainer's coat to mend."

"We have no choice. Her trunk was damaged in transit. I'm sure you can manage something. You always do." And with that, he maneuvered himself to his feet, gripped his cane, and dragged his lame leg back into the shadows of the wings.

The others drifted away as well. Pepper remained. She watched Mrs. Basaraba staring into her lap.

"Mrs. B?" Pepper stood, tossed back the mass of chestnut curls she had roped into a loose braid, and approached the woman who had been her mother's assistant before Bessie MacClair had died and for whom Pepper had worked as an assistant before Stanley gave her a second chance at the stage. "Let me help."

The woman patted at the crown of thin black hair rolled into a halo around her head and released a sigh that could have come from the very tips of her dainty brown boots. "No, bubbeleh, I think no. You have the show."

Pepper settled onto the crate beside the woman, and with a friendly nudge said, "Curtain is an hour off yet. You might be surprised how much I can do in an hour."

• • •

A GUST, UNSEASONABLY COOL FOR THE MIDDLE OF APRIL, caught Pepper as she emerged from Wanamaker's department store, sending the hems of her plum velvet coat and the frock beneath flapping against her limbs. She beat down the unruly skirts, but judging from the disapproving glare of a passing matron, not before exposing a scandalous portion of the black-and-white ringed hose she had inherited from an old pirate act.

"Oh, cheer up. They're only stockings."

The old woman sniffed, pushed through the swinging door,

and disappeared into the cavernous shopping emporium beyond.

"High hats," Pepper grumbled and fussed her garments back into place. She plunged the bag of sewing needles and new thread she'd purchased for the wardrobe mistress deep into her coat pocket, pulled her black bowler low on her brow, and set off for the vaudeville venue she called home.

It wasn't far. She could already see the upper floors over the tops of the streetcars and horse-drawn carriages that choked this part of Broadway at East Ninth Street. From this distance, The Chance Theatre looked like its old self, as grand as it had been when she and her mother arrived on its doorstep, hungry and penniless, thirteen years earlier. Everything had glistened then: the crown of spires at the roofline, the oval windows that ringed the fifth floor like a string of pearls, the orderly arched windows along the third floor. She had gazed up that first day, grabbed hold of her mother's coarse wool skirt, and asked if it was a castle, this place where they were to live. Bessie MacClair had patted her daughter's hand and said, "No, lass, not a castle. Just a theater."

Her mother had been wrong about that. The Chance was not just a theater. It had been a glorious vaudeville theater that Mr. DeGraaf had built into one of the very best on Broadway.

But that had never meant much to her mother.

Pepper melted into the morning crowd, dodging the mucky puddles left from the overnight rain, the reeking residue of horses, and an erratic automobile whose top-hatted driver seemed to mistake the horn for the brake.

No, it was not a castle. But despite the debris collecting in its corners and the grime creeping into the crevices of its brick walls, despite the rust gnawing at the edges of the electrical sign that rose from the third floor to the fifth, it was still a theater. And once it pushed through this slump, it would be glorious again.

It could even happen today. A fresh bill, a fresh start. She squinted to make out the headliner's name spelled out in small electrical lights on the marquee above the main arch. *Madame Bizet?* She repeated it aloud—perhaps the sound would knock loose a memory. But no. Another unknown. Dangling beneath the lights, a hand-painted sign read: *A Most Exquisite Talent. A Parisian Singing Sensation.*

Pepper hoped so. The Chance needed a sensation. She glanced a block farther down Broadway. Already the door to the kinetoscope parlor that had moved into the old cabinetmaker's store was propped open, taking in business. A flashing electrical sign read: *Automatic Vaudeville.*

"Hardly," she muttered. Coins dropping down a metal chute for a peek of flickering black-and-white photographs was not vaudeville. Everyone knew proper vaudeville was a stage with a curtain, with people and props and easel cards, with music and dancing and applause. It was the amusement that had flourished along this part of Broadway before the circuits swallowed all but the hardiest of independent theaters or muscled them into oblivion. All that was left was the rowdy music halls along the Bowery and the circuits' own lavish venues uptown, with little in between.

Mr. DeGraaf said it was only a matter of time before the tide turned. People would tire of paying a dollar, sometimes two, at the big-time stages. If the songs were good and the jokes funny, people would come, he would say, and that was what the theater delivered, five shows a day, six days a week.

Now that Robert would be in charge, she had no doubt better times were ahead, both for her and for The Chance.

She breathed in the earthy aroma of roasted peanuts and followed the scent to a vending cart parked in front of Abernathy's tavern. A grumbling in her stomach was reminding her she had not eaten before the meeting. She was about to pay her nickel for a bag when a fine black carriage stopped beneath the theater's marquee. The ticket window would not open for another half hour, yet the driver hopped down and pulled open the cabin door. Pepper ignored the aproned man shoving the paper bag of salted nuts at her and watched a gentleman in a black overcoat emerge from the carriage.

The sight stopped her cold. Though he was turned away, she knew that profile. The sharp angle of the cheek and upward tilt of the chin. That lean, athletic frame that had not changed so much in three years. It was Robert, she had no doubt.

She was on the verge of calling out when another man alighted from the carriage. The elder DeGraaf? No. This man was trim and silver-haired, certainly not the corpulent Dutchman with the wide halo of frizzy dark hair.

Who was it then?

The two men disappeared into the theater.

"Peanuts, miss?" The vendor shook the bag at her again.

She waved him off and hurried toward the theater's main door, pausing only briefly at a skinny flight of metal stairs climbing the building's north wall to the fifth story. That was where she should be headed. She knew Mrs. Basaraba was waiting for the notions.

But there had to be a few extra minutes to greet Robert. Just a smidgeon of time to see those tender green eyes, like springtime leaves, and that sweet boyish smile.

With an eager hand, she pushed open the main door and peered into the Scarlet Room—that was what they called the lobby, for it was all red carpet and red walls, and sagging red-cushioned benches next to feeble potted palms where patrons might rest before ascending one of the staircases to the balcony above.

She scanned the shadowy alcoves, where two swinging doors opened to the auditorium and another off to the side led to the one-aisle bar that sold whiskey, gin, and sherry to thirsty patrons. There was no sign of Robert nor his companion. She did not see a soul.

She set off toward the auditorium. Halfway across the floor, she stopped. Voices. Too close for a rehearsal on the stage. A light seeped from beneath Mr. DeGraaf's closed office door.

Robert was there.

At once she was standing at the threshold. Only a two-inch width of walnut stood between them. Quickly, she pulled her hat from her head, held it between her teeth by the stingy brim, and coiled up her braid. With one hand holding her mass of curls, she pulled the bowler over it with the other. A pinch on her cheeks and a bite on her lips for color. She raised her hand to rap on the wood, but stopped. He was speaking, and she let that soft tenor wrap around her once again like the cozy wool blanket they had shared on the roof, so inviting and warm. Just to hear it again after all this time.

But there was the other voice. Older and deeper, with a slightly nasal tinge. She tried to place it.

"I rather expected to be meeting with your father," Robert's companion said.

"I assure you, Mr. Ziegfeld . . ."

The name paralyzed her. Florenz Ziegfeld, Jr.? The name appeared in the papers and journals so often he seemed more legend than man, more idea than real flesh, blood, and bone. The whole wide spectrum of the theatrical world seemed to fit within the contours of that name: the Broadway hits and the flops, the fame and misfortunes, the romances and scandals. Even those who turned up their noses at Ziegfeld's arrogance and near-constant courting of the press never disputed the effectiveness of his methods. With his guidance, Anna Held had become a shining light on Broadway, starring for months now in his own musical hit, *A Parisian Model,* uptown.

And here he was. On the other side of this door. She leaned in another inch.

"So you are taking over, are you?" Ziegfeld was saying. "The change, I must say, is long overdue. I remember grand productions here at The Chance. *Vaudeville Stars, Marvels and Delights* was a magnificent spectacle indeed when I booked Eugen Sandow's strongman act through here in ninety-four, fresh from his success in Chicago. He shared a bill with that other World's Fair act, that little Egyptian belly dancer. But the years, I'm afraid, have not been kind to your father's little theater."

Pepper stiffened. Who was he to criticize?

"It's true, Mr. Ziegfeld, but I have plans to change that. Which brings me to the reason I asked you here today. I understand you are developing a new show."

"Good news has a way of traveling, doesn't it? What exactly have you heard, my boy?"

"That it is to be a summer show?"

"It's Anna's idea, really. Something light and fun between the regular seasons. We're calling it the *Follies of 1907.*"

"If you don't mind me saying, I have also heard you were to put it up at the New York Theatre, in the rooftop garden, but that you might have run into a bit of trouble on that front."

There was a pause, then, "Yes, Mr. DeGraaf, you are correct.

Klaw and Erlanger begged for the production and made every promise imaginable to get it. But now that it's time to make good on those promises, I find they are not so forthcoming. I have begun to consider alternative venues, discreetly of course."

What was Robert getting at? He knew The Chance could not accommodate Ziegfeld's production. The theater was home to one show, and one show alone: *Vaudeville Stars, Marvels and Delights.* The players changed, but the show remained constant.

"Then I'll be as plain as I can," Robert said. "I would like you to consider The Chance Theatre."

Ziegfeld was speaking again, but the thrumming in her ears blocked the sound. Consider The Chance? It was impossible. It had to be a mistake. Sure, the theater was in a slump, but the show was not the problem. Robert had to see that.

Her cheeks flushed. The floor beneath her lurched and swayed, and she leaned against the door to steady herself.

By the time she realized the door was not latched, it was too late. She had pushed it, not hard, but enough to send it gaping into the office and to leave her standing, exposed, facing the wall of framed publicity photographs stacked in four long, tidy rows behind DeGraaf's giant mahogany desk. Actors, acrobats, and ventriloquists; animal trainers, magicians, and trapeze artists. They all stared down as if from a vaudeville Valhalla. But it was not their frozen smiles that made her want to crawl into the fibers of the Persian rug beneath her. It was the horrified look on Robert's face.

"Pepper MacClair?"

She forced her gaze to meet his, though every part of her ached to turn and run. This was hardly the reunion she had envisioned. She wanted him to see she was a woman now, a full eighteen years old. And a dancer, a bona fide performer, just as she always told him she would be.

She did not want him to see her like this, bumbling and awkward, a disgrace with no care for proper decorum.

Yet here she was, and she had to make the best of it. She would pretend she had not heard this conversation. She lifted her chin and forced a smile. "Hello, Robert," she said with a cheerfulness spun from the thin shreds of dignity she had left. "I thought I heard your voice. I hope I'm not interrupting."

Ziegfeld was mostly hidden from her in one of the leather chairs arranged in front of the desk, but she heard him chuckle.

Robert, however, appeared too shocked to be amused. Yet it was not the question in those wide, gaping eyes that made her look away. It was simply the sight of that finely angled jaw, the line of that smooth cheek, the blond hair swept back from his brow. It had been so long since she had looked upon him, but the years had not changed him so much. Despite the new sharpness to his face, he was still her handsome, beloved Robert.

"This is a private meeting, Miss MacClair."

Ziegfeld seemed of a different mind. The man was on his feet, rocking on his heels, watching her.

She took his measure. Forty, he appeared, perhaps older, and shorter than Robert, a bit softer around the middle. There was nothing soft in his expression, however. He seemed a typical, well-bred man of business. Tailored tweed suit, crisp white collar, simple diamond pin punched through a striped cravat. His dark hair was gray at the edges and coaxed back with pomade from a wide, smooth forehead. He had a skinny, rigid chin and thin lips that appeared incapable of a smile. But it was those eyes. Deep, dark orbs, under sharply arched brows that stared at her as if she were a thing to be studied. To be judged. She did not like it, and she did not like him.

"I heard voices. I thought . . ." She looked away. She could not bear to say what she thought.

Robert tried to speak, but Ziegfeld stopped him. "What abysmal manners you have, young man." He approached Pepper. "My dear," he said to her, his voice false with warmth and comfort, "allow me to apologize on his behalf." His glance slid from her hesitant smile down the front of her, taking note, it would seem, of each rise and fall of the curves beneath her coat. Then he bowed, as a gentleman would. "My friends call me Flo. And I gather you are Pepper MacClair. Would I be correct in assuming you are a performer at this establishment?"

His scrutiny left her feeling exposed despite her well-fastened coat. "I dance in the deuce act," she said, more to Robert than Ziegfeld. "In the Dancing Dolls trio." If Robert had not been aware of this development, he knew it now. She was pleased to see the glint of surprise in his eyes. Did he know anything that had happened since he'd left? Did he know about her mother?

"I have heard interesting things about your Dolls," Ziegfeld was saying. "Your employer, much like myself, understands the universal appeal of music enhanced by feminine beauty."

"The dancing girls are a house act that has certainly had its advantages from a business standpoint." Robert was on his feet and rounding the desk, but Ziegfeld paid him no attention.

"Young lady," he was saying, "I wonder if your obvious talents"—again his eyes roamed over her in a way that made her arms stiffen around herself—"may be underutilized here. I have a promising opportunity on the horizon that you may find interesting."

Robert forced a laugh and came up alongside Ziegfeld. "I see the rumors are true. Always scouting for fresh talent, hmm? Miss MacClair, please do not let us keep you from whatever it was you were doing. Good-bye now."

Before she could say anything, before she could warn him to veer from this devastating mistake, he had pushed her back over the threshold and closed the door. She was still staring at the swirls in the wood grain, waiting for the shock of being so abruptly dispatched to fade and suppressing the urge to barge back in, when she heard the street door.

"Hey there, doll."

It was Em Charmaigne, the woman who operated the theater's ticket window, though anyone meeting her for the first time might be surprised to learn she was a woman at all, dressed as she was in a man's gray wool suit with her pale brown hair clipped short beneath her bowler and an unlit cigar clenched in her teeth. It was her favorite manly prop next to the silver-handled cane she hooked over her arm while she flipped through her ring of keys for the one that would open the box office door.

"You haven't seen the programs, have you? The printer's boy usually leaves the box out front." Em glanced around. "Or has Stanley cut those, too, to save a few pennies? I expect one of these days he'll decide it's cheaper to keep the doors locked instead of rolling out a show no one wants to see."

"You don't mean that." Pepper knew Em loved the place. She had taken her Uptown Joe impersonation act from New York all the way to San Francisco and back at least a dozen times before retiring, but she always returned to The Chance. And now, when she had her own townhouse on Fourth Street and could spend her time any way she pleased, she still showed up six days out of seven to work the theater's ticket window for a pittance, and would probably show up on Sundays, too, if Mr. DeGraaf had skirted the city's ban on live acts by offering a program of moving pictures, as other theater owners did.

Still, Pepper hoped the comment had not penetrated the office door.

Em noticed her concern. "What are you doing up here anyway? And why do you keep eyeing the office?"

"Robert DeGraaf is in there," she whispered, and was about to explain the whole miserable ordeal when Em's frown stopped her. It had been a long time since they had discussed Robert, and Pepper was quickly remembering why.

"You need to forget about Robert DeGraaf," the woman said in a way that made it clear the young man's return was no surprise, although she had not attended Stanley's meeting. His "no exceptions" rule always made an exception for Em.

The woman removed her hat and hung it from the hook behind her door. "You should be worried about yourself. You can't let Stanley catch you down here and out of costume this close to curtain. You don't want to start the week off with another quarrel."

"We've already quarreled. At the all-hands meeting this morning."

Em had disappeared within her closet of a room, but called out, "What was it this time?"

"The meeting or the quarrel?"

Em reappeared in the doorway. She had removed her cane and her coat. The cigar remained. "Either. Both."

Pepper filled Em in on what Stanley had said about Robert's new role. "But then, you probably know all about that." She waited in vain for Em to disagree. Pepper wondered how much more Em knew.

"And the quarrel?"

Pepper kicked the carpet. "It was that *Variety* notice. Stanley was so . . ." There was no reason to elaborate. She knew better than to expect sympathy from Em when it came to Stanley. "It isn't important." She pulled the bag of sewing notions from her coat pocket and stared at them. "I need to get these to Mrs. B. Stanley told her the headliner needs a gown, and the woman hasn't even arrived yet."

Em closed her eyes and shook her head. "Oh, Stanley, when will you learn? Say, if you're going that way, will you tell him about the programs? I want to get the cash drawer sorted before I open."

"Missing programs, sure," Pepper said, walking backward toward the auditorium doors.

Inside, she sailed down the red-carpeted aisle at a dead run, passing the empty rows of worn cushioned seats and hardly noticing the members of the Shorty Shakespeareans congregated onstage for a dress rehearsal:

"Nay, if Cupid have not spent all his quiver in Venice,
Thou wilt quake for this shortly . . ."

Pepper recognized the lines from *Much Ado About Nothing.* The diminutive Don Pedro's voice rang out clear to the rafters and ended with an emphasis of the final word in a labored yet vain attempt to milk laughs.

By the time the stagehands were restaging for the next scene, Pepper was climbing the half flight of steps to the stage, her heels knocking hard against the wood. She searched for Stanley, but the stool he kept behind the stage-left curtain sat empty.

"Looking for someone?"

She whipped around. A long, lean man in overalls and a white cotton shirt, the sleeves rolled to the elbow, emerged from behind a castle window set piece. Not such an odd place for the theater's properties master to be, yet the sight of Gregory Creighton gave her a start.

She met the awkward moment the way she usually did: with sarcasm. "Is that you, Creighton? I hardly recognize you under all that hair."

It was not true, of course. She would know that low rumble of a voice anywhere. But she had been nagging him on the subject for nearly a month. His sable locks had been neglected so long they coiled around his ears beneath his flat cap and had to be pushed across his brow or they covered his black pebble eyes. She had offered to cut his hair herself, as she had when they were children, when he was the old prop master's apprentice and she roamed the corridors while her mother stitched costumes on the fifth floor. That seemed so long ago now, and she hadn't been surprised when he had refused. "I was looking for Stanley, if you must know."

Gregory made the final push that put the set piece on its mark and slapped his hands together to brush off the dust. "He left for Grand Central a while ago but said he'd be back by curtain."

The train station? The man could not even manage a flight of stairs without complaining. "What's he doing there?"

"Collecting the headliner." Gregory sneered—at her or Stanley, it wasn't clear.

"That Madame Bizet must be something to reduce him to errand boy. Pretty, I assume?"

Gregory shrugged. It was impossible to discern whether he didn't know or didn't care. That ubiquitous frown, that cynical stare. She was so used to it now, she hardly remembered the boisterous boy he had been, the one who'd played hide-and-seek with her in the passageways and storage rooms for hours at a time. But then, they both had changed, hadn't they? And he was still steadfast in his way, and as dependable as they came. That was why, despite everything, she still trusted him, even if he would not say the same of her.

When he spoke again, his voice was so low it didn't disrupt the half-size thespians' rehearsal. "You didn't come to stir up more trouble with Stanley, did you? I think you managed quite enough this morning. Unless you're planning to run off to the Hippodrome like Bart and the rest."

"That's where they're going?"

The Hippodrome was a grand theater that had opened two years before at the corner of Forty-third and Sixth. A monstrosity, really, with a stage so vast it could contain a complete battle reenactment—soldiers, horses, and props. The theater had spread the word about its opening with the usual advertisements, but it had also sent its actors into the streets in costume to talk up the show and hand out souvenir playbills. Pepper had tacked hers to the wall beside her bed. It had been a glorious opening that promised to awe spectators with two productions: *A Yankee Circus on Mars,* and the just as improbable *Andersonville: The Story of Wilson's Raiders,* with nearly five hundred soldier actors, some on horseback, fighting a battle across a river with a thirty-foot bridge. The sheer magnitude of the production boggled her mind.

She had heard rumors it was the Hippodrome poaching The Chance's stagehands, but backstage gossip could not be trusted. Gregory, however, never passed idle words.

"I'm not looking for trouble, Mr. Creighton, and I'm not looking to hire on at the Hippodrome, or anywhere else for that matter."

Gregory dipped his head in a nod. "Then perhaps you should

get upstairs and into your costume before Stanley shows up. Or I expect you'll find trouble whether you're looking for it or not."

"Let him rant. He's not in charge anymore. Robert DeGraaf is." And once she told Robert how Stanley had been running things, maybe they could finally be done with him for good.

"Sure," Gregory said. "If the little prince ever turns up . . ."

"He's already here. I saw him."

Gregory stared hard at Stanley's apprentice. The young man was crawling on his hands and knees along the row of footlights, stopping at each one to check the wires.

"Go back to that last one, Matty. Wiggle it, make sure the connection is good."

Matty grunted but did as he was told.

Without looking at her, Gregory said, "You saw Robert DeGraaf here?"

"In his father's office. He's there now."

She could not say anything else, because Frankie, the theater's piano player, cut between them on his way to the stage. He tipped his chin in greeting. Showtime was near. Everything else would have to wait.

She went to the door that opened onto the stairwell, then turned back. She had nearly forgotten why she had come backstage at all.

"Em says the programs are missing up front. Any idea where they might be?"

Gregory shook his head. "But I'll see they're found." He tipped back his cap. "Will there be anything else, Miss MacClair?"

As the door closed behind her, she called over her shoulder: "Yes, Mr. Creighton. You still need to trim your hair."

• • •

"ARE WE GOING TO THE HARDWARE STORE? OR ARE YOU GOING to stand there gaping after Miss MacClair instead?"

Gregory did not have to turn around to know it was Matty Platt standing behind him. No one else spoke to him that way. No one else dared. The boy hadn't been around long enough to know better. He seemed to figure people found those casual Oklahoma Territory manners charming, but Gregory, for one, had grown weary of them.

Not that Matty noticed. The boy used his thumbnail to scratch muck from an electricity gauge's glass cover, then swiped a rag over the board of levers, knobs, and dials that controlled the stage and house lights before turning around to meet Gregory's glare.

"I am not gaping. Just concerned."

"About Miss MacClair? Hardly seems necessary." Matty stuffed the dirty rag into his back pocket and rubbed his hands against his trousers.

On the stage, the tiny Shakespearean actors were finishing their rehearsal. The dog trainer was standing by, corralling his seven dachshunds for a final run-through on one side of the stage while Alfred and Edwards, wearing just their plaid trousers, suspenders, and undershirts, volleyed jokes back and forth on the other.

"Never seen anybody stand up to Mr. Stanley like that," Matty added. "Did you see the way she stared him down? I thought she'd burn him through with those blue flame eyes of hers. She sure is something, if you ask me."

Yes, she sure was something. . . . "It's not Stanley that worries me."

"Oh?"

He had Matty's full attention now. Gregory shook his head. This wasn't a conversation he wanted to have with a sixteen-year-old boy. "Have you seen Robert DeGraaf in the building?" Already he regretted the question.

"You're worried about the new boss? What's he got to do with Miss MacClair?"

"Nothing. No one said he did." *And it will go better for him if he keeps it that way,* Gregory thought. He stepped back to avoid a dachshund fleeing from the stage. The dog was running through the wings as fast as his three-inch legs could carry him, with his trainer in hot pursuit. Matty, the comedians, the midgets, the stagehands—each man had stopped what he'd been doing to root for the animal, who was easily outpacing his lumbering trainer.

This wasn't going to end well. Gregory knew it as well as he knew the flickering footlight third from the left would need replacing by the end of the night, and that the rigger who was working the ropes had shown up drunk again. There was a time even a whiff of alcohol would get a man branded unreliable and tossed out the stage door with his last paycheck. But not now. These days, The Chance needed every man it could get.

Gregory tapped Matty on the shoulder to break him away from Old Jake, a lanky black stagehand with a thin cloud of salt-and-pepper hair who was taking bets on the outcome of the trainer-versus-dog race. "There's a list of supplies we need on the prop room's desk. Get it and meet me outside."

Matty grudgingly obeyed and headed down the wide passageway.

The dog ran by again. Gregory, his patience wearing thin, pulled Old Jake aside. "When the trainer corrals that thing, remind him it's his job to clean up after his animals. The magician stepped in a pile this morning and screamed at Matty for half an hour. It's in the contract that cleanup is the trainer's job. If he cannot manage it, tell him I'll make sure whatever we pick up ends up in the pocket of whatever I find in his dressing room."

"Done." The glint in Old Jake's eyes said it would be a pleasure.

"Matty and I should be back by intermission. You're in charge while I'm gone."

Old Jake jerked his chin down, at once recognizing and thanking Gregory for the responsibility.

Gregory glanced again at the stagehand still grappling with the ropes. He saw his concern mirrored in Old Jake's expression. "And keep an eye on Laszlo." He made the request, though he knew it wasn't necessary. Old Jake had seen what Gregory had seen, and he would have done it without instruction. That was the way it was at The Chance. They looked out for each other.

"Thanks, old man," Gregory said. More unnecessary words, but he wanted to say them just the same.

Two

PEPPER FLUNG OPEN THE DOOR TO HER DRESSING room, barged in, and found herself tangled in a shin-deep pile of dirty laundry in the center of the room.

"Look who decided to grace us with her presence." Beatrice Pennington turned to watch the commotion, then turned back to her own reflection in the lighted mirror to resume the task of drawing a thin line of black M. Stein paint across one lowered eyelid.

Trixie Small gazed up from the sagging Cleopatra couch, where she was lacing her black dance shoes ballerina style over her cotton stockings. "I told you that pile was a hazard, Bea. What if Pepper had twisted her ankle?"

In the mirror's reflection, Pepper saw Beatrice roll her eyes and lift a brilliant blue medicine bottle to her lips. Finding it empty, she dropped it in the trash bin and pulled its twin from a box beneath the counter.

"Now that would be a shame, wouldn't it?" Beatrice sipped from the bottle—her "cure," she called it—set it down, and picked up a canister of loose powder from the collection of jars and bottles, tubes, and tins assembled around her. She took her time dabbing the powder puff around her eyes, her lips, and her décolletage, dusting away lines and crevices that betrayed the three decades stacked against her. "If we lost the seamstress, Stanley would probably stick us with the old woman who mends our clothes. But then, that couldn't be much worse."

Whatever concerns Pepper had about Robert and Ziegfeld sank beneath the weight of that woman's snide glance. Pepper kicked off the petticoat wrapped around her boot and stormed to the corner, where her costume hung from a row of pegs along the wall. "Don't blame me because he won't give you a solo. It's not my fault you're not as good as you think you are."

It wasn't that she blamed Beatrice for wanting to be a star. It was what they all wanted. The best billing, the best dressing rooms, the best salaries. Admirers and invitations. Stars had all that, and more.

She shook off her coat and yanked down each piece of her costume: the short black dress, the shiny black gloves, the black hose and ballerina shoes.

When the last Doll quit for a job in a legit theater at the beginning of the season, no one had been more surprised than Pepper when Stanley offered her the spot. She knew he had not forgotten her debut. Who could? She had been fifteen and cocky, and she had committed the worst stage sin imaginable: She froze. Dead on the boards, gaping at the audience like a stupid windup toy no one had bothered to wind. The shame of it still lanced her through the gut.

When Stanley had summoned her to his office to tell her she

could have the spot if she wanted it, she knew it was not because she deserved it. She knew the truth: Work had slowed and Mrs. B no longer needed an assistant. If Pepper had not lost Bessie only a few months before, and if everyone had not been feeling so damn sorry for her, he would have turned her out.

It was luck that that dancer had quit as suddenly as she had and put Stanley in a bind. He had his reservations, but Pepper had promised he would never regret the second chance he was giving her. She promised she would be the best Dancing Doll he had ever seen.

She had believed it, too, until she stepped back into those lights. She knew the routine. She knew the music and the cues. But she realized she knew something else, too.

Since her debut, she knew she could fail.

Every day she tried to put that fear behind her, and she was improving, though it hardly mattered to Stanley. He always found something to criticize. If Trixie missed a beat or Beatrice turned the wrong way, he let it pass. But if Pepper even tipped her wrist the wrong way, he complained.

Let him try that now that Robert was back. Once she explained that it was Stanley's incompetence dragging down the show, he would get what was coming to him.

"It really is a wonder when you think about it," Beatrice was saying.

Pepper braced for more insults.

"You live in the cellar—or the Labyrinth or the Lair, or whatever you live-ins call it—yet you still can't make a call time to save your life. Frankly, I find it baffling. Do you get lost in the stairwell? Or do you simply lose track of time when you're squirreled away in Wardrobe, stealing whatever bizarre garment strikes your fancy?" Beatrice swiveled around on the bench and let her gaze drift over Pepper, passing judgment on every miserable stitch of her plain black frock, every black-and-white ring of her stockings, each frayed thread of her worn knuckle mittens.

Fresh heat bloomed on Pepper's cheeks. "I do not steal."

She was prepared to say more, but the sight of the bouquet on the table beside the couch stopped her. A dozen ruby-red roses in a clear glass vase.

Flowers arrived often at The Chance, usually on their way to the headliner's door. They had never come for Pepper. Not yet. But Robert knew that was her dream—to be a performer with a roomful of bouquets. Was this his way of sweetly announcing his return?

"Admiring my roses?"

Beatrice's roses. Of course.

The woman's face brightened with her usual fake stage smile. She sauntered over to the arrangement to caress one bulb's petals.

"They're from a fella I met last night when Trixie and I were at Delmonico's."

Before stepping behind the dressing screen, Pepper exchanged a glance with Trixie, who had slid into Beatrice's place in front of the mirror and was tugging a brush through her frizzy curls. The return glance told her what she'd suspected: "At Delmonico's" meant "walking by Delmonico's repeatedly until the doormen got wise," which was Beatrice's latest method for trying to meet uptown men.

"He's in the business," Beatrice said. "Putting together a show of his own, in fact. That's why he stopped me. Said he could tell I was a performer right off. Says I have star quality. Those were his words, weren't they, Trix?"

"C'mon, Beatrice," Trixie said. "Let's talk about something else."

The room fell silent. Pepper peeked over the dressing screen's curlicue trim and saw Beatrice, arms folded over her cleavage.

"Oh, I see. I can't enjoy a man's attention because you can't get the one you fancy to notice you. Maybe he prefers a woman with a little less meat on her bones. Have you thought of that? Or maybe he needs a little nudge. If you just came out and asked her if she'd say a few words to Tall, Dark, and Moody on your behalf . . . What? Don't wave your hands at me. Weren't you just saying—"

"Beatrice!"

Pepper's ears rang with Trixie's squeal. She stepped out from behind the dressing screen as she fastened the last two buttons in the back. Trixie's eyes were wide with mortification.

Beatrice smirked and went to the couch, where she settled and leaned deep against the single rolled arm. "Oh, was I not supposed to say anything?" A snide glance slid first to Pepper, then Trixie. "Honestly, I don't know what you're worried about. If there were anything going on down there in those dark little basement rooms, I'm sure we would have heard about it."

"Are you talking about Gregory Creighton?" Pepper knew they were. It just did not make sense. Trixie was always sweet on someone. Last week it had been the boy who sold sandwiches at Wanamaker's lunch counter. The notion that Trixie could be sweet on Gregory was absurd. Not that he wasn't handsome. Sure he was, in a gritty, brooding sort of way. But there was that glumness about him. He did not smile. He rarely spoke. When other stagehands gathered in the alley to chat and smoke and throw dice, he holed up in his room. It was a few steps down the hallway from her own, but it might as well have been a whole world away, just him and those machines he was always taking apart and assembling again. Telephones, telegraphs, talking machines—anything he could get his hands on. In all the years she had known him, she had never seen him in the company of a girl, not that way, not once.

The conversation was cut short by the syncopated piano tune that opened the show. Frankie's bouncy ragtime jazz seeped through the floorboards and the plaster walls, and like clockwork the door rattled with three thundering thumps.

"Quarter to curtain," the voice hollered before moving down the corridor and rattling another door.

Pepper pulled up her stockings and fastened the garters. She stepped into her shoes and tied them, then scooped cocoa butter from the tin and smoothed it over her face. Her first time behind the lighted mirror, it had taken a full half hour to apply all the creams: the base, the highlight, the contour, the black to bring out the blue of her eyes—as blue as St. Andrew's Cross, just like Bessie's—the rouge for the cheeks and lips, and dust powder over it all. Now she could do it in three minutes flat, which gave her two more to coil her hair and fasten the black ostrich plume to the back before Beatrice and Trixie were standing at the opened door waving her out.

Trixie hesitated, her fingers dancing at her sides. "I heard the new boss was in the house. Do you think he'll be watching? Do you think he'll like our act?"

"What's not to like?" Beatrice slid her hands suggestively over her hips and twitched her shoulders to make her generously exposed cleavage jiggle. "New management is just what this place needs. It certainly couldn't be any worse than what we've got."

For once, Pepper had to agree. She dabbed a paintbrush in the yellow cream and drew a slender line down the center of her red lips—a trick that made them look glossy in the stage lights—and tried to get that image of Ziegfeld out of her mind. That smug expression, that prickly gaze. She could not say anything about him to Beatrice because the woman was right about the way people talked.

"C'mon, Pepper." Trixie was losing her patience.

Beatrice had already abandoned her. She could hear the dancer's footsteps halfway down the corridor that shot straight down the middle of the fourth floor, with nothing but doors to dressing rooms and dirty laundry hung from sacks on either side.

"Go on," Pepper said. "I'll be right behind."

Trixie gave up and chased after Beatrice.

Pepper checked her reflection again. The pinned hair, the dark paints, the costume. She was ready. Except . . .

Familiar flutters filled her belly. The beating inside her chest.

She clenched her eyes tightly, then opened them, seeing herself as the audience would see her: standing tall, neck long, lips stretched into her best stage smile. To herself she repeated the most important rule of the stage: *Smile, dammit. Whatever happens, smile.*

• • •

GREGORY PULLED THE STAGE DOOR CLOSED BEHIND HIM AND hiked up the collar of his peacoat against the cold. He checked the sky for signs of rain. Only a blanket of silvery white hovered over the rooftops of the brick-and-mortar buildings along Eighth Street, up to the Hudson River on one side and down to the East River on the other, though the road played games in that direction, joining Astor Place and then calling itself St. Marks before returning to Eighth again after Tompkins Square Park.

Despite the gray and the chill, he noted none of the storm clouds that had crept up the seaboard the night before. Good. Theatergoers tended to stay home when it rained.

"Over here," Matty called out.

The boy was leaning against the theater wall between the metal staircase leading up to the upper stories and the concrete one that descended down to the Lair. Home to Matty and himself, Old Jake, Pepper, and until this morning, Bart. The residents. The live-ins.

Though he had worked at the theater longer than the rest, he had not been the first to move in. That had been Pepper, with her mother. They had taken rooms soon after the DeGraafs moved out. That was so long ago now, few even remembered the DeGraafs had once lived there.

The old man had purchased the building in 1890, when it was still a warehouse. He knew what it could become, however. Where that shell of a building stood, he saw the theater's arched windows, the sloping auditorium, two new floors for dressing rooms and rehearsal space. He intended to see it done properly. That was why he had the residence built into the cellar, so he could oversee the work himself. He had spared no expense on that residence, either. As well appointed as anything on Washington Square or Gramercy Park. It had to be. He had a wife to please.

For three years the DeGraafs lived there—through the construction and the theater's first seasons—before Elsa DeGraaf insisted it was not suitable to raise their son. Her husband gave in eventually and arranged accommodations in the St. Denis Hotel a few blocks north.

But that had not been the end of Mrs. DeGraaf's requests. Being a progressive reformer at heart, she saw an opportunity. They should put that grand apartment to use by dividing it into lodgings for employees, she suggested. Give something useful to those less fortunate than themselves.

Her argument proved persuasive only when the old man

realized he could deduct rent from the wages and save a good portion on the payroll. He agreed, which was fortunate for him because his wife had already invited a young Scottish mother, whom she had met at one of her Ladies' Club expeditions to the particularly distasteful and unsanitary parts of the Lower East Side.

DeGraaf directed his work crews to carve five dwellings from the carcass of their grand apartment, and to do it as quickly and inexpensively as possible. The result was a peculiar juxtaposition of a place, with some walls sturdy and some paper-thin, some topped by an uneven gap and others decorated with fine mahogany trim.

This mix of the old with the new, the ornate and the plain, made the Lair a strange, haphazard sort of place. An oddly out-of-place sort of place. But it was home.

And Matty was its newest arrival.

Gregory watched the boy eyeing two burly men heaving crates off a cart along the curb in front of him. Each one clattered with the sounds of liquor bottles.

Matty flashed Gregory a smile that said, *Watch this,* and sauntered up to the gray nag strapped to the cart. He stroked the animal's mottled coat and, in his best frontier drawl, asked, "You boys need help?" He gave Gregory another sly grin. He didn't wait for an answer before he added, "My friend and I would be right happy to lend a hand. If you were grateful, perhaps you might fix us up with one of those bottles that could just happen to disappear from the order. . . ."

The larger and meaner-looking man, bald except for a rim of black stubble around his ears and a mole the size of a penny alongside his flushed, swollen nose, handed a crate off to his partner and rounded on Matty. "Stay away from the bottles, son.

These are paid for by theater management. Any go missing, it comes out of my pocket, see?"

Gregory stepped in and grabbed the boy's arm. "Matty here was just leaving, weren't you, boy? Stanley's not in, but the woman in the ticket booth can sign for the delivery."

The man considered it, then grumbled, "Good enough," and hoisted another crate down to his partner.

Before the deliveryman could do anything more than glare at Matty, Gregory pulled the boy toward Broadway and the parade of pedestrians, streetcars, and horses and carts that flowed along that thoroughfare.

"Now why did you go and do that?" Matty pulled his arm back and tugged on the bottom of the tweed coat he wore like a gentleman, though it was so worn and threadbare at the elbows that you could see the dingy white of the long johns he wore beneath. "It's freezing out here. Another minute, and we might have had a quality libation to warm us."

Gregory rubbed a patch of the day-old stubble on his chin but didn't break his stride. "He was not going to give you any of that whiskey."

"You don't know that; you have not yet seen me at my most persuasive."

"I do know," Gregory muttered. "I wouldn't have let him. That's our stock for the bar. You don't think the theater runs on the price of admission alone, do you?" It hardly ran at all anymore, but he kept that thought to himself. He quickened his pace. "You got that list?"

"I got it." Matty trotted to catch up, brought his hands to his lips, and blew to warm them, making his breath swirl into white billowing wisps. "So this is spring in New York City, huh? I don't mind saying, it's not what I expected."

Gregory kept mum. He never expected anything from the city. It was the place where he had been born, the place he had lived, the place he had not yet left. Sometimes, when he was in a mood for conversation, he liked to hear about the places others had been. He could picture them: Ireland's green patchwork fields or Paris's giant Eiffel Tower, the Dutch canals and the Scottish lochs. It amazed him the distance people traveled to come to this small island, the hundreds of thousands of people, the millions even, who came by boat and railroad and any means available to this tiny sliver of land floating between the Hudson and East rivers. He had been born breathing New Amsterdam air. The island was part of him, and he knew its rhythm—the icy winters and sweltering summers, the blustery autumns and sopping wet springs. He knew the smell of the wharves and the rubbish that collected in forgotten corners, from the factories belching soot up to the heavens. He knew the endless press of people at the southern end and the wide-open spaces that could still be found to the north. He knew this island called Manhattan, and few things could surprise him about it anymore, not even the pie-eyed notions the Johnny-come-latelies brought with them to its shores.

Not that Matty was a typical immigrant. He wasn't. Before landing at Grand Central, the boy had lived on his family's farm in the Oklahoma Territory, a half a day's ride from anything resembling a town. At least that was how he told it. The boy had lived there with his ma and pa, and four elder brothers—a rough bunch who passed the time with whiskey and fistfights. One snowy morning in December, the oldest brother had stumbled home at daybreak to find Matty consoling his sister-in-law in a less than brotherly manner. A particularly harsh beating ensued. Afterward, Matty had gone out to milk the family cows, his usual morning chore, only this time he didn't stop at the barn. He didn't stop at all. He kept walking. Walked a whole day, he said, before hopping aboard an eastbound train. Didn't matter where it was headed. He decided wherever it stopped would be his destination. When it stopped in New York, he figured he'd prefer work in a theater to a barn. A few days later he had persuaded Stanley to make him an apprentice, because as the boy said, he did have a knack for persuasion.

"New York is never quite what outsiders expect," Gregory added.

Only he wasn't paying attention to Matty any longer. He was watching a stubby man with a plump mustache and charcoal-gray derby. He was hovering, this man, over what appeared to be a stacked arrangement of small wooden boxes—one a bit larger than a matchbox atop another three or four times larger than that. These boxes were all set at eye level upon a three-legged stand he had placed in the center of the sidewalk. Judging from the looks of pedestrians flowing around, some found the man and his machine a curiosity. Others appeared less impressed.

One curmudgeonly fellow growled, "Walkways are for *public* use, sir," and gave the tripod's legs a swift whack with his walking stick as he passed.

The man with the machine, as proper as an office clerk and of a somewhat nervous disposition, paid no mind to any of them. He was squatting to examine a brass gear within the largest box. A chain dangled from his wrist, but it was a second brass gear, smaller than the first, that appeared to vex him. He alternated between examining the item and trying to press it into a notch formed a few inches below the other.

"Say, what do you have here?" Matty sidled up alongside the device and was leaning down to peer into its black interior.

"Do you mind, young man?" The man glared at Matty, then resumed his scrutiny of the gear and tried again to fasten it into place. "I'm making a moving picture. If I can just get this . . ." His voice trailed off.

Gregory had been about to pull the boy away—they had wasted too much time already—but he stopped. A moving picture camera? It was smaller than he had imagined. And where was the film? The lamp?

Matty, undeterred, circled the machine. "You make flickers with this, then?" He touched the brass fitting over the lens.

The man slapped away his hand. "Yes, son, animated photographs. Do you mind?"

Gregory pulled Matty back once again. "Sorry about the boy," he said to the befuddled cameraman. To Matty, he added in a hostile tone, "He forgets his manners."

The boy shook free of Gregory's grip. "What sort of flickers do you intend to make out here exactly?" He glanced around at the buildings, the people, the horses and wagons. His lip curled. "Not much to see, really."

"Perhaps." The man peered closely at the gear and the screw. "But the light is good. Diffused by the clouds, you see; reduces shadows. And street views are always popular with the exhibitors. People want to see their neighbors, themselves if they can." The gear dropped to the ground and he cursed as he bent to retrieve it. "I knew I should have brought my own apparatus. Today was not the day to try out this old Lumière model. . . ." He broke off the sentence with a guttural, frustrated sound, then tried again to force the gear and its screw into the notch in the box.

Now that Gregory was closer, he could see the problem. The man's fingers were too thick to hold the gear steady and properly guide the screw into the wood. "A tool might help with that."

"Yes, I'm sure it would if I had one. But since I do not, I shall make do with the tools the good Lord gave me." He raised his free hand and wiggled his fingers to make his point.

Gregory reached into his back pocket and produced a crude little cylinder with a wooden knob at one end and a notch along the side. With his thumb, he slid that notch and produced an inner rod that, when extended, doubled the cylinder's length. He handed it to the man. "You could use mine."

The cameraman took the device and studied it. Four flat screwdriver tips of varying sizes were neatly hinged at the end that had been hidden inside. He fanned them out, then swiveled them back into straight alignment. "What a marvelous gadget. How might I find one?"

"Shouldn't be difficult. It's a Billings and Spencer screwdriver. Any hardware man worth his salt will know how to find them." Gregory held out his hand for his tool, and then the gear and the screw. He selected a driver head.

"You'll need this as well." The cameraman slipped the small chain from his wrist and handed it to Gregory. He brushed at the black grease marks the chain had left on his white cuffs, which only spread the stains, though he hardly noticed. He focused on Gregory's work.

In less than a minute, the gear was in place and the chain stretched neatly over both. Gregory stepped away, and the cameraman leaned down to examine the fix.

"Impressive," he said, rising and shaking Gregory's hand. "I'm much obliged."

"Happy to help." Gregory retracted the screwdriver and slid it back into his pocket.

Matty stepped up. "So these flickers you make . . ."

But the cameraman was gazing skyward. The clouds were

growing dark and threatening. He held up his hand to stop the boy. "You can find me in the studio tomorrow. Come by, if you like, and I'll be happy to answer your questions. I really must be going, however, if I'm to salvage the day." He dug into his vest pocket and pulled out a card. He handed it to Matty, but his gaze was on Gregory. "Edison Manufacturing Company, Twenty-first between Broadway and Park. Ask for Mr. Edwin Porter."

Gregory tugged at Matty's collar as the boy was winding up with another question. "Leave it alone, boy." The truth was, Gregory wanted to see the camera in action. He wanted to know how that machine worked.

Porter, however, was lifting the camera at the joint where the boxes met the stand, and the tripod legs closed like an umbrella. "If you'll excuse me, then." He hoisted the apparatus. "I believe the subway will be a better subject for the day. At least Astor Place Station will offer some protection should the rain return. Thank you again." He bid them good day and tipped his hat before joining the river of pedestrians.

Matty glared at Gregory. "Didn't think I'd see the day you helped a man make flickers."

Gregory wasn't accustomed to being questioned, and certainly not by a boy.

"If it were me," Matty continued, "I'd have tipped it over and smashed it to bits when I had the chance." The apprentice stomped the pavement so there was no doubt as to the violence he had in mind.

"And what good do you suppose that would do?"

Matty looked at him like a brick had fallen on his head and knocked him senseless. "Haven't you heard the performers griping about flickers replacing acts on bills all over town? And now that peep-show parlor moves in. It's going after our own business, our own customers!"

Gregory didn't show it, but he was impressed. He would not have figured such things would matter to a boy. And he had a point. Still, those kinetoscopes, just like the moving picture camera, were astonishing machines. Marvels, really. How did the film feed continuously? Where did it go once it was viewed? What he wouldn't do for a look inside.

He could see that the boy would not let it go. He was watching Gregory, wary. A chill passed through him. The subtle dance of winning over other people had never appealed to Gregory. As a rule, he did not care what other people thought, and since his uncle had taken off to prospect out West and he had become the properties master, he did not need other people to like him. He could get things done because he was the head man. That was enough.

At least he had thought it was until Matty turned up with that eager way about him. He had latched onto Gregory before he figured out most people at The Chance avoided him, and Gregory was surprised to find he didn't mind. Not even the jabs about Pepper MacClair. Right now, however, if he said the wrong thing, if he said what he was thinking, they would have trouble. He considered his words, then said, "Wouldn't do much good to bust up just the one."

Understanding dawned on Matty. He held up the card with one hand and flicked it with his thumb and index finger with the other. "Hot damn, Mr. Creighton. You are a devious devil. Right here we have a certified, grade-A invitation to the candy store. That Porter fellow won't know what hit him."

Gregory snapped away the card, smirked, and glanced away. Let Matty misconstrue his meaning. Let him think he shared that thirst for violence. It might even work in his favor if he could figure out a way to disappear from the theater for a few hours to take Mr. Porter up on his offer. He kept that thought to himself, however, as he tucked the card into his pocket and led Matty up Broadway.

The two of them continued in silence until Matty grabbed his elbow and called his attention to two fresh-faced young ladies in fine wool coats and fine feathered hats walking in their direction.

The boy stopped, tipping his cap with gentlemanly formality. "Hello, ladies. How charitable of you to come out with your pretty faces to brighten this dreary day. I'm sure you are the loveliest things I've seen all morning."

The girls pressed their heads together, giggled, and continued on without a reply.

"If you would like to continue this acquaintance, I'll be at The Chance Theatre within the hour," he called after them.

"Leave them alone." Gregory pressed on down the sidewalk. "We've got work to do."

Matty slapped his cap back over his head. "Now, you see there? One of those lovelies might have been the future missus, if you didn't let her walk right on by. Unless it has something to do with Miss MacClair."

Hadn't they finished with that? Gregory shoved his fists into his pockets and stared straight ahead. The temperature must have dropped another few degrees, for the cold was stinging his nose, his cheeks. The chill had seeped deep within him now, making his toes ache.

They stopped at the corner to wait for a streetcar to pass before they could cross Broadway. The lumbering vehicle slowed, and three men in black suits and bowlers hopped aboard. Gregory was still staring straight ahead when he said, "Miss MacClair has no interest in being the wife of a glorified stagehand."

He was not fool enough to think that was the true reason Pepper would never consider him that way. That truth cut much deeper, and he would never speak of it to anyone, not even eager Matty Platt.

At least he had managed to make his point with the boy.

"Chorus girls," the boy said, rubbing his hands together for warmth. "They all expect some rich bloke to come along and sweep them off their feet, don't they?" He shook his head in a world-weary way that made Gregory chuckle.

When Gregory saw the maple-and-white striped awning of George's Hardware, he held out his hand to Matty. "The list?"

Matty pulled a folded sheet from beneath his coat.

Gregory looked it over: a load of wood planks, canvas, and white paint for the scene drops. "Why more white paint? I bought a gallon last week."

"Used it to paint over last week's scene drops. It's either paint or more canvas, take your pick."

Gregory bit his lip. He would have to speak to the boys about having a care for the cost of things. "How much did Stanley give you to pay for this?"

"He said we should put it on the theater's account."

Gregory closed his eyes and resisted the urge to punch a wall. "You told him what happened last time?"

"Course I told him. Stanley said he fixed it with George. That it shouldn't be a problem."

Sure, it was never a problem for Stanley. He was not the one who had to stare down that German shark, or make promises he could not keep. "Change of plans," he said abruptly, and with enough menace that Matty would be afraid to question. "I'll be back in five minutes, maybe ten. Wait for me here."

"Where are you going? I'll go with you."

Gregory pulled a nickel from his front pocket—the last of last week's wages—and handed it to Matty. "Not this time. Buy yourself some peanuts or a hot chocolate while I'm gone."

Matty took the coin and changed his tune. "Since you're offering, don't mind if I do."

Of Matty's many fine qualities—diligence, intelligence, humor—it was his ceaseless appetite that was perhaps the most consistent and certainly the one Gregory was counting on now.

He did not linger to see which direction Matty's hunger led him. Instead, he went to the corner and when he was out of view, took off at a run. Despite what he had told Matty, he knew it would take him a quarter of an hour, maybe more, to make it up to Brewster's Curio Shop on Fourteenth and back, and that was assuming Mrs. Brewster was in a mood to negotiate. He had already learned it was never wise to assume anything when it came to Lois Brewster.

Three

THREE PEARLY WHITE PLATES SOARED OVER JIMMY'S head and he was kicking up a fourth to add to his air-borne rotation when the three Dancing Dolls took their places in the wings. Pepper didn't have to watch to know they had another four minutes while the clown-faced juggler built up to six plates—maybe seven, if he was on a good streak—because that opening act had not changed in more than a year.

It gave her time to catch her breath. While Trixie and Beatrice bent and stretched to loosen their limbs deep in the wings, she sneaked up close to the curtain, slid her fingers along the velvety red edge, and peeked out to count the house. Not even a quarter full. Weak, even for the first show of the day. Madame Bizet's "most exquisite talent" was certainly not pulling them in.

Still, she could hardly be worse than the other two

acts Stanley had added for the week. She knew the Helzig Family Gymnasts were replacing last week's trapeze act because she had seen them settling into a dressing room on her way down to the stage. Though they were billed as an exceptionally skilled Austrian clan of novelty jumpers and tumblers, she had learned on their first run earlier that year that they were not related and they were barely gymnasts—just seven young and muscular men who pranced and somersaulted around the stage in yellow leotards, with indigo sashes intended to cover the more revealing parts of their costume, though they rarely managed to do so.

The last time they had shared the bill, the Helzigs had appeared in the third slot, just after the Dolls, but Stanley must have bumped them up because it was not padded mats and balance beams being dragged into position behind the first curtain. By the look of the tiny orange hoops and stands, it was the other new act, Alfonse Sneed and His Dashing Dachshunds.

Frankly, Pepper was surprised to see the animals backstage. Although the sausage dogs' flappy ears weren't without their charm, they had to be the worst-trained canines working in the varieties. What possessed Stanley to bring them back again and again?

Pepper glanced at the stage manager, now settled onto his usual backstage stool, his cane in his fist on one side and his steel-braced leg angled on the other. He never spoke about his leg or how he had lost the use of it. The only thing that was known about Stanley was that he had once danced in a concert saloon, like Em, before he moved to management. It was no leap to think that injury of his could have been the result of a barroom brawl or an altercation with someone who took umbrage at his snide and spiteful remarks. She satisfied herself with those theories because she would never dream of asking Stanley outright. He did not care for talk, and he made it clear he did not care for her.

Even now, his head was down, bent over one of the leather-bound notebooks in which he jotted notes about acts in general and performers in particular, and the whole gamut of theater business he shared with Mr. DeGraaf every day. Since his leg made it tricky to manage the notebook in his lap, he had the stagehands devise a short plank on a hinge that could be flipped down to serve as a writing surface when he needed one and flipped up out of the way when he did not. It was where Stanley could be found most of the time, and where he was scribbling now.

He would be furious if she disturbed him, so she stared at the back of his head, the black slick of thinning hair, the limp drape of the vest he wore over a rumpled madras shirt. She willed him to look up. To offer even a hint of permission to speak because curiosity was getting the better of her. Did he know Robert had arrived? Did he know about Robert's meeting with Ziegfeld?

"Pepper!"

Beatrice was standing behind Trixie at the stage's dark edge, waving Pepper to her place. She gave up on Stanley and made her way to her position, tapping her fingers to her lips and then to a framed sheet of paper hanging in the wings: *The Chance Theatre's Cardinal Rules of the Stage.* There were three: *Be punctual, be professional, be polite.* A fourth was added at the end in Mr. DeGraaf's own hand: *Smile, dammit. Whatever happens, smile!*

Her lips stretched into that smile as she waited behind Beatrice and watched Jimmy leave the stage to limp applause. A man in a black-and-crimson uniform—an usher's uniform, for that was the man's primary function—stepped out into the lights to lift away Jimmy's easel card and reveal the one beneath. In glittery and flourished script, it read: *DeGraaf's Delightful Dancing Dolls.*

Trixie cocked her finger like a gun at Frankie at the piano, which launched him into "Frog's Leg Rag." The youngest Doll stepped onto the stage, a sweet picture of girlish grace with her head high, arms wide, wrists and lips gently curved. Beatrice—the sauciest of the three—paraded out next in a way that bordered on burlesque, and then, at the very last, Pepper appeared like an afterthought, just trying to keep up.

Like the opener, the second act performed on the first six feet of the stage, the space between the footlights and the curtain. While the Dancing Dolls worked the crowd, stagehands worked the other side of the crimson velvet, setting up for an act that required set pieces or other complicated preparations. Alternating that way saved time, and if she listened during their act, she could usually make out the scrapes and clatters of props being dragged into place.

Today, it hardly mattered. After the music started, when Pepper should have been concentrating on the choreography, on keeping up and not missing her marks, she was searching the black beyond the footlights for Robert. Was he out there watching? She wanted to make him proud, but her feet felt as heavy as potato sacks, her legs as stiff as tree trunks.

She was paying the price for not warming up. Still, somehow, she was moving. Somehow she was standing beside Beatrice at the center of the stage, waving her arms in time with the plinking piano keys, just as she was supposed to. Kicking right, two, three, hop, then left, two, three, hop. She was dancing all the steps just as she was supposed to, just as she had been doing five times a day, six days a week for the past seven months.

"Stop counting," Beatrice hissed through clenched teeth. Her smile might have looked warm and natural to the audience, but up close it was at its best joyless and at its worst terrifying.

The reprimand startled Pepper out of the rhythm. She

focused on her lips, freezing them into a smile. But she needed to count, especially today. She needed the numbers to carry her through the routine. When she counted, she knew she would land on her left foot when Trixie did her spin, and kick when she was supposed to kick. She tried to think of the numbers without moving her lips: *step, two, three, four, kick, six, seven, eight.*

She caught herself mouthing the steps again during a crossover and her feet tangled. But Beatrice did not notice. She was making eyes at some face in the crowd. The woman was always finding some face in a crowd, some young man or old man—any man would do, as long as he looked at her in that adoring, only-you kind of way. Pepper exhaled the breath she had been holding and focused again on the steps. At least she didn't need to be adored; she only needed to make it to the end of the routine.

She tried to keep her thoughts on the performance, but they kept finding their way back to Robert. Yes, it was troubling that he could be considering a hiatus for the show, but she could rectify that with a conversation.

The greater concern, the niggling one she could not shake, was why, if he was already in town and in the building no less, why had he not found her first?

Had he forgotten his promise?

No, of course not. How could he forget that? And hadn't there been a flash of jealousy in that office? Wasn't that why he had separated her from Ziegfeld with such haste? He cared for her still; she only had to be patient.

She tried again to focus on the routine. *One, two, dip and turn.* She had to focus on the dancing because he could be watching her even now, waiting for her in the wings.

Finally, Frankie struck the last chord of "Maple Leaf Rag," and the trio came together in a line, their arms entwined behind their backs for their bow. Was that Robert beside the ropes? Had he come for her at last? When the bow finished, she skipped toward the shadowy figure. Breathless, happy.

But out of the glare of the footlights, she could see it was not Robert. Just Laszlo, whistling his curtain-up cue over his shoulder and, hand over hand, yanking the hemp to make the red velvet soar to the flies.

• • •

A BRASS BELL JINGLED OVER THE GREEN LACQUERED DOOR when Gregory entered Brewster's Curio Shop. The tiny establishment on Fourteenth Street was nearly hidden from street view, sandwiched between Stockwell's Dry Goods and Bijou Bakery. Even now, the warm aroma of freshly baked bread overtook the store's usual musty smell, making a distant memory of the stale biscuit Gregory had eaten in his basement room before starting the day.

He slipped his cap off his head and held it in his hands as he waited, scanning the shelves laden with delicate porcelain plates and shaving kits, pewter mugs, and silverware. A wall of cuckoo clocks filled the air with insistent ticking.

"Mr. Creighton?" A gaunt woman of mature years peeked out from behind a curtain draped over the doorway to a back room. When their eyes met, she emerged, patting at the thick silver wave of hair piled upon her head and the lacy frill that spilled from her collar. "I didn't expect you back so soon," she said genially. "Have you completed the work already?"

"No, ma'am," he said, suddenly second-guessing his plan. It was too late for that. He proceeded down the tight aisle to the counter, his eyes alighting on the mantel clocks and towering grandfather clocks, parlor lamps and telephones, and cameras. So many cameras. "The talking machine repairs are nearly finished, but there's a gear and a lever that cannot be salvaged and must be replaced. I thought you might . . ."

Mrs. Brewster's tight smile dissolved. Her gray eyes flashed. "We have an agreement, Mr. Creighton." She walked up to the glass case separating them and folded her hands upon it, calmly. "I refuse to pay one penny more than we have agreed."

"You misunderstand," he said. "I seek nothing beyond our agreement. Simply a portion in advance, to cover the expense." There was no need to say more, despite the way she scowled at him. She would not weaken him with that brittle silence. He returned her gaze in kind.

After a long pause, she relented. "How small an advance?"

"Two dollars. Three, if it can be spared."

"A dear price for materials when your fee is five. All that work for two dollars?"

The question annoyed him. "That's my business." But the tone soured her. He tried again. "Once you see that my work will improve your asking price, it's my intention to renegotiate on future repairs." It was close enough to the truth.

She pursed her lips, deepening the lines around them. "Yes, well, there is no benefit to me if I receive a better price only to hand the profit over to you."

"Of course not," he said, but he knew as well as she how much she stood to gain by selling working machines instead of broken ones. On a good day an unusable talking machine might bring in four dollars, while a working one could easily bring ten.

Mrs. Brewster lifted the spectacles hanging from a chain around her neck and placed them on her nose. With her spindly fingers, she pulled a notepad from a drawer, slid a pencil from its nesting place in the fold, and jotted a few words.

His gaze drifted again to the shelf of telephones and cameras. Tucked back in the corner, as if purposely hidden from view, sat a box with a lens and a crank. He couldn't be sure, but it looked somewhat like—

The ringing of the register returned his attention to Mrs. Brewster. She was standing over the money drawer.

"Three dollars?" she inquired again, like a dare.

"Yes, ma'am."

She lifted the coin tray, pulled three bills from beneath, and closed it again. Gregory held out his hand and she counted each one into his palm.

"Is that a moving picture camera you have there?"

Mrs. Brewster followed his glance to the corner. "I believe it is, but it is not for sale. I am merely holding it, you see."

Gregory knew better than to inquire further. Lending money for collateral was not an honorable business, and he would not risk offending her by mentioning it.

Moments later, the fresh bills warm in his pocket, Gregory turned from Broadway toward the hardware store. Matty was pacing the sidewalk.

"You said ten minutes." The boy glowered.

"Did I?"

His impenitence discouraged Matty from complaining further, but it did not stop the sulking. He knew the boy only wanted to be included in his confidence. But it was better this way. He did not want to invite questions.

Besides, Matty rarely held on to a grudge. He gave the boy a tap on the back. "How were the peanuts?" He did not wait for the response, just kept walking.

"How'd you know I had peanuts?" Matty snapped, hurrying to catch up.

Gregory dropped his glance to the boy's coat and its constellation of shell shards. "You must be wearing half the bag."

Matty mumbled something salty under his breath and slapped at his coat to brush away the bits. "I was saving some for you."

Gregory grinned, despite himself. Already the boy's humor was back. "I can get my own, thank you." But it was not peanuts he had in mind. If he had figured correctly, he had enough money now to cover the supplies, with maybe a little something to spare.

• • •

PEPPER LEANED THE CHAIR BACK, BALANCING ON ITS HIND LEGS, and stared up at the rafters, with their tangle of ropes and scaffolding, suspended lights and scene drops. Her mind had wandered back to Robert during the tiny Shakespeareans' scene, and again she pushed him from her thoughts. She had searched for him in the wings. She had searched the Scarlet Room, the office, even the balcony. She had no choice but to wait.

When he chose to find her, it would be easy enough. Anyone could tell him: More often than not, she was here in the stage-right wings, on this wooden skeleton of a chair, tucked back to the wall between the curtain and the mirror where players checked themselves before taking the stage.

He might even remember it himself, for it had always been her place. When other children trundled off to classrooms, she was here, learning the patter of comics before she could read and the proper timing of a bow before she could do sums. Even when the title *wardrobe assistant* had been tacked to her name on the theater's roster, she'd gathered up whatever sewing chore her mother or Mrs. Basaraba gave her and brought it here, to the stage-right wings.

Not the stage-left wings, where Stanley sat and where acts exited the stage. Entrances were always where she wanted to be. It made her part of those moments just before performers strode out to the audience, when there was a glow about them, an attitude. She loved that moment, just as she loved being the one to say "Break a leg," or "You're going to kill them out there."

Today it had taken longer to work her way back to her chair. By the time she had given up on finding Robert, it was midway through Alfred and Edwards's skit, and she was happy to see their old straight man–fool banter getting some laughs, and that Alfred had managed to keep his coattails out of his trousers.

The company of small thespians was up next. She whispered words of encouragement as they waited their turn on the boards, and read that missed line from *Midsummer* as a precaution, and then she watched them maneuver through their selection of scenes. The tiny men milked their lines, but the audience only tittered. Pepper feared for the troupe when the biggest laugh came because the half-size Oberon forgot a line just before the curtain came down.

If Stanley had been paying attention, he would have railed at the Shakespeareans, maybe cut their minutes. But something had him up off his stool. Now that the intermission lights were up and the red velvet curtain was down, Pepper could see he was leaning heavily on his cane with one hand and slicing the air with the other at someone deeper in the shadows.

"What's got his back up?" she asked Laszlo, who had left his place at the ropes to push a broom across the stage.

"Milyen?" the man asked without energy or interest, seemingly unaware that he had slipped into his native Hungarian.

She pointed in Stanley's direction.

"Printer's boy," he mumbled, finally remembering his

English. "Programs." He circled the broom and pushed it back across the stage.

Whatever it was, she wanted nothing to do with it. Skirting the melee, she made her way to the stage door and had pulled it open when a hand landed on her shoulder.

She turned with a start to find Gregory standing over her. "What?"

"You forgot something." He glanced down the front of her.

She followed his glance and shook her head at the grave mistake she had very nearly made. It was one of Stanley's ridiculously fussy rules that costumes were not to be seen beyond the stage and backstage areas. Any player found traipsing about in the Scarlet Room or, worse, outside, without proper cover was docked a day's wage.

Gregory went to the rack at the foot of the stairs that collected costumes to be carried upstairs and pulled out a plain black cloak. He handed it to her.

"This ugly thing?" She went to the rack herself and found nothing with any more appeal. "Fine." She was not about to climb up and down three flights for her coat. She grabbed the cloak from Gregory, wrapped it around her shoulders, and held it tight. "Thank you," she muttered and pushed through the door.

Between the twist of backstage passages and the auditorium doors, the quickest and most direct route to the ticket window was by way of the street, and in a moment she was at the booth's side door, knocking. "Em, it's me."

A moment later, she heard the lock unlatch and the door swung open. "Hi, doll," Em said, and hastened back to the counter in front of the window to accept two coins from a woman on the street side of the glass.

Pepper closed the door behind her and made her way through

the small closet of a room where Em spent her days, filled with boxes of old programs and old playbills tacked to the green plastered walls.

"You will most definitely enjoy the show, love," Em was saying to the woman, leaning forward as though she were conveying a secret.

The woman, not terribly young, though with a pleasing plumpness to her cheeks, was dressed in a white shirtwaist and black skirt, with a simple black ribbon crossed at her throat. A shop clerk or factory worker, perhaps. She blushed at Em's attention, yet lingered until Pepper settled into one of the two empty chairs at the end of the counter.

"I don't want to interrupt," she said, noticing the woman fluster. "I only came to get a program. Don't mind me." She grabbed a folded sheet from the stack beside Em and hid behind it, engrossing herself in the curlicue scrolls and bold black letters touting the wonder and amazement of the week's entertainment.

But it was too late. The woman fumbled for the ticket and program Em had slid into the small dip at the bottom of the window and hurried away.

"Stop by on your way out, dear. I'd love to hear your thoughts on our little show." Em's final words were said to the woman's back as she moved briskly toward the theater's main door. Only when the woman had handed her ticket to the ripper and slipped out of view did Em settle back in her chair and acknowledge Pepper. "I know what you must be thinking. I was merely making small talk."

"You needn't explain. Really. I'm sure Mother wouldn't mind. It's been nearly a year, after all." Had it really been so long? It felt as though Bessie could walk into a room any moment. As if she could be just downstairs. But there was not time to think of that now. "I really didn't mean to interrupt."

"I know, dollface." It seemed Em might say more, but instead she grabbed a program and waved it. "Did you see this? Haven't seen a typesetting mistake like this in years."

Pepper looked at the one she held in her hand. She skimmed down the front, and then, there it was. "Oh my. Madame Bidet?" She giggled, unable to help herself. "I'm sorry. I shouldn't. It's awful, really." She cleared her throat and composed herself. "What does Stanley plan to do?"

"He's told the printer to redo the order, of course. But that'll take time. Until then he says to hand them out as usual. I suppose he thinks people won't notice."

"Perhaps she'll have a sense of humor about it."

"No, not this one." Em gazed out the window, watching the passersby, waiting for someone, anyone to approach the counter.

"Well, it could be worse," Pepper offered.

"Worse than changing someone's name to a lavatory contraption?"

Pepper tensed her lips to keep the smile at bay. "You're right. But maybe she'll be one of those uppity headliners and never leave her dressing room. Maybe she'll never even see the program."

"It serves Stanley right, I suppose." Em still had that thousand-yard stare. "What was he thinking, bringing in a woman with the brass to call herself *Madame*? The Chance isn't a pretty little opera house, for crying out loud. It's vaudeville. It should be fun. It's like that glum Irish lout all over again."

"Have you seen her act?"

"Once. In Paris, years ago. She's no 'Parisian sensation,' I'll tell you that much." She lowered her voice so she wouldn't be heard by a man approaching the window. He slipped two dimes into the dip beneath the window; she handed him a ticket and a program, and sent him on his way with a smile and an "Enjoy the show, sir."

Pepper read further along the program's puffery. *MADAME BIDET—American Debut of the Esteemed French Chanteuse. A Most Exquisite and Refined Talent.*

When the window was clear again, she whispered, "Can she even sing?"

Em lifted her unlit cigar from the ashtray and tapped it. "You know the French. They don't sing; they talk their songs."

"How bad do you think it will be?" Pepper envisioned another auditorium of ladies fleeing from their seats and closed her eyes. Could they survive another week like that?

Em pulled out her pocket watch. "Her curtain should be coming up. What do you say we go see for ourselves?"

"Close the window?"

Continuous vaudeville meant the show ran five times a day, with only brief intermissions and pauses between starts. It also meant a spectator could walk in anytime and stay as long as he liked. It was more convenient for the spectators, but certainly not for Em.

Em, however, was up and at the door. "All that complaining to Stanley finally amounted to something. Watch this." She peeked out and saw Matty talking up Mr. Christopher while the barkeep unpacked liquor bottles. She waved the boy over.

Matty answered the call, reluctantly. Seeing Pepper inside, he smiled, nodded, and pulled the cap from his head. "Hello, Miss MacClair." To Em he said, "You needed something, ma'am, er, sir . . . I mean . . ." His voice trailed off. He wrinkled his face and gave his dusty brown hair a rough scratch, as if that would rattle his brain into better working order.

Pepper turned so the boy didn't see the twitches of her grin.

Whatever kind of life he'd led before coming to The Chance, she was sure it had not included anyone like Em Charmaigne.

"Just call me Em," her friend said gently. "I need you to cover the window for a bit. Can you do that for me, kid?"

"Sure. What do I have to do?"

"Cash, tickets, everything should be in the desk."

Matty pulled out the beat-up drawer and acquainted himself with the contents.

"Should be quick," Em added. "Just a few minutes."

The boy nodded and settled into Em's battered swivel chair. Yet there was a distinct grumbling, something that sounded to Pepper like a muttered "Heard that one before."

Em ignored it, so Pepper did, too, because beyond the ticket booth, Frankie's ivories were signaling the end of the Helzigs' act. By the time they reached the stage-right wings, the Marvelous Marvani's magic act was earning a promising round of applause.

Onstage, the dark and slender Marvani, outfitted in tuxedo, top hat, and satin-lined cape, produced a birdcage from beneath a square of blue silk lying flat upon a table. He followed the trick by placing the blue scarf atop the cage, and when he snapped it away, a blue feathered bird tweeted sweetly within. He repeated the trick with a red scarf, which produced a red bird. And a yellow scarf, producing a yellow bird. Each rendition earned fainter and fainter applause.

Pepper groaned and looked away. She could not bear to watch the man as he struggled to amaze spectators who had grown bored with him three minutes into his ten-minute act. Instead she watched the doorway, eager for her first sight of this "most exquisite talent."

The woman was already late to the wings. Most headliners tended to be, but Marvani's act was nearly half through and there was still no sign of the woman. Across the stage, she could see she wasn't the only one concerned. Mr. Stanley was up and pacing, dragging his braced leg like a plank at his side.

He went to the door as if he meant to collect her from the dressing room himself just as it flung open. The stage manager stumbled back, saving himself from the floor with a quick repositioning of his cane.

"Well, would you look at that."

Em hardly needed to call attention to the rotund woman sauntering through the backstage passage who was now standing as if she were lost, her head whipping around one way and then the other. *"'Alo, 'alo, s'il vous plait!"* she called loudly, despite her proximity to the stage.

"That is our 'most exquisite talent'?" Em muttered under her breath while everyone else backstage huffed an angry "Sh!"

Madame Bizet's heavy jowls turned pink with anger and embarrassment as she stood with her arms crossed over a lavender silk gown. A cape of creamy lace ruffles sat upon her round shoulders. It was a lovely gown, remarkable really, considering Mrs. Basaraba had created it that morning.

From behind the headliner, another woman appeared, a tiny slip of a thing dressed in a gray wool dress and pinafore. She flitted and twittered around the portly singer, puffing lace around the collar and wrists, adjusting the tilt of the wide, ostrich-plumed hat. All the while from her tiny lips issued a stream of coddling words as she took the woman's hand and led her closer to the stage.

Stanley worked his way around, too. "We have what you requested in place," he whispered to Madame Bizet. "I have taken the liberty, however, of speaking to our pianist and he assures me he is quite familiar with Balfe's compositions and would be happy to accompany you—"

"Non!" She glared, her face growing an even deeper shade of red.

The maid inserted herself between her employer and Mr. Stanley. "What my mistress means to say is that she greatly prefers the recorded accompaniment, and I believe there is a mention of this in the contract."

Stanley leveled his glance on the maid. "I realize it is in the contract; however, the piano will offer a superior quality of sound. It was my understanding that the recording was to be present in the event our pianist was unfamiliar with the arrangement."

The maid slid several folded sheets of paper from the wrist of her sleeve. She flipped through pages. "It is mentioned that the choice rests with the artist. Let me find it, yes, here it is." She held out the third sheet to him with her finger pointed to the clause.

Stanley pushed the page away. "Fine. The Graphophone will be ready."

"And the introduction, *monsieur*?"

He mumbled something affirmative and hobbled off.

When the magician took his bow and exited the stage, the easel changer sprinted out and pulled the table toward Stanley. He disappeared and a moment later was back, hoisting the Graphophone and orienting its yawning copper horn toward the auditorium. For its part, the sparse audience was making a music of its own, rustling in the seats and whispering to one another, speculating on the reason for the delay.

Finally, with the machine in place and the music cylinder ready, the easel changer removed the magician's card to reveal the name of Madame Bizet. Then he pulled a folded sheet from his trouser pocket and moved hesitantly to the center of the stage.

Pepper looked at Em, and said with her eyes, "What madness is this?"

Em shook her head, as baffled as Pepper.

The easel changer cleared his throat and with a thin, tight voice and trembling hands, said: "Ladies and gentlemen: We are delighted to present to you an exclusive engagement . . ." He glanced at Stanley, who nodded from his stool and waved for the young man to continue. ". . . an exclusive engagement of a most prestigious talent in her American debut." He cleared his throat again and tugged at his collar. "A chanteuse whose surpassing beauty of both voice and visage has earned her unparalleled acclaim in France and across Europe, and who now brings her exquisite and refined talent to The Chance Theatre. Allow me the privilege of introducing to you . . ." He fumbled a bit with his script and then shot his right hand out, ramrod straight to the side. "Madame Bizet."

He rushed offstage as all eyes moved to the performer, who was beaming with flushing delight as she glided like a great ruffled globe across the stage, reveling in the limp applause as if it were a standing ovation. She stopped to the right of center stage. Behind her, the curtain had been raised on a lakeside tableau, with the white gazebo and fake potted trees and flowers. She smiled a wide, dimpled smile, brought her hands demurely to the spill of lace above her bosom, and serenely nodded to Stanley, who lowered the arm to the wax cylinder.

Anticipation had settled over the theater, both in the auditorium and backstage. Even stagehands were crowded into the wings, angling for a view of this spectacle. The machine's crackles scratched the air, followed by an orchestral overture. Then Madame Bizet spoke as if reciting poetry:

"When other lips and other hearts . . . their tales of love shall tell . . ."

"Oh, good grief," Em repeated again and shook her head.

It was a fine voice Madame Bizet had, a pleasantly lilting soprano that spread through the auditorium like a soft breeze. But that song! It was impossible to imagine a more dreary selection. It not only reached into the chest to wrench the heart, it strangled it, leaving it limp and lifeless. If it had been her intent to fill the audience with despair, she could consider herself a rousing success.

She would likely be the only one, however. Even Stanley appeared dismayed, sitting upon his stool, hands upon his cane. As the song progressed, his fingers tightened until his hands had become fists that seemed intent on snapping it in two. Madame Bizet paid no attention to him, nor to the rustling and whispers that at first could be heard in the lulls between verses but then were evident even above her most ardent and emotive measures.

Again, Pepper thought of Robert. Was he in the auditorium? Was Ziegfeld? Were they witnessing this embarrassment?

Yet nothing, it seemed, disturbed Madame Bizet. Not until the gallery denizens, who had already been sniggering, decided they'd had enough. Those most fickle and demanding patrons paid only a dime for their rear balcony seats and little if any attention to the posted signs reminding them to exercise discretion and proper manners while enjoying the entertainments. They trumpeted their dissatisfaction by stomping their boots upon the floor. The sound unnerved Madame Bizet. It was evident in the way her glance was darting around, searching for the source, even as she continued to recite:

"When hollow hearts shall wear a mask . . . 'twill break your own to see . . ."

From somewhere a throaty man's voice rang out over hers: "A most commodious talent, indeed!" A roar of laughter and then: "The hook! The Hook! THE HOOK!" The words droned on until the whole auditorium had taken up the chant.

It did not matter that The Chance had never employed that most demeaning prop to drag unpopular performers from the stage. The practice that Harry Miner had introduced and made so popular at his rough and rowdy Miner's Bowery Theatre in the lower quarters was now common parlance for theatergoers, at least in New York. Its meaning, however, had not carried across the Atlantic, for Madame Bizet appeared perplexed by the outbursts.

Until, perhaps, the tomato sailed over the lower seats and landed upon the delicate lawn of her lavender silk gown. The shriek that erupted from the woman's lips curled Pepper's toes.

"I'm damn glad I didn't miss this," Em murmured.

Pepper was speechless. She wasn't surprised to see Madame Bizet grab the sides of her ruffled skirt and flee to the safety of the stage-left wings. She was somewhat shocked, however, when the maid took off across the stage in pursuit of her mistress, only to stop midway in the glare of the lights and stare blankly into the auditorium. Such a look came over her, such a horrible, vengeful look, Pepper thought the woman might actually shake her finger and lecture the whole lot of them. But another offstage cry from her mistress redirected her attentions, and in a blink she ran off into the wings.

Stanley was on his feet and gesturing into the shadows behind him. Pepper ached to scream at him to get someone, anyone on the stage. The audience might be rollicking at the gallery's prank, but very soon they would realize the show had come to a complete and utter halt.

Frankie, at least, had the presence of mind to push up his sleeves and launch into one of his favorite numbers, something familiar and upbeat, something that made even the crabbiest toes tap along.

Pepper pushed past Em and Jimmy and all the players who had gathered for a look. She searched until she found Professor Charles Hawkinson, sitting against the black curtain that covered the rear wall, with his easel and its oversize map of Borneo and the Sunda Isles in one hand and a pointer in the other.

"Get out there, Hawkinson," she cried. "Get out there now and fill up the minutes."

There was no time for Pepper's usual well-wishes and encouraging words. She yanked the man up with another single word. "Go!"

The professor—looking every inch the academician, attired as he was in a brown tweed suit and brown bow tie, with an unkempt crown of dusky brown hair—walked hesitantly onto the stage, materials in hand, eyes darting into the boisterous crowd, and promptly slipped on the skin of another hurled tomato. The crowd burst into a fresh roar of laughter.

Pepper hid her face in her hands. Under different circumstances, she would enjoy a bit of slapstick added to this otherwise stale lecture on the indigenous cultures of a set of islands half a world away. But not now, not today. Hawkinson's act needed to hew to its purpose, which had nothing to do with entertainment.

It was another of Mr. DeGraaf's concessions to his wife and her reformist ideals that every bill would include at least one act devoted to audience edification. Yet its first priority and its foremost purpose was to do what any last act on a continuous vaudeville bill was intended to do: prompt patrons to leave. It was how the slot earned the nickname "chaser," as in chasing out patrons who had paid, with the intent of making room for new arrivals, and it was something at which Professor Hawkinson was exceptionally adept.

"I cannot bear to watch," Em said, and edged back with the

others who had lost interest now that the headliner's maelstrom had passed.

Pepper left with her friend, following her through the winding backstage passages to see her off at the stage door before climbing the stairs to the dressing room, where she should have been already, preparing for the next show.

"How foolish we must look to Robert," she said at the door. "What fools we must seem." To herself she wondered how she was ever going to convince him it was all Stanley's doing. Why would he ever want to save a show as dismal as this?

"It may not be much of a consolation," Em said, "but I saw him leave before the show started. Which reminds me, you might have mentioned Ziegfeld was in there with him. Good grief, what a peacock that one is. You should have seen him strutting around the Scarlet Room. Like he owned the place. What do you suppose they were up to in there?"

"I'm sure it was nothing," she said, and hoped Em believed her, though it was taking everything she had to still believe it herself.

Four

THE SECOND SHOW PASSED WITH NO SIGN OF ROBERT DeGraaf. Then the third and the fourth. Waiting in the wings for her fifth, and last, performance of the day, Pepper told herself it could only mean he was waiting for her to finish for the night. He would want her full attention, not something less while she fretted about call times and the usual performance preparations. It had been three years, after all, and there was so much to say, far more than could be contained in a few hurried moments backstage, or even a quiet corner during the intermission.

So why was he not waiting in the wings when she left the stage? Why was there no sign or word from him at all? She could feel the last of her happy optimism slipping as she lingered behind Beatrice and Trixie, hoping he might still call out. In the dressing room, while she rubbed away the greasepaint and slid off her costume's shoulder straps, she listened for his footsteps and a knock upon the door.

There were none.

"Are you going to stand at the sink all night, or can someone else take a turn?"

"Sorry," Pepper said, moving aside so Beatrice could take her place.

Pepper was still drying her face, her skin raw from the scrubbing, but in her mind, she was back in DeGraaf's office, retracing the already rutted terrain of that morning's encounter. Had he said something she missed? Was there some clue to this absence at all?

Only one possibility remained, and it was so simple she upbraided herself for not realizing it sooner. He had always been so private; why should she expect anything different from him now? He would wish for a quiet reunion, wouldn't he? Not here in the theater, with so many inquisitive eyes.

As quickly as she could manage, she slipped back into her black frock and long plum coat, pulled on the ringed stockings and her boots, and settled the black hat with the short violet plume on her curls. She knew exactly what she had to do.

It was quarter past nine when she emerged from the stage door and headed off for Mr. DeGraaf's penthouse at the St. Denis Hotel. She turned north on Broadway and covered the blocks quickly, weaving through the nighttime crowd of pedestrians making visits to dining rooms and theaters, or just out for a late-night stroll. Yet she might as well have been alone on the street for all the attention she paid to anyone else.

As she passed the buildings, all four, five, six stories tall and all nudged up one against the other in endless procession on one side of the street, and Wanamaker's vast department store and

Grace Church, with its Gothic spire scratching the nighttime sky, on the other, she practiced what she would say. She would begin with an apology, naturally, for interrupting his meeting with Ziegfeld. She would not ask why he had feigned interest in the man's show. And under no circumstances would she ask him why she had to hear from Stanley of all people that he was back in town. She had her dignity, after all.

By the time she rounded the corner at Eleventh Street and reached the hotel's elegant sweep of emerald awnings and the twisted topiaries at the main entrance, she felt quite ready to face Robert. Excited, even.

A porter in red uniform welcomed her with a cordial nod and held the door. She pulled back her shoulders and nodded as politely as she could, as though she were used to such fuss, and walked with purpose to the gleaming mahogany staircase inside. She took the steps with smug satisfaction, thinking Sarah Bernhardt had ascended these steps while residing in the hotel during her first American tour. Mark Twain and General Ulysses S. Grant, too. One day, she thought, some young woman might muse, *Pepper MacClair once ascended these steps.*

When Pepper reached the arched door that belonged to Mr. DeGraaf, she lifted the brass knocker and tapped twice.

Gertie Walters, a shriveled spinster who had worked for Mr. DeGraaf since Mrs. DeGraaf died of pneumonia during the winter of ninety-nine, answered with a grimace. "What are you doing here, Miss MacClair?"

"Good evening, Gertie. You're looking well." She smiled her sweetest smile.

"I should look busy, for that is what I am. What brings you round at this late hour?"

"I came to see Robert."

"Young Mr. DeGraaf is out for the evening. I shall tell him you called." She stepped forward to close the door.

Pepper stepped into the threshold. "I'd like to wait, if you don't mind."

Gertie's skinny eyebrows pulled together. "That would hardly be proper. What would your mother say?"

Her mother would be appalled, as Gertie well knew. Yet Pepper was not about to let propriety keep her from her task.

"Who's there, Gertie?" Pepper recognized Mr. DeGraaf's gruff baritone. After two chesty coughs, he added: "Is it Robert?"

She had prepared herself to face Robert, but she had not even considered the possibility of crossing paths with the older DeGraaf. Shouldn't he be in bed? When her mother had been ill, she had hardly left hers.

When Gertie did not respond, he bellowed, "Answer me!"

The older woman took a step back but kept her glare fixed on Pepper. "It's Bessie's girl, sir."

A scraping noise emerged from the far end of the foyer, and Mr. DeGraaf appeared in a wheeled chair in the double doorway of his library. By the strength of his voice, Pepper had expected to see the familiar Old Gruff. But this man with the drawn face, wrapped in a silk robe and slippers, appeared at least a decade older than the last time she had seen him. How weak he seemed, how shrunken and frail. It was impossible not to stare.

"Pepper MacClair?" His voice was still thick with Dutch gravel and more robust than his appearance would suggest. "What on earth are you doing at my door?"

• • •

AT QUARTER TO TEN, EM DECIDED ENOUGH WAS ENOUGH. NO one had approached the window in more than an hour, so what were the chances anyone would notice if she closed up a little early? None. Probably less than none, if there were such a thing.

Besides, she was too itchy to sit in the musty little room another minute. Too downright angry.

She hung the *Closed* sign from the hook above the window and pulled down the shutter before she slid the cash tray out of the desk. She counted out the day's take. Fifteen dollars. Fifteen measly dollars for a whole damn day. She found a pencil deeper in the drawer and noted the number on her log. She wrote it again on a deposit slip, along with the date, and stuffed it in the bag with the cash.

"Not even worth a trip to the bank," she muttered as she grabbed the money and her hat and locked the door behind herself.

Marvani was onstage, but Stanley was not on his stool. She went to his office, which had been a performers' greenroom before Stanley tossed out the stuffed chairs and tables and pulled in a beat-up desk. The door was closed, and she was about to knock when she heard a voice within. A woman's voice. She was trying to make it out when the door popped open and Madame Bizet appeared, looking flustered and more than a little out of sorts. She tipped up her nose at Em and strode past.

Stanley was maneuvering himself up from his chair when he saw her. With a sigh, he fell back and stared at the bare olive walls. Not a framed photograph, not a playbill. Nothing to hide the cracked plaster or even the water stain that spread out behind him like a rusty and lopsided crown. "What is it?"

He was tired, she could hear it in his voice. But they were all tired. Working night and day, day after day. It was no excuse. She stepped up to his desk and dropped the bag with a thud. "Fifteen dollars today. Fifteen dollars and thirty-five cents."

He pulled the bag toward him and dropped it in the drawer beneath his right hand. He did not bother to count it. He knew she was right. She was always right.

"That's it?" He sounded hopeful.

"Hardly."

He sighed. "Of course it isn't."

"I've been trying to make sense of it, Harland. Hell, I've been sitting out front all day trying to make sense of it, and I can't."

"I suppose you're talking about Bizet?"

"Damn right. What the hell kind of name is that anyway?"

He winced and glanced past her to the open office door and the empty corridor beyond. "Would you at least close the door?"

She twisted up her face but did as he asked.

When they were alone, he said, "Fine. Madame Bizet is not perfect, I'll grant you that."

"Perfect? She isn't even in the realm of entertainment."

"I don't agree. She gives the place class."

Em rolled her eyes.

"We need something big, Em. We need something besides the usual chaff if we're going to bring back the crowds."

She threw her hands over her head. "How many big names have been through here, Harland? Carus and Cohen? Beban and Fields? Call in a favor, for crying out loud."

He tilted back in his chair and gazed at the single lightbulb fixed in the ceiling. He sighed again, long and low. "I did, Em. I've written to every blasted performer on DeGraaf's wall, anyone who owes anything to this theater, and you want to know what I got in return?"

He pulled open a low desk drawer and grabbed a handful of white envelopes. From one, he pulled a sheet of paper, unfolded it, and read: " 'It is with the deepest regret that I must decline your invitation to perform again at The Chance Theatre. If my booking contract did not prevent me from appearing on non-Syndicate stages, nothing would give me more pleasure. With kindest regards and fondest wishes, George Beban.' "

He dropped the note on the desk and picked another.

" 'Dreadfully sorry . . .' " He tossed it aside and chose another. " 'Contract prevents me . . .' " He dropped it and picked another and another. "All of them, the same damn thing. 'Cannot help, sorry.' All I can do is bring in performers beyond the circuits' reach. Europeans not beholden to a Syndicate contract, up-and-comers not yet swallowed into Keith and Albee's system, and, yes, the has-beens no one else wants to touch. I thought if we could just find a way to appeal to the ladies, if we could offer the kind of polite entertainment going over at, say, the Hippodrome, then we could carve out a little niche for ourselves. That damn Hippodrome can fill six thousand seats. We only need a tenth of that to survive."

"No one wants to see sappy songs by an Irish blowhard or some Frenchie who looks like a powder puff on legs. There's no fun in that."

He paused, composed himself. "Well, the point is moot. Madame Bizet just informed me she will be on the eleven-twenty train to Boston."

"She can't leave. She has a contract."

"She saw the programs. I believe that would have been enough, but she assures me her maid has shown her at least five instances where The Chance has fallen short of its contractual obligations. She tells me she is prepared to retain an attorney should we try to hold her. So now, I don't have a bad headliner. I have no headliner at all."

Em whistled the equivalent of boy-oh-boy. "That's a tough

break, Harland. But why are you stuck with this business anyway? Why isn't Robert DeGraaf lining up the talent?"

Stanley shook his head, disgusted. "The boy's idea of management is quite different from my own, or his father's. He sticks his nose in files all day, scouring receipts and invoices and bank ledgers for God knows what. He's no help at all."

"What are you going to do, then?"

He leaned back in his chair and stared hard at the steeples he had made with his fingers. "There's one favor I still might be able to call in."

"Oh? Who?"

He locked eyes with her across the desk. "You, Emmalyn."

• • •

MR. DEGRAAF STARED DOWN HIS WIDE, FLESHY NOSE AT PEPPER before turning it on his maid.

"Make yourself useful, Gertie. Get me some coffee. And make sure it is coffee this time. None of that flowery tea business, do you hear me? I'll take it in the library, and you may as well bring an extra cup for our guest."

Gertie disappeared down the hallway, and he swiveled his chair back toward the open double doors from which he had emerged. Pepper assumed he was returning to his guest and she had been duly dismissed.

"Are you coming or not?" he barked.

Her hand retracted from the cold brass doorknob. "Me, sir?"

"Yes, you, Pepper MacClair. Do you see anyone else?"

Instinctively, she glanced to either side to be sure. It was strange to hear him refer to her by name. In all the years of their acquaintance, she had been "that MacClair girl," or more commonly, "Bessie's girl." Otherwise she was nameless to him, and invisible until her association with Robert. It had been awkward enough when Mr. DeGraaf had treated her as a shadow with no form or purpose, but after Robert, it became something worse. He could not—or would not—look at her, let alone spare a word.

"Yes, sir," she stammered. "Of course."

She followed, dutifully, as the man manipulated his chair's wheels and proceeded back to his library. She paused at the doorway, giving her eyes a moment to adjust to the darker space. The last time she had seen the room was years ago, when she had come with her mother to clean while Gertie visited a sick relative. Not much had changed. It was still a dark cavern of richly polished wood with a high, coffered ceiling, a long arched window draped with maroon brocade curtains, and the colossal hearth where a fire crackled and glowed. The light from the flames danced across the glass doors of the bookshelves lining the walls and the glossy surfaces of Mrs. DeGraaf's collection of blue-and-white Delft scattered about the room. Mr. DeGraaf motioned for Pepper to join him beside the fire.

She settled at the edge of an upholstered chair.

"So you've come for Robert?"

"Yes, sir." She watched Mr. DeGraaf's thick fingers tangle together in his lap like the making and unmaking of a knot. She did not want to speak of Robert, not to his father. She knew his feelings on the matter. But she no longer cared that he preferred to send his son away instead of seeing him matched with her. Robert was a man now, and he could choose for himself. That he had returned was proof enough that he had chosen her. So what good could come from revisiting those old complaints?

"I never had a chance to thank you for what you did for my mother," she hurried to say, grabbing at the first thought that occurred to her to put the conversation on a different track.

It had surprised her, and it seemed to surprise him as well. His thick, unruly brows rose. "Your mother?"

"The funeral service. The burial. It was generous." The words almost stuck in her throat, but she choked them out. They needed to be said. He had not had to do it, but he had, and without a word.

He said nothing, only gazed at her, as if he were no longer seeing her, but looking on to something far in the distance. Then he unlaced his fingers and placed them on the giant wheels of his chair. He rolled himself to a cabinet, where he lifted a crystal decanter and poured himself a portion of the clear liquid. With a glance he invited Pepper to have a glass, too.

She declined with a shake of her head.

With the glass precariously balanced in his lap, he returned to the fire. "A jenever from Amsterdam, my native city," he said. "Your mother secured that bottle for me. A gift, it was, though quite unnecessary." He shook his head and that faraway look returned.

Unnecessary, indeed. Pepper recalled the grim occasion, though it was unlikely Mr. DeGraaf ever knew the strife that bottle had caused.

Saving and sacrifice had always been Bessie's way. It was a point of pride for her to get by on less than half her wages, and the rest she squirreled away in her room, in an old sewing basket she kept hidden beneath her bed. That money would do some good one day, she told Pepper whenever the girl asked. Someday she would buy Pepper something so wonderful and so grand, it would make all their sacrifices worthwhile.

But the disaster of Pepper's debut, that shame she had brought on herself and her mother, had changed Bessie's mind. She must have decided Pepper no longer deserved whatever grand thing she had planned because it was a few days after that dreadful occasion when Bessie walked into their rooms with that sewing basket swinging from her arm, empty. Pepper inquired about the money, but Bessie had shrugged off the question, telling Pepper, "It's not your concern."

Pepper had persisted.

"It's doing more good than it was sitting here in a heap," her mother had said.

"You spent it? On what?" The pained look on her mother's face told her that was not it. "You gave it away, didn't you?" Yes, Pepper could see the guilt plainly. "To Em?" No, not Em. But who? Outside of the theater, Bessie knew hardly anyone in New York. "You sent it back to Scotland, didn't you? You sent it back to your people."

"They are your people, too, lass, but that is not the point. That money is needed, now leave it at that."

And Pepper had left it at that, for it was clear that Bessie had shipped that large sum back to Scotland, back to that fishing village, back to a family she would never see again, rather than spend it on her disgrace of a daughter. Still, that had not been the worst of the betrayal. That came later that night when a boy knocked on their door and asked Pepper to tell her mother the fine Dutch gin she had ordered had just been delivered to Mr. DeGraaf, just as she asked.

Pepper was sure her mother had given away those savings to punish Pepper. That Bessie would set aside even a portion for Mr. DeGraaf was the most horrible insult of all. It told Pepper just how much she had disappointed her mother, as if she did not already know.

When Bessie's coughing began the following year, Pepper wondered if her mother had regretted sending the money away.

When the congestion moved deep into her chest and the hot baths and poultices gave no more relief, that money would have paid for doctor visits and any number of remedies. But the MacClair women had no money for such extravagances then, and it had made Pepper angry all over again.

"Bessie was always so proud," Mr. DeGraaf added. "I suppose it had something to do with that Scottish blood, for I see that fire in you as well."

Scottish blood, indeed.

He shifted and took another drink, then set it back in his lap. "I had a reason for wanting to speak with you, however."

Pepper closed her mind to those old thoughts, those old pains. She told herself again they were best forgotten.

Mr. DeGraaf was watching her, every twitch and blink. "What I want to know, Miss MacClair, is how you are faring with the Dolls."

She tensed. "Has Mr. Stanley mentioned something?"

"Yes, he has had quite a bit to say on the matter. But I should like to hear it from you." Those stormy green eyes slid away from the fire to pin her. To dare her, it seemed, to justify her place on his stage.

What wickedness had Stanley spewed to the old man? What venom had he scribbled in his notebooks? "I'm getting along quite well, I believe." She tried to return that glare, to defend herself with her own hard glance. But there was doubt in his expression; she could see it like a beacon shining out from those wide, disappointed eyes. "And I am improving," she continued. "Every day. I know I have more progress to make, but I work hard, and . . ." She stopped the tumble of words. They were not helping.

His frown deepened. "Surely there is something else you might rather do?"

The question hit her like a marble wall, cold and impenetrable. She looked away, to an arrangement of Delft platters above the mantel, the deep folds of the draperies, the bronze statue of a lion atop a pedestal in the corner. So it was true. Her whole body shook with the realization. Stanley wanted her cut, and he had Mr. DeGraaf on his side. He might as well have thrown her into the East River, let her loose upon the swell and sway of those angry tides. "No, sir, there is nothing else I would rather do. The Chance Theatre is where I want to be."

She could not sit another moment. She rose from the chair and went to the window, pulled aside the curtain to look over Broadway and the Grace Church spire. In the span of their talk, a fresh storm had moved in. Rain kissed the glass. She held her hand to the frigid pane and felt the force of the drops hitting the other side. A chill traveled from her palm to every part of her. She looked back to see Mr. DeGraaf staring into his drink. Was he deciding how to deliver the news? Some way to soften the message that there was no longer a place for her upon his stage?

Movement at the door startled her. It was Gertie with the coffee. The old woman moved through the firelight with the utmost care, balancing the tray with the pot and the cups, with the attendant sugar and cream. It all happened so slowly, it gave Pepper time to think.

Before the tray could be settled onto the table beside Mr. DeGraaf, Pepper had already moved away from the window. "I have taken up too much of your time," she said, edging toward the door. "If you will be so kind as to tell Robert I stopped by, I really must be on my way."

Alarmed, Mr. DeGraaf glanced up from the tray. "But, Miss MacClair, I insist—"

"You have been so kind already," she said, cutting him short.

"But I have imposed quite enough. If you'll excuse me, I'll see myself out. Good-bye, Mr. DeGraaf, Gertie." Hastily, she slipped out through the door Gertie had left open.

In the amber glow, Gertie poured a stream of hot coffee into her employer's porcelain cup and muttered, "Strange girl."

Mr. DeGraaf sipped the last of his jenever, set the glass upon the tray, and accepted the cup she handed to him. "Not so strange," he said with a sigh. "But stubborn and proud. Quite like her mother, God help her."

Five

PAUSING UNDER THE ST. DENIS HOTEL'S AWNING, Pepper clutched her fingers to her lips and warmed them with a breath. She was stalling, waiting for the rain to lift.

"Shall I get you a cab, miss?" the doorman asked for the third time in as many minutes.

"No, I'm fine, thank you." It was a lie. She had no money for fare, but she could hardly say so. She did not want more looks of pity. Not from Mr. DeGraaf, not from Gertie, and certainly not from a hotel doorman. Before he could ask again, she pulled her hat low, hunched deeper into her velvet coat, and left the shelter of the awning to press onward, against the rain and the wind.

She turned at Broadway, and the torrent lashed harder still, driven by gusts that passed over her with a feral howl. It brought with it the rancid whiff of the East River docks and dumping wharves, and all the foul muck usually kept to the alleys and back streets of the Lower East Side. A queasiness came over her. The sour stench brought back memories of the months she and Bessie had lived on Hester Street. It was the same stench that had greeted them the day they arrived on the steamer from Glasgow. When they had sat outside Castle Garden with their small trunk, waiting for her father to find them.

"He promised he would come," was all Bessie would say when Pepper asked why he was not among the masses gathered to greet the other disembarking passengers, and again when they set their small black case near a bench on the dock and sat with the steamer's stern to their backs and the Castle Garden administration building and manicured lawns before them. "There are so many people," Bessie said, running her hand over Pepper's ringlets. "It may take a while, lass."

Four hours they had waited before giving up.

Pepper closed her eyes. None of it mattered. Not the father who never appeared. Not the savings her mother sent back to grandparents and uncles whose faces she could not even remember.

Pepper tilted forward against the wind and moved quickly through the rain, ignoring the mad slapping of the awnings over store windows and doors, the scraping and banging of the metal fire escapes overhead.

Though she tried to keep to the driest spaces, the wetness was soaking her and making her skirts cling immodestly to her limbs. She forced herself on, shivering and miserable, and thought of home, of submerging herself to her chin in a hot bath. As if that alone would set everything right. As if that were her only concern.

Of course it was not.

A voice within her whispered, *Where will you go when Stanley fires you?* She had no answer.

Through the downpour, horses ferried carriages along Broadway, but one came to a stop a few paces ahead. The door of the dark, gleaming coach swung open and a man's top hat appeared, his face hidden in shadow.

"Miss MacClair?"

It was Robert.

Her breath caught. She did not want him to see her like this. She stared down and proceeded onward.

"Miss MacClair!" He jumped from the cabin, pulling the back of his coat collar up to protect against the rain.

There was nowhere to hide. She stepped into a shop door's alcove and watched him approach, trying to formulate a reasonable explanation for being out alone and so late on such a merciless night.

When she could see his face, the smooth, strong line of his jaw, the golden gloss of his hair darkened by the night, she somehow found the strength to speak. "Robert, what a lovely surprise."

How cavalier she sounded! How perfectly aloof. Perhaps he would not guess the distress she had suffered that day.

"Good heavens, what are you doing out at this hour? And in this storm, no less?"

There was no reproach in those wide, emerald eyes, or the crinkle along his brow. Only concern. He reached out and took her elbow.

"Come into the carriage," he said. "It's dry, and wherever it is you're going, I'm happy to deliver you. No, I will accept no argument. This downpour might very well sweep you off to New York harbor, and then what would I do?"

Such cheerful tenderness in his voice, as if he hadn't a worry in the world.

"I'm on my way home," she said, giving in to his care. She wrapped her arms about herself and allowed him to guide her back to the carriage. At the door, she ducked inside. Her fingers brushed the wet lawn of her coat. She hoped he would not notice.

After conveying the destination to his driver, Robert entered the cabin as well, taking the seat alongside her.

The sudden proximity gave her a start. The warmth of him, the subtle fragrance of his hair oil and lavender soap. It was Robert. At last.

Perhaps it was a good omen, his finding her this way. It had to be. But she could not allow it to distract her from her purpose. She pushed his father's words from her thoughts and concentrated on the greater problem, for there would be no show to speak of if Robert allowed Ziegfeld to take over.

Robert leaned forward to knock on the wood above the opposite cushion, signaling the driver to be off. Outside, the reins snapped and the coach lurched. When they had settled into a rhythmic sway behind the horses, Pepper could feel Robert's gaze upon her. She turned to see the familiar glimmer in his eyes and that irresistible dimple in his chin.

"You are thoroughly soaked, my dear."

"Yes, I suppose I am." She hoped the darkness obscured her shame. "I was not expecting rain when I set out."

"And where were you off to at this hour?" She read no disapproval in his voice, only curiosity.

"Actually, I was coming from the St. Denis. I was hoping to find you there. I did not realize the meeting with Mr. Ziegfeld would keep you so late." How careful she was to keep the judgment from her voice.

"Ziegfeld? Goodness no, we parted hours ago."

"I was wrong to barge in this morning, on your meeting, I mean. I wanted to apologize."

He chuckled softly beside her. "Yes, that was awkward." His grin returned, telling her the offense had not been terrible, merely inconvenient.

"Does Mr. Ziegfeld have an interest in The Chance?" It required all of her resolve to remain impassive.

"Not really."

"You sound disappointed." She watched him, searching for clues in the way the hazy lights along Broadway played upon his face.

Robert settled into the cushion and was making himself comfortable. "No. I did not expect he would. I had another purpose in mind."

"Oh?" Her muscles tightened. Her ears thrummed.

"It was research, in a way. The man understands a theater's strengths and weaknesses better than most. You see, my father has isolated himself too long. I will not make the same mistake."

"Is that what you've learned at Harvard?"

"Yes, actually. To seek out knowledge when it is needed."

"And what did you learn from Ziegfeld?"

"That the place needs a good cleaning, but anyone can see that. I hardly recognized the place when we drove up this morning. I had half a mind to tell the driver to keep going. But Ziegfeld understands about these things. He could see that the problems were cosmetic."

She bristled at the complaint, but it heartened her, too. "So he does not want to put his own show at The Chance?"

Robert laughed. "Is that what you thought?"

"No," she lied. "Not really. Well, I thought it might be a possibility."

"Oh, Pepper MacClair, still such an odd little thing. Such a firecracker. You have not changed, have you?"

"But I have changed," she insisted. She wanted him to know how much she had changed, how much better things could be between them now. This time she was truly ready to be the woman he wanted her to be. "I have changed," she repeated, "and you would know that if you had not been away so long."

That broken feeling returned. She had not wanted to show him that pain, but it had emerged, unbidden, anyway.

"You know that was not my choice," he said, taking her hand. "It was my father's doing. I would have stayed in New York if I could. You must know that. But three years is not so long, is it?" He inched closer to her. "It was not easy for me, either. These years have been difficult."

She softened toward him. He had missed her as she missed him.

"Keeping up at Harvard was the most challenging thing I have ever had to do."

Her heart sank. Being apart had not been his hardship, not as it had been for her. But he was a man. Men considered these things differently, didn't they?

"I did not have the luxury of wealth or a prestigious family name to get me through," he continued. "I had to earn my place, and keep earning it term after term."

She wanted to tell him they had that in common. It was a feeling she knew all too well, and she was about to say so when he said, "I have thought of you, Pepper MacClair. I have thought of you often."

"You have?"

It was not the confession of love she had wanted, but it was close and Robert always was a more practical sort. She could feel the depth of his feelings in the way he held her hand, gentle and loving. His leather gloves so smooth and comforting against the bare tips of her fingers above her damp knuckle mittens.

"Of course I have," he murmured.

It was maddening to be so close. The sweet fragrance of his skin, the coarse surface of his coat against her arm, the black center of his eyes piercing her, fixing her where she sat.

Reason told her to hold back, but her body was telling her something else. The tingling that began where he touched her was radiating to every extremity, enveloping her in dreamy rapture. She felt safe with him. No harm could come to her with him by her side. He would protect her, just as he would protect The Chance. He would save them both.

"I'm so glad you're back," she whispered into his collar. "The Chance needs you. These last few months have been awful."

He put his fingers to her lips. "That is business, my dear. It has nothing to do with this."

"But it does. You cannot even imagine the damage Stanley has done."

"I can, I assure you," he whispered. His finger caressed the back of her cheek. He worked an arm around her shoulders and was coaxing her closer to him.

She gave in readily. There was such confidence in his words. Harvard had taught him so much. He was a man of the world now, and he would set everything right. If anyone could restore The Chance's glory, he could.

The carriage stopped. Through the window over his shoulder, Pepper could see The Chance's marquee, the shimmer of the brass foot panels on the main door. They had arrived, though he did not seem inclined to release her. He was staring down with wide, admiring eyes.

"I had nearly forgotten how lovely you are, Pepper MacClair." His voice was a whisper that caressed her.

His hands slid from her elbows to her shoulders and around her back, and his touch sent her troubled thoughts wafting into the night. This was Robert, the boy she had loved as long as she could remember. The tender boy she saw only in glimpses when he was home from boarding school. He had not come around the theater much, only to deliver a message to his father now and then. But it was one of those occasions when he had caught sight of her, in the Scarlet Room.

It was the beginning of her sixteenth summer and she was heady with the knowledge she would soon make her dancing debut. She felt like a woman, finally, and then he had smiled at her. Already so handsome and self-assured at eighteen. When the heat made the theater unbearable, she was happy to go with him to the rooftop for the cooler air.

That was how it had begun, that summer they fell in love. He had never meant to harm her. And it did not matter now, because he was back. They would be together as if he had never left, and he would protect her from Stanley, from her loneliness, from everything.

"I have waited so long for this," she whispered.

With a glint in his eyes, he said, "How bold you are, Miss MacClair."

His arms tightened around her, guiding her farther back,

pressing her against the plush cushion. The wail of the wind had calmed and the raindrops had ceased.

She wanted to tell him that she needed his help. But the words died on her lips. When he pressed himself against her, she could think of nothing but him. She closed her eyes and gave in to the rush of feeling coursing through her.

All she could think was that he still loved her. She had not imagined it.

His lips were at her ear. "Perhaps I shall be bold as well. I want to take care of you, Pepper MacClair."

Her heart swelled and pounded in her chest. He had read her thoughts exactly. She waited breathlessly for more.

His lips brushed her throat. "Say you will let me provide for you," he said. "Say you will be mine."

These were lovely words, beguiling words, words that made her pulse quicken. But it was the words he did not say that were casting shadows now. Words like *wife* or *marriage, wedding* or *matrimony*. He veered from them, and the one word he left unspoken was this: *mistress*.

She pulled away.

"As your mistress?" It was not uncommon for girls working in the theater to accept such arrangements. For many, it was the primary goal. But not for Pepper. The feelings she and Robert shared went much deeper than that.

"I know it is sudden," he said.

It was many things, but yes, it was also sudden. She had never considered anything but marriage to Robert DeGraaf. He had said he loved her, that day on the rooftop, and they had been as intimate as any man and woman could be. She had never imagined herself as anything less than Mrs. Robert DeGraaf.

"What do you say?" He breathed gently, tickling her ear, and made Pepper shudder with fresh yearning. "You do love me, don't you?"

That was hardly playing fair. He knew her feelings.

"I want you to have a proper residence," he continued. "I want to free you from that dreadful hovel and those grueling performances."

"I can't quit the Dolls."

"Of course you can."

A strong gust buffeted the coach, shaking her free from the haze of wishful thinking. "It's all I have."

He pulled back. "That's absurd. You have me."

Before she could reply, before she could say anything, the flash of the brass panel caught her eye. The theater's front door had swung open and in the shadow she made out Gregory's form. He eyed the carriage a moment before emerging into the light and making his way over to where it stood.

She pulled back from Robert and cleared her throat just as Gregory's knuckles tapped the glass.

"Mr. DeGraaf," Gregory said gruffly, pulling his hand back and shoving it into his pocket. "Mr. Stanley would like a word."

Annoyed, Robert pulled away from Pepper and threw open the carriage door. He put on his hat and stepped out into the glow of the marquee lights, tightening his coat around himself to fend off the cold. At least the rain had stopped. "Incompetent," he muttered.

He might have meant Gregory. He might have meant Stanley.

"Where is he?"

"The stage." Gregory backed away from the door, giving Robert room to pass.

Had he seen her within? He gave no indication. She hoped not.

Robert removed any doubt, however, when he leaned back inside to say, "I'm afraid we'll have to resume this matter later, Miss MacClair." He touched the brim of his hat in farewell.

Before she could respond, he turned to say something to the driver and then made his way into the theater.

She took her time alighting from the carriage, hoping Gregory would take the hint and leave as well. But he did not. Instead, he rocked on his heels, with both hands pushed deep in his pockets. She fussed with her gloves and her coat before stepping out into the misty night air.

When Gregory gave no sign of leaving, she said, "Are you going to stand there or are you going to help me out?"

He tipped his glance her way. "Since you've asked so nicely . . ." He took her hand and helped to steady her.

Once she'd stepped down from the carriage, she smoothed her coat, hoping Gregory did not see the way her soaked skirt was clinging so inappropriately and unattractively to her limbs.

"Why are you here so late, anyway?" She tried her best to appear composed.

"Replacing a footlight. I was locking up when I saw the carriage. Didn't realize you were inside."

Guilt stabbed at her. "Whatever you are thinking—"

"About what?" He was gazing across the street, at Abernathy's, at nothing. He knew what she meant.

It was not a subject she wanted to pursue. "Why is Stanley still here? The show finished an hour ago."

Gregory shook his head, though he was still gazing out into the blackness. "He isn't. I expect it won't take long for Little Robby to figure it out."

"You shouldn't call him that. He's management now."

"I suppose."

She knew better than to taunt Gregory with what was undoubtedly an unpleasant turn of events. He and Robert had never been friendly, even as boys.

"Why did you lie?"

"Thought you might want to be rid of him."

Pepper felt his black marble gaze upon her. He was studying her. What would have happened if Gregory had not interrupted? If Robert had pressed his advances? Would she have resisted? She knew she should have refused him, but there was part of her that would agree to anything Robert asked.

"Are you angry?" he asked plainly.

"No." Confused, but not angry. "Nothing happened. He saw me walking home in the rain and offered the ride." Why was she explaining herself to Gregory? It was just the way he was looking at her, with such disapproval. "If you'll excuse me." She turned toward the corner, toward home.

"I'll see you to the door."

"Honestly, Gregory, it's twenty paces."

His look silenced her. If she protested, he would, too, and she was too weary for that. She was too weary even for a bath. She only wanted to crawl under the bedcovers and put the day behind her.

"Fine," she said. A fresh raindrop landed on her arm, and then another.

Gregory tugged his cap lower over his eyes and started off toward the corner in long strides, forcing her to hurry to catch up.

When they rounded the building, he pulled a ring of keys from his pocket and searched for the one that would open the cold basement door, the same one Pepper wore on a chain around her neck, next to the one to her own rooms.

He took the descending flight of steps quickly, and by the time she caught up to him, he was inside the long, straight passageway, waiting for her.

He stood there watching until she had worked the lock on her door—the first along the barren corridor—and stepped inside. "I'm in now. All is well."

Still, he looked beyond her into her room, examining its interior by the slant of yellow light cast by the streetlamp through the room's single window, confirming that the couch and chairs, the bed and dressing table, everything within was just as it should be.

"Lock it" was the last thing Gregory said as he headed back to the street.

She did not know what to think when she closed the door. But then, she never knew what to make of Gregory Creighton these days. Such a recluse he had become. Such a stranger to her. It seemed so long ago that he had been her closest friend. The only one who understood how lonely it could be for a child in a theater because that had been his life, too.

How mysterious the theater had seemed to her in those first days. She had done nothing but wander the halls and get in the way until Gregory had introduced himself and made it his job to teach her how the theater worked. He was only nine, but already so mature. He had been sent to live with his uncle, an old prop man named McShane, when he was seven, and he knew so much about the place. Everything, it seemed.

He explained it all to her. How ropes and pulleys raised and lowered the curtains and backdrops, and how the lights went on and off at the flip of a backstage lever, and more important things, like how not to stare at Stanley's braced leg because that made him angry and how to look busy even when you were just watching the show, and, when you could not look busy, how to sneak into the balcony and hunch down in an empty seat so Stanley would not send you off on an errand.

She was grateful for his instruction, even if he had been wrong about the balcony. The wings were always the best place to see the show, watching performers transform when the stage and the lights worked their magic. Back then she had believed it was magic, and it mesmerized her from that very first show, especially the headlining act.

Little Egypt was the name on the marquee—which was painted then; Mr. DeGraaf had not yet installed the lights—but the young woman with a fall of black hair and skin like milky tea introduced herself as Dora when she caught Pepper staring after the show. Pepper couldn't help it. Dora performed the most unusual dance Pepper had ever seen. It was a troupe act, with several dancers, drummers, and other musicians against a backdrop painted with pyramids and sand dunes, camels and a bazaar—an elaborate spectacle brought from the Chicago World's Fair months before. The act was held over for weeks because the crowds never tired of the shimmies and sways, the undulations and shakes that sent Dora's wide skirt flipping and whirling around her knees.

That first day, during the third show, while Bessie was becoming acquainted with the wardrobe workroom, Dora caught Pepper lingering beside her dressing room, gazing at the beautiful bouquets that filled it. Dora had been sitting at her vanity table when she spied Pepper in the glass. She asked if Pepper had something to say. Awestruck and nervous, Pepper wanted to run, but instead she heard herself whisper, "How do you dance like that?"

That was when Dora, gracious as she always was, invited

Pepper inside and gave her that very first lesson. Swaying her hips, she showed Pepper how to draw an invisible figure eight upon the floor. Other lessons followed, every afternoon between the third and fourth shows, until Pepper had learned a good portion of Dora's routine.

The lessons came to an end a few months later when the dancer announced that she was pregnant. Her husband, the darkly handsome Egyptian who managed the troupe, took the act out West, where the weather was more temperate and the others could perform without Dora until after the child's birth.

Pepper had lost track of them then. She always hoped they might return to The Chance, but they never did. And she never forgot her lessons. For months after their departure, she told anyone who would stand still long enough to listen that one day she would be a star like Little Egypt, a famous dancer with her name on the marquee and a dressing room filled with flowers.

Everyone laughed—except Gregory.

After Dora left, Pepper practiced alone on the roof after her laundry chores, repeating what she had learned and picking up new dance steps she mimicked from other performers. Sometimes Gregory stole away to keep her company as she hung damp petticoats and linen shirts on the clothesline and then she would dance for him, for practice, as if he were a real audience.

Unlike Bessie, who believed Pepper was good only for a needle and thread, he had believed in her.

At least he had until that sweltering September. That awful afternoon when she proved she did not deserve any of the good things he had thought of her. Since then, he hardly turned her way. Not that she blamed him. He was still cordial, certainly more than he tended to be with others, but there was a gulf between them that widened every day.

She pulled the chain and the keys from her neck and hung them from a hook by the door. Dwelling on that gulf was not going to do her any good tonight. She crossed the floor to the window that looked out at the street, pulled the linen damask curtains closed over the sheers, and peeled off her wet coat and dress.

Maybe it no longer mattered at all, because now that Robert DeGraaf was back, everything would change.

Six

GREGORY LINGERED IN THE DARK RECESS BESIDE the Lair's staircase and watched the narrow rectangle of a window that opened into Pepper's room. He saw it brighten and then dim when she pulled the curtain over the glass. Good girl. Safe and snug where she should be. Where she should have been all along.

He couldn't think what would have happened if he hadn't noticed Robert DeGraaf's carriage on the street. He upbraided himself for holding back so long, debating whether to confront the man. To be fair, he hadn't known Pepper was within.

But when he saw them together, his blood ran cold. He kept his distance as long as he could, but he knew better than most how Pepper, for all her fire and spark, could be taken in by Robert DeGraaf.

If his intervention irritated her, so be it. He had done

what he had to do. And he wasn't finished yet. The rain had turned to a cold heavy mist as he made his way to the front of the theater, intent on tracking down Robert.

There was no need. The carriage was still there, and the man was, too, locking the theater's front door. When he heard Gregory's footsteps, he stiffened, which gave Gregory a twinge of delight.

"Your idea of a prank, I suppose?" Robert's voice was rough, yet too strained to disguise his fear. They both knew Gregory's greater size would give him an advantage in a fight, should the moment come to that.

"Did you find it amusing?"

"Hardly," Robert said. "If you try anything like that again, I can assure you, you won't find it amusing, either. Not while I'm in charge."

"And how long will that be, I wonder?"

"As long as my father needs my help."

Gregory had his doubts on that score. "Why involve Pepper MacClair, then?"

"Anything between Miss MacClair and myself has nothing to do with you. It never has. You really must get that through your apelike skull."

Gregory's fingers curled into fists. If only Robert were closer. . . . But the rat kept his distance. "You haven't changed, have you? Pepper MacClair is my friend. I intend to look out for her, especially when it comes to you."

"Me?" Robert's chin tipped back and he gazed at Gregory over the slope of his nose, trying to look down upon him, though Gregory's height exceeded his by four inches at least. "Are you saying you have a claim on her?"

"I said nothing of a claim."

"Then I believe she is free to associate with whomever she chooses."

"I've warned you."

Robert reeled back. "Warned me? You have not changed, have you? Still the same cretin. Honestly, does Miss MacClair even know what kind of monster you are? What kind of vile, sinful blood runs through your veins? Tell me, what did she say when you told her how it was you came to call this wretched place home? Did she tell you it didn't matter to her? Oh, but your expression gives you away. You have not told her, have you? Why is that, cretin?"

Gregory gritted his teeth. How did Robert know about that? Of course Mr. DeGraaf knew the details. McShane would have had to explain. Perhaps even Stanley knew. But Robert? "If you do not leave her alone, I will—"

"Now you are threatening me? Well, the apple does not fall far from the tree, does it?"

It took all of Gregory's self-control not to land a fist on Robert's cheek. "Stay away from her or we'll have trouble."

Robert met his glare and held it. "You forget your place. You're a stagehand, a worker bee. Nothing more. Stop buzzing around where you aren't wanted." Then he swept by Gregory, his fine wool coat brushing against Gregory's grimy overalls as he passed.

"And," he said when he had opened his coach door, "if you do not stop, I assure you I will see to it that Miss MacClair learns exactly what sort of guttersnipe you are. I will turn you out and make sure you are turned away from any other theater in the city. I do hope I make myself clear."

Gregory scowled and stalked away.

"I hear the union is looking for men. You might give it some thought."

Gregory ignored the threat and continued on. Finally he heard Robert clamber back into his shiny black carriage and watched as it drove past him.

He shoved his hands in his pockets and kept his pace, imagining all manner of violence that might be visited upon Robert DeGraaf. He passed the photographer's studio, the piano shop, and a rug seller before his hands stopped forming fists. The angry thoughts subsided. At the corner, he paused in front of that damned kinetoscope parlor that had moved in. He gazed into the window of the locked shop for distraction.

A dozen bulky kinetoscopes lined each wall, each topped with its peephole viewer. Across the window, a banner announced the week's views: *Sioux Ghost Dance, Sandow Muscular Posing,* and *Frolicking Seminary Girls.* Pepper might say it was not vaudeville, but the only thing missing was the piano and the worn-out seats. He might have gone in for a look around, but the door was locked. The place was closed. At this time of night, everything was closed. He walked on.

What needled him, the thought he could not shake, was not that Robert could fire him. It was the question of whether that rat had the clout to blackball Gregory from any other theater. He never would have believed it, but all those blue bloods stuck together, didn't they? Theater managers had banded together in their syndicates and their circuits to crush performers' efforts to organize for higher wages. And they had tried to do the same with backstage employees. Mr. DeGraaf never had anything to do with those efforts, but Robert? Gregory chewed on the possibility as he turned up Waverly, then made it back around to

Eighth. As he approached Broadway, he checked the shadows around the stage door and the descending stairwell to the Lair. He searched the darkness around Abernathy's Bar.

That corner spot had belonged to a cobbler for a decade before Abernathy moved in. Gregory frequented the establishment, but he had not welcomed the change, not when it meant drunks now came and went at all hours within feet of Pepper's room.

He knew her well enough to know she would never tolerate a suggestion that the room was no longer safe for her, so, to soothe his own mind, he spent most of his restless nights out here in the moonlight, shooing the louts away.

Tonight, he trudged through the usual triangles of light cast down from the windows above the tavern, their edges blurred and indistinct in the foggy mist. He peered along the stretch from the trash barrels and wagons abandoned at the curb. The street was empty and quiet but for the crunch and scrape of his own footsteps.

Still, Gregory paced the length of the building to ward off the chill. Long, strong strides, with his chin up and his eyes narrowed, replaying the argument with Robert.

Until a scraping perked his ear. He froze midstride, then turned toward the stairs leading to the Lair. In his pocket, his fingers twitched with dangerous expectation, although he saw nothing but shadows.

The sound came again. Behind him. He whirled to see a figure, hunched and lurching from the stoop of the printer's building behind the theater. Too dark to see clearly, just a blackened figure, a man of significant size. Something flashed in the man's hand. A knife?

Gregory slowed. In the cold, hazy moonlight, he watched the stranger bring the thing he held to his mouth and tilt it back. A bottle, not a blade. Gregory strode forward with greater determination and grabbed the man by the coat collar, nearly knocking him off his feet.

"Just a cotton-picking . . ." The stranger's arms flung out, searching for balance.

Gregory leaned to the man's ear. "Take it somewhere else, friend."

The man wheeled around. He was hatless with a scruffy beard and greasy dark hair that stood off his head at odd angles. He reeked of cheap whiskey, urine, and sweat. "Who are you?" the stranger slurred with an attempted sneer.

"A concerned citizen. Now I asked nice: Leave and we won't have trouble."

"You're no copper." The man pushed away from Gregory and stumbled again.

Gregory had dealt with this kind before, but he had no patience for it tonight. The anger that had simmered all day in his gut had reached its boiling point. If he could not rid the theater of Robert DeGraaf, he could at least rid the street of this vagrant. With his head still low, Gregory reached up with both hands, tipped his cap with one and pushed the black wisps from his brow with the other. He settled the cap back into place.

The man watched Gregory's eyes, not his fingers, and the distraction gave Gregory time to slide the Billings and Spencer screwdriver from his pocket. In a fluid motion, he extended the sharp tip and brandished it like a blade. "I may not be a copper, but you will leave, have no doubt of that."

The drunkard's eyes widened like a deer caught in a trap. He raised both hands, the bottle still clutched in one, and backed into the street. "No need for that, mister." His eyes glazed with terror. No sign of the slur or the sneer. "Why don't you put that knife away?"

Gregory closed the space between them in three rapid paces and grabbed the vagrant before he could move. The man cried out as Gregory spun him around and locked his neck in the crook of his arm, the tool's tip nudged up sharp against his throat, nearly piercing the skin.

"Let me go. I'll be on my way. Just let me go. Please, sir."

" 'Sir' now, is it?" Gregory said, his breath coming fast and his limbs tingling with the rush of the moment. He envisioned Robert bent in his arm, squirming. The fingers around the screwdriver twitched.

The man cried out, and Gregory felt something wet and warm trickle over his hand. He snapped it away. Blood covered his knuckles. The man dropped his bottle and clutched his neck with both hands.

Gregory froze. His glance darted between his hand and the cowering man. "It wasn't . . ." But his voice died in the night's cold, damp air.

The stranger shuffled back two steps, turned, and half fell, half ran into the darkness.

Gregory stared at the blackness smeared across his hand. He turned and shot a glance toward Pepper's door. He half expected to see her there, a frown upon her pretty face, a disapproving shake of her head. He had not meant to harm the man, yet he had. If the vagrant had not squirmed away, what else might Gregory have done?

A queasiness rose up from his stomach and he closed his eyes. He had done what he had to do. That was all. He bent to pick up the surprisingly intact bottle and poured a portion of the whiskey over his hand to wash away the blood. He poured more over his screwdriver and dried it with a wipe on his thigh. His heart thrummed in his ears. The bottle trembled in his hand. He raised it to his lips and gulped. The liquid burned his throat. He gulped again and dumped the rest into a puddle, then tossed the empty bottle into a trash barrel. He slid the tool closed and shoved it back into his pocket.

When the street's stillness had calmed the beating in his ears, he folded his arms across his chest and settled onto the printer's stoop. Sitting there on the stone, in the moonlight, watching for movement in the shadows, he thought about Robert DeGraaf's words. Was there truth to what he had said? Was Gregory like his father? No. Little Robby would say anything. But still, Gregory could not dispel those words from his thoughts. They kept him company on that lonely stoop like the blackest of shadows.

• • •

PEPPER HAD BEEN STARING AT THE DARK CEILING FROM beneath her bedcover for an hour when she finally gave up on sleep. Every thump of a closing door, every creak of the boards, even the occasional snore from Old Jake's side of the wall two rooms away pulled her back from the brink of slumber. She would find no comfort here tonight.

Too many thoughts churned within her. Too many questions. Why had Gregory behaved so strangely? Why was Robert proposing something less than marriage? Why was Stanley pushing her out? Each was a greater mystery than the last. Each a greater heartbreak.

No. It was just the darkness, the silence playing tricks on her. She struck a match to light the lamp she kept on a trunk pulled up alongside her bed as a table. Grabbing her kimono robe to pull over her nightdress, she made her way through the mullioned pocket doors that divided what had once been the DeGraafs' drawing room from a narrow hallway. It led on one side to a lavatory and a small kitchen, and on the other side to the part of the DeGraafs' dining room where Bessie had kept her bed.

Passing the curtained doorway into her mother's makeshift space, her bare feet skimming the cold wood floor, Pepper kept her gaze low, as had become her habit. Every time she passed, she thought of that empty sewing basket.

She closed her eyes. Best to keep those memories shut away behind the curtain with Bessie's things. The sewing machine and the mirror where she had pinned up her auburn hair, her dresses and the bed where she had languished all those months. Better not to think of any of it. Especially now.

She hurried to the kitchen, which had been half of the DeGraafs' kitchen. On the other side of the thin plaster wall, Old Jake possessed the other half. He had the original sink. She had one that had been hastily added, jutting awkwardly from the wall with its metal pipe descending like a naked tail. It was just large enough for the teakettle Pepper positioned beneath the spout. She filled it with water, then set the kettle on the cast-iron stove and lighted the flame.

The stove had belonged to the DeGraafs, and it had been Bessie's pride and joy. She had never had more than a hearth for cooking and baking in Scotland, and not even that when they had lived on the street. Before the sickness sapped her strength, Bessie was always in the kitchen if she was not up in the wardrobe room or with Em.

When Pepper inhaled, she could still smell the savory stews and Scotch broths, the fresh bannocks and oatcakes, even the occasional meat pies. But to Bessie, meat was dear. "Tatties and carrots do just fine," she would say.

She would chop the bruised potatoes and flaccid carrots she bought for a pittance from the grocer and stir them in a cast-iron pot over the stove with a bone she had sweet-talked from the butcher. For hours she'd tend it until the whole concoction had melded into a dark, delectable broth.

It was usually when she cooked that Bessie spoke of Scotland. Of how life had been for a fisherman's daughter in a tiny village populated by fewer souls than were held in any Lower East Side tenement. She spoke of hard winters and desolation. Of hunger and hopelessness. However the stories began, they always ended the same way: with a reminder to be grateful for this small basement home. It was true enough.

The problem with her mother was she never wanted more. They lived beneath a whole world of possibilities, where anything seemed within reach. But Bessie never reached; she would not even try. She had reached across an entire ocean for a better life, from the old world to the new, then stopped. It never made sense to Pepper, just as the hours Pepper spent dancing and dreaming made no sense to Bessie.

Finally the kettle rattled to a boil. Pepper poured the steaming water into the teapot she had placed on a tray, along with a cup and the sugar bowl, and returned down the hallway. Holding the tray with both hands, she closed the pocket door behind her with a nudge of her big toe—all the way, so not even a smidgeon of a gap remained—and took the tray to the velour couch the DeGraafs had left, along with the cherrywood table beside it.

While the tea steeped, she examined the dress and coat she had pinned to a clothesline strung from one wall to another in front of the fireplace. The clothes were still wet to the touch. She debated whether to move the line as she went to the oak shelves behind her bed. They had once held Mr. DeGraaf's library and now served a more universal use. Several messy stacks of folded shirts, skirts and petticoats, corsets and chemises. A basket of combs, hairpins, and ribbons. Scarves. Hats. Extra candles and wicks for the lamps. One entire shelf held treasures the DeGraafs had left behind: a silver tea service, a rotating globe, and a brass birdcage. Pepper ran her hand over the empty place where the broken music box had been. Her music box.

She could feel it calling her to practice.

From the shelves, she tugged free a ruffled black skirt she had inherited from a singer who had a falling-out with her manager during their three-week run. The manager had held the woman's costumes hostage when she stormed out, and then abandoned them when she refused to return. Mrs. Basaraba had kept the trunk in the wardrobe room for a month, waiting for it to be claimed. Then she had sent the skirt down to Pepper, along with an embroidered shawl with long flossy fringe, several thick metal bracelets, and a pretty pair of pearl ear bobs.

Pepper pulled an amethyst blouse with a drawstring collar over her head and wrapped the shawl around her waist. Like a Scottish Esmeralda, she thought, checking her appearance in the mirror. She finished her tea and went to the door.

The corridor was so dark at this hour, it was nearly impossible to see. But after thirteen years, she knew the way to the stage well enough. Twenty-six paces, door, four paces, stairs.

When she entered the stairwell from the backstage wings, a faint glow greeted her. It came from the light stand with the single bulb placed every night in the center of the stage: the ghost light. A nightly offering to keep The Chance's spirits content. It guided her. She sometimes thought, in these silent hours, that the spirits themselves guided her.

Of course, who would believe her? Most didn't believe in the spirits, not really, even if they were careful not to wish players good luck before a performance and avoided saying the name of Shakespeare's Scottish play inside a theater. Even if they tucked lucky trinkets in their pockets and engaged in all manner of pre-show rituals to ensure a fortunate turn. But if asked (and Pepper had asked, many years ago, before she had learned such things were not to be said), they would tell her, "There are no such things as ghosts. Do not be absurd!"

To Pepper, however, it was not such a leap of the imagination to believe phantoms roamed these halls. Or that they played upon the stage in the small hours of the night. If there were phantoms, and if they could haunt any place they liked, where else would they go? What better place could there be?

But tonight it was not the theater's phantoms she was thinking about when she approached the table beneath the rows of levers, gauges, and switches, and bent to push aside a crate filled with dusty coils of thick rope. It was Robert, who wanted her to abandon the only place she had ever belonged. It was her mother and Gregory and Mr. DeGraaf, who had all measured her and found her wanting. It was Mr. Stanley, who wanted to send her back to the street.

Yes, tonight she needed her practice, perhaps now more than ever. But she also needed to still her thoughts.

Slowly, she tugged at the box that sat near the crate. She guided it out and pulled off the canvas that kept the music box hidden from view. She touched its smooth, glossy lid, inlaid with pink and yellow flowers, as enamored with it as she was the day Gregory had returned it to her. It was one of the discarded belongings the DeGraafs had left behind, and she still marveled that Gregory had taken it, broken, worn, and abandoned upon those shelves and, with a little tinkering and polish, created this. "Restored," he had said, but to her it looked as good as new.

She lifted the lid to reveal the shiny silver comb mechanism that could pluck ten lovely melodies from the tiny constellation of divots in the brass cylinder. She considered "España Waltz"; it was her usual favorite. But no, that was too cheery for tonight. "Don't Let Her Lose Her Way" was a better choice. She cranked the lever and padded quickly to the stage-right wings.

She closed her eyes and imagined the stage alight. The music was not the usual rag, but she fit the Dolls' routine to it, moving through the choreographed skips and kicks, pirouettes and *ronds de jambe*. When the music wound down two minutes later, she padded back to the wooden box and cranked the lever. Again and again, she practiced the steps, keeping her limbs strong, her neck long, and her mind silent.

On she went, drilling her routine. Then it happened, as it always did. Her mind wandered and her limbs followed. Without thought, she grabbed her skirt in both hands, and like a tide pulling out, all the weariness and fretting left her. Only lovely nothingness remained as the music filled her. She was not dancing for Stanley or Beatrice or even Robert. She was dancing for herself. Little Egypt's sways and shimmies. A flamenco dancer's sweeps and stomps. A ballerina's graceful dips and turns.

Then her body began to move in strange and new designs. It was the theater's spirits, she told herself—guiding her, teaching her their own ghostly dance.

She knew it had to be the ghosts because she had that odd, familiar feeling of being watched. The sensation sent a tingle up her spine.

She danced until her legs trembled and her breathing came in gasps, until she could not dance another step. Only then did she pull the sheet back over the music box, maneuver it back into its hiding place, and replace the ghost light at the center of the stage.

"Good night," she whispered to the phantoms and padded back to her room.

When she was gone, when the sound of her footsteps had faded and only stillness remained, a man, hunched low in the last row of the balcony, rose from the shadows and stretched his limbs. He bid his own farewell to the theater phantoms and quietly made his exit.

Seven

THE NEXT MORNING, A STICK STRUCK PEPPER'S windowpane and startled her from sleep. Boys. Why did those children living above Abernathy's find it so amusing to batter her glass? She rolled over, pulled the pillow over her head, and fell back into that wonderful numbness.

Tat-tat-tat. It wasn't the glass, but the door. A voice called, "Pepper, doll, it's me."

Squinting over the covers, Pepper noted the feeble gray light hugging the edges of the window curtain. It was early. She jumped up, alarmed. Only something dreadful could draw Em out before nine. She scrambled to the door.

Her fingers, clumsy and still half asleep, fumbled with the lock. A fire? Sickness? Death? Finally, it unlatched and she threw open the door. "What's the matter? What's happened?"

Em swept in and gave her closed umbrella a rough shake that sent drops flying through the room before leaning it against the door. "I couldn't sleep," she announced as she hooked her bowler hat on the coat rack and ran a palm over her slicked-back hair. "Did I wake you?" She dropped into the old pine-colored cushion.

Pepper might have been annoyed by the intrusion if it were not for Em's eyes. They were swollen and dull, void of their usual verve.

"I was awake," she said cautiously as she crossed the room to collect her robe.

"Of course you were. Who could sleep through this racket?" Em propped one trousered leg on the cherrywood table. "The rain is beating, *beating*, on my window. Just listen to it." She paused dramatically and attended to the gentle plinking against the glass. "It's maddening. I couldn't stand it so I went out for a walk. I couldn't stand being cooped up. I couldn't stay in those rooms another moment. Anyway, darling, I had a feeling you would be awake. Are you having trouble sleeping? I've noticed shadows beneath your eyes, and you've always been such a sound sleeper. Not like your mother, God rest her soul. The tiniest sound could awaken her."

That was when Pepper knew. It wasn't the rain keeping Em awake. It was memories of Bessie.

"I was just about to make a pot of tea. Will you stay?"

"Yes, something warm would do these old bones good, I think. That dress looks like someone tossed it in the Hudson. What happened to it? Is this place leaking?" She searched the ceiling and the walls around the windows.

Pepper debated how much to tell Em. How much of a lecture

was she willing to abide? She settled on a half-truth. "I went out last night."

"You went out? You?"

Pepper made her way to the kitchen and returned with a serving tray but did not answer.

Em tried again. "Who was it? Do I know him? Someone from the theater? No, it couldn't be. A new young man? Oh, your mother would be so pleased."

"It was not a young man." Pepper did not want to explain the business with Robert. She would not even know where to begin.

Em's eyebrows shot up, and her lips pulled into a sly grin. "A young lady, then?"

"No, nothing like that. Must I explain myself? Really, I'm a grown woman." It was her standard response and the beginning of their usual argument.

"I'm only concerned about you," Em said softly. "You haven't been yourself, not since . . ."

Not since Bessie died. Only those were words she never uttered. Neither of them did. Instead, with her pert nose upturned, Em glanced around at the paneled walls, the unkempt bed, the trunks and crates stacked and pushed against the wall. "I know it was difficult while you were caring for your mother. But you need to put that behind you. There's a whole world outside this theater. Don't hide from it."

"No one is hiding." Pepper sat in the cushioned chair alongside the sofa and leaned over the tray to spoon a portion of sugar into her teacup and another into Em's while the tea steeped.

She was not hiding, but she could not deny the truth in what Em said. When Bessie was ill, she relied on Pepper's constant care. Pepper made tea and fed her biscuits, the only things she could keep down near the end. Pepper helped her to the lavatory and bathed her, applied the belladonna plaster to her bare chest and back on the nights when the coughing pained her most. When the coughing subsided enough that Bessie could sleep, Pepper sat on the couch with mending for Mrs. Basaraba. But mostly she listened to her music box, danced, and dreamed of Robert and the better life that lie ahead.

Only Robert was back and nothing was turning out the way she had planned.

"What's knocking around that noggin of yours, doll?"

That was why Pepper loved Em. The woman always saw through her.

Pepper set down the teapot and stared at its shiny white surface. "Stanley wants to cut me from the act." The words dropped like stones at her feet.

"Why do you say that?" Em leaned forward, angling her elbows on her knees.

Pepper nibbled a corner of her fingernail.

Em took her teacup. "You know how he is. All blather. A mean dog with no teeth. You cannot let it worry you."

Decades of experience gave weight to her words. No one knew Stanley longer or better than Em. It heartened Pepper.

"The show is in a slump," Em continued. "He's desperate. And that high and mighty Madame Bizet? She walked out on her contract last night."

"We have no headliner?"

"I didn't say that. But we don't have her, not that it's much of a loss, really." Em sipped and set down her teacup.

"Then who? Who could he get on such short notice?"

"You're looking at her."

"But your retirement?"

"Exactly. Because every good retirement needs . . ." She threw her arms out wide. "A comeback! Yes, siree, The Chance Theatre will have the distinct honor and privilege of showcasing the highly anticipated return engagement of the amazing and always fabulous Uptown Joe."

Pepper nearly choked on her tea. "That's wonderful. It's the best news I've heard in a long time. When do you start?"

"Today. Just have to train someone for the ticket window. But you see, you needn't worry. Stanley is neck deep in worries, worries he's never even dreamed of. But things are finally turning around for him. Once Little Robby settles in, maybe Stanley can relax a bit. Things will go back to normal. You'll see."

"Then why would Mr. DeGraaf ask me if there was anything else I would like to do?" Pepper bit another fingernail. She waited for her friend to assure her she was overreacting, that there was no reason to fret.

"You spoke to Mr. DeGraaf?"

"Last night after the show. I went to the St. Denis to speak to Robert. Mr. DeGraaf saw me." She shrank at the admission.

The news settled on Em. "And he told you Stanley wants you out? He said that exactly?"

He might as well have. Pepper nodded.

Em's frown deepened.

It was not the response Pepper wanted. Where was the optimism? Where was the reassurance?

"What did you tell him?"

Pepper stared into her cup.

"I didn't tell him anything. There is nothing else I care to do."

Em did not meet her gaze.

Pepper's thoughts went back to the carriage, back to Robert. Perhaps she should let him take her away, before Stanley had his way. She sipped her tea and settled the cup back on its saucer.

"You need to stop antagonizing Stanley," Em said. "If you would only try to work with him, instead of quibbling all the time."

"I don't quibble. Only when it's necessary to draw his attention to something he has overlooked, or when he's incorrect."

Em drummed her fingertips on the sofa's arm. "You can be right, and still get it all wrong. Maybe he isn't perfect, but he is the boss. You must find a way to work with him."

"Or I could ask Robert to fire him."

"Oh, doll, don't be spiteful. It doesn't become you."

As much as she wanted to argue, Pepper knew Em was right. But it was tempting.

* * *

GREGORY HAD PACED THE LENGTH OF THE GRAY BRICK BUILDing at Forty-one East Twenty-first Street for the fourth time when he stopped, slumped down on the concrete stoop, and tried talking sense into himself. He had told Stanley that a leaky pipe had damaged the park scene backdrop and that another emergency run to George's Hardware was required. But what was the point of doing so if he was not going to venture inside the building?

That silent debate was disrupted, however, by a *chug-chug-chug* of an automobile pulling up to the curb. Gregory watched the driver park the forest-green Ford Model B and hop out to open the short panel door for the rear-seat passenger, a gentleman with a black handlebar mustache, a fur-trimmed overcoat, and a pair of leather shoes so shiny they looked like mirrors.

Gregory stood and nudged his cap in greeting as the man

passed with his ivory-tipped walking stick and pulled open the glass door. It was inscribed with the words *Edison Manufacturing Company* in golden paint. The gentleman was halfway over the threshold when he turned back and said, "Are you here about the position, son?"

"No, sir." Gregory yanked his cap from his head. "Mr. Porter invited me."

"I am quite certain he would prefer you not loiter about, then. Come with me." And he disappeared inside.

Gregory followed, assuming that was the man's intent. He skipped up the stoop's stairs and caught the door before it closed. Inside, he followed the man's black heels up a tight stairwell, keeping a polite distance as they ascended three, then four flights. At the very top of the stairwell, Gregory found the man waiting in a doorway that opened onto the rooftop—and there stood the most amazing structure he had ever seen. Not only were the walls made of glass, but the whole roof—which had to stand twenty, maybe thirty, feet over their heads—was made of glass as well.

He realized he was gaping like a yokel when the man in the overcoat said, "Welcome to our skylight studio, son. She is something, isn't she?"

"Not bad at all," he muttered. His gaze settled on three walls—solid, not glass—at the room's center, which formed a partial room. An office, it seemed. Above, lights housed in cages moved along an adjustable track fastened to the ceiling, and inside the partial room, a man in a suit frantically paced between a rolltop desk and a spin-lock safe as two other men looked on. One of them—Porter it was, in a crisp white shirt and vest—sat upon a folding chair. Behind him, another man in a coat and tie cranked the lever of a moving picture camera that was larger and boxier than the one Porter had used on the street.

"You in moving pictures?" The man was giving Gregory the once-over, taking in the low state of his dress, the black duck overalls, the rumpled shirtsleeves, and work boots.

Gregory stood straighter. "No, sir, theater."

The answer must have been sufficient, for the man draped his coat on a hook, pulled a cigar from a pocket, and mumbled something benign as he wandered off to a row of closed doors. When he passed behind Mr. Porter, he tapped him on the shoulder, jabbed his finger at Gregory, and kept moving.

Even from this distance, Gregory could see the question on Porter's face. He didn't remember Gregory. Still, he lifted his hand and hailed him with a twitch.

Every one of Gregory's instincts told him to walk out the door. What business did he have here in this odd glass warehouse? He shouldn't be wasting his time with these moving pictures, where everyone dressed in clean wool trousers and starched white shirts. And collars and ties, for Christ's sake. The theater was where he belonged. Where a pair of overalls did just fine. Where a spot of paint or grease here and there didn't matter a whit. Where no one ever summoned him with a twitchy hand.

He would have been gone in a hot second if Robert's pasty face had not been at the edge of his thoughts, reminding him that his days at The Chance were numbered. Sure, he had always known the rat would be back eventually. He had just figured it was a ways off yet. That there was still time to turn things in his own direction. It was his own fault he had squandered the years. He couldn't squander any more.

And it was too late to leave now. Porter rose, causing the man behind the camera to straighten as well. "Keep going," Porter said, then turned to the actor who had stopped his pacing. Porter held out both hands and clutched the air in front of him. "You are ruined, Edward. Ruined! Let us see your despair, your torment! Search the desk. Search the safe. Yes, my good man, like that, the eyes are marvelous. Keep going!"

Porter turned from his crew and settled the full weight of his attention on Gregory. "Who are you, boy?"

Boy? He was a man of twenty-one years, certainly not a boy. He straightened himself to his full height and towered over the shorter man, who seemed so much more at ease and confident here within his own surroundings than he had been on Broadway. "The name is Creighton. Made your acquaintance yesterday."

Porter rubbed his thumb on his jaw, coaxing the memory. "Oh, yes. You used that clever tool to fix that Lumière model. You had a friend, as I recall."

"He couldn't make it," Gregory said. He had taken great care to avoid Matty that morning. He certainly did not want him along. "I wouldn't mind seeing how you make these moving pictures, if the offer stands."

This seemed to please Porter. "Of course. I see you've already met the boss."

Gregory glanced across the room at the man who had ushered him in. The older man with the Fifth Avenue walk, who smelled of money and expensive tobacco, was pacing the floor, looking over shoulders, asking questions. So that was the Wizard of Menlo Park? One never could trust the newspapers' engravings. "Mr. Thomas Edison?"

"Goodness, no. Mr. Edison has no time for moving pictures. These days he prefers the company of lawyers, or so it would seem." He chuckled at something, then thought better of it. "No, that, young man, is Mr. Alexander T. Moore, vice president and general manager of Edison Manufacturing Company. He runs things here."

"And what is it you do here, if you don't mind me asking?"

Amused, Porter threw up his hands. "We make moving pictures! If you want to see how, pull up a chair. But just so we understand each other, you can watch all you like, but we don't stand for jibber-jabber. Especially today. Too much to do. We have four more scenes to get through before the sun goes down." He scratched his forehead where his hairline was in retreat and murmured something to himself. He glanced up to the gray clouds, then to his pocket watch, and then the clouds again. "Yes, not a moment to lose." He hurried back to his chair. "Very good, Edward, very good."

Not one of the workers paid Gregory any mind, and Mr. Moore had disappeared into an office at the opposite end of the warehouse. He was on his own, it seemed, so he grabbed the nearest chair and sat a short distance behind the cameraman—close enough to see which levers the man cranked and which knobs he turned, yet far enough that they hardly knew he was there.

• • •

EM LEFT PEPPER'S ROOM SOMEWHERE AROUND NINE, DESPITE Pepper's offer to steep another pot of tea. She had refused, kindly, of course.

"The old legs need a stretch before they begin the day," she had said as she grabbed her damp umbrella and headed out into the midmorning sun.

Pepper didn't blame her. Em was returning to the stage after years away, and when she could have been fretting about the lyrics and banter for her own act, she had remained in Pepper's room, trying to come up with a plan to save her place in the act. They had stayed at it for nearly two hours without getting anywhere. It seemed impossible. What could Pepper do in a day or two to convince Stanley that she deserved her place when he had been making up his mind about her for months, maybe years?

At least Em agreed she had to try. At least she had someone on her side.

It was a small consolation when the door closed behind Em and she was left alone again with her thoughts and the distant clatter from the street, an occasional creak of someone walking across the floor above her head. Pepper ignored the noises and the tea tray that needed to be returned to the kitchen, and set about her usual morning routine. A quick bath to start and then a change into a pair of cotton drawers over black stockings. She put a claret-colored camisole trimmed with black lace over her corset. No reason to waste time on a fussy getup if she would only be stripping it off the moment she stepped into the dressing room.

Of course, Bessie would be horrified. She had insisted that Pepper cover herself at all times with proper undergarments and overgarments, usually three layers or more. But like everything else, those old rules hardly seemed to matter after Bessie was gone. Pepper made her own rules now, and no one upstairs cared what she wore, so why go to the trouble? Not when a coat could cover everything that needed to be covered. From the shelves, she pulled down an old colonial costume retired from a Founding Fathers bit, slipped on the azure frock coat edged in black trim, scooped up her carpetbag, and was out the door in three strides.

But before she made her way to the dressing room, there were two things she had to do first. One was to get a peek at the marquee. It brought a wide, goofy grin to her face to see her friend's name up in lights: *Uptown Joe.* And the smaller, painted sign beneath: *Em Charmaigne as the Randiest, Dandiest Man on Broadway.*

She was still grinning when she took the outside stairs past the fourth floor to the fifth and made her way to the door of the wardrobe room. She still owed Mrs. Basaraba a proper apology, at least something better than the apologetic note she had left with the bag of notions on the woman's desk the day before.

She scanned the stacks of bolted fabrics—wools and taffetas, satins and cotton—arranged in the shelves along two walls. A third wall was covered in tiny spindles, each sheathed by a spool of thread. All around, costumes, finished or near finished or needing a mend, hung from racks placed along the room's perimeter. The worktable stood at the center of the room, beside the sewing machine where Mrs. Basaraba sat, working the pedal, guiding a length of velvet beneath the needle's rhythm.

Pepper waited for the woman to look up. Mrs. Basaraba finished the seam, backtacked the stitch, and, as she cut the thread, said in her coarse English, "What is wrong, bubbeleh? Why do you stand there?"

"Are you angry with me?"

Mrs. Basaraba pulled the garment from the machine, shook it out, and scrutinized Pepper. She pushed back a hank of wiry tendrils that had broken free of her rolled crown and, with only kindness in her dark eyes, said, "Worried, yes. Angry, no."

Pepper stepped closer. The garment was a miniature Elizabethan doublet. A Shorty Shakespearean had burst a shoulder seam, by the look of it. "You needn't worry about me."

Mrs. Basaraba's thin eyebrows dipped into a scowl.

"Why do you look like you don't believe me?"

"I will tell you why." It was one of the woman's endearing

qualities that her Ws sounded like Vs. It always made Pepper smile. "Two words: Robert DeGraaf."

Pepper's sheepish grin faded. She had never spoken of Robert to Mrs. Basaraba. No one had known about them. Only Mr. DeGraaf and Gregory. Of course Em might have suspected; probably her mother, too. But no one else. Robert had insisted they be careful that way. Pepper forced the smile to return. "What a silly thing to say. I think it's wonderful he's back. He cannot do worse than Stanley."

"We shall see."

"You worry too much, Mrs. B. I only came up to see if you needed anything. If there was any way I might make up for yesterday."

Those black eyebrows twitched again, telling Pepper the woman had more to say, but she only glanced at the clock beside the door. "You should not be here. You should be downstairs, in costume. You know this."

Pepper backed out of the room. Why was everyone always lecturing her? "I have time," she argued. And besides, the less time spent in that dressing room, the better. It meant less of Beatrice's harping.

Still, she obeyed, and by the time she made her way to the fourth-floor corridor, her partners were already on their way to the wings.

"Late again?" Beatrice sauntered by. "Don't worry, we'll be sure to tell Stanley you're just running behind. Again."

A snide objection was on Pepper's lips, but she didn't voice it. Instead, she said, "I'm sorry, I'll only be a moment." It was the first time she had ever apologized to Beatrice. She clenched her teeth and hoped it sounded sincere. "Five minutes."

Beatrice's eyes narrowed, suspicious. "See that you are."

And she was, although she was still fussing with the stubborn button at the lower back of her costume when she burst through the backstage door and joined her partners behind the curtain.

Jimmy was up to his third plate.

"See? I made it. With time to spare."

Silently, Pepper congratulated herself. But if she thought Beatrice would be impressed, she was mistaken. The woman only glared.

It hardly mattered. It was not Beatrice she was trying to impress anyway. She peered over the top of Trixie's bushy curls to the opposite wings, where Stanley sat on his stool. He watched Jimmy with his typical frown. Then the juggler kicked the fourth plate into his juggling rotation, and Stanley checked his pocket watch and opened his notebook to record his notes on the act.

When it was the Dolls' turn, Pepper tapped the Cardinal Rules of the Stage as she always did, and mentally added one of her own: *Don't think, just dance.*

She repeated it to herself as Frankie's fingers plinked the syncopated *tatap-tatap-tap-tap* and she paraded out with her partners, smiling wildly at the audience. And she kept repeating it through the full first song and then the second, and even the third. As the "Maple Leaf Rag" wound down, she realized she had not missed a step. Not a single kick or turn. She had not even moved her lips to count.

When the girls came together for the final bow, Pepper's breath came fast. For the first time, she had danced without a misstep. A perfect turn, her very first. The grin stretched her cheeks till they hurt, and it was not the facsimile of a smile. It was the genuine article, an honest-to-goodness grin.

She could not wait to get to the wings. What would Stanley

say now? No one could find fault with that performance. Even Beatrice seemed satisfied.

"You were marvelous." Trixie grabbed her around the waist and whispered in her ear as they made their way off the stage.

"You think so?" She knew it, but it was glorious to hear. She wanted to hear it again.

As they followed Beatrice into the wings, Pepper waited for Stanley to look up from his notebook. She had not expected much from him, but she did expect something, even a glance to acknowledge her triumph. He gave her nothing.

Fine, if that was how he wanted to be. She would be perfect at the next show and the next. Let him ignore her every time. He would be forced to acknowledge her eventually.

And at the next show, she was perfect, too. Maybe it was her new rule, or maybe it was the thrill of seeing Em back onstage entertaining the crowd. Whatever it was, it was working.

At the end of the second turn, she was prepared for Stanley's silence. But when she walked by, lagging behind her partners on the slim chance he might let a compliment slip, he spoke. He did not look up, and his voice was so low, so nearly imperceptible, that she had to ask him to repeat himself.

"There is a stain on your hose," he said. "I want it out before the next show."

She looked down and grabbed the hem, searching for the offending mark. There it was, at her left knee, a tiny smudge of flesh-colored greasepaint on the cotton. After all that, this was his complaint? A stain so minuscule even he could not have seen it from the stage.

A calmer voice subdued the one screaming spiteful remarks inside her head. *What good will it do? It's only what he wants*. She dropped her hem and forced a smile. "I'll see to it straightaway."

She left before he could say another word.

Immediately, she enlisted Mrs. Basaraba's help to remove the greasepaint stain and hung the stocking in the wardrobe room's open window to dry. It was still damp when she had to return downstairs for the third performance. Perhaps Mr. Stanley would find a way to criticize her for that as well. She was quite sure he would find something. It rattled her, and she forgot to repeat her rule. During the second song, she turned the wrong way when she came out of the spin and nearly collided with Beatrice.

"Pay attention," the woman hissed through her fake stage smile.

Pepper counted herself lucky. Beatrice might have said much worse. When they were finished and she was preparing to walk by Stanley, she braced for his criticism.

He was sitting with the fingers in his lap. For once the notebook was set aside, the pencil tucked in his shirt pocket. He watched her approach, yet he did not say a word. Even as she passed, he did not make a sound. She might have wondered if he had seen the mistake at all, but she could see the reproach staring back from those sunken, unhappy eyes. They left no doubt.

The two evening shows passed just as uneasily. After the last bow, Pepper lagged behind her partners. Instead of going up, she made her way to the stage-right wings to watch Sneed and his dogs. While she watched the Shorty Shakespeareans, she called over Alfred and helped him untuck the coattail that had lodged up in his waistband again.

By the end of the comedy bit, she figured it was safe to go up to the dressing room. The girls would be well on their way for the evening and she could undress in peace. She could not face any more of Beatrice's insults tonight. She had no fight left.

When she opened the door, however, she found Trixie still within.

"There you are, I've been waiting for you. I wanted to show you my new look."

Trixie was so cheerful, Pepper could only smile. And her partner did look lovely in her smart dusty rose town dress with a small feathered hat that tipped to the side.

"Aren't you a vision," Pepper said, and she meant it.

Trixie beamed and twirled, giving Pepper a view of the whole affair. "It is a vision, isn't it? Beatrice gave it to me. It's too large for her, but it nearly fits me. As long as the corset doesn't give out."

Pepper noticed the strain along the side seams and around the shoulders, and there was a distinctly breathless sound in her friend's voice. Trixie gazed at herself in the mirror and her face clouded. "Beatrice is right, isn't she? I need to reduce."

But the cloud passed just as quickly and the cheerfulness was back. "I should be going, though. She's waiting. We're celebrating, you know. We're to be roommates, Beatrice and me, and she's treating me to dinner at Annabelle's Tearoom." She stopped, realizing she might have said something she shouldn't.

Annabelle's, just two blocks down Broadway, was more restaurant than tearoom. Nothing fancy, just a small establishment where a hot roast beef sandwich and a side of potatoes were on the menu every day for just a few coins. What made the place special, however, was that it kept its doors open late, making it especially appealing to entertainers looking for a bite after a long day on the stage.

"You're welcome to join us, if you like," Trixie added sweetly.

Pepper could not imagine a more unpleasant way to spend an evening than sitting across a table from Beatrice Pennington.

Fortunately, she had a dinner date of her own. "I'm dining with Em. But thank you."

"Of course," Trixie said, in that odd tone people sometimes took when she mentioned Em.

Pepper could see the questions in Trixie's eyes, the tilt of her head, the nibble on her lower lip.

"Aren't you keeping Beatrice?" Whatever curiosity Trixie had about Em or the time they spent together, it was not anything Pepper wanted to discuss.

On cue, Trixie's anxiety returned. "I told her I would be right behind her, too. Oh, she hates to wait, absolutely hates it. I better hurry. See you there, then."

Eight

IT WAS NEARLY AN HOUR LATER WHEN PEPPER strode into Annabelle's, refreshed by a quick bath and a change of dress, but still stinging from her failure with Stanley.

She loosened the embroidered shawl she had tied around her shoulders for the brisk walk over, but did not remove it or hang it with the coats on the rack by the door. The soft wool against her skin was soft and comforting, and she enjoyed running her fingers through the flossy fringe that dangled from the edges. She played with the fringe as her gaze hopscotched across the dining room's black-and-white checked floor.

The place was already divided in the usual way. Musicians in the black cushioned booths to the left, openers and middle billers in a matching row of booths to the right. Gawker alley—the square-top tables and chairs in the center—held everyone else, mostly civilians hoping to see a famous face. They need not have bothered, however, for anyone important who happened in was instantly whisked to the private room in the back. Pepper had glimpsed behind that frosted-glass door just once, when she was nine years old and on an errand from Stanley to find Mr. DeGraaf. She had marched into that posh dining room without a thought, clueless that she had broken any rule until the owner scooped her up and marched her out.

That day had also marked her introduction to Stuart McManus, the retired concert saloon manager who operated Annabelle's. (Exactly who Annabelle was, no one knew. A wife? A mistress? A pet?) The dining room was his domain, and every night you could find him there, for there was nothing he loved so much as the bluster and blather of vaudevillians. You might see him at the front welcoming new arrivals, or behind the polished oak bar nursing a scotch and swapping stories with the veterans. Sometimes, if a fresh-faced ingénue happened to visit and if he had already tipped back a good amount of scotch, he would dote upon the lady until she or some chaperone shooed him away.

Tonight, McManus was huddled at the end of the long walnut bar with a chubby old comic whose specialty was the bawdy jokes they loved down in the Bowery. When the proprietor saw Pepper, he hollered hello in the fake French accent he had adopted some years ago. She waved to him and to Frankie, who was sitting with a few men who peddled songs from the Tin Pan Alley music houses up on Twenty-eighth Street. She scanned the place. No sign of Em; but not Beatrice or Trixie, either. She counted that a small blessing and slid into an empty booth along the right wall.

The wizened waitress, another new one it seemed, was setting down a hot pot of tea with two cups and a platter of oysters on the half shell when Em swept in. She glided over to the booth, bent for an air kiss and plopped down in the seat across from Pepper.

"Oysters and tea, just the thing for my comeback celebration," she said, scooping up a shell, tipping it back, and slurping down the contents.

"I thought you would like that," Pepper said, pleased that her selection had been well received. "How does it feel to be back?"

Em squeezed a section of lemon in the cup and drizzled honey in the tea, a restorative for the vocal cords she insisted upon after every show. "Wonderful, doll. Like I never left." She leaned to catch the restaurateur's eye. "You are a credit to your profession, McManus," she hollered, though she was hardly the loudest in the room. McManus lifted his glass in her direction. She picked up a half shell and offered it to Pepper.

"No, thank you. I have a sandwich on the way."

"Not even one? You aren't still holding a grudge about Coney Island, are you? It was years ago, doll. You must let it go. You're only depriving yourself of one of life's greatest pleasures." Em pulled the half shell back and slurped the briny contents herself.

Pepper flinched. It was difficult even to watch someone else eat that slime. "Believe me, I feel no deprivation. And it is not a grudge. They do not like me, and the feeling is mutual. I have never felt as near to death as I did that day. There was an hour or two where I might have preferred death, actually."

Em chuckled, which turned into a cough when she tried to swallow. Tears welled into the red rims of her eyes, but still she was laughing when she grabbed for her tea. "I remember. You were so miserable on the ferry home. I have never seen anyone turn quite that shade of green. Your poor mother, she insisted you eat more to settle your stomach. I fear it only gave you more to hurl into the river. Oh, I am sorry, I should not laugh, but you recovered."

After a day of being unable to keep anything down, yes, she had recovered, although her stomach had ached for more than three days from all the heaving.

"I will stick with my sandwich, thank you."

"The usual brown mush, I suppose?"

Pepper did not nod, but she did not deny it, either. She could not. The waitress was collecting it now from the kitchen overpass—a roast beef sandwich smothered in brown gravy.

Em read her silence. "You always run to your roast beef and gravy after a bad day. What happened? Tell me."

Pepper took a moment to consider her answer while the waitress slid the platter in front of her. When the woman walked away, Pepper lowered her voice. "Today was miserable," she said at last, trying to make it sound light and of little concern. But she couldn't forget Stanley's glares, his disappointment. It all massed into a hard stone in her throat. She had had plenty of bad days before, days far worse than this even, but she knew her time was running out.

She could see Em was holding back, pretending to pick through her oysters, then gingerly peppering the one in her hand with fiery red sauce.

"I danced a perfect turn, Em. Not a single mistake. Twice, I did it twice. But did that finally make him happy?" Her voice broke. She leaned back and closed her eyes, willing herself not to cry here in the booth. She opened her eyes and stabbed her fork into the sandwich, cut off the corner with her knife. "It didn't make any difference. You know what he said? After the second show, he told me I had a smear of greasepaint on my hose. A lousy little smear."

She waited for Em to say something soothing, but she only stared at her plate of oyster shells nestled in the rock salt.

"You can't defend him, Em. Not this time." She stopped. Beatrice was at the door with Trixie in tow. They were approaching, on their way to an empty table in the back.

"Hello, Pepper," Beatrice cooed with a saccharine smile. "Trixie wants to know if we can expect to see your friend, Mr. Creighton, this evening."

Trixie looked appalled and batted Beatrice's shoulder. "Bea, you said you wouldn't."

"Don't be silly," Beatrice said. "You were just saying . . ."

"Don't mind her," Trixie said by way of apology as she tried to pull Beatrice away.

Beatrice pulled her arm back. "I will speak for myself, thank you." To Pepper, she added, "Now, please, you were saying?"

"I wasn't saying anything." Pepper speared another piece of gravy-soaked sandwich.

"Why? Have I struck a nerve?" Beatrice's eyes glittered.

Em, watching the exchange, wiped her lips with the napkin and rose from the table. "It's Beatrice, isn't it?" Before she could respond, Em added. "Yes, Beatrice Pennington. I believe we have a friend in common, you and I."

"I hardly think so," Beatrice said, as if the notion disgusted her.

"No, I'm quite sure. You used to dance with the Saloon Sally girls, didn't you? Benny Jedders has spoken of you. Surely you remember Benny."

Was that fear that flashed in Beatrice's eyes?

"I don't believe so," she said. "You must have me confused with someone else."

"Beatrice Pennington? No, I remember that name. You must

remember Benny. Tall, lanky fellow. Terrible chewing-tobacco habit. He told me he picked it up in mining town saloons. Oh, the stories he has about those mining towns." Em smirked and rolled her eyes to the ceiling. "He and I split a bill up in Ithaca after Sally sent him packing for shacking up with one of her girls. He never misses my salons when he's in town. I just love when he can attend. He has the absolute best stories. Perhaps you'll remember this one: He said you and he—"

"Oh, Benny! Of course, I remember Benny. Such a chatterbox, that one. But he and I didn't cross paths out West. It was here, up in . . ." Beatrice seemed to draw a blank. "Albany, it was. Yes, I'm sure it was Albany. You see, I've never performed in a mining town."

A wide, sly smile spread across Em's face. "Albany? So it was. How could I have gotten that wrong?"

Beatrice eyed the room anxiously. Every part of her seemed trained on an unoccupied table at the back and the single goal of putting distance between herself and Em Charmaigne.

"Look what I have." Trixie, unable to stand the tension, produced a small medicinal vial from her purse. She held it up for Pepper to examine. "It's a tapeworm," she announced with equal parts pride and surprise.

Pepper was glad she was not holding the vial, for she was sure she would have dropped it when she heard its contents. She looked closer to see the tiny worm resting at the bottom of the liquid. "What are you doing with it?"

"It'll help me reduce. Beatrice took me to her apothecary. The druggist says it's absolutely safe. I can eat what I want, and it does all the work for me. Isn't it marvelous?"

Beatrice tapped Trixie's hand. "Best not to wave it around, dear. A lady should keep her beauty secrets secret, you know."

Trixie's smile faded. "I shouldn't have said anything, should I?"

"Never mind that," Beatrice said, feigning graciousness. "You'll excuse us, won't you?"

With a glance, Beatrice urged a still-puzzled Trixie toward a back table.

"You've never mentioned Benny Jedders before," Pepper whispered when she and Em were alone.

Em slurped down another oyster with red pepper sauce. "Never had a reason to. I know a lot of people. The salons are quite handy that way. You should come to one, you know. You might enjoy yourself."

Em's salons drew a diverse crowd, but it hadn't always been that way. When she began inviting friends to her parlor, her guests were other performers, like herself, with certain preferences. Men who enjoyed the company of men and women who enjoyed the company of women, and all of whom enjoyed the privacy of a cozy and accepting parlor over the public bars and corner taverns that afforded little shelter from prying eyes.

Over the years, word of Em's bohemian gatherings, with her impromptu performances and political discussions—not to mention the free flow of alcohol and other diversionary substances—led to an ever-widening guest list. These days, the only thing her guests had in common was a mutual affinity for high-spirited debauchery and decadence of any stripe.

It had been a surprise when Bessie began attending, sometime around Pepper's thirteenth year. Though Em and Bessie had become friendly soon after the MacClairs arrived at The Chance, it was only after Bessie's first salon that the two of them had become something more. The following day, Em had sent red roses. The following night, she had collected Bessie in a gleaming white hansom cab like a fairy-tale carriage.

It wasn't something Bessie talked about, not with Pepper. Not with anyone as far as she could tell. Em simply became part of their family, like a new aunt—or uncle, as the case may be—who came round for dinner a few times a week, and received her own visits in kind.

It was not long afterward that Em retired her act and settled into civilian life. Her salons, which up until then had been held sporadically, became a monthly event, and Bessie returned home later and later, until she was arriving only moments before she thought Pepper would be waking for the day.

Naturally, Pepper was concerned at first, but Bessie was always so cheerful after one of those long nights. She never questioned her mother about what she did at Em's or why she went. It was enough to know that Em and her salons made her mother happy. They seemed to be the only things that did.

Though she was gone now, it wouldn't feel right for Pepper to attend Em's salons. Those nights belonged to Em and Bessie, and it was best to keep it that way.

"Last week, someone brought absinthe," Em said, as if that might change Pepper's mind. "Now that's a kick in the pants."

"I wouldn't know."

"Never danced with the Green Fairy?" Em clucked. "You should at least once, you know. For the experience, if nothing else."

Pepper did not have to respond, for Frankie was settling in behind the upright piano at the end of the bar. After a quick consultation with Jimmy, who had his elbow on the piano's top, he started up a rag tune. A bouncy melody Pepper could not place.

"No, not that one. The other one," Jimmy corrected, then tipped back something amber in a shot glass.

Frankie slid his fingers from the ivories. "Right, I know the one you mean. Here." He launched into another melody.

Jimmy cleared his throat, draped an arm across the top of the piano, and announced to everyone and no one in particular, "A little something for my friends." And then the mild-mannered Jimmy, the Jimmy who usually kept to himself when he wasn't sporting a big clown-faced grin, that Jimmy was gone. This Jimmy was filling the room with his own crazy smile and wild, buggy eyes. This Jimmy was lifting and dropping his shoulders to Frankie's wild rhythm, making his big plaid coat move as if of its own accord. He stepped into an open space between the piano and a table, swept his hat from his head, held it over his chest, and sang in a strong tenor, "One dark and stormy night, the rain was falling fast. . . ."

"Who knew he could sing?" Em whispered.

When he neared the song's end, he came up to Em and Pepper, dropped to one knee, and put his hat to his ear. "Is that the sultan's song I hear?"

Pepper dropped her head into her hands. She knew what was coming next.

As if on cue, Frankie plucked a ditty that had become nearly as famous as Little Egypt's shimmies. When the crowd was like this, all keyed up and eager for entertainment, it was impossible to refuse an invitation to perform. Trying only prolonged the torture. Pepper had learned it was best to give in quickly and get it over with. So that was what she did. She took Jimmy's hand and let him lead her back to the piano, where she took the embroidered shawl from around her shoulders and tied it around her hips in the Arab style. Once Frankie had Little Egypt's tune in full swing, she danced for Annabelle's diners. She circled her hips and her shoulders, she swayed back and forth, but it was her shimmy—which made the shawl's fringe jump and twirl—that always made the crowd cheer.

The dancing had been hesitant at first, but as the music and the crowd's enthusiasm filled her, it emboldened her, too. She danced for the joy of it, with no need to count steps or kicks or turns. She forgot about Stanley and his reproaches. About Beatrice and her insults. The music lifted her above all of it, made her part of the laughter and the cheers and all the happy clatter of people having a very good time. She was so lost in it, she hardly noticed him walk in. Robert DeGraaf, standing at the door. He did not speak, he did not nod. He simply stood and frowned.

* * *

"IS THAT TYPICAL, THAT MAYHEM?"

Pepper winced. Robert had not looked at her when he said it, but as they walked side by side, through the circles of light cast by the streetlamps along this part of Broadway, she could sense the trouble. It was a simple question, spoken plainly and without emotion, yet the disapproval was thick in his gait and the way his hands plunged deep into his pockets.

It was late, and a fog was pushing in from the east. Though she had pulled her shawl from her hips back up to her shoulders when they had left Annabelle's—after a quick good-bye to Em and an attempt to leave payment for her meal, which Em spurned—the thin fabric did little to defend against the chill. She shivered and pulled it more tightly around herself.

"Well?"

"I would not call it mayhem," she answered.

"Oh?" He glanced at her sideways but did not slow his pace. "What would you call it?"

At this hour, it was so quiet on the street. A distant clopping of carriage horses carrying residents to their homes, the hollow echo of their footsteps. Only the thrumming in her ears remained from that raucous music and laughter. "We were just having a good time. There was no harm in it."

He stopped then, in a space sheltered between a lamppost and a resting hansom cab. "You see, that's where you're wrong." His hands emerged from their pockets and he took her gently by the shoulders. His hard expression softened. "Don't you see you are going down a wrong road? Don't spoil yourself."

She flinched. How was dancing and laughing spoiling herself? But she could not say it. His concern was earnest. She could see it in the way his emerald eyes stared down at her.

"I can give you more than this, but you must let me."

All at once her anger, her embarrassment melted away. She remembered why she had fallen in love with him. He was strong and sure of himself in a way she never was. He never doubted himself or worried about the future. It was why she'd followed him to the rooftop three summers ago, why she knew he was telling the truth when he said they were meant for each other.

Looking up at him, she could see that he wanted what was best for her. She only had to trust him. He could set everything right, and how wonderful that felt. All the day's difficulties meant nothing next to this. Just the two of them. As it should be. She leaned against him, smelled the soap on his skin, the musky scent of his hair oil. She breathed it in and let it draw her closer. She lifted her chin. . . . He dipped his. . . .

"Perhaps this is not the place," he whispered. "Out here in the open." He glanced again at the carriage beside them. He stepped back from her and up to the driver's raised bench, where a man sat hunched and apparently sleeping. "Sir," Robert said, knocking on the wood siding. "Are you for hire?"

The man roused with a grumbled, "Waiting for a return fare." He gestured with a tip of his head at the dining establishment across the street.

"I will double your fee for a turn up to Washington Square Arch."

"S'pose there's time for that," the driver said, taking up the reins.

Robert turned back to Pepper and gestured to the cab's step. "Shall we?"

She might have felt scorned, but she knew he was right. Again, he was only looking out for her interests, as a gentleman should. It was how ladies should be treated. He helped her into the cab.

"That's better, wouldn't you say?" Robert settled against the tufted leather cushion and spread out the lap robe that warmed their knees. When he had shifted and arranged himself, she felt his palm come to rest upon her thigh. She expected him to move it once he realized his trespass, but he did not. His fingers rested, content, it seemed, to conform to the curve of her limb.

As the horse trotted up Broadway, Pepper fought the inclination to remove his hand. She forced herself to ignore it, and when she still could not ignore it, tried at least not to appear as unsettled as she felt. It was only a hand after all. Robert's hand.

"You have said nothing of my offer." He was looking into the distance. Into the heart of the park. "It's a very good offer."

Her mouth went dry and she stared into her lap. She had known this moment would come, yet still she dreaded it.

Robert turned from the majesty of the George Washington memorial arch, partially hidden by the sycamore and maple trees, to face her. He lifted his hand from her leg to push aside a tendril of hair that had fallen loose over her eye and stroked her cheek. "You are so beautiful, Pepper MacClair. Your sweet little nose, your tender little lips. You know I have always admired you."

Thoughts of them together came crashing back, the longing mingled with the shame. There was nothing to be ashamed of, as long as they were together. "I want to be with you," she said at last. "Nothing would make me happier. But . . ." Her voice stalled. How could she tell him she wanted more? In the darkness of her own room, it seemed so simple, but not here in the moonlight. What right did she have to ask anything like marriage from a man like Robert DeGraaf?

But he was waiting. His gaze full of expectation.

"I do not want to leave The Chance." It was only a partial truth, but it was enough.

He leaned closer. His lips warmed her ear. "Am I not enough?" He was playing with the words, stretching them out, teasing her with them. "We could be together. Is that not what you want?"

Her heart pounded. Could he hear it? Under the protection of the lap robe, she could feel his hand find her waist and then move upward. Even through the layers of her dress and camisole, the corset, she could feel the press of his thumbs along the sides of her breasts, sending a shiver that traveled down to her toes.

"I do want it," she breathed, sitting stiff and still and helpless.

"Then tell me you accept."

He watched her. Yet he had to know she could not refuse. He knew her circumstances as well as she. He had claimed her on that balmy afternoon on the rooftop, under the scratchy picnic blanket. Her choice had been made that day.

She pushed back against the cab's cushion and brushed at her shoulders where his fingers had been. She knew she had no right to want more from him, yet she did. This helpless feeling did not suit her. "Please ask the driver to return me to Annabelle's."

He pulled away, surprised by her detachment. Then he did as she asked and took a cigar from his coat pocket.

The driver changed course and they sat together in hard, prickly silence, she watching the townhouses and the trees, he puffing on his cigar.

When they neared the restaurant, the driver brought the carriage to a stop. Robert hopped down and helped Pepper out. When her boot touched pavement, she tried to remove her hand from his grip. He held it and said, "Your answer, Miss MacClair."

There were no soft glances and sweet caresses now, only the hard will and resolve of a man negotiating a deal. Yes, college had certainly left its mark on Robert DeGraaf.

She tilted her face up defiantly, holding his gaze. "I believe my answer is exactly what you've known it would be, Mr. DeGraaf. I accept."

Before he could respond and before she could change her mind, she retracted her hand and hurried toward Annabelle's front door. At least she had gotten the last word.

• • •

INSIDE, EM WAS LEANING AGAINST THE PIANO BELTING OUT A suggestive verse from "In My Merry Oldsmobile," while one of Frankie's Tin Pan Alley pals pounded at the keys. Alfred and Edwards were in the aisles, cakewalking and pulling ladies from the crowd for a quick turn. The place had devolved into its usual late-night revelry.

Mayhem, indeed.

Pepper slid onto a stool at the bar and watched. Em finished her song and tapped the upright. "That's it for me, Cornelius."

By the time Em had joined Pepper, Alfred was winding up a new song. She leaned down to Pepper before taking the empty stool beside her. "I didn't expect to see you again tonight. Everything all right?"

Pepper watched Alfred crooning in the center of the room. "I suppose you should congratulate me," she said.

"Oh?"

Still with her gaze straight ahead, she said, "Robert DeGraaf has made me an offer." *A very good offer,* were those not his words? She knew what he had meant: A girl like her, a theater girl with no prospects to speak of, was lucky to get an offer at all.

"Marriage?"

Her heart broke again. "No, not marriage."

"I see."

There was a world of reproach in those two words. But what did Em know of these things? What did she know of the love that bound Pepper to Robert? "He wants us to be together. That's what is important." She pretended to be caught up in Alfred's performance. It did not matter if it was not a proposal of marriage. It would be soon enough.

"So you're happy with it, this . . . offer?" Em picked up a toothpick and poked between her side teeth.

"I am."

"Sure you are."

"Fine, I am not completely satisfied. But isn't it all the same?"

It was what she had decided on the silent ride back from Washington Square. And despite her misgivings, the idea had taken hold. She wound and unwound a silky strand of the shawl's fringe around one finger and told Em what she was telling herself. "Robert loves me. He came back, didn't he? All that matters is that we're together."

Em hailed the bartender. "Gin, neat. Make it a double." When the glass was in front of her and she had taken a good long sip, she turned to Pepper. "So he loves you. And he doesn't mind that you are a performer? High and mighty Robert DeGraaf is fine with his lady love hoofing in front of a crowd six days a week?"

"Sure he is." She coiled the flossy fringe of her shawl around and around her finger. Even as she spoke, Pepper knew her friend did not believe her. Em could read the truth on Pepper's face.

"Don't fool yourself, doll. You're not fooling anyone else."

"I really have no other choice, do I? Stanley has it in for me. He wants to fire me, and he will one day. No, don't deny it. You can't defend him this time. If I don't do something, he will toss me back on the street. But Robert will protect me. Stanley wouldn't dare to touch me with Robert by my side."

That was the truth of it. However she might yearn for marriage or whatever silly notions of love she had had as a girl, this was the truth of her life: She could not demand more from Robert because even his stingy offer of affection was the best she was likely to get. And maybe it would be enough to save her from Stanley.

Em toyed with her glass. "You deserve better than this."

It was more than Pepper could tolerate. She pulled her finger from its silky floss cocoon as the frustration welled up inside. Then she turned it, squarely, on Em. "It's easy for you to say, isn't it? You have a home that cannot be taken from you. You never have to worry about being turned out on the street. You have an act you could take to any other stage. I have none of that. So if you would not mind, I'd rather you stopped sticking your nose in my affairs."

She paused to breathe and only then realized the ruckus

around her had come to a halt. Even the music had stopped. She glanced around the silent dining room. Every eye in the joint was looking back. When she looked at Em, the woman held her glass frozen midsip.

All of Pepper's anger dissolved in the face of that frozen horror, and only one thought remained: *What have I done?*

For the second time that evening, she gathered herself together and ran out into the night.

Nine

BEATRICE WAS ODDLY SILENT WHEN PEPPER WALKED into the dressing room. Pepper had not expected a warm welcome, but she had thought an early arrival for a change might merit at least a pleasant word. But Beatrice only stared at her reflection as she tapped her cheek with the rouge stick and smeared the color with her fingertips.

"Don't mind her," Trixie said, poking her head around the dressing screen. "She's just cross that those didn't come for her." She poked her finger at a bouquet of lavender roses sitting in a vase on the table beside the couch.

"Oh, Trixie." Pepper went to the bouquet and touched a single perfect bulb. "They're beautiful. Who sent them to you?"

"Not me, silly. They came for you. Look at the card."

She slid the white envelope from beneath the corner of the vase. Her name was scrawled there in flourishing, cursive script. She pulled out the linen stock square:

You've always deserved the best.

"We saw you leaving last night with Mr. DeGraaf, the *young* Mr. DeGraaf," Trixie gushed.

Pepper winced. What else had they seen? Last night had not been one of her proudest moments.

"Are they from him?" Trixie continued.

"I don't know." And she didn't. The card was unsigned. She turned it over and checked the envelope again. "Who brought them to the room?"

"Matty," Trixie said. "He said they were delivered by the florist's boy. Well, they must have come from Mr. DeGraaf. Just look at them. It's the biggest bouquet I've ever seen. And you know what lavender roses mean, don't you?"

"Admiration?" It was a blind guess. Pepper had never learned the language of flowers.

"No, silly. Love at first sight." Trixie giggled. "Isn't that just so romantic, Bea?"

Pepper turned to the roses to hide her embarrassment, though it was a happy sort of embarrassment. Romantic, indeed. And to think all night she had wrestled with her decision, letting Em's words plant doubt in her mind. She should not have lost her temper the way she did, she knew that, but Em had to accept that Pepper was a woman now. She knew what she was doing, and she knew what was best.

And whatever lingering doubts she might have had about Robert melted into sweet nothing beside these beautiful flowers.

Beatrice slammed her tube of lip rouge down on the vanity counter, making the other paints and brushes clatter. "Good grief, they're only flowers. Flowers die, so you better enjoy them while you can." She sneered at her red roses in the corner, already wilting and tinged with black edges. "Flowers don't amount to a hill of beans."

Pepper caught Trixie's glance from the dressing screen and nodded. They had worked together long enough to understand this silent communication, and they had worked with Beatrice long enough to know it was best for all if Pepper's flowers disappeared from the room as soon as possible.

"Did you notice how Matty lingered?" Trixie said from the screen. "I think he might be sweet on you, Bea."

While Trixie chatted up Beatrice, Pepper gathered her card and the vase.

"Sure he is," Beatrice said in her weary way. "But he's a boy. Hardly worth the trouble." She dragged the color over her lips and rubbed them together.

"Maybe. He does have a certain charm, though, don't you think?"

The last thing Pepper heard as she hurried down the corridor was Beatrice saying, "Charm doesn't pay the rent. As soon as my fella gets his financing together, he's going to give me the best gift a girl can get: He's going to make me a star."

Not likely, Pepper thought as she came upon three Shorty Shakespeareans in the corridor. She asked them to hold the door to the stairwell.

"Sure, peaches," barked a fourth smallish man, dressed in a courtly doublet and sounding like a Bowery tough. "Need help with those?"

The small admirers followed behind her. One gazed up at her in wonder as the others took the opportunity to brush against the short hem of her skirt. One tiny bold hand reached up beneath that hem and planted itself against her rump. She squealed and wheeled around. "Who did that?" She scanned each of the four innocent faces pressed around her. "Well, knock it off or I'll thump the lot of you."

The diminutive men shot glances back and forth, feigning surprise. "What's she talking about?" "Do you know?" "I don't, do you?"

She left them on the fourth floor and was smiling again by the time she reached the backstage. She passed Laszlo and Old Jake, then the professor. Then she heard that old, familiar grumble.

"Some flowers you have there."

She peeked around the side of the arrangement to see Gregory on his way out of the prop room.

"They are, aren't they?" She held the vase proudly.

"Who are they for?"

"Me. Is that so difficult to believe?"

"S'pose not. But who would send something so grand?"

"Isn't it obvious?"

"Not really." A smile twitched his lips.

Gazing at the bulbs again, she said, "Robert DeGraaf, of course." When she looked up, that irritating, smirking smile was gone.

One of these days, he would have to accept that he had been wrong about Robert. Then maybe he would accept that he had been wrong about her, too.

She left the roses in her room, grabbed her plum velvet coat, stiff from its hanging but at least fully dry, and left by the street door. She passed the ticket window, where one of the ushers was searching through the top desk drawer for God knows what, trying to make sense of the job that had been thrust upon him the day before.

She walked up to another usher standing like an aged sentinel inside the door, ready to rip tickets that had not yet sold. "Is Mr. DeGraaf in?"

The old man in the black-and-red uniform leaned back and considered Mr. DeGraaf's closed office door. "If you mean the younger one, he's in there. Hollered for a coffee a few minutes ago and said he wasn't to be disturbed."

"Is he alone?"

She couldn't risk repeating her earlier mistake.

"Far as I could tell, but he didn't seem in a mood for visitors."

"It's all right. He'll want to see me."

It probably should not have given her so much pleasure to say those words, but it did. The smile on her face made her cheeks ache as she made her way across the crimson carpeting toward the office door.

She knocked.

"What is it?" Robert barked from within.

She took it as an invitation to let herself in. She found him behind the desk, one hand on a short stack of files, another rubbing his temple. He was reading something in a folder on his desk and mumbling to himself, "This hardly makes sense. Is there another account? It must be a mistake."

She waited for him to look up.

When he did, reluctantly, his eyes widened slightly in surprise. "Pepper, I wasn't expecting you." He did not smile.

"I hope I'm not disturbing you." But she had the distinct impression that was exactly what she was doing.

He leaned back in the tall leather chair and stretched his hands out in front of him, as though he were unfolding from a position he had been holding far too long. "No, I suppose I need to break from this mess anyway."

"What mess?"

He glowered at the stacks on his desk. "These damn ledgers that never add up. And the dismal receipts. It's difficult to fathom how anyone could sit back and watch it all fall apart. Money wasted on sewing notions and Graphophones and recordings when we have a pianist on salary. Does Stanley not see that money should be put toward advertising and pulling in new patrons? But no, the man seems happy to do nothing but sit on his stool just as he's always done. No innovation, no imagination, nothing." He glanced up and shook his head. "But that's not your concern, is it?" He smoothed back his hair and composed himself. "I'm glad you've come by, actually."

Her smile returned.

"I want you to have dinner with me tomorrow night." He spoke as he rose, grabbed a handful of files, and slid them into a leather satchel.

"I would like that. I would like it very much." She nearly ran across the room and threw her arms around him to show just how much, but she managed to suppress the urge and maintain some semblance of decorum. "What time shall I be ready?"

He was glancing around his desk, perplexed. He did not seem to have heard her, so she said again, "The time?"

"Let's say quarter past eight." He grabbed another file and stuffed it into his case.

"That's too early."

He frowned.

"What I mean to say," she added hastily, "is that I won't be off the stage until quarter till nine."

He sighed and turned back to his case. "Of course, the show. Nine is later than I prefer for dinner but I suppose it will have to do."

She could see that the accommodation annoyed him. She moved closer. "I'll be looking forward to it."

He clasped the satchel and turned to her. His expression softened and his eyes held that old glimmer they'd had when she stole away from her chores to meet him on the roof. When they had stood at the ledge and held hands and . . . If only they could run back up there now, to gaze out at the horizon and each other. If only they could replay that last scene, rework it, give it a proper finish. She would have thrown her arms around his neck and begged him to go with her if the sound of Frankie's fingers on the piano keys had not slipped into the room.

The show was beginning. There was no time. She had to leave.

She pulled away.

"I know. The show." There was no enthusiasm in his voice.

"I'll be looking forward to tomorrow night." She smiled and let herself out. She was halfway to the auditorium when she remembered the flowers. She had completely forgotten to thank him for his gift.

• • •

GREGORY WAS STALKING THROUGH THE SCARLET ROOM ON HIS way to see Robert DeGraaf when he saw Pepper emerge from the theater manager's office. The sight of her nearly stopped him cold, but it was the smile on her face that tore through him like a blade. He hardened himself to it.

A pair of patrons had entered and were heading toward the balcony stairs when Pepper passed him. "Late again?" He regretted it instantly. Why could he not say something nice?

Pepper hardly noticed. She hardly noticed him at all.

Her eyes shimmered with a happy glow. It had been so long since they had done that. She was still smiling when she paused, tilted her ear toward the ragtime coming from the stage, and said, "Jimmy just walked on. I have plenty of time."

Another sarcastic comment nearly passed his lips, but he held it back. Instead, he nodded and said, "You're worth a wait."

But Pepper was already off.

There was no time to think about Pepper MacClair, however, not when he had been summoned by Robert DeGraaf. As he approached the door, he saw the man pulling on an overcoat.

"You asked for me?"

Robert turned, and his eyes narrowed when he saw Gregory in the open doorway. "I did." He went to the leather case standing at the edge of the desk and pulled out a thick folder. "I've been auditing the theater's accounts and there appear to be several inconsistencies pertaining to the purchase of supplies for your department. I thought you might have something to say about that."

"Not a thing." He thought back over the days. Hadn't he told George to keep his invoices? He was sure he had, or had he asked Matty to do it? Damn, why couldn't he remember?

Robert opened the folder and thumbed through the sheets. A dozen, possibly more. "All these statements say 'paid in full,' yet the account ledger shows no record of a payment being issued to this . . ." He glanced to the top of the page. "This George's Hardware, not for the last six months. So you have no knowledge of these transactions with this establishment?"

"Can't say that I do."

Robert's eyebrows peaked. He shoved the statements back into the folder and then back into his case. "That's hardly an acceptable answer from a properties master. Perhaps the job is a bit much for a simple stagehand like yourself." He grabbed his hat from the coat rack.

Gregory waited.

"Nothing to say for yourself? Interesting. Tell me, cretin, have you taken my advice and filed that application with the union yet?"

"That's not your concern." It took every ounce of self-control to keep his rage in check. The worst of it was, he only had himself to blame.

Robert grabbed his case and made for the door. "Time may not be on your side, cretin. I understand there is a waiting list."

"I'm not going anywhere."

"Yes, well." Robert checked his fingernails and the position of his cravat. "Circumstances have a way of changing."

Gregory's fingers curled against his palm. They itched to wind themselves around that scrawny white neck and squeeze.

He was still feeling the burn of that desire five minutes later when he pushed through the prop room door and clipped Matty.

"What's the big idea?" the boy wailed, grabbing his arm and rubbing hard at the spot where the door had slammed him.

"I thought Stanley told you to clean away those boxes around the light board."

"He did. I mean, I am. But if you have a moment . . ."

Gregory pushed by the youth to the rows of shelves holding the theater's stockpile of props and building supplies. The theater didn't keep much of an inventory of its own up front, not since the old days when Mr. DeGraaf had money to burn on extravagant pageants. These days, it was mostly construction supplies and storage space for the props the acts brought with them: extra bird cages for Marvani's performance, tiny ramps and hoops for

Sneed's dogs, padded mats and blocks for the Helzigs. Gregory grabbed a box at random and sifted through its contents. Nails, it turned out: thick framing nails, carpentry nails, finishing nails—nails, it seemed, for every job imaginable. "When we went to George's, you took the invoice, didn't you?" he asked Matty.

"Invoice? No. Doesn't he save them up and send them once a month?"

"But I asked you to take that one."

"No, you didn't," Matty insisted.

Damn.

"Why, something wrong?"

Gregory stared hard at the nails, pretending to search for something in particular. "So what's Stanley want with me?" He braced for more grief, more bad news.

"It's not him who's looking. It's me."

Gregory slanted a look at the boy. There was fear in that tender face, but he was in no mood to coddle. "Why?"

"I can see this is a bad time. I'll come back later." He made a hasty retreat toward the door.

"Stop."

Matty turned back.

"Tell me what you came to tell me." If the boy had more bad news, he wanted it now.

Matty's fingers hooked and twisted. "I only wanted to check with you about . . ."

"Just say it, dammit."

"Trixie." The boy stepped back, expecting a swing to the jaw.

Now it was Gregory's turn to be surprised. What did he have to do with Trixie Small? "What about her?"

The boy straightened like a steel rod had been shoved up his backside. "I know she fancies you, but since you don't seem inclined toward her, I was wondering if you would mind if I called on her." The boy somehow mustered the gumption to look him straight in the eye.

"Trixie? The chorus girl?"

"You know who I'm talking about; don't pretend otherwise."

So the boy had a boiling point after all. Gregory sucked in his lips to keep the smile off his face. But he could not tell the boy he had never had a spare thought for Trixie Small. Had never given her a second look. There was nothing in that package of frizzy brunette hair and bubbly chatter that appealed to him, and he certainly had not known she was sweet on him.

"I won't stand in your way."

Matty looked at him sideways. "Only if you're sure."

Any other day, he would have taken the opportunity to tease the boy. But not today. "If you're fond of her, you have my blessing. For whatever it's worth."

The boy's chest swelled with happy relief, and he rocked back on his heels. "Just doing the gentlemanly thing, is all."

From the stage, Frankie's plinking piano heralded the end of Jimmy's last juggle. Gregory glanced across the boards to the opposite wings just as the usher changed the easel card and the Dancing Dolls took their places at the edge of the stage. Beatrice and Trixie, and Pepper behind them.

"Excuse me, will you?" Matty elbowed him in the side as he tried to catch Trixie's eye. When he had it, Matty cocked his head in hello. Trixie blushed behind her hand. Gregory's gaze followed Pepper. He moved closer under the pretense of checking one of Laszlo's knots and watched her tap her fingers to her lips and then to those ridiculous stage rules.

• • •

ON THE OTHER SIDE OF THE BOARDS, PEPPER WAS REPEATING HER fifth rule to herself: *Don't think, just dance.*

And she did, again. And again Stanley hardly took notice. This time it was because the printer's boy was back, and by the look of it, Stanley was no happier to see him.

When the turn was finished, and the Dancing Dolls sashayed off the stage, Pepper lingered to overhear the argument.

"You may as well dump them in the trash bin on your way out because I don't need them, I don't want them, and I am certainly not going to pay for them. I ordered one thousand programs."

"But sir, you said you would need double the order with the Uptown Joe reprint."

"I said I would need 'another' order, you dimwit."

There was a crowd accumulating around the pair now. No one wanted to look like they were eavesdropping, but there seemed to be a hundred necessary tasks that required doing in the space around Stanley.

Pepper edged by. She wasn't listening anymore. She was thinking about those programs. Had she heard correctly? Two thousand programs? If Robert was vexed by the usual expenses, what would he say when he heard of this?

"Take them out back and put them in the trash, just get them out of my sight." Stanley maneuvered himself onto his feet, grabbed his cane, and hobbled back to his office.

The printer's boy threw up his hands and stormed out the stage door.

More money wasted that could have gone to advertising. That was what Robert would say. Money that would just sit out back rotting with the rubbish.

Unless . . .

And then it came to her. Call it innovation or imagination, it did not matter. She knew exactly how to put those programs to use.

She moved fast, leaving Beatrice and Trixie in the wings in her rush to get upstairs to the dressing room. As quickly as she could, she cleaned the greasepaint from her face and dabbed herself with powder—her face and her décolletage, which her costume displayed much more than her usual street garb. She blew down the front of her corset and camisole to relieve the heat from dancing. Then she threw a black shawl over her shoulders so it draped down her back and smoothed the long fringe so it hung neatly.

Altogether it was still less—much less—than she would wear on even the warmest summer day, but comfort and warmth had nothing to do with what she was about to do. For this outing, she was not Pepper MacClair, she was merely a Dancing Doll, taking a bit of the stagecraft to the street. That was how she would lure in the passersby.

Just like the actors on the Hippodrome's opening day.

She checked herself quickly in the mirror and was on her way out the dressing room door when Beatrice strode in.

"Where do you think you're going?" The woman wasted no time unhooking her dress and letting it slide to the floor. She stood in her corset and undergarments, fanning herself with her hand.

Pepper was wondering how much to say when Trixie entered and, seeing Beatrice half naked in the center of the room, quickly closed the door. She settled on, "I'm going to do some advertising."

Beatrice snorted, "I know the pay is bad, but honestly, have some decency."

"Not for me, for the show," she snapped. As if she needed lessons on decency from Beatrice. "I'm going to pass out programs, talk up the acts."

"So you're some sort of floozy newsboy now?"

Leave it to Beatrice to make her feel foolish.

"Say what you like, at least I'm doing something." Maybe she would do what even Stanley could not do: fill The Chance's auditorium again.

Quickly, Pepper found the abandoned box of programs by the stairwell, scooped up an armful of them, and pushed through the stage door. The rain clouds had drifted west, leaving a gaping expanse of cool blue sky. Let Beatrice make fun. If it could work for the Hippodrome, why could it not work for The Chance?

She was imagining Stanley thanking her, smiling even, as she hiked her shawl over her mostly bare shoulders, when a man in a brown tweed suit passed her on the sidewalk. She held out a program. "May I interest you in one of these, sir?"

He stopped. His glance slid from her chest to the bundle in her arms. "What's this?"

She gave him her best stage smile and pressed the program toward him again. "A preview of the fine vaudeville entertainments inside The Chance Theatre, sir, five shows a day, six days a week."

The man took the proffered sheet and glanced at it too quickly to see anything more than the curlicue scroll and the theater's name in black letters across the front. His gaze returned to her as he smoothed the grain of his black-and-silver mustache. "A show, you say? And would you be one of these fine vaudeville entertainments?"

"Aren't you clever?" She feigned amusement. "I dance in the deuce act, but I suppose I would leave it for you to decide whether it's a fine entertainment or not. The next show begins in two hours. Plenty of time to get yourself a good seat."

The man pulled a shiny golden watch from his breast pocket. "Perhaps I will." He glanced at Abernathy's swinging door. "And plenty of time to stop in for a nip as well. You will join me, won't you?"

He must have assumed the offer was too compelling to refuse, for without a word from her, he stepped forward to guide her toward the tavern. She sidestepped the palm he tried to place on the small of her back and gave him an apologetic grin. "I would be delighted, sir, but I've work to do." She tapped the stack in her arms.

Surprised but undeterred, he said, "Perhaps I might help? The boys inside would welcome a diversion."

She caught the glint in his eye that said *diversion* was not the first word to cross his mind. That hardly mattered, though, for she could picture the roomful of men with money to spend on drink and time to warm Abernathy's seats. Would they not find more enjoyment at The Chance? "Now that you mention it, I think that would be lovely, Mr. . . ."

"Garrett. Wilbur Garrett." He plucked his hat from his head to reveal a thick tuft of black hair on the otherwise smooth terrain above his forehead. "At your service."

"That would be lovely, Mr. Garrett. Shall we?"

Together they entered the dim tavern and as soon as they were inside, Pepper separated herself from her companion, leaving him stranded at the door. Quickly, she made her way to each table, leaving a playbill in front of every man, whether he was in the midst of conversation or slumped over a lonely cup. "Guaranteed laughs, gentlemen," she said with a bright and—she hoped—

captivating smile. Or, "A show you won't want to miss," or "Just across the street, couldn't be more convenient."

She was not too naïve to think this was an acceptable manner of promoting The Chance, not by any measure. Entering Abernathy's or any establishment of its kind was a risk for a young lady. It made haste essential. Even moving with all possible speed, there was the occasional scrape of callused fingers along her leg, searching beneath her hem. It required discipline not to slap each offender's face. These were not the Shorty Shakespeareans she could threaten with a scowl. She made do with stepping aside and moving on to the next table.

The serving woman, whose red kerchief held back long, unkempt hair, stood behind the counter watching every move. When she disappeared down a corridor only to return a moment later with a short, greasy man in a soiled apron, Pepper knew it was time to leave. She was already at the door, thanking Mr. Garrett for his assistance, when the man called out: "No solicitors allowed, yeah? Says so on the blasted door!"

Behind her, the wood plank floor rumbled with approaching footsteps. She reached out a grateful hand to her companion. "I do hope to see you at the theater. Good-bye."

Before he could utter a response, she was gone, back among the parade of pedestrians on Broadway, doing her best to blend in with all the black bowlers and feathered hats, to pretend her pulse did not race or that her skin was not tingling like a live electrical wire. She knew she should have felt chagrined by her conduct, even ashamed. But she didn't. A few of those men would end up at The Chance ticket window before the day was out, of that she was sure.

Why had no one else thought to advertise this way? It was so simple, and so much better than pasting posters to a wall or paying for those tiny boxes at the bottom of a newspaper page.

She crossed Broadway after walking past Wanamaker's department store, just before the bend at Grace Church, and made her way back on the eastern side of the street. Along the way, she stuffed a program in the hand of every man, woman, and reasonably aged child she passed, saying with a happy, toothy grin, "I do hope you will come to the show."

By the time she had made her way back to the theater, she had distributed all but a few of the programs she had carried out—and to her delight, a line eight men deep had queued in front of the ticket window. As she neared, she had to smile. She recognized half of them from the tavern.

One recognized her as well: a burly man in black overalls and work boots who slapped his neighbor on the back when he saw her approach. "There she is, boys," he said. Three jowly, swarthy faces turned her way.

"Hey, honey pot, give us a taste. Don't be shy," another one called out, waving his folded program at her.

The others chimed in, begging for a teaser.

She skirted the sidewalk, keeping a distance between them and herself. "No, no, no," she said playfully, as though she were not a little afraid of these men now that she saw them in the harsh daylight. "Wouldn't want to spoil the show."

The roughest-looking one, the one who had called out, stepped out of line and staggered toward her. "The fellas and I want to know what we're gonna git for our money, darlin'. Let's see a bit, just a little bit. C'mon now. We're all friends, ain't we?"

Pepper hurried to the stage door. "You'll see plenty inside. Take my word for it." The smile on her face felt stiff and heavy.

"Yer word, huh?" With a wink back to his buddies, he added,

"That's not the first thing I'd like to take. How about a little kiss, then?" He had quickened his pace, too, and had nearly reached her.

"Oh, you flatter me." She hurried on, steering clear of his advances and trying to keep the fear from her face. "I'm late getting myself ready for the stage, however. Want you to see me at my best, you understand?"

"Will you be stripping down to your whatnots, then?"

The men sniggered.

Pepper glared—at least she hoped it was a glare. She was trying desperately to appear stern. "That most certainly is not what I meant, sir."

"C'mon, darlin', just a little kiss," he coaxed again. He had broken from the line and was now close enough she could see the chip of his front tooth, the cracks in his dry, scabbed lips.

Pepper hastened her stride, trying to reach the stage door before he did. How big he was, yet how quickly he could move. He cut off her path. She stopped and wished she had the security of knowing Em was in the ticket booth, watching over her. But the usher on duty was so consumed by his new job that he did not even raise his head from the cash drawer. She straightened against the ruffian. "That will be quite enough, sir." She stabbed her finger into his giant barrel of a chest. "You've had your fun, now go back to your friends. Let me pass."

But he did not let her pass. He stood solid as a mountain, rubbing his jaw. "Some fire in ya," he drawled. "I like that."

"You had better think twice before you do something you'll regret," she said. Admittedly, she did not sound convincing, even to herself.

His hand swept from his face to the back of her head in a move so fast, so bracing, it nearly knocked her to her knees. His fingers clutched a cloud of her curls and swept her head closer to his own. The stench of him turned her stomach, a rancid brew of sweat and urine, whiskey and malice.

She was about to beg him to release her when something yanked him backward. The noose of fingers gripping her throat released and he was stumbling, eyes wild, arms flailing against his attacker.

She could not see the attacker's face, but she knew that overgrown sweep of dark hair.

Wrapping one arm around the man's neck, Gregory pulled his prey back so his lips were alongside the man's neck. The hoodlum lurched to break free, but he could not break Gregory's hold. Pepper saw Gregory whisper into the man's ear, and in an instant, the fight drained from him. He hung slack and awkward against Gregory, his wide eyes shooting fearful pleas to his buddies.

Those buddies exchanged their own worried glances. Should they intervene, should they run? They did neither. They stood, watched, and kept mum.

Gregory tightened his grip on the man and said loudly enough for even his friends to hear: "Is there a problem, fellas?"

The man choking in his embrace shook his head and tried to respond, though only a gurgle and spittle passed his lips. The others shook their heads and dodged Gregory's glare.

"Did he harm you?" Gregory was looking at her now as he held the man firm.

She adjusted her shawl, which had slipped from her shoulders and hung slack down her back. "No harm," she grumbled, angry despite herself. He was trying to be helpful; she knew that. But she could have handled this herself. She was not one of those silly, helpless girls. "I'm fine."

"Lucky for you," Gregory spat against the man's cheek, then released his hold and pushed the man away.

The tough righted himself and rubbed at his neck where Gregory had pinned him. "So the lassie's yers, yeah? Coulda said so."

Pepper opened her mouth to correct him, but Gregory stopped her. "She's mine. A little wild, but not bad to look at." A cocky grin slid across his face.

He glanced at her and, noting her outrage, shook his head, almost imperceptibly.

"Didn't mean to trespass on another feller's territory," the man added. "We were just teasing the girl. Weren't we, boys? Meant no harm."

At the corner, his friends shrugged and shook their heads, but they had broken from the line and were working their way down the sidewalk.

"I'm quite sure you didn't," Pepper said in a huff. "If you'll excuse me." Again she moved toward the stage door.

Again the ruffian blocked her. "Hold on there. Yer man's gone to all this trouble on yer behalf. Seems the least you could do is show a little gratitude, maybe a kiss for his trouble. Right, boys?"

The mocking tone was back. And his friends were around him, backing him up. The blood drained from Pepper's face. Gregory's, too.

"That would hardly be appropriate, Mr. . . . ," she began.

"Call me Harry," the man drawled. "But you needn't be shy. We're all friends now."

"Friends? Of course." She was stalling.

"That's not necessary," Gregory said, but there was a hesitation. He had lost his advantage.

"Oh, come now. Just a kiss." The man's meaning was clear: She would kiss Gregory or there would be trouble.

Fine, she thought. If a silly kiss would bring this nonsense to a conclusion, so be it. "A kiss then." She approached Gregory, tilted her head and closed her eyes. She waited for the brush of his lips over her own.

And she waited. She squinted open one eye to see Gregory looking not like Gregory the man at all, but rather like Gregory the boy—eyes wide, anxious, uncertain.

"Kiss me already," she muttered.

Still he did not move. So she grabbed his shoulders, popped up on her toes, and kissed him.

She had meant it to be quick. But at the touch of their lips, she lingered. His lips were warm and soft as two pillows, not the ice-cold things she would have imagined them to be. She was aware of nothing beyond this joining of their mouths, until Gregory's arms circled her waist and pulled her closer.

She snapped her head back and covered her mouth with her hand. Her glance dropped to the pavement and she tried to think what to say. Finally, she mastered her faculties and shot a look at the ruffians behind her.

"There. Shall we see you inside, then?"

Harry tipped his cap. "We shall see you inside."

Pepper's arm brushed Gregory's as she pushed by him. She could feel him watching her, his gaze burning through her, but she did not have the courage to meet it. She forced her feet to move, to take her away from him, even as every part of her throbbed with the memory of his touch. At the stage door, she heard Harry chuckle. She drew out the turning of the doorknob.

"You're right about her," she heard him say. "She's a wild one."

There was a scuffling, and Pepper glanced back to see Gregory holding the man's collar in his fist. He pulled him closer. "Never speak of her like that again."

Pepper opened the stage door and hurried in. But she did not go far. She closed her eyes, waited to hear the latch behind her, and leaned against the hard, smooth wood, trying to calm her racing heart.

"Miss MacClair?"

Her eyes shot open. Stanley stood in front of her, squared up for a fight.

From behind him, Beatrice smirked. "I told you, Mr. Stanley. I told you she was up to something."

Ten

"HOW LONG HAVE YOU BEEN SITTING OUT HERE, doll? You must be freezing."

Pepper was trying to stand, but her feet and limbs refused to cooperate. They had gone numb from sitting on the cold concrete steps.

"Edda would have let you in. Did you knock? Isn't she here?" Em skipped up the stairs past Pepper and tried the black handle of her brownstone door herself.

"I didn't knock." Pepper was still unfolding herself and feeling silly now for staying out in the cold and the dark. It had just seemed easier to wait on the stoop. She had not wanted to disturb Em's housekeeper, and she had not minded the cold. She had not even noticed it until she'd tried to rise.

"Let's get you inside. You're going to catch your death out here."

"Edda," Em called once she had entered the foyer.

A round woman with a small chignon at the base of her neck emerged from a swinging door at the end of the hall. She had a towel in one hand and was using it to wipe down a large white platter she held with the other.

"Edda, make us some tea, will you, dear?"

The woman nodded, and turned back to her task.

"Some of those sweet pancakes, too, if it's not too much trouble," Em called after her. Then she waved Pepper in. "Here, give me your coat. I have a wrap in the parlor that should keep you warm."

Maybe it was the chill, or just the way the day had gone, but Pepper was having a difficult time accepting all this fuss and attention after she had treated Em as she had. "Aren't you angry with me?"

Em was still hanging the coat Pepper had handed her on the rack in the hall.

"What for? Last night?" She led the way into the front parlor, where a fire burned low in the grate. "Have a seat, get comfortable."

Pepper followed, but she could not sit. It felt good to stretch her legs now that the blood was flowing through them again. And there was always so much to see in Em's parlor. Equal parts bordello and opium den, or at least that was how it seemed to Pepper. It was Em's sanctuary, where she held her salons, and where she surrounded herself with all the things she loved.

Pepper trailed her finger over the ivories of the upright piano while Em tended the fire.

Em poked at the embers. "Is that why you're here?"

"I was not angry at you, not really. It was just . . ." She gazed up at the oriental parasol suspended from the ceiling and blinked back guilty tears.

"That isn't necessary, doll. You should know that." Em settled into the crimson velour couch that dominated her parlor, removed her boots, set them neatly to the side, and pulled on a pair of soft Chinese-style slippers that had been waiting there.

Maybe it was Em's kindness in overlooking her crude behavior, or maybe it was just everything that had happened that day, but if Pepper opened her mouth, if she tried to say anything, she was going to sob. Instead, she stared at the parlor lamp atop a glass cabinet containing mementos Em had accumulated during her touring years. If Em's stories were true, back then her act took her out West and across the Atlantic, even as far as Shanghai and Cairo and Bangkok. Pepper stared at the brass Buddha, the shard of papyrus engraved with hieroglyphs, the small drawstring pouches made of glossy silk. Each strange wonder held hints of Em's former life.

Pepper's favorite corner, the one she gravitated to now, held a small claw-footed cabinet containing a collection of mementos honoring Annie Hindle, the male impersonator who inspired Em to follow that calling. Em had told Pepper she was a chorus girl when she met Annie. They had shared a bill and became friendly. It was Annie, Em said, who'd trained her in the art of male impersonation, coaching her on how to wrap her chest and her waist to achieve the masculine silhouette, and how to study a man to learn how he moved and carried himself. Together, they had dreamed up Uptown Joe. And it was a lovely tribute, this collection of engravings and notices, framed playbills and advertisements Em had kept all this time. She never spoke of those early years, but there was love in the way the items had been arranged along a glass shelf, every wooden frame carefully cleaned and worn at the side where gentle thumbs had held it for closer inspection.

"I heard you had a falling out with Stanley," Em said from across the room.

How benign it sounded. So insignificant. Yet there was concern in her eyes. She knew the truth.

"He told me he has never known anyone less qualified to perform on a vaudeville stage," Pepper told her. He said other things, too, about her lack of talent, her ignorance, and her general disregard for rules. It had started as a scolding for venturing out in costume, but when she defended herself by explaining what she had been doing with the programs, it had taken a worse turn. He accused her of undermining him, of secrecy and arrogance. He said so many things, and they echoed in her head while she was on the stage and when she had sat in the wings wishing the other players well.

Long after he stormed off, his slights and accusations had remained with her, consuming every thought and growing more vicious with every one of his hard glares and the pitiful glances from the players and stagehands who had overheard. After the last performance, when she could finally escape, she had not sought the solace of her room. There would be none there. She came here, to wait for Em.

Her heart sank all over again. She slumped against the cabinet and gave in to the tears that had been lodged all day in a hard lump in her throat.

"Stop that now," Em urged from the couch. Not callously, but in a way that made it clear she meant it.

Em couldn't abide crying. Usually, she left the room at the first sign of it. Even when it was someone she held dear. She could not force herself to coddle and coo. It wasn't in her nature.

With a soft knock, Edda entered the parlor with a tray. She set it on the table beside Em and glanced at Pepper. "Shall I pour?"

"No, this is fine. And you made the sweet pancakes. You are a treasure, my dear. Thank you." Em lifted the pot's lid to check the tea, and, finding it sufficiently steeped, lifted the pot to pour into the porcelain cups.

By the time Edda left the room, Pepper had swallowed her sobs. "I know it does no good. I just wish . . ." Her breathing fluttered as another sob sought escape. She mastered it, forced it back. "I'm better now."

Em sipped from her cup and leaned down to add a cube of sugar from the silver tray. "The pot's a bit bitter. Sorry about that, doll."

Pepper settled into an overstuffed chair and accepted the cup Em handed her. She welcomed the strong brew and breathed in the earthy aroma, feeling the warmth travel deep within her.

Em tested her cup again, and still finding it lacking, pulled a silver flask from behind a stack of books on the small table beside her. "I need something more fortifying than tea leaves, I'm afraid." When she had poured herself a portion, she offered the vessel to Pepper, who waved it off. "Suit yourself." Em wedged it back into its hiding place behind the books. "Shall we begin at the beginning? Tell me what Stanley said, exactly."

Pepper did not blame Em for requesting the recap. She had exaggerated their squabbles before. But not this time. She recounted it all again.

" 'Never known anyone less qualified to perform on a vaudeville stage,' those were his words? Well, that is a pile of horse manure. You didn't take him seriously, did you?"

Pepper closed her eyes and spoke again only when she was sure her voice would not waver. "Perhaps it's time I did."

Em nearly sputtered her tea.

"Don't put any stock in that venom of his," she told Pepper. "He's had a very difficult time these past few months. You would not believe the pressure he's under just keeping this theater going. I'm not making excuses for him, but—"

"You *are* making excuses for him." All the pain and hurt and confusion she had accumulated all day balled up in her stomach, and she hurled it at Em. "You always do. Why? He's an awful stage manager and he's hateful to everyone, except you. Is that why you defend him?"

"I am not defending him," Em countered. "But you cannot understand how it has been for him."

"Why? Because he's a cripple? Because he hates everybody and everything? Because he's a miserable, mean-spirited human being?" Pepper shot up from her chair and nearly toppled her tea. She caught it before it spilled, and brought it to rest on the table in front of her, but the commotion only frustrated her further. "Why can't you be on my side for once?"

"I am on your side, doll."

Pepper knew Em was right. It was just the pain of the day, the anger that had been simmering within her like one of the stews her mother kept on the stove for hours on end. She paced and tried to calm the roiling within her.

Across the room, the mantel clock chimed midnight. Em stared at it, a long hard stare, then pulled the flask out from its hiding place again. She opened it and lifted the vessel in toast. "Here's to our Bessie. May she be looking down upon us with a smile." She tossed back a long gulp. And then another.

Pepper watched in confusion, and then she understood. April eighteenth. The anniversary of the day Bessie passed.

She had been so consumed by her own worries, she had not spared a single thought for her mother. She stared at the flowering vines of the Persian rug beneath her. The carvings in the mantelpiece. A whole miserable year.

Em replaced the cap on the flask. "Will you take the ferry with me to New Calvary?" The cemetery where Mr. DeGraaf had purchased a plot for Bessie was in the Queens borough. "We can be back before the first show."

Pepper had not returned to the grave site since the day Bessie had been interred. She nearly skipped that day, too. She had still been angry. Bessie might have weathered the illness if they had had money for medicine and a doctor's attention. She might not have died at all if she had not shipped their savings back to Scotland to help a family they would never see again.

"I can't," she said. "I'm to have dinner with Robert and I have nothing suitable to wear. I pray Mrs. Basaraba can help me find something."

"If a man requires a change of wardrobe, you're better off changing the man."

"It's only a gown; it isn't the end of the world."

"The end of the world?" Em stared down into her empty cup. "Don't tell me about the end of the world. I know that tricky bastard all too well. He never makes good on his threat. Just sits on your shoulder, taunting you while life goes on and on . . ."

Em was sinking into one of her dark moods again.

"Don't be sore that I'm not going to the cemetery," Pepper said. "I'll go another time. I will."

"Soon?"

"Soon."

After another pot of tea—and one last pour from the flask into Em's cup—Em said, "Doll, you do know you are always welcome here, don't you? There's plenty of room. You could even help me fix up the place. I've been considering turning that top floor into an apartment or two. You could help me."

Pepper stared into her lap. She knew it was pity, the well-meaning sort, but pity nonetheless. "Thank you. But I can't leave The Chance. It would feel like giving up, like my mother and Stanley were right. The Chance is where I belong."

It was the one thing she had always known. People came and went, but the theater remained constant. Not just the stage, but the long passageways, the dim stairwells, all the dressing rooms and storage rooms, Wardrobe and Prop and the Scarlet Room. Her own room. Like a snail's shell, the theater was what protected her from the rest of the world.

It was her home, even if she could not shake the feeling that it was slipping away from her.

• • •

GREGORY SLID INTO HIS USUAL BOOTH AT ABERNATHY'S, THE farthest in the rear, with his back to the wall. In this rank and dusty room, he found it wise to keep his eye on the door. He'd witnessed enough of its scuffles to know trouble could swagger in anytime. It wasn't as rough as a Bowery bar, but Abernathy's still attracted a good number of roughnecks who worked the construction sites, where steel skeletons climbed high into the sky. The men who wrestled girders a hundred, even two hundred feet above the ground were a scruffy lot. They worked hard and at the end of a long day, they tended to have more than their fair share of steam to vent. Who was to say they didn't deserve a little leeway? Theirs were the hands that were shaping this city.

It was good, honest work in a place where cheats and con men were all too common. More than once, Gregory had considered the work himself. But he always talked himself out of it. Told himself he could not leave The Chance. Could not leave Pepper.

Not then.

He tipped up the frothy beer. He had not known what to expect when he showed up at the Edison Manufacturing Company, sitting in another man's shadow. It had reminded him of his first days at The Chance, watching his uncle. Porter did not chew tobacco like McShane, he did not spit, but he had the same gritty dedication to the job at hand. Of making something.

The time had passed quickly as Gregory sat there behind Porter, watching the man spew directions at the actors and the cameraman for hours. And then later watching while he met with the men who took the spools of film and ran them through a chemical bath. They laid the celluloid strips around wide wooden drums to dry before they were ready to be snipped and spliced into the form that would run through a projecting apparatus in some darkened theater, or those peep-show boxes called kinetoscopes. There was much he could learn in that glass warehouse, and he felt the excitement of being part of something entirely new. The hours had passed quickly. Porter had all but ignored him until, during a break for an actress to change her garments, Gregory had asked if the company ever needed an extra man to run those moving picture cameras.

"The men aren't hard to find, it's the cameras that are rare." Porter had said.

Gregory had asked what a moving picture camera set a man back. He had thought it a reasonable question, but it seemed to take Porter by surprise. The man swiveled around in his chair and laughed. "More than most men make in a year, I can tell you that."

Gregory had sat back in his chair and mumbled,

"Interesting," or something just as vague. They didn't speak again until the sun reached its peak, and he rose at a pause in the filming.

Porter heard the rustle behind him and turned. "Leaving already?"

The excuse of returning to the hardware store had bought Gregory only a few hours, but that was not the explanation he gave Porter. "Theater business," he said and left it at that.

"You're welcome back anytime," Porter said when they shook hands. "If you think you might give processing a try, we have a new facility opening in the Bronx. We might be able to work something out."

Gregory nearly broke into a smile. "I might take you up on that," he said as Porter walked him to the door. He did not mention the plan that had already begun to form in his mind. The one percolating as he sat later that day behind a tankard of beer in a corner of Abernathy's.

"Pour you another, love?"

A dark-haired woman with bloodshot eyes and a red kerchief tied around her hair had planted her hand on the table and was leaning over him, the bulge of her bosom on the same level as his gaze.

"If you'd be so kind, dear." He knew the woman's name was Charlotte, but he never used it. He also knew she had two young boys she told to stay in their rooms upstairs, but they could be found most afternoons in the street outside playing stickball, usually substituting whatever rubbish they found against building stoops and alcoves for the ball. Liquor bottles, broken bowls, wadded-up newspaper pages. He knew Charlotte exiled the boys to the front steps sometimes at night when she joined a fellow for a drink after her shift, which tended to lead to an invitation upstairs. He also knew Charlotte had a husband somewhere, maybe locked up or prospecting out West.

Since Gregory found himself in Abernathy's more than a few times a week, he was sure she had come to know his name, too. But like him, she kept it to herself. It was better that way. She scooped up his mug and a moment later placed it in front of him again with a sway that sent a thick stream of tan foam down one side.

"I'm nearly finished for the night, love. Want company?"

He glanced up. Her lips blazed with fresh rouge, and kohl rimmed her eyes. She was jutting her hip in a way that made her meaning clear. He shook his head. "Not tonight, dear. Work to do."

She smiled a sad smile. "You work too hard, love." She patted his shoulder and wandered back toward the bar.

When he stepped out into the brisk night air, his head was fuzzy and his limbs were warm from drink. He glanced at Pepper's window to be comforted by the amber glow behind the curtain. But tonight the window was dark. Asleep? Unlikely. She did not sleep much these days. The stage, more likely. Dancing in the ghost light to her music box. He would check, just to be sure she was safe. Of course, he knew this was another lie he told himself. He wanted to see her, and to see her dance in those midnight hours was to see her at her best. There was none of that sadness that clung to her like soot these days. None of those rough edges. It was the only time she seemed happy.

Maybe tonight he would tell her exactly why he had interrupted her and Robert DeGraaf. And he would tell her the truth about his mother and his father, so it would not matter what that rat told her, if he told her anything at all. The beer had stirred a reckless courage within him. Perhaps once he told her everything, she would put her arms around him and whisper sweet words. Maybe she would tell him she loved him.

His head was buzzing with these thoughts—these wild, wonderful thoughts—when he unlocked the theater door and entered the dark Scarlet Room. Even without light, he knew where to step so the floor did not groan. He knew how to make his way up the staircase, to the polished walnut doors that opened to the gallery, where he could watch Pepper without fear of being discovered.

At the door, he strained to hear her music. Nothing. Still, almost eagerly, he pulled the brass handle and trained his vision down below, to the stage. There was only the lonely standing lamp, the ghost light.

The theater phantoms whispered in his ear, "She's with Robert DeGraaf."

• • •

EM KNOCKED HARD ON THE DOOR AT THE END OF THE LONG, dingy corridor and covered her nose. The window overlooking Waverly had been dark when she approached, but she had made her way up three flights of stairs to the bachelor rooms anyway. It was late. Very late. But she had wanted to be sure Pepper was asleep—tucked soundly into a spare bedroom at the brownstone—before she had ventured out. At this hour, Stanley would surely be inside.

She knocked again. What *was* that smell? Rat droppings? Dead mice?

"You've got the wrong door," she heard a voice bellow from inside. It was Stanley.

"It's me, Harland. Let me in."

There was a creak of floorboards. A *thump-thump.* A fumbling with locks. Then the door opened a mere few inches.

"What is it?" He squinted, trying to focus in the darkness.

She pushed the door open and strode inside. She did not care if she knocked him over. In fact, she might feel better seeing his lousy carcass sprawled on his sitting room floor. "I want it to stop, Harland. I'm sick of this vendetta you have against Pepper MacClair."

He had already stepped back, though, leaning heavily on a crutch wedged beneath his armpit. He always was good at staying out of her way when she was hot. "Vendetta?" He glanced down the hallway before shutting the door. "Is that what that girl told you?"

He was ready to square off, but now she was distracted. A single candle flickered in the room, on a table pulled up beside the bed against the far wall. But why was the bed in the sitting room, blocking the doorway to the corridor and the other rooms? She whipped around. The small kitchen was still there, shielded by a curtain strung along a length of twine. A plain table and chairs pushed to the window. His leg brace unhinged and resting atop the old traveling trunk he had used when their act jumped cities.

He maneuvered to a chair and sat, his lame leg protruding straight in front of him. "You've been drinking."

Good old Stanley. Master of the obvious. "Of course I have. That's hardly the point. What happened to this place?"

"Didn't need the other rooms. Only this one." He picked up a tin pitcher from the table, poured something into a mug and handed it to her. "Sit down and drink this."

She leaned her nose to it first. Just the metallic scent of cheap tin. She sipped. It was water. But she was too angry to sit. She paced instead.

So he was living in one room now. God knows why. That wasn't the reason she was here. "I want you to back off Pepper. I don't know why you've gotten it into your skull to harass her the way you do, but I want it to stop." She stopped. The room was spinning. She went to the empty chair and sat.

He shook his head and massaged the spot above his knee where the brace usually rubbed. "She's not keeping up. I'm not being any harder on her than I would on any other dancer. It's business."

"Hogwash. We both know it. No one in that joint is exactly at the top of their game. And Pepper shines out there, you know it. She might flub a step or two, but she sparkles."

Stanley made a sound like a growl deep in his throat as he worked the place near his knee. Then he leaned back. "Remember the time we performed at The Trigby in—where was it? Syracuse?—and we followed that fellow who danced like a wet noodle? God, I yelled at that manager. Who puts up dance acts back to back like that? That guy was good. Now *he* sparkled."

Em remembered the act. The man defied gravity with those rubber legs of his. The audience had eaten it up, too. Clapping so loudly it was nearly impossible for the performers to hear their own opening music. "We did all right. He was going for laughs. But we had style."

They did, too. Stanley had been so debonair then, just twenty-five, and she a handful of years younger than that. She had thought herself the luckiest girl in town when he asked her of all the girls in the music hall chorus to team up on an act. They kept working at the music hall until they found an old tuxedo and top hat for him, and a ball gown for her. The Swells, that was what they had called themselves. It was her first taste of a real traveling act.

"Yes, we had style." He pushed himself up and pulled a whiskey bottle and another glass out from behind the cupboards behind the curtain. He returned, set the glass on the table and pulled the cork from the bottle. He filled her glass halfway when she presented it, then his own. "Those were good days, weren't they? A good six months." He was smiling as he sat back in his chair, tipping his tin cup to drink.

Em could not remember the last time she had seen Stanley smile. He looked like his old self again. Not the snarly old coot who constantly harassed his players, and Pepper most of all. He was her old dance partner again, a man who had taught her the joy of the traveling vaudeville life and who was never happier than he was on a stage. The man who had been her best friend for a time.

And who knows how far their act could have gone if things had gone differently. If she had not made them late to that train to Baltimore. If she had not forgotten their tickets and left them on the chair of that Boston hotel, he never would have run back the way he did. Or darted into the street without looking, right into the path of that spooked carriage horse that had appeared out of nowhere.

She had seen the whole thing, but it was so dark and it had happened so fast it was still a blur. The animal had come barreling through the street, but the music from the hall next door masked the driver's shouts of warning and the furious tattoo of the animal's approach. Harland was simply there one moment, and then he wasn't.

When she'd screamed, everyone had looked at her. Only when they turned to see what held her spellbound did anyone seem to notice the man lying in the street. He was lying unconscious, with the tickets in his left hand and his right leg twisted at an unnatural angle.

They never made it to Baltimore.

Em had stayed at his bedside for a week before he told her he was sick of her. That he had family coming and preferred she not be around.

She did not believe him, but Harland could be stubborn, even then. She had packed up her trunk and returned to that old music hall in New York. Got her job back, and it wasn't long afterward that Annie Hindle joined the bill and changed everything.

Em wrapped her fingers around her cup and stared into it.

He must have seen her shiver, for he said, "You're cold, aren't you?" Before she could answer, he maneuvered himself up, grabbed his crutch, and limped to the room's small fireplace.

The room was cold, much colder than it had been outside. Or maybe it was just the liquor playing tricks on her.

He pulled the iron poker that hung on a hook and jostled the ashes, trying to revive a flame.

She sipped from her cup. "Do you ever miss the dancing?" she asked. It was something she had wanted to ask him for a long time.

He stared into the fragile fire. "Not the dancing. I miss you, Emmalyn. What about you? Ever miss those days?"

"Sometimes." They'd had such laughs back then. Dancing and laughing. And he had always treated her square. Not like a girly-girl who needed a man to watch out for her. They were partners. Equal down the line. It was the first time she had ever been treated that way.

The firelight caught his eyes again. He returned the poker to its place and lumbered back to his bedside table, pulled out a drawer, and took out a frame. He moved back to her and set it on the table.

"Remember this?" It was their old publicity shot. Two bright-eyed youngsters dressed up as swells, posing and grinning like mad for the camera.

"Haven't seen this in years." She picked it up, ran her fingers along the frame. "We were young, weren't we?"

"I never should have let you go, Emmalyn. It was the biggest mistake of my life."

She waved him off. "That's the liquor talking. We had a good time for a while, but nothing lasts . . ." The last word caught in her throat. *Forever.* It never came.

Stanley stood at her shoulder. His fingers twitched, and then he set them, reluctantly, on her shoulder.

"I was thinking, now that Bessie is gone, that there might be a chance you and me could try again."

She let go of the photograph and it tumbled back on the table. "Try what?"

"That," he said, pointing to the image lying flat and askew. "Being together again. We were good together. I know you and Bessie had . . ." He looked uncomfortable as he searched for a word. "I know what you two were, but she's gone, and you've had time to grieve—"

She jumped from the chair and away from Stanley's hand. "You and I danced together, Harland. We were friends. We were never—"

"Don't say that, Emmalyn. Don't say you didn't love me. I know you did. We had good times, the two of us."

"We did, but . . ." How could she tell him that even then she had no interest in him. Not that way. She preferred the company of women, even before she understood why. Back then it was easier to avoid those longings by immersing herself in the act, in chasing a dream. "If I ever made you think . . . I never meant . . ."

He sank back into the chair. The effort of staying upright on that crutch was too much. "It's the MacClair girl, isn't it? She reminds you of Bessie. That same stubbornness, those same icy blue eyes." He grabbed his cup and tipped it back. He wiped his lips with the back of his hand. "You'd think different if she weren't around."

"Is that what all this is about?"

His gaze locked on hers. "Would it really be so bad if she moved on?"

All of her sympathy for him, all that old, lingering guilt, vanished on the spot. "Harland Stanley, I swear to God, if you do anything to harm a hair on that girl's head, you will regret it. Don't forget who talked you up to Mr. DeGraaf in the first place."

She stormed out the door before he could say another word. She had nearly reached the stairwell when she heard the shattering of glass, like a picture frame hurled against a wall.

• • •

PEPPER AWAKENED WITH A START IN A ROOM FILLED WITH SOFT morning sunshine. A strange room, a strange bed. But then she remembered. It had been hours past midnight when she had decided to make her way home. Em would not hear of it. She insisted Pepper stay. The guest room's bed was already prepared, and it was only for a few hours after all.

Before retiring, Pepper had opened the window so she would awaken at first light. It was already well past dawn. The sun had crested the roofline, making the windows of the brownstones across the street blaze a raw coppery red. Clopping horses pulled wagons and carriages, and birds squawked their morning complaints from the trees. The whole city was awake, it seemed, and Pepper was late.

She had undressed to her camisole and drawers to sleep, so as quickly as her sleepy fingers could manage, she worked herself back into her corset and black frock. She yanked on her stockings, turned inside out since they had not been washed, and shoved her feet into her boots. She checked her hair in the room's mirror, found a rat's nest, and groaned. Grabbing the curls in her fist, she worked her bowler over the mass. It would hold well enough.

Then she hurried out, quietly so as not to wake Em or disturb Edda, who was chopping and humming in the kitchen, and set off for home.

The blocks passed quickly, but the closer she moved toward the theater, the more unsettled her thoughts became. The thought of seeing Stanley made a knot in her stomach.

"Where have you been?"

The low grumble gave her a shiver that had nothing to do with Stanley. It was Gregory. She had not noticed him sitting on the stage door steps. That feeling of kissing him returned. That perplexing, inscrutable kiss that had taken place only a step or two from this spot. But she had neither the time nor the patience to sort through that tangle just now. "What business is it of yours?" She hurried by.

From around her neck, she pulled out her pair of keys and let herself into the Lair and through her own door. She hung the chain on its hook and crossed the floor to open the curtain, letting light shine in through the lacy sheers, though it did not change the empty feeling in the room, or the squeeze of the walls that seemed to tilt in on her.

This was her home, but it gave her no comfort today. It was Stanley's fault. Just like everything else. He was the reason she was so miserable.

She shimmied out of her day-old dress and pulled another from the shelves. It was nearly as rumpled as the one she was wearing, but at least it was clean, and it was good enough for getting upstairs. Her gaze skimmed her collection of old costumes and cast-offs. No, nothing there was suitable for dinner with

Robert, but Mrs. Basaraba would have something. If she could make a woman like Madame Bizet look good enough for the stage with only an hour's notice, surely she could do something for Pepper.

The more difficult task would be getting through another day with Stanley.

• • •

MATTY WAS BEGINNING TO SUSPECT. GREGORY COULD SEE IT IN the way the boy looked at him when he said an errand would delay him an hour, maybe more. The boy had asked what errand. One sharp look had stopped that line of questioning, but Gregory knew he had to be careful. These absences were beginning to draw attention.

It relieved him when Matty asked bluntly: "You aren't fixing to leave, too, are you?"

No, he told the boy. Just an errand. He had tried to laugh, to change the subject, but only received another suspicious look.

But he could not think of that now. Mrs. Brewster was scrutinizing the talking machine. Did she expect to find a flaw? She wouldn't. He had taken care to ensure that the machine performed as well as a new model. But she was turning it over and over. Only after her meticulous inspection did she go to the cash register and open the drawer. She pulled out two bills and extended them to Gregory, then held them back. "I wonder, Mr. Creighton, if you might be interested in another sort of job. Something more lucrative?"

"Happy to entertain offers."

She placed the bills in his waiting palm and pulled something else from beneath the counter. Something shiny and metal that she pushed across the glass in his direction.

A gleaming pair of brass knuckles, with long spikes extending like canine teeth from between the finger holes.

"We're having a problem with a client's payment."

She told him the job was simple, really. Merely accompany her son on a visit. Junior would do the talking. It was hardly anything, this job she was asking him to do, and it would pay double what she had paid for the talking machine.

"Will I need those?" He gestured at the brass knuckles.

"Unlikely, but one can never be certain of such things."

How primly she had said it, as though she were speaking of the weather or the availability of pears from the grocer.

How still she stood behind the counter. How serene.

"What do you say, Mr. Creighton?"

Eleven

WHEN THE GLEAMING BLACK COACH TURNED FROM Broadway to Eighth shortly after nine o' clock, Pepper was already standing in front of the theater, waiting.

"I didn't expect to find you out here," Robert said when the driver had brought the horses to a stop and he hopped down from the cabin.

"It's such a pleasant night, I couldn't resist the fresh air," she said. The truth was, after spending a good deal of her time between shows tidying up her room, she had decided it was best not to remind him she lived in a basement. And she certainly didn't want him coming up to the dressing room to collect her. She smiled sweetly and loosened the black silk shawl hugging her shoulders so it drooped to better reveal the crimson satin and black lace of the gown Mrs. Basaraba had produced from a corner of her workroom. The garment had required only a few tucks and stitches to bring in the waist, and the alterations were masked quite nicely by the addition of a black sash tied into a bow at the back.

When Robert's gaze lingered on the delicate trim around the neckline, she smiled to herself with pride.

His glance darted away when he saw her watching him. He fussed with the cashmere scarf around his neck and coaxed the ends beneath his overcoat lapel. "I suppose I should have realized you would require something appropriate to wear. I should have arranged for something."

Her glance dropped to her chest. "Is this not appropriate? Is there something out of place?" She glanced down. What flaw had she overlooked?

"The style is fine, I suppose. But the color, don't you find it glum?"

After her mother's funeral service, she had fed to the fire every garment of a cheerful color she had owned. There were no happy pinks or corals, no marigolds or greens. She did not always wear black—though she found it particularly comforting—but she had kept to a more subdued palette since that bleak day. "While I've been mourning my mother, I find the darker shades suit me." She hoped he read no criticism in the comment, but it occurred to her that he might still be unaware of her mother's passing. They had not spoken of it, and she did not want to embarrass him by bringing it to his attention.

That, however, did not seem to be the case.

"Yes, I was sorry when I heard the news from my father, but surely enough time has passed. Let me arrange a fitting for you with Mrs. Cecil. Let's cheer up this wardrobe of yours. What do you say? Will you indulge me?"

"Of course," she said.

The offer should have delighted her. What young woman would not be thrilled at the prospect of a new wardrobe created especially for her by one of the city's most favored dressmakers?

Robert patted her hand and wrapped it around his arm to guide her toward the coach. "It gives me pleasure to see you so happy." Then he whispered in her ear, "And I will confess a secret: I have more surprises in store for you this evening, my dear. Terrific surprises, indeed."

Pepper beamed as he helped her into the cabin. Already she was feeling better. Perhaps he was taking her to a candlelight dinner for two at Delmonico's, or that jewel box of a dining room at Barbetta. Someplace wonderful and opulent. Someplace where they might sip champagne next to New York's elite, an Astor or a Rockefeller or Lillian Russell and Diamond Jim. Perhaps even Ziegfeld and Anna Held, though in truth she hoped she had seen the last of that man.

At last Robert settled them into the coach and it lurched into motion. How different it was this time, Pepper thought, without any of the awkwardness or despair of their ride from the St. Denis Hotel or the frustration of the turn around Washington Square. Everything had changed. Tonight, it seemed anything was possible.

Robert leaned forward and slid open the small window to the driver. "I'd like you to skip over to Fifth Avenue." He closed the window again. "No point getting caught up in the delays around Herald Square."

"But it is so lively at this time." She could envision all the dazzling electrical lights touting the shows at The Savoy and Herald Square Theatre, all the shops and restaurants and hotels. All the music and chatter and laughter.

"I think we can do without that clamor tonight. All that chaos."

She settled back against the cushion. "Yes, of course."

Robert settled back beside her. He placed his hand upon hers, which were clasped in her lap. "Don't be cross. Your face is so pleasing when you smile. Come now. Yes, there it is. That smile I adore."

When he turned those sweet green eyes upon her, it was impossible to deny him anything. They sat together, in a warm, comfortable silence, until he leaned in close and whispered. "We're here."

At that moment the coach came to a stop along a street of stately brownstones and elegant hotels on a small street off Fifth Avenue.

"Here?"

Robert wiggled his eyebrows with impish mischief. "This is my surprise." He scooped up her hand and planted a kiss upon her fingers.

His delight infected her. She scanned the street, trying to surmise what form this surprise might take.

"Isn't it a grand building? I was fortunate that a friend alerted me to a vacancy."

So he had found a place of his own, something away from his father and Gertie Walters. "It's lovely," she said. Four stories of red brick with white shutters over the windows, and a private garden behind a wrought-iron fence.

He opened the carriage door and held out his hand to help her down.

"We're going inside?"

"Does that disappoint you?"

"No, I only thought we were on our way to dinner."

"And so we are," he said.

Perhaps it was the confusion on her face that made him continue. "We can't very well walk into a public dining room together, can we? Imagine how that would look." He chuckled as if the notion were absurd.

But if they were not to dine at Delmonico's or Barbetta or any other dining establishment, then where?

She let go of her vision of the champagne and the happy faces, the smiling and nodding at New York's elite, and put her hand in Robert's.

He led her to the door, where they were greeted by a uniformed doorman.

"Good evening, sir, madam," he said without making eye contact.

Odd. She leaned toward Robert to remark on it, but he stopped her with a finger. "Discretion, my dear. Discretion."

Inside, the modest lobby opened to a sitting area arranged around a fireplace. On the other side of the lobby stood a reception desk, where another uniformed attendant sorted mail into wooden cubbyholes built into the wall behind.

Robert approached the desk. "I'm Mr. DeGraaf. I have secured apartment three-oh-six on my sister's behalf." He glanced at Pepper, implying, to her astonishment, that she was that sister. "I trust there will be no problem?"

The man had not smiled at Robert's approach, and he did not smile now. "None, sir. Miss DeGraaf, kindly let me know if there is anything you require. It is our aim to make our residents as comfortable as possible." He delivered his speech with a persistent frown and in a rote manner that suggested it was not the first time he had uttered those particular words, and likely would not be the last.

Before she could ask Robert about the meaning of this, he was guiding her up the walnut staircase that dominated the back portion of the floor. It was not until they were safely closeted within the apartment that she trusted herself to speak calmly.

"What have you done?" Somehow she managed to hold her tone steady, although her thoughts were as scattered as a spilled bag of beans.

Robert had removed his coat and was draping it on the rack in the vestibule. "I knew you would be pleased."

Was she pleased? No, that was not the feeling at all. Bewildered, appalled, queasy, even. Not pleased. "It is unexpected."

Robert came up behind her.

"And this is for you," he said. He took her left hand by the wrist and in her palm placed a shiny brass key. "This is yours because all of this"—his gaze swept a full circle—"is yours."

Pepper turned to face him. "It appears that someone else already lives here." She did not know why she whispered it, as if they were trespassing on some stranger's solitude.

"It's a fully furnished apartment, and I took the liberty of adding a few extra things myself. Shall I show you around?"

"Yes, I suppose," she said, although it was not what she was thinking. She had imagined there might be an apartment, but not now, not so soon.

Pepper had to admit that it was exciting, though. All this attention, all this fuss for her.

He stepped beside her and scanned the front room. "The parlor is quite well outfitted, as you can see: fireplace, furnishings, and the wallpaper is new, I'm told."

"It's charming." And it was. The green flock quite nearly matched the shade of his eyes, and it was set off nicely by the mahogany moldings and fireplace mantel. There was an unmistakable newness to everything. A freshness. As if everything had only just sprung into being the moment they entered the room. There was no musty smell, no layers of dust. This was nothing at all like the Lair.

Robert took her hand and led her to a door in the corner. "Here you have a small kitchen, with an icebox and stove." He opened a few cupboards, which were full of glasses and plates and cookware. "I believe you'll find everything you'll need here. And you must see this." He took her to the next room. "A tiled washroom with all the amenities."

It was a lovely lavatory, not as large as the one she had in the Lair but entirely clean and new. A shelf held a stack of towels, as well as a small inventory of soaps and lotions and brushes.

Pepper tried to enter for a closer look, but Robert was already pressing her onward.

"I hope you'll find the sleeping chamber to your liking." The room was not large but it was cozy. At the center stood the bed, a massive construction with rich reddish-brown drapes tied to the end posts and covered in deep stacks of crisp, inviting pillows. She moved to the armoire against the wall and opened one drawer after another, finding tidy stacks of white undergarments and other feminine essentials. There were a number of dresses and a shelf of hats, and even a jewelry box filled with baubles and other pretties. On the opposite wall, a vanity table was just as well appointed. "I cannot think of anything else I could need."

He moved closer to her and took both hands in his. "That was my hope. I want you to stay here. Starting tonight. I can't think of you living down in that awful basement."

She wanted to argue, but the way he looked at her now, she could not. She would do anything he asked. It was as though he were seeing far more than her hair and eyes, her lips and lightly rouged and powdered cheeks. It was as though he could see all the nights she had lain awake with thoughts of him and wondered if he ever thought of her, all the little moments when something reminded her of his smile or the touch of his hair. It was as if he could see the culmination of all that, as if he could see her love for him.

In truth, she had never felt so exposed, yet she welcomed it. She submerged herself in it eagerly. They were together, just as they were meant to be.

"I can hardly believe this is real."

He took her words as an invitation to embrace her. His hand came up to her bosom and caressed her, softly at first, but growing more insistent and urgent. His breathing came faster, as did her own. She wanted to give in to him right there. To surrender to these feelings, and to him.

If only she could banish that image of Gregory and the memory of that kiss. Had anyone seen them? What if Robert learned of what happened?

"What is it?" he whispered, looking down at her. Would he see her guilt? She turned away.

"It's just so much." In all her dreaming, she had never imagined it quite like this: the perfect man, the perfect room. She would change absolutely nothing. This foreboding she felt was only fear.

She was safe here. From Stanley. From Beatrice. Even from Gregory and whatever it was she had seen in his eyes out there on the street.

Robert came up behind her and slid his fingers between hers. "I knew you would like it. This is only the beginning, my darling. There are grand things to come."

A knock on the door interrupted them.

Robert's eyes brightened. He pulled away. "I believe I know what that is."

He went to the door.

She lingered in the bedchamber. This lovely room that smelled of fine wood and luxury, of tender care and better days ahead. This room that was now her room, and her new life. At the dresser, she opened a drawer and made a space in front of a stack of scarves and gloves. From her small reticule, she pulled out the long chain with her two dangling keys and placed them gently inside.

She was still gazing at the keys when she heard the men's voices grow quiet and then the front door closed.

"Pepper, come here, please."

Her fingers lingered on the chain.

"Pepper?" His voice was more insistent.

"Yes, I'm coming."

When she returned to the front room, the table had been transformed. Upon a white linen cloth had been set two plates covered by silver domes, and all the amenities: salt and pepper shakers, a vase with a red rose, glasses, and silverware. As unaccustomed as she was to such indulgences, there was something familiar about this table. She lifted the dome over a plate and realized why.

"McManus's finest oysters. I hope you enjoy them. It cost extra for the delivery."

She nodded and forced a smile.

Robert hurried around to pull out her chair. He looked so happy, so eager for her to approve of this gift.

"Just because we cannot dine out together, there's no reason we can't enjoy a nice meal. I'd say we've outsmarted the busybodies, wouldn't you?" He turned to her. "Darling, you haven't said anything. Are you pleased?"

"Of course, I am. Why wouldn't I be?"

Robert looked proudly over his table. "It is wonderful, isn't it? I told you I would spoil you."

It was wonderful. She repeated it to herself again to silence that insistent voice within her. The one demanding how he could spring this upon her. But she was being foolish. One did not seek permission to present a wonderful gift. And that was what this was. A wonderful, extravagant gift.

"Oh, I nearly forgot." He disappeared around the corner to the vestibule and returned with a standing ice bucket. When he set it down beside the table, he lifted the champagne bottle nestled in the ice. "We are celebrating, after all."

He pulled the cork and filled their glasses. And then he toasted her. "To the most beautiful dinner companion in all of New York." They sipped, and he leaned close. "I must admit, I rather enjoy having you all to myself. It's so much nicer this way, don't you agree?"

She smiled and sipped from her glass.

He pulled out her chair and they sat down to the meal. He grabbed up one of his half shells and slurped heartily.

"You aren't eating. Was the surprise too much?"

"I suppose so." Should she tell him the truth? Should she simply smile?

He set down his shell. "Are you disappointed?"

She shifted under his gaze. The truth burned on her cheeks. "I know you went to all sorts of trouble, and it's lovely. It is. It's only that I was looking forward to going out with you, going somewhere special."

He dabbed at his mouth with the white linen napkin. "My dear, I know you are accustomed to doing as you please. But this is not the theater. There are certain rules we must follow."

He had not always been so concerned about rules. "Common rules do not apply to true hearts," that was what he had written in his letter after he had returned to school. After that afternoon on the rooftop. She nearly reminded him of that, but instead she told him she understood. "I wonder, though, will we ever be able to dine together outside this room?"

He mulled the question, much longer than Pepper thought necessary.

"Perhaps we can arrange something."

"Truly?"

"Yes, I think so. Monday evening. I'm obliged to attend to a bit of unpleasant business first. A banquet at Delmonico's, of all things."

He said it as though he would be obliged to sit through one of Professor Hawkinson's lectures or a tooth extraction.

"That hardly sounds unpleasant."

"It will be, I assure you. The banquet is being held by Marcus Klaw and Abe Erlanger. A contrived occasion so they can crow about a new partnership they've forged with the Shubert brothers."

"I thought the two sides were mortal enemies."

Robert chuckled. "They are, or they were. If they have something big enough to bury this feud of theirs, it cannot bode well for the rest of us independents."

The feud was only a couple of years old, but it was vicious. According to rumor, it began when the middle Shubert brother died in a train wreck and Erlanger used the occasion to back out of a deal with the family, saying he could not do business with a dead man. It was a cruel accusation, but then Erlanger had a reputation for cruelty.

"Isn't it better to avoid those men? That's what your father has always done."

"And look how it has isolated him," Robert said. "Every manager in New York has been invited to this banquet, from the remaining independents like us to the biggest circuits. I hear that even Keith, Albee, and Proctor intend to be there."

The powerful Keith-Albee vaudeville circuit had operated dozens of theaters throughout the eastern states for years but had entered New York only the year before, when they allied themselves—and more importantly, their venues—with the city's most powerful vaudeville theater owner: F. F. Proctor. That uneasy alliance had formed shortly before Mr. DeGraaf fell ill, and there were some who considered that something less than a coincidence.

"My father has hidden his head in the sand all these years, and I'm not going to make that mistake. Keep your friends close and your rivals closer. You cannot simply wish them away."

He spoke with such conviction. It heartened her.

"I intend to put in an appearance," he continued, "and then we'll have the rest of the evening to ourselves."

She glanced down so he did not see the burn of her cheeks. "Thank you, Robert."

Robert finished his meal and if he noticed her uneaten oysters, he did not remark upon them. Lucky for her, there was also a fresh loaf of bread and butter, along with a tureen of French onion soup.

All day she had told herself she could not ask for Robert's help with Stanley, but now that they were sitting here, so cozy and comfortable, and he seemed so satisfied with the apartment and the meal, perhaps it would do no harm to broach the subject.

She dabbed at her lips with her napkin and settled it demurely in her lap. "May I ask you something?"

He refilled his champagne glass and hers. "Yes, of course, darling."

"Have you ever considered whether the theater's troubles might stem from flawed management? Perhaps a new stage manager would inject some new thinking, new enthusiasm into the show."

He leaned back and cocked his head. "A new stage manager?"

She forced herself to meet his gaze and not shrink from the suggestion, bold as it was.

Robert nearly chuckled. "I could never replace Stanley, my dear. He has been with The Chance from the beginning. My father would never allow it."

"Of course he would, if you explained it. If you told him Stanley is ruining his show, because that is what he's doing. I'm sure you can see it." She stopped herself. Her words were coming fast; she was losing her composure.

"No, my dear. I appreciate that you are trying to help, but Stanley is not going anywhere, I'm afraid. Frankly, I don't know what I would do without him. I certainly don't want to deal with the booking agents and all those dreadful performers myself. I have enough to do just trying to get the accounting in order." He pushed away from the table and pulled his watch from his vest pocket. "Which reminds me, I have an early meeting at the bank."

"But it's still so early." He couldn't leave, not yet. Not before she had convinced him.

"It is hardly early. It's nearly midnight. We are going to have to do something about these odd hours of yours."

He went to the rack to retrieve his coat. "McManus said he will send someone in the morning to collect the dishes. And I'll see about getting a woman to come in and help you. There's that extra room, and you need someone, I think."

"Yes, that would be nice," she said, joining him in the vestibule. He was fastening the buttons of his coat. She pulled her own from its peg.

"Darling, what are you doing?"

She froze. All these new rules. Which had she broken now? "Should I have let you put it on? I thought you were in a hurry."

"No, my dear. What I mean is, you needn't go anywhere. You're staying here."

• • •

BY MORNING, PEPPER HAD MADE PEACE WITH HER NEW HOME. IT had not come easily. She had tried to rest within the covers of that extravagant monument of a bed, but the strangeness unsettled her. It was soft and clean and new, but she missed the comfort of the Lair, the musty smells and the squeaks, the particular shadows and the way the light seeped around the edges of the drapes.

Her new rooms had felt so empty after Robert left, and when he said he could not dine with her that night, she had sulked. Of course she did not expect to join him at his father's table, but what was she to do without him in this strange, new place? Not even the dollar bills he pressed into her palm to cover the expense of whatever meal she cared to buy gave her solace.

He had left her alone with her thoughts and the vexing matter of Harland Stanley. Robert would do nothing, it seemed, to hold the man accountable for his failures. So where did that leave her? Safe from being sacked, but still under Stanley's thumb.

It was the thought of Stanley that kept her staring at the canopy of her bed and then forced her up to pace the floor. She could not seek the comfort of the stage, so she was forced to wander the small apartment. She opened every cabinet door, looked in every crevice and corner.

A dozen times she laid herself down again, trying to force her slumber. She tried to think of Robert and their future, but those thoughts always led her back to the same place. What was she going to do about Stanley?

She struggled with the question in the darkness, but when the sun came up and she set about the task of getting ready for the day, her thinking on the matter improved.

She felt better after the bath in her gleaming new tub with the fresh bar of soap that smelled of lemons and sunshine. She was pleased, too, to find so many appealing dresses—she counted a half dozen. It hardly mattered that the colors were softer and lighter than she would have preferred; each was a lovely and stylish affair. She selected a lavender-gray wool skirt with a pigeon-breasted blouse in the same shade.

She pulled on a new pair of stockings, so delicate and soft they had to be silk, and her old pair of boots, then braided her hair. She nearly left with it dangling down her back, but caught herself at the door.

This was no longer the Lair. She had to present herself appropriately. Here she was not even Pepper MacClair, at least not beyond this threshold. She was the virtuous Miss DeGraaf. The unattached sister to Robert DeGraaf. She must not forget that, whether she had passed a sleepless night or not. She had to behave accordingly.

Quickly, she tucked the braid up with pins. But not grudgingly, as she might have done. Because she was a lady now. Not a theater urchin. Not just a seamstress or a chorus girl. A lady.

After all her restless pacing and wandering, she realized that was the true gift Robert had given her. Let Stanley say what he would. Let him rail and jeer. He had no hold on her if she did not fear him, and she no longer had to fear him. She looked around at these fine new furnishings, the clean walls and bright windows. It was a fine apartment, and as Robert had said, it was her home now. And Stanley could never take it away.

When he gave her the usual cool treatment after the first show, she was ready for it. He had hardly had a chance to sneer and tell her she had fumbled the crossover step when she faced him squarely and requested a private word.

The turnabout had its desired effect. He huffed and gave excuses. He could not up and leave in the middle of a show. After all this time, didn't she know better? And on and on.

"At the intermission, then," she said. "If you can make the time." She turned and walked to the stairs without looking back.

By the silence of the stagehands and the players standing around, she knew she had made an impression.

When she reached the dressing room, a thrilling new feeling coursed through her. And it was still coursing through her an hour later when she made her way to Stanley's office.

He was already behind his desk when she approached.

"If you have something to say, Miss MacClair, come in and close the door."

She did as he said, then clasped her hands behind her back, straightened and expressed it as plainly as she could: "I believe you treat me unfairly, Mr. Stanley."

"Is that right?" The contempt was plain upon his face.

"You single me out for minor offenses when greater ones committed by others are ignored." She stopped. She struggled to remain calm. "I demand that you stop."

Oh, the look he gave her. Like a boot heel hovering above a beetle.

"Let me be sure I understand you, Miss MacClair. You propose to tell me how I should manage the stage I have been managing for the past sixteen years?"

She could feel her confidence crumbling, but she would not be intimidated, not anymore. "I only ask that you show me the same courtesy and respect you show other players. It's only fair."

"Fair?"

"Yes, sir."

He paused and pushed about a pile of black-and-white publicity shots scattered upon his desk. A dancer, a strongman, an actress. He rubbed at his jaw. "How many years have you managed a stage, Miss MacClair?"

"That is hardly the point."

"The correct answer would be none. Isn't that right, Miss MacClair? You have never managed a stage. Yet you seem to believe yourself qualified to instruct me?"

"I was not instructing, merely suggesting—"

"Yes, suggesting. You are always suggesting, aren't you? A know-it-all chatterbox who can never hold her tongue. No better than your mother that way. Well, I won't have it. Not anymore."

"What are you saying?"

"I am saying, Miss MacClair, that your services at The Chance Theatre are no longer required."

* * *

JUNIOR BREWSTER WAS STANDING OUTSIDE WANAMAKER'S south entrance just as his mother said he would be. An olive vest over his white shirt, his tie hanging loosely around his neck and his bowler tipped down in the front. The Friday sun was near its highest point when Gregory approached. "I'm Creighton. You waiting for me?"

The man took a bite of his red apple, tossed it into the street, and extended that sticky hand to Gregory in greeting. "Good to meet you, Mr. Creighton. Ma was right. You'll do fine. Ready?"

Except for the pair of brass knuckles in his pocket, Gregory was not sure what he was ready for, but he nodded and allowed Junior to lead the way.

The man was a brawler, he could see that. Older than Gregory and built like a brick wall, with a scar that ran down his right cheek like a knife fight souvenir. What, Gregory wondered, had he gotten himself into?

Once again, Gregory cursed Robert. None of this would have been necessary if the rat had not discovered those invoices from George. It would not matter that the discrepancies came from Gregory paying for supplies out of his own pocket. The numbers did not add up; that was the only excuse that rat needed to dismiss him, if he even needed an excuse at all.

Gregory was trying not to think about any of that when he and Junior boarded a streetcar headed uptown. Junior paid both fees without a word. Since the car was empty except for a businessman and a lady with her maid, the two men slid into separate seats at the front.

Gregory settled back and watched the buildings pass. The photography studios and auctioneers, the music publishers and dry goods stores. Their names all painted across buildings four, five, six stories over Broadway. And then Union Square, a small oasis of leafy trees, green lawn, and paved walkways nestled in the middle of it all.

At the square's north end, Junior rose, so Gregory did, too. They hopped off and headed west on Seventeenth. They had walked hardly a block when Junior stopped and turned to Gregory.

"I'll do the talking, yeah?"

So they were close. Gregory glanced around. A piano purveyor and carpentry shop on one side of the street. An apothecary and a flophouse on the other. Junior led him past these to a storefront that did not yet have a sign, but through the front window Gregory could see it was filled with kinetoscope machines in nearly identical arrangement to the one near The Chance. The floor was strewn with wood planks, paint pails, and tools that seemed to have been abandoned midtask.

Junior approached the door, turned the knob, and, finding it unlocked, poked his head inside. "Anyone here?"

When no one answered, he ventured in. Gregory followed.

"Hello," he called again, more loudly.

An answer came from a back room, and in a moment a curly-headed man with long dark sideburns appeared in a rear doorway.

"You must be the fellows from Edison. I say, you are quick. I only ordered the views this morning."

"We're not from Edison," Junior said. "We're here to see Joe Harvey."

The man's good-natured grin slipped away. "He isn't here just now. Perhaps I may be of assistance. I'm his brother, Ned. We're partners here."

Junior strolled around the floor, peered into a kinetoscope's viewer.

"Nothing to see yet, I'm afraid," Ned said. "That's why I thought you might be from Edison."

"Nice place you have here." Junior gazed around at the fresh wallpaper. The place still smelled of glue. "What is it now, your third parlor or the fourth?"

"This will be our fourth Automatic Vaudeville location."

Gregory made the connection. This fellow and his brother must own the parlor near The Chance.

"Where might we find your brother, Ned Harvey?"

"I wish I could help you, but I haven't the slightest idea."

Junior strolled across the floor toward the anxious proprietor, his stride quick and deliberate.

"That's a shame, Ned Harvey, because your brother owes my family a good deal of money. Left us with a big clumsy camera as collateral and seems to have skipped out."

"A moving picture camera? He gave it to you?" He covered his face with his hands. "He pawned it?"

"Seems he did," Junior said, gripping Ned's shoulder and startling the man. "So I'm going to ask nicely one more time, Ned Harvey. Where can I find your brother?"

"I really don't know." The words came out in a shaky, fearful whisper. "He told me he was taking the camera to Niagara Falls to make views for the parlors. Exclusives, he said. I should have known better."

"Sorry to hear that." Junior turned to Gregory. "Close that door."

When it was done, Junior glanced at the window. Anyone walking by would have full view of what transpired in this room. Junior seemed to note that fact as well and, with his hand firmly on the man's shoulder, turned and walked him toward the door to the back room. "I'm done being nice, Ned Harvey."

Harvey was standing in front of Junior so he did not see the blade emerge from Junior's front pocket. But Gregory did. He had a terrible feeling this would not end well.

When Gregory reached the rear room—no more than a small office with two desks and a back door—Junior already had the man on his knees. His head was in his hands and he was whimpering, "I don't know, I don't know where he is."

"Then I s'pose it would be the good, brotherly thing to do to settle his debts. Don't you think, friend?"

It took Gregory a moment to understand that Junior was speaking to him. "Yeah, the debt should be paid."

Ned sobbed. "He took everything. Joe took it all. Cleaned out the money drawers at every shop, the bank accounts, everything." He looked up, searching for mercy from Junior. "The machines aren't even paid for."

The more Ned begged, the more disgusted Junior seemed to become. He stepped behind the man, grabbed a fistful of curly hair and yanked back his head. He placed the blade against the man's throat.

Gregory stared dumbfounded. How far did Junior intend to go?

"You see, I think yer holding out on us. I think you do know where we can find that brother of yers. Do you s'pose you might tell me if I took one of those lily-white fingers?"

"Please, don't do this. You can have whatever you want. I beg you, please don't do this."

"You hear that, friend? Ned here says we can have whatever we want. I think I want that finger. Or maybe this ear." He moved the blade up beneath the lobe. Ned screamed and grabbed at his ear. Blood dripped over the cuff and down to the elbow of his white sleeve.

Junior's barrel chest rumbled with an awful laugh.

Gregory's stomach dropped. He had promised to keep quiet, but he could not remain quiet through this. He stepped forward. "If you don't mind me saying, I think you'll like my idea better."

Junior and Ned both looked up in surprise.

"Set the knife down for a moment and hear me out."

Twelve

BY THE TIME PEPPER ARRIVED AT ANNABELLE'S, THE dining room had filled with the usual Friday night crowd and McManus was jumping from one table to the next, chatting with patrons. When he spotted her at the door, he threw his arms in the air in a grand greeting.

"Madam Charmaigne—or should I say Monsieur? I never know—she says you are leaving us? But I say no, this cannot be true!"

His fervid attentions made Pepper the object of curiosity throughout the dining room. The gawkers watched and whispered, "Is she somebody?"—which made even the other theater folks take note.

Pepper smiled to hide her discomfort.

"Have you seen Em? She told me to meet her here after the show, but I don't see her. I don't see anybody from The Chance."

He leaned forward with a conspiratorial grin. "The party is in the back, mademoiselle. The room is reserved special for you tonight."

Incredulous, she pointed at the frosted door to be sure she understood.

He nodded, with a smile that stretched his lips all the way to his fuzzy black sideburns. "They are waiting for you." He nudged her toward the door.

What had Em done?

When Pepper walked out of Stanley's office after their conversation, she had gone directly to Em's dressing room.

Her friend turned from the lighted mirror. She could see it was trouble. "What happened? Why aren't you in the wings?"

Pepper was still collecting her scattered thoughts. She tried to sit in the ladder-back chair that Em kept along the back wall, but each time she lowered herself to it, she rose again. She couldn't be still, she had to move. "He cut me," she said at last.

"No, that's impossible. It must be a mistake."

Pepper tried to explain as calmly as she could. She told Em about the new apartment, and about everything Robert had done. About the cabinets filled with dishes and the wardrobe filled with clothes. "He's arranged a fitting with Mrs. Cecil in the morning."

"But what does that have to do with the show? What does that have to do with Stanley?"

"It's all for the best, don't you see? I've had it all wrong. I thought I belonged at The Chance, but I don't, not anymore. My place is with Robert."

A knock rattled the door. "Quarter to curtain."

Em ignored it. "Stanley is behind this, isn't he? He's convinced you of this. Doll, don't be hasty. Don't do something you will regret."

But Em was wrong. How could she regret this? All the fear she had been carrying melted away. For the first time in longer than she could remember, she could breathe. She nearly dropped to her knees. "I am so tired of being careful. I'm tired of being afraid. I don't know why I didn't see it before. I don't need The Chance. Robert will take care of me. It's the only way we will be happy."

"But your act? What will happen to it?"

"The Dolls existed before me, and I'm sure they will go on without me." She wondered when Stanley would break the news to Beatrice and Trixie. She could not imagine there would be any tears.

Em leaned back against her vanity table and crossed her arms, her disappointment thicker than the M. Stein rouge upon her face. "So you're really leaving?"

"I am."

"Will I still see you at Annabelle's after the show?"

She had not thought that far ahead. She had not had time to think of much at all. Robert had said he would be with his father, so there was really no reason she couldn't. "Of course. The usual time?"

"Make it eleven. I'll want to freshen up a bit."

So they parted and Pepper made her way to the dressing room, thankful her partners were not within. She changed back into her street dress, hung her costume from the peg, and left behind everything that was not her own.

Quietly and quickly, she made her way through the backstage. No one glanced her way; no one yet knew. Without a word, she slipped out and down to the Lair. She intended to spend the afternoon packing what she needed from her rooms, but when she entered and looked around at that old familiar space, she realized there was nothing she wished to take.

So she had made her way to the place all the ladies went: Wanamaker's department store. She entered its cavernous halls and lingered among the glass cases of trinkets and jewelry, the shelves filled with teapots and serving sets, the rooms filled with parlor sets and lamps of every size, shape, and description. She even visited the fabric displays and marveled at the expensive silks, velvets, and laces.

She used the bills Robert had given her to buy a roast beef sandwich at the lunch counter, and stuffed the rest back in her reticule. When she was finished, she walked the neighborhood and found herself standing in the Automatic Vaudeville parlor, of all places. She broke a dollar with the attendant, plunked her nickel down the metal chute, and gazed into a wooden box at the flickering images of a woman with a shroud of long curls and a gauzy dress waving her skirt like wide, billowing wings in a lovely butterfly dance.

There was something captivating to these moving pictures, but they left her with the feeling of an unfinished experience. She moved on to different views: General Lee's procession in Havana, a drawing that seemed to come alive, and a trick film of a man moving backward through his day called "Catching an Early Train."

Each had its charm, but without sound, without the experience of seeing live performers, the pictures left her amused yet unsatisfied. Still she plugged her nickels, watching the images again and again, until it was finally time to make her way down to Annabelle's.

She had expected Em would try again to dissuade her from leaving. She had not expected a party.

Pepper thanked Mr. McManus, and despite herself, she felt some of his ebullience rubbing off. When she reached the door, she paused and peered in. Jimmy had pulled up a seat at a table with the diminutive thespians. Frankie and Sneed were there. Marvani and Mr. Hawkinson. Even Beatrice and Trixie. But it wasn't just players. There were backstagers, too. Mrs. Basaraba was there. Old Jake and Laszlo and Matty. They were all laughing and talking over flutes filled with bubbly champagne.

A hand took her shoulder. It was Em. "Are you going in?"

"What did you tell them?"

"The truth. That you are too good for that small-time joint. That you finally wised up to that fact and were moving up in the world."

"That makes it sound as if I'm headed to a bigger theater."

"Does it?" Em feigned innocence.

"Did they believe you?"

"Of course they did. We've all known it was just a matter of time. They think it's the Hippodrome. Someone mentioned Ziegfeld's show. I left it vague, and I recommend you do the same."

"Stanley will tell them he fired me. I can't believe he hasn't done so already."

"Oh, he did. For insubordination. Said it a dozen times at least. But no one believes him. Everything sounds like sour grapes coming from him. I told them he's just trying to save face. That they believe."

"Thank you." Pepper's words hardly seemed sufficient to express her gratitude, but there was no time for more because Em had taken her by the arm and together they entered the back room. Every head turned. A hearty round of congratulations and "Well dones" filled the smoky air.

It was something, seeing them all here like this. All smiling and congratulating her. Pepper went to Mrs. Basaraba first. She leaned down and hugged the small woman.

"Oh, bubbeleh," the woman cried. "I knew you would go one day. Your mother, God rest her soul, would be so proud."

She made her way around the room that way, accepting congratulations she did not deserve but could not refuse. When she reached the table where Beatrice and Trixie sat, some distance from the others, she braced. She could see fear on Trixie's face. That told her all she needed to know about how Beatrice had taken the news.

Pepper put her hand on Trixie's shoulder. "I'm so happy you came."

"This works out best for us, really," Beatrice snapped. "You aren't the only one headed for greener pastures, you know."

"I'm sure you're right," she said, though that was not at all what she was thinking. "Will you excuse me?" She hurried to catch up to Matty, who had just passed on his way across the room to join the other stagehands. "Is Mr. Creighton expected?"

"Haven't seen him today, Miss MacClair." She could see he was troubled.

"That's certainly not like him. He's probably consumed with one of those little projects of his." She smiled to mask her disappointment. But what did she expect? Why would he want to see her after the way she had treated him? Her last words had been so careless and rude.

"You're probably right, miss. I'm sure you're right."

"Well, when you see him, please let him know I wanted to say good-bye." The word nearly stalled on her lips. How could she say good-bye to Gregory? Seeing more faces appear at the door gave her an excuse to move on, so the boy did not see the strain of her smile. She did her best to focus on the Helzigs and Alfred and Edwards, the ushers and Mr. Christopher. Everyone who had come out to see her off.

At some point Em slipped a fluted goblet into her hands, and the champagne's magic was keeping the conversation flowing. Soon, Pepper was laughing along with the rest. When she drained her glass, she went alone to the table where more bottles sat nestled in a tub of ice and poured herself more. When she turned, the whole room stood before her. In her tired and tipsy state, she realized it was perhaps the first time she had ever seen the players and the workers all gathered together voluntarily. Not by call board decree or any other forced measure. And they were happy, like a large, wonderful family.

"Not having second thoughts, are you?" Em had broken away from her conversation with Sneed.

"Not at all," she said, then repeated it, just to be sure. "Would you help me quiet them down? I'd like to say a few words."

"Splendid idea." Em raised a butter knife from the table and tapped the side of her glass. "Everyone! Your attention, please."

The chatter and laughter diminished to murmurs and then to silence as the faces turned in Pepper's direction. Perhaps it was the champagne, but there were no butterflies or any of the nerves that struck her onstage. So much had happened in a day. More than she could have thought possible.

"I just wanted to thank you for being here tonight," she said. "As many of you know, The Chance has been my home for longer than I can remember. It was a tremendous gift when Mrs. DeGraaf offered my mother a job and a few rooms to call our own, but the true gift has been being part of The Chance all these years. We've had some difficult times lately, but I know there is a brighter future ahead. With Robert DeGraaf to lead you, I know *Vaudeville Stars, Marvels and Delights* will be back on top very soon. My only regret is that I won't be here to share that with you."

Em had heard enough. She stepped forward, waving her hands and shaking her head in her typically brash fashion. "Oh no, you'll be off strutting with the high hats, and I for one say it's about time you were. You're one in a million, doll; The Chance has monopolized you for far too long." She paused, and the wide smile faded. She looked directly into Pepper's eyes and said, "We were lucky to have you while we did. So don't go and forget us, you hear me?"

Em must have seen the tears welling in Pepper's eyes, for she didn't wait for a response. She grabbed a champagne bottle in each hand and started making rounds. "Now let's celebrate. Everybody, drink up!"

Pepper accepted the round of applause but quietly declined a refill. She gravitated to the back of the room and sipped what was left in her glass as she watched the party. The joy of her friends touched her and made her feel better than she could have imagined.

She drifted through the room and watched these people she had worked with and lived with, the people she had fought with and talked with and laughed with. It didn't matter if they were stars, marvels and delights, or fools, misfits and deviants. They were good people, her people.

It warmed her, this overflow of well-wishes. Yet for all these happy faces, she could not help missing Gregory. She could not leave without seeing him one more time.

If only she had not said those hasty, angry words on the street. But like everything with Gregory, she could never say what she meant to say. She could never tell him that his kiss had frightened her. That it had excited her and turned her thoughts upside down. She could say so many things to him, but she could never say that, just as she could never tell him how sorry she was about that September afternoon on the roof, when she had proved herself to be less than he had believed her to be. That she had been a stupid girl with love in her eyes instead of sense in her brain. She could not tell him how much she regretted what she had done that day.

She had always meant to tell him, but the time just never seemed right. There always seemed a reason to put it off. But maybe now that she could tell him she had made an honest girl of herself, he would finally forgive her.

It was worth a chance.

She set her glass on the table and waited for Em to reach a pause in her debate with Sneed and the professor over the optimal amount of water to add to scotch. A moment passed, and another. Everyone was busy. She didn't want to interrupt to say good-bye. But if she was going to do this, she had to do it now, while she still had the courage. And while the other Lair boys were occupied here in this room.

Without a word, she slipped out of Annabelle's and made her way back to the theater's basement and to Gregory's door. She stood there for a moment, listening for any sign that he was holed up inside with his machines, lost in his world of gears and cranks and coils. There was only silence within.

She knocked.

Silence.

"Gregory, it's me," she whispered and knocked again.

Silence still.

She tried the knob. It opened. Horrified, she closed it again. "I'm so sorry, I didn't—" but she was apologizing to nothing. She peeked inside again and gazed at the emptiness. The stripped bed, the dresser with the empty drawers hanging open, the shelves bare of anything that might have belonged to him. He was gone.

She closed the door and stood behind it, too stunned to move. It didn't matter, did it? They had not been friends for ages anyway, not really. Though it had always seemed there would be time to patch their friendship. But that time had run out.

The music box. It was the only thing he had ever given her. A moment later she was in the darkened wings, only the ghost light and the distant sound of the street penetrating the walls around her. She pulled the box from its resting place, and the theater ghosts called to her once again. But she did not want to dance. Not now, maybe never again. She tucked the box up beneath her arm and made her way back out into the night.

• • •

A BANGING STARTLED PEPPER AWAKE. IT TOOK A MOMENT TO orient herself. To remember why she was in a strange chair and not her bed, or why she was still wearing her clothes.

It had been nearly two in the morning when Pepper finally arrived home in the cab and retired to her room. She was still missing Gregory as she made a place for her music box on a table partially hidden by a lush fern and then settled into the chair. Her feet ached from all the day's walking. She had lifted them onto a small stool and must have fallen asleep.

The banging returned, an insistent rapping that bounced off the walls. Pepper ran her fingers over her face, trying to wipe away the remnants of sleep. She was at the door when a new round of banging began.

"Who's there?" she whispered through the wood, leaning her cheek against the cold, hard surface.

"It's me, doll," Em said, more spritely than she had a right to be so early in the day. Pepper pulled back the metal bolt. When she pulled open the door, Em presented herself in a chocolate brown bowler with matching tweed coat and trousers. Two white collar points topped a black bow tie. She was dressed to the nines, but that wasn't what surprised Pepper.

"How did you find me?"

Em winked. "I have my ways. By the looks of things, it's a good thing I do, too. I wanted to make sure you weren't over-sleeping after last night. You did mention a fitting with Mrs. Cecil, or don't you remember?"

She pushed in with her typical zeal, gazed around, and whistled low. "Well, this is a fine gilded cage he's stuck you in."

"It's hardly a cage," Pepper muttered, and closed the door.

Em was still looking around as she plopped down on the couch. "Were you asleep, or is that arrangement of your hair a new style choice? Interesting, but you may want to reconsider. Say, if you have a pot of tea in the works, yes, I'd be delighted to join you."

"I suppose you'd like tea, then?" Pepper said, unnecessarily. She moved toward the kitchen.

Em shot up again. "You get dressed, doll. I'll get the tea and fill you in on what you missed last night after you gave us the slip."

"It wasn't the slip," she hollered from the passageway. "It was late."

"Call it what you like, it was probably for the best. That pal of yours, Beatrice what's-her-name, made a big to-do with her own little announcement."

Pepper hurried back down the hall and craned around the doorway. "What announcement?"

"Go, get yourself together. You can't show up at Mrs. Cecil's looking like that. And, for God's sake, do something with your hair."

"Fine." Pepper drifted down the hall once again, patting her unruly mane. "What did she say?"

"She quit."

Pepper ran back down the hall. "She quit?"

Em was filling the kettle. She scowled at Pepper when she saw her back in the doorway. "Yes, she quit. Her new beau, it seems, is opening a burlesque hall on Park Row. He's giving her a song and dance act, with a chorus of girls to back her up. She's taking Trixie to be the lead girl."

Of course she would. She certainly wouldn't want anyone with an eye on the top spot. "But Beatrice doesn't sing," she hollered from deep in the passage.

"That doesn't matter in burly-q. The customers are drunk and loud, and she'll have a chorus backing her up."

She wanted details, but the chiming clock told her she didn't have the time. It was already quarter past eight. How had she slept so late?

She went to the armoire and pulled out a rust taffeta ensemble that looked promising. When she had shimmied into it, she pinned her mass of curls into submission and topped them with a brown velvet hat. She checked her reflection. It wasn't perfect, but if she'd already had suitable town dresses and gowns, there would be no need of the fitting, would there?

"That is much better," Em said as she emerged into the parlor with a tray.

Pepper glanced at the clock again. She had only minutes to spare before her appointment and several blocks yet to walk. "Should we leave the tea for later?"

Em settled onto the couch. "Of course not. There's always time for tea."

Pepper released the breath she had not realized she was holding, and felt a bit of tension leave with it. She dropped into the chair to enjoy her cup. "Yes, Mrs. Cecil be damned."

It was nearly half an hour later when Pepper, with Em by her side, approached the broad glass window on which *Mrs. Cecil, Professional Dressmaker, Est. 1897* was emblazoned in gold-and-white lettering. She tried the door and found it locked. She tapped the wood with her knuckle.

A young, raven-haired girl opened it, standing before them in a plain wool dress and with an exceptionally large white bow on her head. "Mother has been expecting you. I'll show you to the salon." Her voice was hardly more than a whisper.

They followed the girl through a rear doorway that opened to a larger room. There, a small, roundish woman with a knot of black hair on the top of her head was at a rack of gowns, flipping through the bright silks and taffetas, lush velvets and lace.

The girl stopped Pepper and Em inside the doorway, then continued alone to the woman, who gave no indication she had heard anyone enter. Pepper gazed around at the pale-pink-and-ivory sanctuary of tufted velvet benches and gilded mirrors, generously draped changing rooms, and a white lacquered tree arrayed with a profusion of hats festooned with ribbons, flowers, and feathers. It was the most feminine space she had ever seen.

After a long moment, the woman turned from the flocked skirt she had been examining and leveled her gaze on Pepper. She was a woman of indeterminate years, for the golden rimmed spectacles upon her nose obscured the typical signs of age that rest in the corners of one's eyes. Her jet hair was so fine and smooth that even the light from the sheer-covered window reflected off its glassy surface and gave it a glow. Yet it was her dress, as one might expect, that was most remarkable. It was a masterpiece of violet silk in the modern pigeon-breasted style, tailored to hug her generous form and sumptuously trimmed in lace without appearing gaudy or at all inappropriate for its function.

Pepper had not noticed the length of measuring tape around the woman's neck until Mrs. Cecil yanked it off, snapped her fingers at Pepper, and pointed to a raised platform in the center of the room. "Stand there," she commanded with the severity of a schoolmarm.

Pepper glanced at Em, and Mrs. Cecil noted her hesitation. The crevice between her brows deepened. "You arrive late and still make me wait?"

"No, of course not," Pepper said. "We didn't mean—"

The woman's hand fluttered. "No excuses."

"Yes, ma'am," Pepper whispered, afraid even that might earn her a rap on the wrist. But Mrs. Cecil was no longer paying attention to that end of her. Instead, she was stretching the tape in lengths from her waist to the floor, then around Pepper's waist, and calling out numbers to the girl, who sat at a white writing desk with a pencil, committing the numbers to paper.

As the daughter of a seamstress, Pepper knew this ritual well, yet from what Pepper could gather, the woman was doing it all wrong. "Would you prefer I undress?"

Mrs. Cecil ignored her and went about her ministrations.

Em seemed amused by the woman's strange methods. Several minutes passed this way, with Pepper standing atop the platform and Mrs. Cecil buzzing around with the measuring tape. Finally, the woman stood. "Step down."

"Thank you," Pepper said, patting her skirts and her sleeves, making sure everything was still in its proper place.

Mrs. Cecil was studying the measurements she had taken from the girl. Without looking up, she said, "Anne, you may show the"—she looked at Em from above the rim of her glasses and paused—"the ladies out."

"But we have not discussed colors or styles. Are there samples or drawings I might see? How am I to choose?"

Mrs. Cecil turned that somber glare once again upon Pepper. "There is no need for you to choose. Mr. DeGraaf has done so."

"But my preference—"

Em, perhaps sensing the collision of wills, stepped between the women. "Mrs. Cecil is a professional. You can see the quality of her work for yourself." She glanced about the room, where gowns hung from the walls like portraits in a gallery, each grander than the last.

Pepper heard the warning in Em's voice. She mastered her temper. "I certainly meant no disrespect."

"I'm sure you have nothing to worry about, doll. Whatever Mrs. Cecil creates will be top-notch. Isn't that right, Mrs. Cecil?"

Mrs. Cecil grimaced. "You can be assured my gowns will transform the young lady."

"There you are," Em said. "All will be well."

"If you will excuse me." Mrs. Cecil turned her back to them and returned to her rack.

That could not be the last of it. "So I'm to have no say at all?"

Em guided her toward the door. "Doll, I believe we should be on our way." Before Pepper could protest, Em hooked her arm and pressed her toward the door. "We thank you again for making time to see us this morning." Deftly, Em maneuvered Pepper into the front room and to the door. "Good-bye now," she said, opening it and squeezing Pepper's forearm, reminding her to say something pleasant.

Pepper did her best to smile. "Yes, good-bye, Mrs. Cecil. I look forward to seeing—" She winced at the warning pinch Em applied to her arm. "Good-bye, now."

Young Anne closed the door behind them. Pepper waited until they were out of view of the shop's window to yank her arm away. "Why would you not allow me to speak?"

"Were you not listening? Your preferences are not her concern. She is working for Robert DeGraaf, not for you. You've put yourself in his hands now. You must accept it."

Before she could argue, Em changed the subject.

"So what do you have planned for today?"

"I have not considered it," she said truthfully, gazing upon Grace Church as it came into view. She could not remember a time when she had so many open hours spread out before her.

Em pulled her watch from her pocket. "Whatever it is, enjoy. I'm off to dazzle the crowds." They parted and she sauntered down the sidewalk with her walking stick, ignoring the curious looks cast her way.

Pepper strolled on. How wonderful it seemed to have nothing but time to enjoy the crispness of the springtime breeze and the wide blue sky. She was imagining Trixie and Beatrice rushing to get into costume and makeup before she remembered: They were gone, too.

What was Stanley doing for a deuce act? It would be a mistake not to bring in a last-minute act. He needed girls, maybe not in the deuce slot but somewhere, because the bill was already too heavy with men. Dancers, singers, comediennes, any discipline would do. But would Stanley know that? She wondered if he had any theatrical sense left at all.

She nearly turned and headed back toward The Chance, curious to see what she would find. But she stopped herself. It wasn't her concern, was it? She had to leave it alone.

It was an odd feeling, but she compensated by strutting along the sidewalk, enjoying this new status as a lady with time to promenade during the day. She smiled to herself, thinking that if it felt this good being a fake Miss DeGraaf, how much better it was going to be when she was the real Mrs. DeGraaf.

She was still feeling the glow of that prospect when she walked up the brick pathway to her new apartment building and greeted the man with the persistent frown behind the desk. He saw her and looked away. She brushed off the rebuff. What did it matter if an attendant greeted her or not?

Upstairs, she pulled her new key from her new reticule and let herself in. The table with the dirty dishes awaited her. She could wait for McManus's man to collect them, but the truth was she had nothing better to do. She set down her purse and went about the task of washing them.

When she finished, she looked around for something else to occupy her. She made the bed, she set aside the laundry, she even straightened the towels and soaps in the lavatory. When she found herself straightening the corner of a painting in the passage, she decided it was time for tea.

At least Robert had thought to stock the cupboard with a nice Darjeeling. She pulled down a teapot and the tin, but found that the dried tea leaves were little more than dust. She proceeded with it anyway. Once she had the tray together, she took it to a chair in front of a window overlooking the street.

There she sat, sipping from her porcelain cup and watching the breeze play with the leaves of the sycamore trees until she realized what was making her anxious. It was the quiet. Except for the clopping of horses pulling carriages and wagons in the distance, there were no sounds in her room. There seemed to be none in the building at all. It was utterly and unnaturally quiet. Certainly not like the Lair, with its squeaky boards and the rattle of slamming doors, even Old Jake's snores in the middle of the night.

It left her feeling empty. Like Gregory's room. She sighed. It was still difficult to believe he was gone. But what did it matter if he had left without saying good-bye? She had Robert. They were together as they were meant to be. It no longer mattered what they had done on the rooftop that afternoon, not what Gregory had seen or what he had thought. Not what anyone thought. It would only be wrong if they were not in love and not together now. He was making an honest woman of her, slowly, yes, but surely.

The clock struck three. The third show would be starting, if Jimmy was on time. Whoever the new deuce act was would be queued up in the wings.

When she caught herself missing those moments, she reminded herself what she did not miss: Stanley and all his complaints. She was better off. She was a hundred times better off.

And if she wanted to dance, she could still dance whenever she pleased. Yes, that was what this place needed. Some music to lighten the mood. She pushed her chair to the wall. A moment later she had the couch and the low tables pushed aside, and she pulled the music box from its corner. She untied her boots and kicked them off to the corner, cranked the brass lever, selected "España Waltz," and danced.

It was not the stage, and there were no theater ghosts to keep her company, but still the music filled her, pushing out the boredom and the silence, even the memory of that attendant's grimace. It seeped into all the parts of her that missed the Lair and her old friends.

A knock at the door stopped her. She stopped the music and opened the door to find the attendant from downstairs.

"Excuse me, Miss DeGraaf. There has been a complaint about the noise."

"I'm not making noise. It's my music box—"

"Yes," the man interrupted. "There has been a complaint about the music. And, a clatter of furniture moving or some such thing?"

"Well, yes, but—"

"We strive to maintain a quiet environment for the convenience of all residents. I'm sure you understand. Good day." He nodded briskly and returned down the corridor.

No, she did not understand. But once again, it seemed her preferences were hardly the point. She closed the door and tucked her music box away.

After McManus's man carted the dishes away, Pepper bathed and made herself ready for Robert's arrival.

Finally, she could hear him in the corridor. His footsteps first and then the knock. She hurried to answer, eager to see his face after such a long and trying day. Eager to hear a friendly voice.

But it was only the man from downstairs again. "This arrived for you, Miss DeGraaf," he said and presented a telegram. When she took it, he nodded stiffly and retreated down the hall.

Miss Pepper DeGraaf. How strange it appeared, there in black and white. She opened the envelope.

My dear,

A business matter will detain me this evening so I cannot make my visit. I am looking forward to seeing you Monday evening.

Robert

P.S. I have good news from Mrs. Cecil. She promises to deliver at least one of the gowns Monday morning.

Pepper closed the door, and without removing the light rouge on her cheeks or her lips, or the pins from her hair, or even her gown or slippers, she made her way into her bedchamber, grabbed a pillow, and buried her sobs deep in the down, muffling them so they made no inconvenient sound.

• • •

THE NEXT MORNING SHE STAYED IN BED UNTIL SHE COULD NOT stay in bed another moment. It must have been noon, or sometime thereafter. It hardly mattered. There was no reason to rise. Not when she had a day filled with nothing to greet her.

Not the sounds of stagehands at The Chance whistling their cues, or the loud banter and chatter of players running their lines. Not even the creaks and squeaks of the theater's loose floorboards. Just the stifling, oppressive quiet of this well-to-do part of town.

She even missed the racket of the boys playing stickball in the street.

It would not be so tiresome if Robert were to be expected, but he had made it clear she would not see him again until the next day. That would come soon enough—and with it so many preparations. There was the banquet at Delmonico's, after all. And Mrs. Cecil's dress. Tomorrow would be an exciting day, indeed, when it arrived.

She just had to get through today.

At the theater there was always something to do or someone to see. And when there was not, she had the music box and her practice. Here, she did not even have those.

Yet it would not always be like this. Once she and Robert were married, she could do as she pleased. She could even go back to the theater, if she chose. When she was alive, Mrs. DeGraaf had certainly visited often enough, though her concerns always lay more with the fitness of the working conditions and employees' hygiene, not whether the lineup should be shuffled or the headliner hit the right note.

Once she was Mrs. DeGraaf, Stanley would not be able to touch her.

The thought of that alone got her through an hour. But then the thrill waned. She considered dressing and leaving her rooms, just to stroll and feel the sunshine upon her face. She would have done it if she couldn't already imagine the frown she would see on the attendant's face. The silent reproach of a single young woman going out alone.

When Robert sent the maid he mentioned, she could ask the woman to accompany her. Then it would be all right. Then she would not have to sit at this window, gazing out at the street and the budding trees, at the carriages and the pedestrians walking and talking and laughing beneath her. All day she watched that window as if it were a flicker peephole with the same loop whirling around and around.

When night came, she realized she had eaten nothing but a biscuit with her morning tea. If she went downstairs, she was sure she could have the attendant arrange for something to be sent up. But it hardly seemed necessary. She had no appetite at all.

Monday was different.

She rose early, eager for the day. Eager for the banquet and Delmonico's. She thought of Beatrice. Would she and Trixie be loitering out front, pretending they could walk inside, when Pepper arrived on Robert's arm? As he led her into that happy haven of wealth and privilege, where champagne glasses clinked their music through richly appointed rooms? Where oil magnates and railroad tycoons paid handsomely to dine on pheasant and oysters beside literati and the latest stage sensations? No, Beatrice had a man now, wasn't that what Em had said? He had even given her a show. Pepper felt a twinge of jealousy.

But she had all this. She looked around at her wonderful apartment, her expensive, lovely apartment. This was better than a rowdy burlesque show. Far better.

She also had Robert. This banquet would be both their new beginning and their happily ever after, for once she appeared on his arm, their match would be known. It would be as legitimate as any marriage certificate.

And she would look so lovely in her new gown. Mrs. Cecil had said it herself: *It will transform the lady.*

Pepper took her place again at the street window but this time with a purpose. She was watching for the delivery. Soon after the nine o'clock chime, it arrived, ferried by private carriage in the hands of young Anne. Pepper sailed down the passageway at the first sight of the girl and the box.

Pepper found her in the lobby, holding the package that

measured nearly half as long as Anne was tall. It was marvelous—all white with a silver trim and bow. Pepper found it difficult not to tear it open right then and there, but the attendant with his persistent frown was watching.

When Pepper had taken the box, Anne fished a delivery receipt from the small bag she pulled from a fold in her skirt, along with a nub of a pencil, and asked Pepper to sign.

A moment later, Pepper was back in her room with the giant box. She placed it on the table and with a pair of shears gingerly, reverently, clipped through the silver ribbon. She lifted away the top and sat back at the first sight of her new gown.

A breathtaking gown made of the softest and most sumptuous sapphire velvet.

The color was bold—not a pale blue or sky blue. But a strong and vibrant shade. The color of her mother's eyes, the color of her own.

She lifted the gown by the shoulders. She could see now that the sapphire velvet constituted only the bodice and cap sleeves. A netting of linked rhinestones with a crisscross of gold-encrusted embroidery covered the lower part of the bodice and was attached to an ivory sheath of a skirt embroidered down the center, where the skirt was slit to the knee, revealing more sapphire velvet beneath. It truly was a remarkable garment, and she loved it utterly.

This gown would transform her, she had no doubt.

There was still more within the box. Beneath the layers of tissue paper were ivory silk stockings and delicate evening slippers. Folded in the corner was a pair of long silky gloves and a smart hair ornament made of beads and ostrich plumes in blue and gold and ivory. An entire evening ensemble.

She carried it all to her bed, tugged the blanket flat, and arranged it just as she would wear it. The dress, the gloves, the stockings, the slippers, the hair decoration. She stepped back and gazed at the invisible woman lying upon her new mattress and imagined she was looking at herself. She could be that woman, alighting from a coach, pressed to Robert's side as he escorted her through Delmonico's rooms. This was a woman others would admire. One they would respect. Not a theater urchin, not a chorus girl.

This woman would be demure where she was bold, sophisticated where she was scrappy, smooth where she was rough. In this gown, there would never again be a question that she would be the lady Robert wanted her to be.

She stripped off her day dress, then worked herself into Mrs. Cecil's creation. She could hardly believe that the woman's strange measuring method had produced such a pleasing fit. She went to the mirror and admired its drape. She slipped on the gloves, the stockings, the slippers, then piled up her hair and pinned in the ornament.

In the mirror, that invisible lady gazed back, fully formed. The lady Robert would be proud to lead on his arm.

• • •

IT WAS SOMETIME AROUND SEVEN THAT PEPPER MADE HER FINAL preparations and took a seat beside the window to watch for Robert's carriage. It would be early, she knew, but she did not want to keep him waiting.

She watched the darkness settle over the street and the lamplighter make his nightly visits to set the streetlamps ablaze.

At eight, she checked the color on her cheeks and lips, the upsweep of her hair, and the placement of the feather. At nine, she checked it all again and resisted the urge to walk down to the lobby and ask if any message had come for her.

Finally, at half past nine Robert's black carriage came to a stop in front of the building, and she watched him make his way up the walk. A few moments later, he was knocking at her door.

Brimming with the excitement of the banquet and her gown, she threw open the door to greet him, presenting herself to finest advantage. "Robert, good evening, how wonderful to—"

He strode past her without seeing her. "Yes, it will be a good evening, but not quite yet. Is there a liquor cabinet in this apartment? I swear I saw one. Yes, there it is."

She closed the door and found him at the open mahogany cabinet that held a trio of crystal cut decanters and matching short glasses. He poured himself a ration of what looked like scotch or bourbon as the brass pendulum of the grandfather clock beside him swayed. There was something strange in his manner. Something definitely off.

"Should we be on our way?" The banquet must be well under way by now. If he intended to make a showing, they had no time to waste.

He finished pouring, replaced the stopper, and took a long drink. "On our way where?" He wiped his lips on the back of his sleeve.

"The banquet, of course."

He took another gulp and finished off the glass. "The banquet? It completely slipped my mind." He reached for the decanter to fill his glass again.

She was too shocked to speak. What could she say? That attending that banquet with him had been the single happy thought she'd had these past two days?

He tossed back another sizable gulp and lowered himself onto the edge of the velour sofa.

"You're worrying me, Robert."

He set the glass on a white lace doily on a side table and patted the spot beside him.

She obeyed. Not out of duty, but to give him no reason to delay an explanation.

"My father died today."

The words were plain, but they struck Pepper like firecrackers.

Her hands flew to her mouth. "Oh, dear." She reached out to him, to comfort him. Who knew better than she the pain of losing one's parent? Instantly she felt the guilt of thinking only of herself, and of a party no less, while Robert so clearly suffered. She remembered how it had been for her in the first hours after her mother had died. The word had spread quickly, and the visitors had come at once. Em, of course, and Mrs. Basaraba, Gregory, and Old Jake. Frankie. Everyone had streamed through that afternoon. She never could have guessed so many people could fit in their small rooms. "You should have told me. We should be at the St. Denis. There must be family and friends paying their respects."

His face twisted. He looked at her as though she spoke nonsense. "Friends? My father had no friends, and we certainly have no family to speak of."

It was the grief. Pain did such ugly things to people. "Were you with him?" She made her words soft and consoling. She wanted him to know she understood.

Robert stared into his empty glass. "I was there. Gertie was there, and Father's attorney."

"An attorney?"

"It was only a formality, really. There was no reason for Father to work himself up. But you know how stubborn he can be, how bullheaded when it comes to the theater."

Something changed in Robert's voice. It turned raspy, desperate.

Still he stared into his glass. "He's an old man. Was an old man." He stopped, dazed, as if the reality of his father's death still had not sunk in. "Old people die, don't they? It's what they do."

This was not Robert. This was the shock speaking. It was the pain. She covered his hand with her own.

"It was just like him, really," he continued, "to be so concerned about The Chance's welfare and not mine. I suppose I shouldn't have been surprised. I've always come in second. But the deal makes sense for us, and what good was the theater to him when he was an invalid locked up in his rooms?"

She was trying very hard to follow the logic of his words, but he was not making sense. "What did your father want you to do?"

He stared at her as if it were obvious. "He wanted me to reject the best offer anyone has ever made on that old stack of bricks."

She pulled away. He was talking about the theater. "But you told me Ziegfeld had no interest in The Chance? That it was only research, an assessment?"

He threw off her hand and rose to pace the floor. "Who's talking about Ziegfeld? Though he certainly helped in his way, once word got out that we had spoken. I'm talking about Benjamin Keith. He has big plans for his Union Square Theatre, and he doesn't want a little nobody theater like The Chance getting in the way. Do you understand what that means? He wants to buy it, the whole damn building. He's offering top dollar."

"What would he do with it?" She knew the answer, she just could not believe it.

"Who knows, and who cares? It isn't my concern."

And it wasn't. She could see it in his sneer, his stony glare. He did not care about the theater, not the show, not anything that mattered to her.

"Is that what your father thought?"

"Hardly." Robert took his glass to the cabinet again and poured another drink. "He flew into a rage and wouldn't stay in that damn rolling chair. He actually tried to throw the agreement letter in the fire."

A numbness was settling over Robert. His words had lost their strength. Pepper remained silent; she did not trust anything she might say.

"When I wrestled those papers from him, he clutched at his heart and began to gasp—all very theatrical, very dramatic, just what you would expect from an old show horse like him." He gulped from his glass. "He made such a scene that Gertie flew in and threatened to throw me out. Can you imagine? The maid throwing me out of my own home? She demanded a doctor be called, but I told her it would be done after my father signed the papers. You see, I know his tricks. I knew it was a bluff." He shook his head. "I thought it was a bluff." He drank again. "As it turns out, it wasn't." He paused, then added, "I suppose I won't need his signature now. The theater shall be mine by inheritance."

Pepper could not move. This was too much to take in. "And you intend to sell it?"

"Have you not been listening? Of course I am going to sell it. What do I want with a shoddy old theater? That old-fashioned vaudeville is dead. People want flash and sparkle, they want something new. Ziegfeld has it right and so does Keith and the others. That's why the patrons are moving uptown."

But it was The Chance. The theater that had once showcased the best vaudeville in New York. Where Pepper had been dazzled by Little Egypt and all the amazing talents that came after. The theater that had sheltered her and entertained her, that had been with her through every good day and bad. That theater was as much a friend to her as Gregory and Em, closer even than her own mother at times. And it had a future, surely. It only needed someone who believed in it.

"If you don't want to save it, we could do it together. I know what needs to be done. And then we could run it together. It would be no bother to you, really."

"I hardly think so. How would it look to have my mistress carrying out my business? I'd be laughed out of town."

The words hit her like a slap. "I'm more than that, aren't I? We were once as close as a man and a woman could be. And all the time you've been away, I've been faithful to you. I have never strayed, not once. Does that not make me more than a mistress?"

"Like what? A wife?" He laughed, a deep, hollow sound that scraped through her. "You have spent far too much time in the pretend world of that silly little theater if you believe that. The real world does not operate that way. A man in my position could never marry a theater girl."

"No?" She jumped to her feet. "Ziegfeld married Anna Held; any one of Lillian Russell's suitors would be happy to walk her down the aisle."

He laughed again, a sarcastic laugh, a mean laugh. "You put yourself in that league?"

She crossed her arms. "Of course not. But what has changed? You said you wanted to marry me once, on the rooftop that day. Before we . . . Wouldn't we be married now if your father had not prevented it?"

"I was a boy then." The liquor gave his eyes a glazed, rheumy look. "I would have said anything."

Yes, she could see that now. He did not love her and he never had, not as she had loved him. "Your father did not send you away that day, did he?"

He said nothing, but she could see the guilt in his expression.

Her limbs and every part of her trembled. "Did you even send those flowers to my dressing room?"

How tired he was of this conversation. How tired he was of her. He rubbed his eyes and sighed, "What flowers?"

Thirteen

THE LAST OF "ESPAÑA WALTZ" PLINKED OUT OF THE music box, but it would do no good to start it again. Her limbs could not find the rhythm tonight. Even the theater ghosts, it seemed, would not be stirred. Perhaps they already knew it was the end.

She should not have run out on Robert as she had. It was rash, and she regretted it. Not because she forgave him. She could not imagine she ever would. He had made her folly so clear to her. She could see she had been naïve. He was not the man she thought he was, and he never would be. And maybe he was correct when he accused her of having been in this little theater too long. Such folly must be inevitable when you call a theater home.

Still, she knew what had to be done. She had known it when Robert made no move to stop her as she stormed out of apartment three-oh-six with the only things that mattered to her: her old keys to the Lair and her music box.

She cursed that music box, but she could never leave it behind. For twenty blocks she had suffered for it as she made her way back to the theater in those short cap sleeves in the cold middle of the night. The dainty heel of one shoe broke somewhere around the fifth block, and the other somewhere near the tenth. She hurled both into a rubbish heap behind a grocer's shop and continued on in what was left of her silk stockings.

When she finally made it back to the Lair and her own room, however, it was not the comfort of her old bed she craved. It was the stage.

After removing her gown and carefully placing it on the couch, then changing into an old pair of drawers and striped stockings, camisole, and shawl, she made her way to her only true sanctuary. She did not know when Robert planned to sign over the theater: perhaps tomorrow, perhaps the next day, but soon, of that she had no doubt.

He had said he did not know what Keith had planned, but there would be no reason to keep The Chance as it was, which to Pepper even now—despite its dull and faded wood, the patched curtain, the fickle footlights and worn carpet, despite every flaw and fault—was perfect. Standing on the lip of the stage, she looked out onto the sea of seats, the gentle curve of the balcony, the walls of scarlet-flocked wallpaper and frosted globe lanterns. The smell of sweat and mildew, greasepaint and turpentine, the dogs, the birds, the whole mess of it. She took it all in. And she loved it.

How could she have thought she could leave it? Robert had called this her pretend world, but it was not here where she was forced to present herself as Miss DeGraaf or be hidden away like a shameful secret. It was only the world beyond these walls that forced her to pretend.

The truth was, this was the only place she could be herself. A theater urchin, a wardrobe assistant, a chorus girl—a bit of all three. These were the people who accepted her for the woman she was. And in a few hours, she would have to tell them they were losing this shoddy little theater they called home.

She found a pencil and a sheet of paper on Stanley's desk ledge and wrote out: ALL-HANDS MEETING. TEN O'CLOCK, STAGE. She took it to the call board and pulled everything else off—the notes on laundry times and whose mended garments were ready to be picked up, who had a spare trumpet to sell and a menu from Annabelle's. She tossed them all in the trash bin and posted hers dead center.

She had believed Robert would save them, and that had been a mistake. Em had been right not to trust him. Even Gregory seemed to have known that night he interrupted them in the carriage. He had given her the means to get away and she should have stayed away. If only she could tell him that. Maybe that was her greatest regret of all.

It pained her still that Gregory had left without a word or a note. And if not to her, then to someone. But then, maybe he had. Old Jake or Stanley? Matty?

Matty. If anyone knew what had happened to Gregory, it would be the boy who had followed him like a shadow. Quickly, she returned to the Lair and knocked softly on the boy's door.

There was a rustling, then nothing. She rapped again.

"We'll be quiet, Jake. Go on back to bed."

"Matty, it's me," she whispered into the doorjamb.

More rustling, and then the door opened just enough for her to see one tawny brown eye. "Miss MacClair, what are you doing here?" He was breathless and careful to keep the door as closed as possible.

"Do you have company, Matty?" She could not help but smile, for it was obvious he did.

"That would be against the rules, wouldn't it? What are you doing here? I thought you left."

"I'm back."

A distinctly female giggle inside made Pepper stop, and she expected him to snap the door closed on her nose. Instead, he appeared genuinely worried. She should leave him to his guest, but she had to know: "Do you know where Mr. Creighton went?"

"He didn't say. Not to me, anyway."

Another giggle, and then a girl's arm wrapped around his neck from behind and a rosy face with curly brunette hair leaned out. "Hello, Pepper, come in. Have a drink with us." More giggles.

Matty tried pushing her back inside but not before Pepper saw that it was Trixie Small—a very drunk Trixie Small.

"No, thank you. I was just leaving."

Matty looked horrified.

She leaned closer to him and whispered, "I didn't see anything." Then she said good-bye.

Let the boy have the pleasure of his room at least while he still could.

• • •

PEPPER HAD BEEN CONSIDERING A BATH FOR AT LEAST AN HOUR. It would be nice to sink down in the warm water of her old tub, to feel something besides the dull ache of her feet, her head, and everything in between. But she could not distract herself from the symphony of sounds above her. Instead, she rolled under the covers to hide from the pale gold sunlight seeping below the curtain and drank in the joyous clatter she'd thought was gone forever. The scrapes and creaks of the stagehands sweeping the aisles and cleaning the Scarlet Room. The stomps of the players hurrying to their dressing rooms. All the hammering and hollering and whistles that went on in the early hours before the theater opened its doors.

She lay on her old lumpy mattress, wrapping herself in the sounds around her, holding them tight, until she heard the one that told her she could no longer delay: Em's footsteps in the ticket booth above.

Though Em was back in the show now and Matty and an usher were swapping turns at the window, the woman still insisted on doing the daily accounting. It was still the box office where she started her day.

Reluctantly, Pepper rose and pulled a burgundy cotton frock over her head. When Em opened the ticket booth door, she greeted Pepper with a surprised "Good morning, doll," but she sensed the trouble in a heartbeat.

"He's selling The Chance," Pepper blurted. And just like that, the delicately phrased explanation Pepper had planned as she lay in bed vanished. She sank against the desk and spilled it all, through gasps and sobs and wipes of her nose on the back of her black knuckle mittens. Em did not try to stop her. She did not even frown. She listened without interruption as Pepper recounted all the hours she had waited at the window, waiting for Robert and the banquet he had promised to take her to, about the callous way he had recounted his father's death and his plans to sell the theater quickly to B. F. Keith.

Em threw up her hand. "I have to stop you. You said Mr. DeGraaf is dead?"

Pepper had kept company with that news all night, long

enough that it felt familiar now. But for Em the wound was fresh. Pepper dropped her face into her hands. "I should have realized. . . ."

Em stood and paced. "Just give me a moment." Her hand trembled at her mouth. She had not been at such a loss for words since the day Bessie passed, when they were gathered in her room in the Lair.

"Let's walk, shall we?" Pepper said. "We need fresh air." She ignored the clock and the fact that it was already ten. "The meeting can wait."

"What meeting?"

Something else she had forgotten to mention to Em. "I put a note on the call board for an all-hands meeting at ten. I wanted to tell everyone at once, after you, of course."

Em checked the clock. "Then you're already late."

"You're more important."

Em shook her head. "Let's just go and deliver the news. Before the rumors start. They deserve to hear it from you."

The usher knocked on the door, ready to take the window.

"Not going to need you today, son," Em said. "Head on back in."

The pudgy young man shrugged and did as she said. The *Closed* sign was not lifted away from the theater's ticket window by ten. No one sat behind the glass to take coins, and no one dispensed tickets to be ripped at the door.

When Pepper caught up to Em, she was already across the Scarlet Room floor, holding open the auditorium door. Pepper could see that everyone was there, waiting. Old Jake was sweeping the stage and Laszlo was beating dust from the curtains with a cane swatter. Professor Hawkinson and Marvani conversed in the back. Sneed circled the stage with a dachshund cradled in his arms, cooing into one big, flappy ear. Matty darted out from the wings.

"I knocked on her door, but there was no answer. Should I check with Mrs. B upstairs?"

"And what do you want with Mrs. B?" Mrs. Basaraba was sitting quietly at the back, pulling a needle and thread through a white blouse.

He turned, chagrined. "Miss MacClair, ma'am. Have you seen her?"

"I'm here," Pepper called out.

Stanley sauntered out from behind the curtain, cane in hand. He sneered, "I told you that you weren't welcome in this theater."

Em stepped forward and pounded her walking stick into the crimson carpet. "Don't say another word, Harland. She has every right to be here and you're going to want to hear what she has to say."

Stanley straightened. His lips clamped, making him look like his face had been pinched between a giant thumb and index finger. "This isn't like you, Emmalyn. Can't you see the trouble she causes?"

"No one is causing any trouble right now but you, so sit down and listen to her."

"You're taking her side?"

"I am."

Whatever other conversations had been going on stopped. Pepper could hear only Stanley's angry huffing and the thumping of her heart against her ribs. She watched Stanley turn and settle himself onto the stool at the stage's edge.

Pepper did not know where to begin. She wanted to break the news gently, more gently than she had managed with Em, but she could think of nothing to say as she stood in front of

Stanley and everyone, for now even more faces had appeared—two ushers and Jimmy, the Shakespeareans and a few Helzigs, Alfred and Edwards. How could she tell them it was over? It had taken all she had to tell Em.

Em nudged her. "You're on, doll."

Her eyes stung. She couldn't breathe, she couldn't think.

Everyone was watching her. They already knew it was bad news.

Somehow Pepper told them. All of it, and again it came out in a rush of words, but this time she began with the most significant information: Mr. DeGraaf had passed. As that settled in, she told the rest, about Robert's plan to sell the theater, most likely to a man who only intended to shut it down.

At this, Stanley pulled Matty aside and whispered something into his ear that sent the boy hurrying off into the wings. There were other mumblings, too, of surprise and dismay, confusion and disbelief, but it was Jimmy who stepped forward.

"I can't leave," he said. "I have nowhere to go. Where am I supposed to go?" It wasn't defiance, merely a question. He looked to Pepper and Stanley, the other players.

No one answered.

Pepper chewed on her thumbnail and silently asked the same question. Where would she go when she was turned out of the Lair? And Old Jake and Matty, what would become of them? "I don't know," Pepper said at last.

Before she could say more, the auditorium door flew open and Matty stood there, shaking a fistful of notices. "These were nailed to the door when I was locking up." He raised them, two to each hand. Heavy black letters spelled out *Notice to Vacate.* "They're signed by Mr. Robert DeGraaf."

Em snatched one from his hand. "The lout couldn't even give us a day to sort our affairs."

"I don't think the folks in line saw them," Matty said. "But should I tell them the show is off?"

"May as well," Stanley said. "The show's dead, by the sound of it." All the anger he had directed at Pepper had drained away, leaving him with nothing.

"Now just hold on." Em was still reading through the fine print. "Let's not be hasty."

Stanley pushed his chair back to its corner. "What's to think about? I think it's clear we're not wanted."

"I know. . . ." Em was pacing and pinching her bottom lip, deep in thought. "But are we just going to give in?"

"Do we have a choice?"

Stanley might have uttered the words, but no one wanted to know the answer more than Pepper.

Em was still pacing, still pinching. "I'm no lawyer, but this smells off. It's too soon. I doubt he's even had time to unseal the will."

"What does that matter?" Stanley grumbled.

"It matters a great deal. Without that will, he has no right to do anything, not yet."

Pepper read the notice over Em's shoulder.

Em continued. "I say we have a valid argument that, at least for now, Robert DeGraaf has no authority to enforce this order."

The murmurs multiplied, though Stanley's voice rose above them. "You want to keep operating as though we know nothing of this? He'll send the law. They'll shut us down. It'll be a scandal."

"It's already a scandal," Pepper said. "Or it will be once the newspapers hear of it. But we can't let him close The Chance this way. It isn't right."

There was a time when the theater was as good as any on Broadway. A stage anyone wanted to play. But if it closed now, it would only be remembered as a run-down theater on the wrong side of town. An embarrassment.

"It deserves better," Pepper added.

Em put her hand on Pepper's shoulder. "What do you have in mind, doll?"

The idea was just a spark, just a seed of a plan. "We could give the theater a proper farewell. A send-off, like you did for me."

She caught a questioning glance from Stanley. He had not known about the party.

"We could do one last show," she continued. "Something grand, something marvelous. Something like Mr. DeGraaf would have done in the old days."

Matty was scratching his head. "So we put on a big show and hand all the money over to Robert DeGraaf?"

"Couldn't we keep the money?" Jimmy asked.

"No, Jimmy," Em said, "we couldn't keep the money. That would be stealing. But who says we have to charge admission?"

The suggestion was met roundly with snarls and frowns. No one liked the idea of working for free, but Pepper could see the sense of it. "I don't want to slink away, defeated. Do you? And who would hire us anyway? Not after that *Variety* notice. We have nothing to lose, and if we do it right, if we put on a good show, maybe we can restore our own names as well. Prove we are more than a band of fools, misfits and deviants. We can prove we are professionals."

"And if we call it a tribute," Em piped in, "Little Robby will have to go along. He'd be too ashamed to shut us down."

"How exactly do you propose we finance this grand and marvelous production?" Stanley sneered.

To Pepper's surprise, Old Jake stepped forward. "The storage rooms are full of bits and pieces from those old shows. There might be something there worth dusting off."

"Splendid idea," Pepper said. "Thank you, Jake."

"We have trunks full of old costumes in Wardrobe. You are welcome to any of them."

"Thank you, Mrs. B. We'll definitely need costumes."

Em stepped forward and held out her hands. "Before we go further, let's just get something out of the way: Is everyone in? This isn't going to be easy, but it'll be a lot harder with dead weight. So decide now. If you're in, you're in. If not, now is the time to say so."

The players and workers looked around, nodding with each other, murmuring, deciding together they were in.

All of them but one. Without a word, Stanley rose, shook his head and dragged his lame leg into the wings.

Everyone watched him leave. No one spoke, and it took a moment for the departure to register with Pepper. Perhaps she should have expected it, but she hadn't. Despite all his vitriol and all the hard times, he had always stuck by the theater. They had never had a show without Stanley. How could they put this one on without him? For a moment, she considered giving in, too.

But only for a moment.

"Everyone else is in?" she asked.

There were nods and affirmative murmurs.

Marvani darted glances around the room. "Our stage manager just quit. Does that not concern anyone? Who will run the show?"

"I will," Pepper said.

Her offer hardly seemed to instill confidence. Their gazes conveyed only surprise and doubt.

Defiantly, she added, "You all have enough to do, and frankly, we don't have time to get anyone else, even if we could find someone willing to work for free. So, I'm saying I'm willing, unless anyone has a better plan."

Old Jake glanced away as he murmured, "She's always spouting her opinions anyway."

It might not have been the endorsement she would have liked, but it would have to do. "Then let's get started."

Over the span of the next two hours they decided three things: that they were going to stage a single show on Saturday night, that every player who wanted one would have a place in that show, and that planning a grand production without Mr. DeGraaf or Mr. Stanley was going to be far more difficult than anything they had ever attempted at The Chance.

Old Jake and the other stagehands excused themselves to take an inventory of the old props, and Mrs. Basaraba left to do the same with costumes. Everyone else pulled up a chair or a crate or anything handy and set out to plan the show.

Jimmy suggested they build it around a circus theme to set it apart from the usual format. Sneed concurred.

"Yes, but not circus. Circus is common," Marvani scoffed. "We should elevate the entertainment, perhaps something like *Magic Through the Ages*? That has a more elegant appeal."

The Shorty Shakespearean who played Don Pedro leaned forward on his crate and planted his hand on his small knee. "What's the ta-da, Marv? Making the audience disappear? As it is, your magic can't hold the house's attention for ten minutes. We need variety. I say we need something like *A Night of Courtly Entertainments*. You could have your dancers, your singers, your pantomimes."

When Professor Hawkinson's ears turned red as beets

because someone suggested he would be perfect as a stumbling jester, Pepper suggested they break for lunch.

Em and Pepper lingered, and when everyone else had gone, Pepper spoke the question that had been building up within her for the better part of an hour. "How can this ever work?"

Em was sitting at the edge of the stage, her feet dangling over the side. She pulled her knees to her chest. "I haven't a clue, doll. But you can't back out now. You've convinced them it will work. They believe in this show now, and they believe in you."

"They deserve better. They deserve someone who can give them a real hit."

Em craned her head around and gave Pepper a funny look. "Someone like Florenz Ziegfeld, perhaps?"

"I suppose." The name still sent a chill down her spine.

"I doubt he'd be up for managing the show, but if the rumors around town are true, Little Robby has given him a good reason to steer us in the right direction."

Fourteen

PEPPER AND EM STEPPED OFF THE STREETCAR NEAR Forty-first Street as it approached the Broadway Theatre, a stoic building of red brick capped with a white Federal-style pediment. If not for the electrical *Broadway* sign that climbed the face and the flickering marquee over the rounded arch windows, one might assume it housed some somber city function and not the season's lightest and silliest musical comedy. But *A Parisian Model*, starring Anna Held, was doing a brisk business here, and had been for months. Already the box office was selling tickets to the evening show.

But that was not Em's destination.

She led Pepper past the window, hooked around the corner, and headed directly for the stage door, a shiny black affair two steps above the sidewalk. Perched on a stool at the foot of those steps, a husky man with a grimy shirt and loose vest sucked on a toothpick.

"Follow my lead," Em whispered to Pepper. "Pardon me, sir."

He pushed his bowler back and took a long moment to focus on Em.

She ignored the smell of whiskey, which was so strong it forced Pepper to turn away. "My client has an appointment with Mr. Ziegfeld. He said you could direct us to him."

The man gave Pepper a long look. "He said that, did he? Squeezing in another audition during the wife's rehearsal? Mighty convenient for him, wouldn't you say?"

"I wouldn't know about that," Em said. "But my client is a dancer."

"Is she?" The man's greasy gaze traveled down Pepper's legs as if he could see through her clothes: the plum velvet coat, black-and-white skirt, petticoat and drawers. "But it puts me in a bind, you see. I'm supposed to stay right here. On this stool. Management docks my pay if they see me wander off." After giving his shoulder a good scratch, his hand settled, open, in front of Em.

"Perhaps a little something for your trouble is in order?" Em suggested.

The man's pockmarked face stretched into a clownish grin. "A little something would be rightly appreciated."

Em pulled out a bill and pressed it into the man's palm.

He shoved it into his pocket. "Let's go see if we can't find Mr. Ziegfeld, shall we?"

He led them through the stage door and a labyrinth of passages and stairways until they arrived by a side door at the theater's auditorium. The sheer size of the place stole Pepper's breath. From the rear rows, where they were standing, the stage seemed a half mile away—a half a mile of lush, new red carpeting, gleaming theater seats, a cascade of golden balconies, all topped by not one but three enormous chandeliers that had been dimmed to a deep amber glow.

"Sir, your appointment is here."

Pepper turned. The man was speaking to the shadows in the very last row. Em was straightening her coat, fixing her hat, preparing for the inevitable defense of this outrageous trespass. The man in the shadows stood. Yes, it was Ziegfeld: sharp gray suit, black cravat, smudge of a mustache above his lip. He nodded to the guard, who turned and left without another word. Slowly, deliberately, he turned to Pepper: "I am delighted to see that you have taken me up on my invitation, Miss MacClair."

Em wheeled on Pepper. "What invitation?"

Pepper felt her ears and cheeks burn. "We're here on another matter, sir."

"Oh?" He scrutinized Em. "Madame Charmaigne, I have not had the pleasure, though I have heard wonderful things about your Uptown Joe."

"Thank you. I only recently revived the act, but it is a thrill to get back to the stage."

Was Em blushing? Had Ziegfeld charmed even her? But then she snapped back to her old self.

"I wish we could stand around and chat, but frankly, Mr. Ziegfeld, we've come for a more desperate purpose. It concerns The Chance Theatre."

His gentlemanly smile vanished. "I have heard the unfortunate news about your theater. Very disappointing news, indeed."

He had harsher words on the matter that he was keeping to himself; Pepper could hear it in his voice.

"So you know Robert DeGraaf intends to sell?" Pepper blurted.

His dark eyes flashed. Was he surprised, or was he surprised she knew? "Yes, I heard something to that effect."

"It isn't right," she said, her voice rising despite her effort to control her anger. "It's not a fitting end for a theater like The Chance. So what we'd like to do, what we intend to do, in fact, is give it a proper farewell. We're planning a tribute, a one-night show, to send it out in style."

Ziegfeld looked at her with kindly doubt, as if she had just declared she could fly to the moon. "I understand the young Mr. DeGraaf plans to divest himself of that theater immediately." Again there was a curtness that suggested there was more he could say, but would not.

"That may be his plan," Pepper continued, "but we have the theater, and we won't give it back until after our show."

"I'm sorry, did you say you *have* the theater?"

"Yes, we have it and we're keeping it."

She explained the notices, the injustice of it, and exactly what she and the others planned to do.

At the end of her speech, Ziegfeld laughed, a deep, reverberating sound that filled the auditorium. "Miss MacClair, you surprise me. You have an enchanting determination for such a pretty chorus girl. And I admit I have a selfish motive for wishing you success in this endeavor. I know who spread the word that I was seeking an alternate venue for my *Follies,* and I do not appreciate being taken advantage of that way." He glanced around to be sure they were alone in the auditorium and lowered his voice. "Of course I must admit that it worked to my advantage. Since Mr. Erlanger caught wind of it, he has gone to a good deal of trouble to be sure the *Follies* debut at the New York Roof, which he has agreed to christen the Jardin de Paris for the occasion."

"As that is the case, sir," Pepper said, "what we need most urgently is a bit of advice."

He glanced at the stage. "I'm happy to offer it, if you don't mind sharing my attention. We can discuss it now if you like, while I keep an eye on Anna's rehearsal."

Pepper's gaze followed his to several girls in leotards and blouses tied at the navel, who were shuffling, kicking, and tapping through a bit. One of them was the great Anna Held, though at this distance, it was impossible to know which. "You can see so little from back here. Wouldn't it be better to sit closer to the stage?"

"Not at all. That's why we pack the house. I know it will all look good to anyone sitting down there," he jutted his sharp chin toward the front rows, "but if it doesn't sell up here, we've disappointed half the house. That would not do."

"Exactly!" Em pounced with enthusiasm. "That is exactly the kind of thinking we need to make our show a knockout." Out of the side of her mouth, she added, "And we're certainly not opposed to embarrassing the little brat DeGraaf, either."

"I like the way you think, Em Charmaigne. Have you considered going to the papers?"

"An advert for the show? Sure."

"I'm not speaking of advertisements. Those are fine, but you have a publicity gold mine here. Scrappy theater underdogs squaring off against a big, bad manager refusing to let them pay tribute even to his own dead father. Could there be anything more despicable?"

Pepper stepped in. "But that isn't exactly the truth. . . ."

"When it comes to publicity, my dear, the truth is not your concern. That's for the boys and girls at the newspaper to sort out. People want a story, and it doesn't get better than good guys versus bad."

Pepper could see the wheels turning in Em's head.

Ziegfeld settled back into his seat and thought for a moment. "What you must do is embrace the notoriety of the thing, make it work for you. You might even name this show of yours something outrageous, like *The Utterly Unauthorized and Entirely Unofficial Last Chance Show.*"

Em slapped her knee. "Damn, that's good."

"Personally, I have always been partial to James DeGraaf's early shows. I particularly enjoyed that little Egyptian belly dancer from the World's Fair. Do you have anything of that nature?"

Em and Pepper exchanged a look and shook their heads.

"Then what do you have?"

For the next half hour they ran through their lineup and their ideas.

"What I have found useful," Ziegfeld said, his eyes focused on the stage, as they had been throughout most of the conversation, "is to start with a story already known to the audience, something familiar, and twist it, make it new, make it your own. It worked when we revived *A Parlor Match* at Herald Square. And with this production, we've really given them a twist. Everyone said the romantic dance number between Anna and Gertrude Hoffman dressed up in men's garb would cause an outrage, but I believe we've sold a fair number of tickets for that act alone. People simply have to see it for themselves."

When the stage cleared and the girls paraded out, Ziegfeld rose, indicating their consultation had reached its end.

"We appreciate your time, Mr. Ziegfeld," Em was quick to say, and it was true. They were leaving with a good many more ideas for their show.

What they still lacked, however, and what gnawed at Pepper

when they reemerged from the theater into the glare of the midday sunshine, was a way to distinguish the tribute show from the same old *Stars, Marvels and Delights.*

She and Em spoke little during the streetcar ride back to The Chance, and Pepper could not tell whether Em was worried or just letting Ziegfeld's wisdom sink in.

When they strolled through the auditorium doors, Jimmy was in one corner of the stage juggling billets, while Alfred and Edwards tossed lines back and forth on the other. The Shorty Shakespeareans were there, too, throwing dice against their castle wall prop with Marvani, Sneed, and the professor huddled close behind.

Pepper saw Em frown.

"At least they're here," Pepper offered.

"I suppose that's something." Em clapped her hands sharply as they made their way down the aisle. When they had the men's attention, Em poked Pepper's elbow. "Go ahead, tell them."

"Me?"

"You're in charge, remember? Stage manager . . ."

Stage manager. She had nearly forgotten. "We just called on Mr. Ziegfeld."

That got their attention.

"The good news is: He's as vexed by Robert DeGraaf as we are—or nearly so. And the better news is: He's willing to help us out with the show." Everyone liked his idea for the show's title. Everyone agreed that the bigger the spectacle, the better. But exactly what form that spectacle might take? That was another matter.

"We just have to come up with a story."

There were murmurs of assent all around.

"I've been thinking about that, doll. Ziegfeld told us his best successes came from taking an old idea and giving it a twist. *A Parlor Match,* for example. That got me thinking. In *Parlor Match,* the whole séance gag is a ruse for getting acts on the stage. So, what if we did something like that, say, an *Arabian Nights* where Scheherazade could spin tales for the king and each one would be an act?"

Pepper could see it instantly. A dazzling set, vibrant fabrics, exotic backdrops. Everything she had loved about the old *Little Egypt* show. "It's perfect. And you would play Scheherazade?"

"No, doll. You would."

Pepper braced. It was bigger than anything she had ever done on The Chance's stage. Bigger than anything anyone had done in a long time. There was no question she wanted it. But she had already committed herself to being stage manager. "I do want it. More than anything. But I'm filling in for Stanley."

"Who says you can't do both?"

"Do you really think so?" She knew Em read her meaning.

Em had been in the wings for Pepper's debut. She had seen the entire horrifying incident. The way Pepper had started strong, shuffling, bouncing, and swaying to "Up in a Coconut Tree," but by the time she reached center stage, her mind had gone utterly blank. And she could feel it, the pain in her deepest parts, the reminder of what she had done up on the roof with Robert.

If she had not been so overconfident, so sure she was ready. She'd told herself, *This is how it feels to be a star, how it feels to be a woman.* But even when Robert had reached up beneath her skirts and worked his fingers inside her drawers, she'd known it was wrong. She'd tried to pull away. She'd told him she had changed her mind.

"It's too late for that," he'd said. "You said you loved me, so you must. It's the only way I'll know you do."

So she had. Because he had said he loved her, too.

Afterward, as she was trying to get her skirts back into place, Gregory had come up to the roof looking for her and found her with Robert beneath that blanket. He knew; she could see it on his face.

She had not let herself think about it after Robert left with a kiss and a promise to see her soon. She even managed to get into costume and out on the stage the next day, after she heard Robert had gotten into a carriage and been whisked away from her that morning. But then that tiny voice inside had started speaking to her out there on the stage. *They can all see your shame*, it whispered. *They know what kind of girl you are.*

That was when the dizziness began. She lost her balance during a spin and stopped to get her bearings. She did not remember much after that, only that she had stood there dead still, staring into the black, wondering if everyone out there knew the terrible thing she had done with Robert.

Em had been the one to rush onstage, dressed up as Uptown Joe because her own slot was farther up the bill. Em had grabbed Pepper by the hand and whipped her around as if they were a couple dancing a funny jig, which suited the song but must have looked ridiculous to the audience. Somehow, Em had managed to twirl Pepper offstage, and Frankie finished the song by hamming up the end.

Everyone had felt so bad for her—they knew how long she had been working on that act, how long she had wanted to be onstage—no one had said a thing, not even Bessie, when she'd retired to her bed and did not leave it for a full week. They all thought it was simple stage fright, and that made it easier in a way.

But now the stage fright was real enough, and who knew what

would happen if she tried to go out on the stage alone. She did not have the strength to face that kind of humiliation again, not for herself and not for the theater. "I don't know if I can do it."

Em stepped in front of Pepper, put her hands on both shoulders, and waited until Pepper met her gaze. She held it for a long moment, then said: "You can, you will, and I'll help you. The way I see it, you will have an opening number, something to get the show going, and then you'll hardly be more than a fancy mistress of ceremonies. The king will preside from a grand throne, and you'll be at his side. Instead of sitting offstage like Stanley did, you'll be onstage, looking ravishing. Matty can be standing by to pass along whatever notes or instructions you have. Heck, let's make him assistant stage manager, it's what he's been training for."

"Maybe it could work."

"Besides, who else knows that snaky *danse du ventre*. That wiggly-squiggly belly dance?" She gave an exaggerated shake of her hips and shoulders to make her point, which made everyone around them laugh. "Who else, my dear, can say she trained directly with the legendary Little Egypt?"

"I hardly trained," Pepper corrected, sheepishly. "I was just a girl."

"It's really no different from Annabelle's. I don't see any reason at all why you can't do this. And it's what you've wanted, isn't it? It's what everyone wants. To be a star! This is your chance."

"But what about you? What will you do?"

Em looked at her as if she had just suggested she grow a second head. "I will be the king, of course."

No one argued, not even Pepper.

"So is it settled?"

"Yes—"

"Good, let's move on to the next item on the agenda. What we need to do next is take stock of what we have for props and backdrops." She paused. "And costumes, we'll have to see about costumes." She paused again. "Someone needs to write up the program copy, too. . . ."

Pepper jumped in. "How about this: Em, go to the prop room with the stagehands and see what we have for props. I'll go to Wardrobe to see what we have there. Matty, you get the program copy together, and then we'll meet back here in an hour to decide what we have and what we still need. Players, come up with a way to put an *Arabian Nights* spin on your routine, and then we'll figure out how to pull it all together."

Em winked and gave her a proud smile. To the others, she barked, "You heard the stage manager, get to work and be back here in an hour."

In Wardrobe, Pepper and Mrs. Basaraba worked quickly and soon had the worktable stacked with garments and folds of fabric. So many vibrant colors: magenta and persimmon, violet and chartreuse, azure and carnelian. All luxurious, all shimmering, all enchantingly exotic. Pepper ran her fingers over the rich assortment.

"A good start," Mrs. Basaraba said, pushing her eyeglasses back up the bridge of her nose.

"I'd say it's more than that, Mrs. B. It's wonderful."

"I dug around and found original harem outfits, only three, but the design is simple so I can make more. And there's a sultan outfit, too, that we can use for the king. And whatever fabrics we don't use for costumes could be used for pillows or draped across the stage for a harem effect, no?"

"Absolutely," Pepper said, as though that had been her intent all along.

"Little Egypt, did she wear one of these?" Mrs. Basaraba searched the pile for the harem costumes—an emerald vest with spangles and matching pantaloons, and another set in copper and one in turquoise.

The costumes brought back a flood of memories. Pepper remembered the first time she saw all that glamour and color. All the hours spent huddled in the wings, when she did not even have a chair, just the floor. It was everything she loved about the theater all wrapped up in one act: costumes, dancing, music, whimsy. All those afternoons when Little Egypt welcomed her into her dressing room and taught her that Egyptian dance.

Pepper shook her head. "Little Egypt's costume was magnificent—beads and coins and shimmering, full skirts." Pepper could see it all again in her mind, as if she were back in that old dressing room, when the plaster was new and the carpets were plush, when the furnishings gleamed. Back when the golden frames of the mirrors still sparkled and the couch's middle cushions did not sag, when the air did not yet smell of age and failure and disappointment. When everything was still fresh and bright, without even a hint of the muddy browns and grays that now settled over everything like a plague.

"Beads and coins." Mrs. Basaraba frowned. "We have nothing like that. Here." She plucked a pencil from a cup beside her sewing machine and a sheet of blank notepaper. "Describe them."

For the next half hour, Pepper recounted what she remembered of Little Egypt's costume. Using the harem pieces as reference, she explained how the vest was more richly embellished and how Little Egypt wore a silky skirt instead of the pantaloons the other dancers wore. And while they wore belts around their hips that dripped with ribbons and tassels to their knees, Little Egypt's was fuller, the tassels thicker and threaded with beads of solid gold—at least that was how it had seemed to Pepper.

Mrs. Basaraba stared at the image she had drawn.

"You don't like it?"

Mrs. Basaraba glanced up. "It is beautiful." The woman put her hand on a fabric pile. "But I have nothing here to make it. It will be impossible."

Pepper left after telling the wardrobe mistress that she had every confidence that whatever the woman created would be just as marvelous, just as dazzling, if not more so. But the truth was, she had her doubts. Little Egypt's costume had been as popular as the dancer herself. And since she would be trying to fill that legendary dancer's shoes, a stunning costume would be necessary.

Maybe Mrs. Basaraba did not have anything to make such a costume, but there was one more place Pepper could look.

She flew down the metal staircase to the Lair. On the street-side door, she found another eviction notice. *Notice to Vacate: All Residents. Immediately.* She ripped it down and crumpled it in her fist.

She was still fuming when she let herself into her room and scoured her shelves, searching the messy stacks, pulling down anything that Mrs. Basaraba might use: an amethyst taffeta skirt, a claret bolero, a teal peasant blouse, anything that was not black. She threw open the trunks and filled a basket with brooches and baubles and ostrich plumes. She searched the bed and the floor, kicking through the piles for anything she might have forgotten.

Then she opened the pocket door to the passageway and lifted the drape to her mother's room. She tied it back to let in the meager sunlight from the front room, but still it took a moment for her eyes to adjust in the windowless space. Slowly, the bed and the dressing table came into focus. A thick layer of dust shrouded the dresser and the shelves she had not looked upon since the day the funeral home men took her mother away.

She pushed through the veil of those old memories and hastily made her way to the trunks. Throwing back one lid, she searched through the lace table covers, the long swaths of uncut wool, and all the odds and ends her mother had stashed away. She dropped the lid and searched the other trunk and found nothing there either. The empty sewing basket she left in the corner untouched.

Disappointed, she left the room—and that was when she caught sight of Mrs. Cecil's sapphire-and-cream gown draped over the back of the couch. She lifted it, felt the weight of the beading, the embroidery. So beautiful and sophisticated. It was everything she had hoped to become. Yet what good would it do her now? It deserved to be seen at balls and salons, opening nights at the symphony or opera. It did not belong here with her old costume pieces. That is what it would become, just another costume, like the others, folded and stuffed onto a shelf. But if she could persuade Mrs. Cecil to take it back, maybe then it could do some good.

• • •

SOMEONE WAS IN THE SCARLET ROOM TO SEE PEPPER. THAT WAS the message Matty brought down to the stage Wednesday afternoon, when Pepper was watching Marvani's attempts to change his magic act into a snake charmer routine. She told him stringing up a fake cobra so it floated out of a basket was not enough, and, no, he absolutely could not bring in a live serpent, even if he could find one.

"What you need is a girl," she snapped. "Get a girl in the act, and then you can keep that fake snake."

The show needed girls. Not just Marvani. The whole show was men, except for her and Em, and Em hardly counted.

She would have been more discouraged if the acts had not been making such good progress. In a day, the stagehands had assembled a harem room set with pillars and shimmering veils that swayed in a gentle breeze Laszlo created by working the giant bellows. They also had made a golden throne and scores of pillows, cut from inside the dressing room couches and chairs, and a good deal of Mrs. Basaraba's fabrics. The Persian rugs had been taken from the dressing rooms, too, and swatted till they were as free of dust as they would ever be, and strategically overlapped onstage to obscure their holes and tattered edges. It wasn't a perfect set, but when the painters finished the backdrops—they had decided on a trompe l'oeil of a palace window overlooking a desert oasis—it more than rivaled the old *Little Egypt* show.

Still, Pepper knew they could do better. They had to do better. That was all that was on her mind when she told Matty, "If it's another lawyer, send him away and lock the door. Tell him we'll leave when Robert DeGraaf can prove he's the owner."

"It's not a lawyer, Miss MacClair."

She turned. "Did the ushers finally turn up?"

The two men had disappeared the day before without a word. But the way the boy shifted and dropped his glance told her it was not the ushers, either.

"Who is it then?"

"If you'll pardon me for saying, I think you'll want to see for yourself."

Fifteen

WHEN PEPPER STEPPED INTO THE SCARLET ROOM with Matty on her heels, she could see the visitor as a silhouette against the sunshine slanting in from the open doorway.

It took only a moment to recognize Gregory Creighton.

"Miss MacClair, I hope you aren't angry." Matty sounded apologetic, almost fearful.

"I'm not angry." She was too stunned to be angry.

"Hello, Pepper."

How strange Gregory sounded. So unsure and unlike himself. She wished she could see his face.

"Good bit of ink you've got here." He lifted a newspaper he held folded in one hand. "Ziegfeld's protégé now, huh?"

"Ziegfeld's what?" She crossed the floor with her

hand out to see what he was talking about. When she could finally see him, all of him, it nearly derailed her again. He wore new wool trousers with a crisp white shirt, a light checked coat, and a small tuft of silk at his collar. His hair was slicked back, and it was shorter. Distinctly shorter. He looked . . . respectable.

"New clothes," he said, shifting under her scrutiny. He handed her the *Tribune*.

It was more than the clothes. This was not the same man who had left the theater the week before. She took the paper and saw the headline: *Ziegfeld Cheers Chance Rebels.*

Chance rebels? She scanned the article, mostly quotes from Ziegfeld. According to the writer, Ziegfeld had taken pity on The Chance's struggling band of players and workers and was lending his considerable expertise (Ziegfeld's words) to their fight against a greedy heir to hold one last show, a final tribute to their downtrodden theater. Not everything in the article was true, but as she knew, the truth was never Ziegfeld's primary concern.

She glanced up when she reached the article's end, and their eyes connected. "This is why you came back?"

Matty took two quick steps backward. "I'll just lock up here and see if Miss Charmaigne needs anything."

Neither Pepper nor Gregory paid any attention to him as he took the key to the lock and disappeared through the auditorium doors.

"It's not why I came back. I want to help, if you want my help."

"Why did you leave? Without even saying good-bye, without telling anyone where you were going. You just left."

Gregory's face twitched. He started to speak but stopped. Finally, he tipped his finger at the article. "It says your fight's with Robert DeGraaf. Is that true?"

What did that have to do with anything? "He wants to sell the theater as soon as it's his, sooner if he can manage it. And he's kicking us out."

"That's what this show is about? To change his mind?"

After everything Robert had said of the theater, everything he had said to her? She shook her head. "We're doing it for the theater. And I suppose we're doing it for ourselves. We want people to remember The Chance as a proud stage, not what it's been the last couple of years."

"So you've broken with him?"

"Yes, of course I've broken with him. Is that what you want to hear? That I was foolish and wrong and that you were right all along?"

"I don't think you were foolish."

How could he stand there so calmly? She was angry now, and the longer they stood, the more furious she became. She wanted to scream or cry, or both. And still he stood there, unfazed. How could he? She was thinking she could make him hurt just as he had hurt her when she whipped back her hand and aimed it for his freshly shaved cheek.

He grabbed her by the wrist, and held it, midstrike, staring into her eyes, watching her pant and huff. She speared him with her glance, daring him to say a word.

But he did not. Instead he pulled her closer, still gripping her arm with one hand and encircling her waist with the other. She could feel his breath. Coffee, oranges, and turpentine, or something just as pungent, mingled with the warm, woodsy fragrance that was his alone. His dark eyes stared into hers, searching for resistance.

There was none.

When she did not pull away, he loosened his grip and let his hands slide down the length of her sleeve, from her elbow to the shoulder and down the side of her, his fingertips pressing against the corset beneath her shirtwaist.

If he bent even a little, he could kiss her. But he didn't. Why was he waiting? But then she realized. She rose on her tiptoes, wrapped her arms around his neck and met his lips with her own. Their first kiss had been an accident, something thrust upon them by a stranger. This was no accident. They entered into it equally and completely.

Even when the kiss ended, neither pulled away. They stood there in the Scarlet Room, embracing each other. All the years played back like a flicker. Pepper saw it all differently now. "You knew, didn't you, about Robert. You knew Mr. DeGraaf didn't send him back to school. He fled all on his own, didn't he?"

"I knew," he whispered, and ran his thumb over the soft rise of her cheek.

"Why didn't you tell me?" That old shame returned, clawing its way into this happy moment.

"It seemed easier for you. I didn't want to cause you more pain."

They had never spoken of that day, but there were words she had to say to him. Words she should have said then, but had been afraid. "I know I made the worst kind of mistake. I know I disappointed you."

He pushed back. "Disappointed?"

"I thought he loved me. I thought he wanted to marry me. It sounds naïve now, but I believed him." She paused, so ashamed she could hardly continue. "I know what it makes me, though. If I'm not with Robert, I'm ruined."

"No, not ruined, not to me."

Yet he pulled away. She could see the darkness gathering on

Gregory's face, and she wanted to make him understand how sorry she was. Maybe it did not matter, but she wanted him to know how much she regretted what she had done. "If I could go back and do things differently, I would. I would change it all." How she missed the old days, when he looked at her with admiration and pride. When she lost his respect, she had lost her own.

He closed himself to her. He paced and retreated into his darkness. She wanted him to understand, but words seemed so futile now.

Several strides away, he turned. "Don't you see? I should have stopped it. I should have protected you from that." His eyes found the door, the ceiling, the black spot in the carpeting beside his toe that no amount of scrubbing could remove. "I should have protected you from him." He dropped his head back and closed his eyes, as if he were seeing it all again. "I was jealous, and I hated myself for it. I had no claim on you; I had no right. And then I saw you with him on the roof. I knew what he had done to you, and I wanted to beg you to forgive me, but what good would it have done? I should have warned you. I should have done something, but it was too late. I failed you."

Pepper leaped from the bench and went to Gregory, took his hand and forced him to look at her. "You never failed me. It was my own doing. But you changed. You would not . . ." Her voice caught. "You would not even look at me. I knew you hated me because I had disappointed you." Just as she had disappointed her mother. And herself. She had disappointed everyone.

He took her shoulders and squeezed. "I did not hate you. I hated myself." He buried her in an embrace.

"Then why did you leave?" she whispered into his shoulder.

He pulled back to look at her. "I could not be here if you were with him."

She could see that now. She pulled him to the cushioned bench. "Why did you never say anything?"

"What could I say?"

"You could say, 'Do not love Robert DeGraaf, he is rotten and terrible and selfish—' " She stopped. Gregory was shaking his head.

"No one could tell you that."

"You should have said it." She tipped her chin, defiant. "Where did you go?"

He looked down. Had he defected to the Hippodrome, too? They had heard the night before from McManus that that was where Stanley had gone. A job he had been courting for weeks, it turned out.

"I took a position at Edison's moving picture studio," he said. "Training to work a camera and processing the photographs. It's not vaudeville, I know, but it suits me, and there's a future there."

She glanced around at the Scarlet Room. Even swept and polished, the wood oiled and the glass cleaned, it was still shabby. It hardly rivaled the Broadway or any of the new playhouses uptown. "I'm glad for you."

He took her hands. "I can take care of you now, Pepper. I want you to come with me. Not right now. I know you will finish what you've started here. But after?"

She had not considered what would come after the show, after Saturday. There had not been time. And she had been afraid. She was still afraid. She started to speak, but he stopped her.

"Don't tell me now," he said. "Think about it."

Had her hesitation hurt his feelings? He was closing off again, so it was impossible to know.

He rose and held out his hand to help her up. "We should get inside. I'm sure they're waiting." When her hand was in his, he closed his fingers and squeezed.

"But Edison's studio? Won't they be expecting you?"

"Not for a while. I told them I have a show to do."

• • •

THE NEXT MORNING, PEPPER TOOK MRS. CECIL'S GOWN OUT OF the box for the third time in an hour and held it over her nightdress. Where could she ever wear such a thing? It would be silly to keep it. Selfish, even. She should return it. Whatever Mrs. Cecil gave her could pay for something Mrs. Basaraba could use toward a proper Scheherazade costume.

If she intended to do it, however, she had to do it quickly. Rehearsals would be underway within the hour, and Mrs. Basaraba would need time.

With resolve, Pepper returned the gown to its box, along with the hair feather and the gloves. She hoped Mrs. Cecil would not dock too much for the missing stockings and shoes.

A half hour later, when she pressed the buzzer, young Anne with her giant white bow answered. She left Pepper at the door to inquire if Mrs. Cecil would see her.

"No returns," was the message Mrs. Cecil sent back with her daughter.

"But it's in perfect condition. And I'm not looking for full compensation, but perhaps something?"

The young girl left, only to return with a more emphatic message that made her wince to convey: "Absolutely no returns, miss."

Pepper retreated, dazed. She had not expected much, but she had expected something. She was still stunned by the outright refusal when she returned to the theater to find Matty and Gregory in heated conversation under the marquee. They did not notice her until she was nearly upon them.

Gregory saw her first and spoke loudly, to drown out Matty's words. "Miss MacClair, hello, good morning. This is a surprise. Let me help you with that."

As he moved to relieve her of the giant box, there was a tenderness in his look that eased some of the morning's disappointment. Still, she tightened her arms around her package. "I can manage, thank you. But I know that look. You're up to something. What is it?"

Gregory pretended to be surprised by her accusation.

Matty, however, was not so skilled at obfuscation. He appealed to Gregory: "We should ask her. Where is the harm in asking?"

"Ask me what?"

Gregory shook his head, but Matty paid no mind. He turned to Pepper. "It's Miss Small. She wants to come back. Can she come back?"

"What happened to her show?"

Matty's face twisted. "They played two nights down on Park Row, and then Beatrice's fella disappeared. Turns out it was a swindle from the start. He took off with everything."

"I'm sorry to hear that." And she was. Trixie deserved better.

"You've been after Marvani to add a girl. Miss Small could do it. She wants to."

Gregory had been staring off, up Broadway, into the cotton-candy clouds parked over Wanamaker's and Grace Church. "Tell her all of it."

Matty kicked the ground. "Miss Pennington wants back in, too."

She nearly dropped her box. In all the madness of the past

week, one small consolation was being free of that woman. "Why? She despised this place."

"They've auditioned everywhere, but nothing is panning out. They need a break."

"Why here? We can't pay them. Why on earth would they want to come back?"

"The show has a buzz. Beatrice thinks if they can get in, they can move up to something better when it's done. Miss MacClair, they don't have anything else. Miss Small has been staying with me"—the sudden look on his face told her he had not meant to divulge that—"because she can't pay her rent. She's been dodging her landlord for a month."

"They've hardly been gone a week."

He shrugged.

She had hoped to have seen the last of Beatrice, but she could not do that to Trixie. And the fact was, they did need girls. She sighed. "Tell them to report to rehearsal at six and they can have Bart's old room. We'll get them started after the dinner break."

He was still beaming when she left to check on the rehearsals getting under way inside. She found Em standing atop a wooden crate with Mrs. Basaraba hunched around her ankles taking measurements, and all the players gathered around for instructions on the final number, which Em had choreographed as a big dance bit with every player onstage.

When Em finished and the players went about their business, Em motioned Pepper over. Mrs. Basaraba was on her knees, marking the hem on a pair of silky white pants.

"What is that?" Em gestured to the box Pepper had left at the edge of the stage.

"The gown Mrs. Cecil made for me."

Before Em got the wrong idea, she added, "I tried to take it back. I thought she'd give me something for it, something we could put toward a Scheherazade costume. But she wouldn't even see me."

Mrs. Basaraba's head perked. "May I see it?"

Pepper retrieved the box. She pulled out the garment and held it by the sapphire velvet shoulders. The rhinestones and golden embroidery shimmered under the stage lights.

Mrs. Basaraba's hand went to her mouth. "It's so beautiful."

"Tough break." Em grinned. "You must be a little glad you don't have to part with it, though."

"It's the finest gown I have ever owned, but I have no use for it. And it's a reminder of something I'd just as soon forget." She glanced into the wings, where Gregory was showing Matty how to help Laszlo with the ropes.

Gregory caught her look and winked.

"The way you two carry on, making your lovey-dovey faces, it's a wonder you can concentrate on the show at all."

Mrs. Basaraba tried to smother her giggle with her hand. "I'm done with the measuring. If you'll excuse me." She hurried off the stage toward the stairs to get back to her workroom.

Pepper ignored them both. She knew they were teasing. They were both pleased by the match.

"What I came to tell you," Pepper said, "is that I've made a decision. A stage management decision."

"Oh?" Em stepped down from the crate.

"I have invited Beatrice and Trixie to rejoin the show."

Em spun around to face her. "You did?"

"Marvani needs an assistant and Trixie will be a good one."

"Agreed. But Beatrice?"

Yes, that was the problem. Where could she put Beatrice? The show needed harem girls, but it was not likely Beatrice would ever agree to a background role. She would demand something grand and preferably with a dance solo. "I haven't decided that yet."

"You know what role she'll want."

Pepper was very well aware. "She can want it all she likes, but she cannot have it. Scheherazade is mine. I'm not giving it away, and certainly not to her."

Em gave Pepper's shoulder a friendly, proud squeeze. "That's my girl."

• • •

PEPPER WAS RIGHT ABOUT BEATRICE WANTING TO BE SCHEHErazade. When Matty ushered the two women into the theater after the break, Trixie could not have looked happier to be there. She gushed over everything. How great the theater looked since they had cleaned it up, and the auditorium. And she gushed over Matty, who had clearly replaced Gregory as the object of her affection.

Beatrice, however, was another matter. She was guarded and aloof. And when Pepper asked what role she thought she might play, she said, "I think it's obvious, don't you? Who really believes you could be Scheherazade?"

Was it possible that in her short absence, the woman had become even more irritating?

Pepper could see Em and Gregory both itching to come to her defense. She smiled and reminded herself that they needed girls—and it was not likely they would find any others who could pick up a routine quickly or be willing to work for free. Beatrice would give her two days of grief, and then she would be gone for good.

"We're thinking a three-minute solo wedged between the dog act and the Helzigs. A combination of a traditional routine spiced up with some of Little Egypt's old moves. I need to meet with Sneed, so perhaps you and Em can go up to the rehearsal room and get started. I'll be up when I'm finished and we can go over some of the new steps."

Beatrice's mouth gaped, just as Pepper had expected it would. The woman had not expected to take instruction from Pepper. That the prospect seemed to pain her was at least one small vindication.

• • •

"I HAVE AN IDEA FOR SCHEHERAZADE'S COSTUME."

Mrs. Basaraba's announcement was the best news Pepper had heard all morning. It was already the day before the show, and it was beginning to seem possible that Scheherazade would have nothing special to wear. But Mrs. Basaraba had come through, just as Pepper knew she would.

Except the woman would not look up from her worktable. And she was fidgeting with the measurement stick.

Pepper glanced around the wardrobe room at the profusion of Arabian-inspired costumes hanging in every nook and corner—a rainbow of pantaloons, vests, and wide circle skirts. It was a Cairo street bazaar in here, but there was nothing that had the grandeur of a Scheherazade costume. "Are you hiding it?"

"I have only sketches, but what do you think of these fabrics?" Under her hand was a small pile of rich silks and satins. "Imagine a snug coat in the cranberry and gold silk over a bodice, with embroidery and beading here"—she indicated a panel across the chest and along the sides of the coat—"with a pair of golden pantaloons beneath a wide indigo skirt that switches around to become plum. Each piece independent and reversible to be easily changed throughout the show to suggest the passage of days."

Pepper could envision it perfectly, and it was marvelous, but—how could she say this without insulting Mrs. Basaraba? "Beading and embroidery require so much time," she began cautiously. "The show is tomorrow night."

Mrs. Basaraba was staring at the pile, frowning. "It is why it is only an idea. You see"—she paused and flipped up the cranberry silk, and then the gold—"it would be possible, if the embellishment could be appliquéd, perhaps. You see, I was thinking that, if you were not opposed . . ." Again she paused. Then tentatively, "Mrs. Cecil's gown has such exquisite detail."

"My gown?"

Mrs. Basaraba glanced up. "Yes, your gown."

• • •

THE FINISHED COSTUME WAS MORE MAGNIFICENT THAN ANYthing Pepper could have imagined. The velvet was carefully cut and reassembled as a snug bodice, and the cream sheath became sumptuous trim for the coat. When Pepper saw it completed, she hardly recognized the original. Mrs. B's creation had the whole jewelry box of colors: sapphire, cranberry, persimmon, and gold. It was marvelous, and Pepper told the wardrobe mistress so.

"Mrs. Cecil would curse me for what I have done to her gown," Mrs. B said, but there was not an ounce of regret in that proud grin.

Pepper ran a finger along the soft sleeve. "It's more glorious than anything Little Egypt ever wore."

Mrs. Basaraba came up beside her and wrapped a tender arm around her waist. "I did it for you, bubbeleh. You were my muse."

Pepper dropped her arm around the woman's small shoulders. "Thank you. And not just for this. For everything." She pulled away. The day was passing much too quickly, and there was still so much to do. "If anyone comes looking for me, tell them I'll be back by noon. No later."

When she reached the Broadway, the stage door guard did little more than tip his cap as she breezed by. He was used to seeing her now, and she no longer needed his help to navigate the labyrinth of passageways. She found her way easily to the theater's back row, where she knew Ziegfeld would be at this hour. On the stage below, the girls, a full stage of them, were learning a new choreography that required them to break apart and come together in complicated formations.

"Miss MacClair," he said in his relaxed, genial way when she dropped into the seat beside him. "So lovely to see you again."

This was only her third visit, but he seemed to have expected her.

"So I'm your protégé now?"

"The reporter enjoyed that immensely." He chuckled. "I knew he would use it. But you cannot blame me, you know. The publicity was irresistible."

"I don't blame you."

"Then to what do I owe the pleasure?"

"Our dress rehearsal is tonight."

"And that concerns you?"

She dropped her face into her palms and rubbed her eyes. Every inch of her was weary. All day she had worked with the acts, and seen to the details of the show, and only had time to rehearse her own numbers when everyone else had turned in for the night. "There's still so much to do. How do you know if you're ready?"

"There will always be more to do, my dear. If you care at all about what you are putting on that stage, you will never feel completely ready. You must do the best you can in the moment. Be sure the players have what they need. Be sure everyone backstage has clear instruction. Beyond that, just let them see your passion. It will inspire them. Apathy is the true enemy of any artistic venture, not nerves or lack of preparation."

They were silent for a moment. Then for the first time since she had arrived, his eyes moved from the stage and rested solely and completely upon her. "Tomorrow," he said, "I wonder if you might keep a seat for me. I might like to see this show of yours."

• • •

THE DRESS REHEARSAL WAS NOT GOING WELL, AND PEPPER HAD no one to blame but herself.

Half the set pieces seemed to be missing, though no one could account for them or even seemed to notice. But that was not the worst problem. She was. She had botched the Helzigs' cue because she had been whispering instructions to Matty in the wings, and then she had missed her own cue for the duet with Em while she tried to remind Laszlo to get the bellows in position for the next act.

No one said anything, but she could see the worry in everyone's eyes. Everyone but Beatrice. The woman did not even try to mask her delight in Pepper's failing. It fueled Pepper's resolve to do better, but the truth was, she was already doing the best she could.

When the final dance number ended and Em belted out the last lines of her song, everyone came onto the stage in two lines for the big bow. Pepper, in the front, broke from her line and waved her hands over her head. "Stop. No bows, not until the performance. It's bad luck. But bravo! It was wonderful. You were all wonderful."

They had been, and they were proud of what they had done, despite her mistakes. Even Beatrice was smiling. They were all so busy congratulating each other that they did not hear Pepper trying to get their attention once again.

She pulled out a chair from the wings and stood upon it, waved her arms, and yelled as loudly as she could: "Let me say something!"

The chatter stopped. Heads turned. Even Old Jake, Laszlo, and Matty poked their heads out from behind the curtain.

"I expect I will not have a chance to get you all together tomorrow," she began, "so I want to tell you how much I appreciate the work you have done and the time you have put in to make this show happen. I know it was a lot, but in less than a week, we dreamed up a show from scratch.

"Let them call us fools or misfits or deviants or even rebels. This show proves we are professionals who can put on a damn fine show." The last word caught in her throat. She did not want to become emotional, but she was having a difficult time avoiding it. When she saw Em wipe her eye, she nearly lost what was left of her composure.

Thankfully, Em came to the rescue. "Oh, shut up, will you? Let's get over to Annabelle's. The first round is on me."

Everyone laughed, which at the moment was the perfect thing.

Pepper caught a tear with her finger and smiled. "I'll be along in a little while."

• • •

PEPPER HAD BEEN SITTING IN A NINTH-ROW SEAT, IN THE SHADows, for a quarter of an hour when Gregory strolled up the aisle and dropped into the seat beside her. "Why the frown?" he asked. "The show is in fine shape."

He rested his elbow on the wooden arm between them. On

the stage down front, Old Jake was pushing a broom across the boards and someone offstage was pulling backdrops to the flies, but Pepper felt sheltered in the auditorium's darkness. She leaned her head on his shoulder. "No, I'm afraid it isn't. I've made sure of that."

He rubbed his cheek against her hair. "You are being too hard on yourself."

"I fear I haven't been hard enough. I will hate myself if I'm the reason the show flops."

"Nothing will flop. But if it would make you feel better, you could let Matty handle the stage. The boy's bright. He can handle one night."

She nodded. It was clear to her, as she was sure it was clear to Gregory and everyone else, that she could not both perform and manage the stage. Tomorrow night would be a disaster if she tried.

"I only want everyone to be able to leave this place with their heads held high."

"I know." He touched her hand.

"Would it be terrible to admit that I'm also looking forward to putting this show behind us?"

"No, not terrible. But aren't you being missed about now? Em and the others must be wondering where you are."

"I can't face them, not tonight. Would you stay with me?"

He answered by draping his arm over her shoulders. It felt good to be there in the dark and the quiet, just the two of them. They had so little time alone. Though he had moved back into his old room temporarily, it had hardly mattered. These past couple of days they had returned to the Lair so late, it was impossible to spend time together. He would kiss her at her door, and then she would go into her room and he into his. The only time they spent alone, it seemed, was dinner. Last night they had shared sandwiches in the rehearsal room, looking out the windows over Broadway, and it had been lovely. The best part of the day.

He must have read her mind. "Should I ask McManus to send something over? Another roast beef sandwich?"

"Open face with gravy?"

"Whatever you like."

"I would like that very much." She nuzzled in closer, the top of her head nudging against his cheek.

He shot up and shook out his legs. "None of that now. Not if I have to run over to Annabelle's."

She giggled. "Spoilsport."

"Meet you in the rehearsal room in half an hour?"

"Good. Gives me time to change out of this costume." She stood and looked down at the shimmering cranberry coat, the golden skirt. "Mrs. Basaraba will have my hide if I drip gravy on any of this beautiful work."

• • •

GREGORY WAS NOT IN THE REHEARSAL ROOM. WHEN SHE ARrived, she found a note tacked to the door. "Dinner on the roof."

The roof? She had not been up there since that awful afternoon. It was the last place she wanted to go. She did not want to think about Robert or that scratchy blanket or any of it. Especially not tonight.

But when she opened the door to that wide-open space where The Chance Theatre ended and the nighttime sky began, she saw that Gregory had gotten her far more than a roast beef sandwich with gravy.

She stepped out to see a legion of tiny oil lamps, a scattering of oriental rugs, fabric billowing from pipe frames created for the harem set pieces, and a profusion of shimmering, comfy pillows. All the set dressing that had been missing from the dress rehearsal. And at the center of this special production, a small round table set for dinner with two chairs and an ice stand with champagne chilling to the side.

The staging was beautiful, but the best part was Gregory, standing in front of it all, under the half moon with the rooftops behind him, watching her, waiting for her reaction.

She had no idea what to say. What she heard leave her lips was, "How did you get permission to use all this?"

Gregory cocked his head. "What makes you think I asked?"

And there he was: that playful, amazing boy who had been her best friend. The boy who had always seen the best in her. The boy who had grown into the man she loved.

Sixteen

PEPPER WAS UP AND DRESSED AT DAWN, AND standing in front of Bart's old door shortly thereafter. She rapped softly.

"Go away." The woman sounded as if she were speaking into her pillow.

"Beatrice, I need to speak to you."

"Sleeping. Come back . . ." The last words were lost in the muffle.

Pepper tried the knob and, finding it unlocked, let herself inside. It was bold and improper, she knew, but she had been up all night thinking about this and she was not going to wait another moment. In the dim light from the corridor, she searched the room until she found a candle on a small table. She lighted it.

The single room still looked much as Bart had left it. Besides the table and a single chair, there was a shelf upon the wall holding a tin of biscuits, a bag of peanuts, and a half-full bottle of what looked like whiskey. A chest of drawers and the slender bed were pushed against the wall, where Beatrice lay somewhere beneath that pile of blankets.

Pepper pulled the chair up to the bed. "Beatrice," she whispered. "I have to ask you something."

The woman pulled the pillow from her face and her grimace made her displeasure clear. "Now?"

"I want you to take over as Scheherazade."

Beatrice dropped the pillow and sat up. "You're giving me Scheherazade? Why?"

Pepper clenched her teeth. She had made the decision while lying in her bed beside Gregory. While he lay sleeping, she considered doing as he said and turning over the stage management to Matty. The boy was bright. He could certainly do a passable job. But she was good, she knew it. It came naturally to her. Dancing had been her dream, but despite all her practice and all her hard work, she knew she would never be as good as Beatrice. Just as she knew no one would run the show better than she would.

As much as it pained her to admit it, she was not the best dancer for the job. She was the best stage manager. And as the best stage manager, she knew the best dancer was the woman in front of her, fighting her way out from under her bedcovers and scowling at this early intrusion. "What are you up to, MacClair?"

It took every ounce of Pepper's resolve not to back down. "Do you want the part, or not?"

"Don't be stupid. Of course I want it."

• • •

PEPPER SAT IN HER USUAL WOODEN CHAIR IN THE WINGS, HEAD bent over her notebook, pretending to be absorbed in the hefty list of details that still needed attention before the show began. What she was really doing was taking deep breaths, fighting back the dark hole that threatened to engulf her. Somehow, after checking in on the rehearsal room, where Em was coaching Beatrice through the Scheherazade choreography and the lines, and then on to Mrs. Basaraba in Wardrobe, and then back to the stage to be sure Matty had chalked the marks where the set pieces would be placed, she had let her gaze drift out to the auditorium.

That was when the doubts came crashing in. Were they ready? Could they pull this off? Would anyone come?

The lights went fuzzy and her chest fluttered. She could feel the floor beneath her begin to sway.

"Tell her, go on, tell her."

Her head popped up. It was Old Jake, and he was dragging Laszlo by the arm. Laszlo dodged her glance.

Something was wrong. She knew it in an instant.

"Tell her what you told me." Old Jake gave him a warning look.

Laszlo stared at the floor.

Frustrated, Old Jake spoke for the man. "He was out front replacing some marquee bulbs when a carriage stopped in front of the theater. Men got out and one of them was Robert DeGraaf." He bumped Laszlo at the elbow. "Tell her that's who you saw, Robert DeGraaf."

Laszlo nodded.

Pepper was not surprised. She had expected that Robert would try to do something, but she had expected it before now. What did he think he was going to do? In another hour, the doors would open. "Are they outside?"

"Yes, ma'am."

"Then let's see what they want."

She marched up to the front, ignoring the way her stomach tightened with each step. She had not seen Robert since they had parted at the apartment. When she pushed through the front door, she saw what Laszlo had seen: Robert, accompanied by three stout and serious-looking men. All in black bowlers and matching overcoats, they turned at the sound of the door.

How different Robert appeared to her now. Still the same angle of the jaw, the same oiled hair, the same green eyes. He was still handsome in his tailored suit, but he no longer made her heart race. She no longer yearned to be wrapped in those arms. The look he turned on her was hard and unfeeling, with no memory of the tenderness that had once existed between them.

"You're too early for the show, Mr. DeGraaf," Pepper said by way of greeting. "But if you like, we'll be happy to reserve seats for you and your colleagues."

"We do not require seats, Miss MacClair, because there will be no show. You are violating my notice to vacate. I suppose it's no surprise there's no mention of that in this publicity rag." He waved a copy of *Variety* at her.

She pretended to be shocked. "I don't know what you're talking about. Have they published something about us?"

Since Wednesday, each of the theater periodicals had dedicated ink to The Chance and its plight, as had a fair number of the daily newspapers. The latest *Variety* had come out only that morning, and though she had not seen it, she had expected those folks would write something. After that last bad notice, she only hoped it would not be more of the same.

Robert's expression gave her hope. By the look of it, it did not favor him. His face blazed redder than she had ever seen it.

"I've had these snippy stories hounding me all week, but this? It stops here." He crumpled the issue and threw it at her feet.

She picked it up. It was open to a page with a headline that read, *Chance Rebels Stage Coup Against DeGraaf Heir's Greed.* She glanced up. "*DeGraaf Heir's Greed.* It has a nice ring, doesn't it?"

How delightful it was to watch him squirm.

"You won't think so when tomorrow's headline reads, *Rebels Shown for Criminals They Are,* or *Chance Rebels Tossed in Jail for Holding Theater Hostage.*"

He was sputtering, and she had to look away so he did not see her grin. When she composed herself, she said, "I hardly think the editors would use either of those. They don't have the same appeal."

She had pushed him too far. He rounded on the men who had loitered behind him and shot his finger to the door. "I want you to clear it out and shut it down. Now."

"You have no authority here."

Pepper turned. She had not heard Gregory come up behind her, but here he was in his old overalls and white linen shirt rolled to the elbows. His arms folded over his chest. And not just Gregory, but Old Jake and Laszlo, and Matty, too.

"These lawyers say I do," Robert shot back.

Gregory did not back down. "You will not bully Miss MacClair or anyone else associated with this theater. We'll have our show, and then you'll have your building. If you know what's good for you, you'll see that this is your best option."

Robert's glance darted between Gregory and Pepper and back again. Understanding dawned upon him. "So you've done it, have you? You've claimed her. I suppose that means you've told her everything?"

In the whole history of that word, it had never conveyed the malice it did now.

Gregory stepped forward, eclipsing Pepper. "That is between us. It has nothing to do with you or your lawyers."

Robert's lip curled as he walked to within an inch of Gregory's face. "Doesn't it? Until you're off my property, I believe it is my business."

"Step back, Robert." Gregory's fists clenched at his sides. His shoulders squared.

Robert, his head angled up to meet Gregory's glare, raised one black-gloved hand and stabbed at Gregory's chest with his index finger. "It's *Mister* DeGraaf to you, stagehand."

Gregory grabbed that hand and in an instant had twisted it behind Robert. With his other hand he revealed the spikes of Mrs. Brewster's brass knuckles, which he made sure Robert could see.

Robert's face drained of color.

Pepper's did as well.

"Gregory, no!" she cried. She could see what he meant to do and she could not allow it.

Gregory glanced at her. There was confusion upon his face, then the creep of shame.

He unwound his arm from Robert's neck, slipped off the knuckles, and dropped them back into his pocket.

Robert straightened and adjusted his coat and hat. "Try that again, cretin, and I'll have you tossed in the Tombs. But then, that would be something of a family reunion for you, wouldn't it?" He paused, and watched Pepper. "He has told you about his father, hasn't he, Miss MacClair?" He turned back to Gregory, a hint of a smile upon his lips. "Are you still trying to keep those awful family secrets? Yes, I'd say you are. I can see it on your miserable face." He clucked and shook his head. "Cretin, you didn't expect to keep something like that a secret forever, did you?

Gregory wasn't paying attention to Robert. He was watching Pepper.

She was staring back at him, her eyes wide with questions. "What's he talking about, Gregory? What secrets?"

Gregory ran his fingers through his hair, pain and confusion etched on his face. He turned and stormed off.

Pepper watched with the others as he left and yanked open the door to Abernathy's. She yearned to run after him, but she could not leave. She could not risk letting Robert inside.

When Gregory had disappeared, she turned back to Robert and with her hatred at a boiling point, she sneered at him. "After everything your father has done for you, after everything he gave you, you want to ruin the only good thing he left in this world? This is the legacy you want for him?"

"He's gone. I have my own future to consider."

"Have you ever cared about anyone but yourself? If I'd had even half of what you've squandered . . ."

But she could not say more. Another carriage came to a stop in front of the theater and a man in a tan wool topcoat emerged. He paused, scribbled something in a notebook he pulled from his pocket, then approached the gathering. "I hope I'm not interrupting. *Variety* sent me. I'm looking for Miss Pepper MacClair."

Pepper glanced at Old Jake, and he stepped forward. "And what do you want with her?"

"An interview, if she has a moment."

To Old Jake, she made a motion with her eyes toward the Scarlet Room.

Old Jake approached the man and put out his arm to lead him toward the door. "I may know where to find her. Come with me."

When they had disappeared inside the theater, Pepper turned to Robert. In a low and measured voice, she said, "If you leave now, I won't tell him you came here to bully us. If you would prefer I explain it in detail I'm sure I could provide plenty of fodder for another fascinating article."

Robert turned to his lawyers. "I am not paying you to stand there. Do something."

They looked at each other with blank, confused faces. One stepped forward. "We cannot prevent her from speaking to a journalist. Of course if it turns out what she says is false, our recourse is to file a claim of slander, and the penalty—"

"Oh, shut up," Robert said, his patience, his confidence, his composure, all of it lost. "I want something done now. Right now!"

Pepper knew she was getting the better of him. "I could tell this man why you're here, or I could tell him you're here to wish us well and that we have come to an amicable understanding. You may not care about this theater, but you seem to care about your reputation. What do you say?"

Robert dropped his head back. Then he chuckled, a mean, hateful sound that rumbled through him. "Seems we have attracted quite an audience."

Pepper followed his gaze and saw the faces peering out the third-floor windows. Everyone who had been inside the theater seemed to be up there, staring down. A movement caught her eye. She turned. Gregory had emerged from Abernathy's, and he was not alone. He had Harry and a handful of burly friends behind him.

Robert shook his head. He could see he was outnumbered. And with the journalist inside, he had no choice. "Fine. You have tonight. But I want you"—he glanced up—"all of you out by tomorrow morning."

Pepper might have agreed and taken it as a victory, but she did not. If he was backing down, it could only mean Em had been right all along. He had no legal right to the theater, not yet.

"We are not going anywhere until your father's will is read and the inheritance is official."

She expected more argument, but Robert only adjusted his hat. "Fine." He was already in his carriage when Gregory came up beside her with his companions.

"Seems Robert didn't want to meet our new ushers," Gregory said, watching Robert's retreat.

Pepper leaned toward Gregory and whispered, "But we can't pay them."

"They'll be paid," he said. "I told them when the show's over, they can have all the liquor still locked up in the bar. It's a couple of cases at least. But only after the show, right, boys?"

There was a hearty round of affirmative acknowledgment.

Gregory pointed at Robert's carriage. "And I hope you all got a good look at that man. If you catch sight of him around here tonight, see that you send him on his way."

• • •

AT THE EDGE OF THE RED CURTAIN, PEPPER WAS COUNTING THE house through the gap she had created between the velvet and the wall. The auditorium was already two-thirds full of spectators eager to get a seat. Ziegfeld was right—all the publicity was paying off. She glanced at the two front-row center seats she had cordoned off with ribbon, the ones with the small *Reserved for Mr. Ziegfeld* sign she had inked herself. Those were still empty, but there was a half hour yet till showtime. Surely he intended to come or he would not have requested a seat.

There was a tap at her shoulder. "Doll, we have a problem."

Em was already in costume, her makeup done and a thin black mustache glued above her lip. She was ready for the stage, a perfect Persian king in a golden coat cut at the knees, white peg-leg pants beneath, and curly-tipped slippers and a turban fixed with a giant center jewel. She appeared calm, which calmed Pepper. She pointed to the curtain. "Have you seen the house? I think we might sell out."

"We aren't selling anything, remember? The show is free."

"But people are here. They want to see it." And it was going to be a grand show. A show that would have made even Mr. DeGraaf proud. If her mother could have seen it, maybe she would have been proud, too.

Em's calm strained.

"What is it?"

"It's Beatrice. I think you should have a look."

They went to the dressing room the Dancing Dolls had once shared and found Beatrice sprawled on the couch, which could not have been comfortable considering the stuffing had been cut out and used to make pillows for the stage. Beatrice was making do with her laundry. She reposed upon wrinkled shirtwaists and skirts, petticoats and drawers, which in itself was not a cause for alarm, but the usually composed Beatrice was in worse shape than the room. Her golden hair hung in hanks where it had come unpinned. And she was not in costume. In fact, she was not wearing much at all. All but a couple of hooks of her corset had come undone so that it gaped about her middle, and her petticoat had been hiked up so far on her thigh that anyone could see the pearly-white skin above her black stocking.

Pepper stared, horrified. "What happened to her?"

"It would seem she has become unreliable." Em went to the dressing table, picked up a bright blue bottle, and waved it at Pepper. "Here's your culprit."

Pepper recognized the bottle. "No. That's just some cure she gets from the apothecary down the street."

"Shiloh's Cough and Consumption Cure is more curse than cure, I'm afraid. It's nothing but liquor and opium, with a bit of prussic acid and chloroform tossed in."

Trixie leaned through the door, fully dressed in her new emerald harem outfit, her hair pinned up, her greasepaints applied. "A party before the show? Why wasn't I invited?"

Then she saw Beatrice on the couch. She pushed by Pepper and Em. "What happened to her?" She took Beatrice's hand and tapped it. "Wake up, Bea, honey, come on, wake up." She looked up, frantic. "What did she do?"

Em wiggled the blue bottle again. "Too much of this, if I were to hazard a guess."

"I told her to leave that bottle alone. I told her it wouldn't help."

"Help what?" Pepper moved closer to see if Beatrice was rousing at all.

Trixie looked down on her friend and tucked a loose curl behind her ear. "She was so happy, you know, when you gave her Scheherazade. And she really wanted to do a good job. She knows how important it is. Just one solo act was all she needed to get to the top, that's what she's always saying, right? Well, now she got it. This is her last chance and she knows it. She said the cure helped ease her mind, helped her cope. She said she needed just a little to get her through."

"Quarter to curtain— Hey, what happened?" Matty craned his neck through the door, trying to get a look at whatever was causing the commotion. "Is Beatrice all right?"

The slow creep of fear was inching up Pepper's spine. She looked to Em. "Can't you do something?"

Em nudged Trixie out of the way and bent down to Beatrice's ear, smoothed her hand over her brow and said softly, "Hey, there, dear. Are you in there?"

Beatrice's eyes fluttered.

"There you are. How are you, dear?"

A euphoric smile spread over Beatrice's face. "Em," she said at last, the syllable lingering on her lips.

"Yes, it's me, dear. How are you feeling?" The words were more insistent, more hopeful.

"Em, Em, Em. Have I ruined everything, Em? Is it all over? Please, tell me it's over."

Em smoothed her brows. "You lie right here, love. Don't you worry about a thing."

Beatrice's eyes fluttered closed again, and a faint snore rose from her.

How could Em treat her so gently? It was all Pepper could do not to take the woman by the shoulders and shake her, a good hard shake to snap her back to her senses.

Em pulled Pepper out to the hallway and left Beatrice to Trixie's ministrations.

"She can't go onstage like that," Em said.

"What can we do? Get her a pot of tea? Coffee? Dunk her in a cold bath?" Pepper's own bathtub would do nicely. Should she head down and run the water, or send Matty?

Em leaned closer and whispered. "You don't understand, she can't go onstage *at all.*"

"She must."

Em shook her head. "You know what I'm going to say next."

Pepper felt her blood drain to her feet. "No. Absolutely not. I can't."

"You have to. Or we don't have a show."

"I'm not prepared." She swallowed hard and bit a fingernail. "I'll ruin everything."

Em brushed off her protests. She was pacing and tapping her

lips with her thumb. "You won't. You're plenty prepared and if you forget anything out there, we'll improvise, you and me."

"You know I can't." If Pepper had steps, she could count. If she at least had that, then maybe. But to improvise? Never.

"Doll, just follow my lead."

• • •

WHEN THE HOUSE LIGHTS DIMMED AND THE STAGE LIGHTS went up, Em sauntered out in front of the first curtain in her Persian king finery to begin the show.

"Well, what have we here?" she cried out to the crowd. "I'd say it's a full house."

She paused for a round of applause.

"Let me say up front how pleased we are to see so many fine faces here at *The Utterly Unauthorized and Entirely Unofficial Last Chance Show.*" She paused for more applause. "What happened to the good old *Vaudeville Stars, Marvels and Delights,* you ask? Well, I'll tell you. For sixteen years—sixteen long and tumultuous and wonderful years—Mr. James P. DeGraaf, the founder of this proud theater, dedicated his life to giving you the very best show he could.

"Perhaps you knew Mr. DeGraaf, perhaps you didn't. Perhaps you even liked him, though I suspect you wouldn't." From the side of her mouth, she added, "Most of us didn't."

There was a tittering of laughter from the auditorium.

"We may not have liked him, but everyone who worked in front of this curtain and behind it respected him. And we listened to him. Because there was never a man who loved theater more. He was hard on us because he wanted the best from us, for his theater and for his *Stars, Marvels and Delights.* He wanted the best for you. So tonight, in his honor, we are going to push ourselves once again, and we are going to give you the kind of show Mr. DeGraaf loved—big and splashy, bright and flashy. That is our tribute to him, and our gift to you.

"So sit back and let us, the whole Chance Theatre family, transport you to a palace in a distant corner of exotic Persia, where you will meet me, the king"—she paused and raised her arms in a pose that earned another round of applause—"and, unless I'm mistaken, it's time to welcome today's bride—" She stopped and looked both directions, then again out of the side of her mouth said, "Don't ask about yesterday's bride. The poor thing went and lost her head, along with, oh, the hundred or so brides who came before her. Don't say anything to Scheherazade, but in the morning she will meet the same fate."

There was a long, low whistle backstage, and then Old Jake and Laszlo raised the red velvet to the flies to reveal the Desert Palace set. Em, with arms folded across her chest, paced in front of what appeared to be a pillared throne room with gauzy fabrics swaying in Laszlo's billowing breeze. A Shorty Shakespearean dressed as a courtly servant entered from stage right and, on bended knee before the king, said, "Scheherazade has arrived, Your Highness."

"Welcome her in. Let's have a look at this vizier's daughter."

Frankie commenced his version of Nikolai Rimsky-Korsakov's *Scheherazade,* enthralling the audience with the serpentine melody. Pepper felt a jab in her back ribs.

"That's your cue," Trixie whispered harshly in her ear.

The reminder gave Pepper a start. She had been so caught up in Em's introduction and in making sure the Shakespearean and Frankie hit their marks that she had forgotten she was next up. She ran her fingers down the sides of her coat to be sure the costume was in order, checked that the bodice sat in its proper place and that the gauzy gold drape spilling from the upsweep of her hair unfurled as it should over her shoulder. She breathed deep, glanced up at the Cardinal Rules of the Stage, and repeated her fifth one to herself: *Don't think, just dance.* She kissed her fingertips, tapped the glass, and stepped out onto the stage.

She was not bursting with confidence as she strode out into the glare of the footlights, but she did her best to look as though she were. And she danced her solo, all the steps she could remember, and when she faltered—and she did, but only for a moment—she smiled harder and looked to Em, and the warm, supportive smile she saw on her friend's face helped put her back on course.

When the little voice inside tried to tell her that all those faces out in the auditorium could see she did not belong there, she ignored it. And it helped when she saw Trixie and Matty, holding hands in the wings, cheering her on, and Mrs. Basaraba and Old Jake. Her friends, her family, helping her through.

Everyone was there but Gregory. He had avoided her after Robert had left, and still there was no sign of him. But she could not think of that now. There were too many smiles. She could not hold on to that worry, and she could not even muster any anger when she looked into the dark haze beyond the footlights and saw a young couple brazenly pull away her *Reserved* sign and settle themselves into Ziegfeld's seats. If he were coming, he would have been there by now.

And then her solo was over and her arm was threaded through Em's, and Em was speaking again, urging Scheherazade to join her in a cozy palace nook.

It was Pepper's next cue.

"But Your Highness," Pepper said in a strong voice that began in the depth of her belly. She went on to introduce her special wedding-night gift: a display of physical and vocal skill by a singing juggler whom she beckoned with three regal claps. Then Jimmy appeared in full Bedouin attire.

Em took her place upon the throne and Pepper upon a nest of jewel-colored cushions alongside, and she whispered in a way that would appear to the audience to be friendly banter with the king but was in truth instructions to Matty, who sat crouched on the other side of the backdrop, listening.

"Sneed and the dachshunds, are they ready?"

Two knocks on the floor indicated yes.

"Make sure Marvani and Trixie are ready as soon as the dogs are onstage. And be sure Alfred's coattails are not tucked up in his trousers."

Another two knocks, then a scuffling as he hurried off to do her bidding.

When Jimmy had given his bow, Scheherazade announced to the king that she had another special gift, an even grander entertainment, but alas, he would miss it because dawn approached. At that, thanks to Gregory's clever rigging, a light shone against the oasis backdrop speckled with stars in such a way that it created the illusion of first light. The king, tantalized by this missed opportunity, begged Scheherazade to present her gift the following night.

"If that is your wish," Pepper said, fluttering her eyes in the exaggerated way Em had taught her.

And so the production went, with each new entertainment ending with a promise of something grander and more spectacular—the trained dogs who performed tricks of agility, a magical snake charmer and his beautiful assistant, a comedy skit between dim-witted desert raiders, tiny minstrels who performed a pantomime of *Ali Baba and the Forty Thieves,* and an enlightening survey of the beautiful and exotic women of the indigenous

Southeast Asian tribes. After each one, the king extended Scheherazade's life for another day, and between acts, Mrs. Basaraba's laundry girl, outfitted in harem garb, crossed the stage in long strides, tearing off days and months at a time from the oversize calendar prop she held.

And on it went until Scheherazade was forced to confess she had no more entertainment to present. By then, however, the king was smitten and Scheherazade's life was saved. He serenaded her with a love song and a waltz, culminating in a palace celebration that brought every performer to the stage.

At the end, Pepper could hardly believe they had gotten through it, but they had, and the audience was on its feet. It was almost more than Pepper could bear. The whole night had passed so quickly, too quickly. She did not want it to end. Mr. DeGraaf would be proud, she told herself. And her mother would be, too. If only Ziegfeld had seen it.

When they made their way to the wings, Em grabbed her. "You were wonderful, doll, wonderful! But get back out there. The crowd wants another bow."

That night there were five bows. And through it all, Pepper could see the *Variety* scribe writing in that notebook of his. She felt good. She felt happy. She felt exhausted.

In the wings, the pop of champagne corks punctuated the din of cheers and laughter. But where was Gregory?

"Star material. Definitely star material."

"I couldn't agree more."

Pepper spun around. It was Ziegfeld, with Em at his shoulder. He was dressed in full tuxedo, with top hat and walking stick.

"Look who I found wandering around our place for a change."

"Mr. Ziegfeld, I didn't think you had come." Pepper nearly stumbled over her words in her rush to get them out.

"That hefty usher of yours told me of the front-row seat you reserved, my dear, but I preferred to find something less obtrusive in the back. I was fortunate enough to find a young couple willing to exchange with me."

Instantly Pepper regretted the harsh things she had thought of that couple.

"Quite an enjoyable production," he added. "The duet between you and Miss Charmaigne struck me as a tad familiar, however."

"Don't blame her for that," Em piped in. "That was my doing."

But his grimace was already replaced by a smile. "Imitation may be the sincerest form of flattery, but it's also good for publicity. If you would, please be sure to mention your inspiration to that writer fellow."

"Of course," Em said quickly. "It was the plan all along."

"My hat's off to you and your colleagues. In fact, I'm relieved to know it's a one-night show. I wouldn't want my *Follies* to have to compete with you. That belly dancing, especially, was quite something. Should you ever decide to expand your horizons, I wouldn't mind adding a bit of that to my show."

"Thank you," she said. "But I believe I'll be hanging up my dancing shoes after tonight. Should you find yourself in need of a stage manager, however . . ."

Em shot her a quizzical look, but before she could speak, Old Jake appeared out of the crush of people and slipped a champagne bottle into her hand, along with three glasses. "The party's moving to Annabelle's," he said, and melted back into the crowd.

Em turned to Ziegfeld. "We'd be delighted to have you join us, Mr. Ziegfeld."

"I appreciate the invitation. Truly. But I am meeting Anna at Del's after her show. I do hope you understand."

When he said his good-byes and was gone, Em turned back to Pepper. "What's this about hanging up your dancing shoes? You killed out there."

Pepper smiled. She had done a fine job, better than she had expected. But the truth was, the moments she was in the lights, her thoughts were still backstage. If she had been back there, she could have made sure the dogs were out on the boards on time, and not two beats late, as Matty had done. And she would have caught the awkward tuck of Alfred's coat in his trousers before he sashayed out onstage.

Her feelings surprised even her. The golden moment she had craved, when the spotlight was on her and she was not afraid, had still felt empty. Lonely. It was not like the wings, where she was needed. Where she belonged.

She hugged Em quickly. "I have to go. I'll catch up with you at Annabelle's."

Em seemed to understand. "All right, doll. But do come. You've worked too hard not to celebrate."

She smiled, but she could not tell Em she did not feel much like celebrating. She could only think of Gregory. She knew it was not her imagination—he was avoiding her and she knew why.

She found him in the prop room, huddled with Old Jake, Laszlo, and Matty. She held back, not wanting to intrude. When he saw her, he did not smile. His face told her nothing as the others hurried their good-byes.

"I've been looking everywhere for you," she said when they were alone.

"I was telling them I paid a visit to the stage employees' union office yesterday. They're all expected down there Monday morning. Told them to cite me as a reference. I'll vouch for them."

"Will they get work?"

"Sure. They're as good as they come. They'll get work."

She was glad to hear it, but it was still difficult to accept that they were all parting ways. But that was not what she had come to discuss. She wandered to a shelf of prop clocks. Reached out and spun the brass hour hand of one from six to twelve.

"About this afternoon," he began.

She turned. His sadness nearly broke her heart. "Don't, Gregory. I was terrible. I know I was, and I'm sorry."

"I should have told you about my father." He rubbed his forehead, as if the thought of the man pained him. "He was not a good man, Pepper. He took up with a gang and he drank. People say he killed a man over a wager. I was young when it happened. Only five, but old enough to remember. I thought it would be better when he left, but my ma had no one. She drank, and it got so bad that when she looked at me, she only saw my father. She told me I was just like him. Then she stopped looking at me altogether. That's when she sent me to my uncle; it's why I came here. I never saw my father after he was convicted. Robert says he's still in the Tombs, but I don't know. He might be dead. He's probably dead." He slumped against the prop shelves, his gaze locked on the floor.

This was the darkness that enveloped him, she could see that now. This secret had become so much a part of him, as much as the callused fingers and the soft, dark eyes that had now turned from her. She put her hand on his arm.

"You are not your father," she whispered, and took his hand in hers.

He pulled away. "But I am. There's violence in me. I know it, I feel it. One day I might not be able to control it."

Pepper went to him again. She could see the pain on his face, the fear. "That isn't true. Even today. You did not harm Robert, even when he goaded you. You did control it."

His gaze moved to the ceiling. "I know it was wrong not to tell you. I just couldn't stand the thought of . . ." He paused. "It doesn't matter. Now you know, and it's probably best that we leave it at that. You should steer clear of me. There was a reason my mother didn't want me around."

She pressed herself to him and lifted her eyes to meet his gaze. "Pardon me for saying so, but your mother did not know you as I know you. You were with her for, what, seven years? I've known you more than twice that. I know you would never hurt anyone."

"But you must be afraid of me."

In his eyes, she could see that was his fear. "No, Gregory Creighton, I am not afraid of you."

The words were hardly out when he folded her in his embrace and kissed her, a tender kiss that was sweet and long. When he pulled away, she wiped away the wetness that had spilled from her eyes, and saw him do the same. They smiled at each other.

"We should join the others, don't you think?" His voice was rough and thick with emotion.

"Let's celebrate our own way. Just the two of us."

Seventeen

THE NEXT MORNING, AFTER SEVERAL LOUD AND prolonged raps, Em finally answered her door. "Come in already." Dressed in a man's striped silk pajamas with matching robe and a sleep mask hiked up over one eye, she pulled Pepper and Gregory into her foyer. "Tell me the theater hasn't burned to the ground. Wait. It's Robert DeGraaf's now. Or maybe Beefy Keith's. So, who cares? Don't make me guess. Spill it, why are you pounding on my door at dawn?"

Gregory took his cap in his hands. He wanted to do this right. "Sorry to wake you, Miss Charmaigne, it's just that we didn't want to wait—"

Pepper shifted and fidgeted at his side. "We want to get married," she blurted.

Gregory put his arm around her, in comfort and a bit

of constraint. "But only if you'll give us your blessing. You're the closest Pepper has to family. . . ."

Em pulled off her sleep mask and rewrapped her pajama robe. It was rare for her to be caught off guard, but she appeared to be now. "I suppose that explains why neither of you showed up at Annabelle's last night."

Gregory glanced away. He could feel the burn that told him he was turning at least a hundred shades of crimson. "Last night," he explained, "or this morning rather, Pepper did me the honor of saying she would be my wife."

"Wife?" Em took her head in her hands. "This is too much so early in the morning. Edda! Where are you, Edda?"

The husky Nordic woman trundled out in a robe. "Yes, mum?"

"A pot of tea, if you please, and make it strong, will you? I'm going to need it."

With another "Yes, mum," the woman disappeared behind the kitchen door.

"Come into the parlor. I want to be sure I have this straight."

Em dropped into an armchair and motioned for them to take the couch. "So, you're to be married?"

"Yes, ma'am," Gregory said, taking a place beside Pepper and trying his best to sit straight and proper. "With your permission."

"How can you manage it?" Em leaned back and kicked her heels up on a table. "Didn't we all lose our jobs last week?"

"I've taken a position with Edison Studios." His fingers wrestled in his lap. "Started last week. It's a good job. A solid job. And I have plans. I'm learning to work a moving picture camera. I've recently come into possession of one." That was enough. He did not need to explain that he had gotten that camera by assuming Ned Harvey's debt, and that he had also made the man promise to close the Automatic Vaudeville parlor beside The Chance. Of course, that was when he still cared about The Chance. It hardly mattered now.

"You have a moving picture camera?" Pepper looked up, surprised.

He took her hand in his. "I know how you feel about them, but you must see that animated photographs are not going away. And it's not just street views and silly things. You can tell a whole story in a flicker, sometimes better than you can on a stage. You should see what they can do."

"Flickers will never be vaudeville," Pepper said, but she was thinking of the hours she had spent in that parlor looking through those viewers. She had been surprised by how captivating those images were. They had lacked something, yes, but if there had been sound. . . . Perhaps in a theater with music or actors speaking the lines.

"Can we get back to this wedding business?" Em said. "You know you don't need my permission. It's entirely Pepper's decision. Is this what you want?"

Pepper took Gregory's hand. "More than anything."

"Then let me just say this: Why the rush? You could marry now and scrape by. But if you take a year, save your wages, and then when you have a good foundation, then we could have a grand wedding."

Gregory looked at Pepper. "I would wait, if that's what you want."

"I don't care about a grand wedding," Pepper said. "I only care that we're together. I did not like being apart, and I certainly don't want to be apart for a year."

Gregory tried to be more practical. "We wouldn't really be apart. And it would only be for a short time. I want to do this right."

There was another knock on the door.

"Oh, for the love of God. What is this, Grand Central?" Em rose and went to the door as her maid brought in the tray of tea. Pepper and Gregory were helping themselves when they heard Matty.

"I've been looking everywhere for you, Miss MacClair." Gasping, the boy handed her a sealed envelope, then pulled his cap from his head and wiped his face. "This came to the theater. The messenger made a big racket nailing it to the Lair's door. It has your name on it."

"What is it?"

She stared at it in her hand.

"I didn't open it," he said. "Thought it was probably important, though."

She broke the seal and read. It was a letter requesting her presence at the reading of Mr. DeGraaf's last will and testament at the offices of a Mr. Jonathan J. Peabody, with an address on East Seventh Street.

When she had read it again to be sure, she looked up. "I believe Robert DeGraaf wants to have the last word."

• • •

MONDAY MORNING WAS UNUSUALLY SUNNY AND NOT AT ALL suitable to Pepper's grim mood as she set off from the theater in full mourning attire for Mr. Peabody's office.

She glared at the indecently cheerful sky and kicked a crumpled newspaper that had drifted into her path. "Where's a rainstorm when you need one?"

"Careful what you wish for," Gregory said, and pulled her closer. He had extended his leave from Edison Studios until the business with Robert DeGraaf could be finished once and for all. "You never know when you just might get it. That's how you ended up with me, isn't it?"

She batted him away, but she was smiling.

"Consider it a nice day for a stroll," Em offered, twirling her walking stick at her side.

"Then I would prefer a turn around Union Square Park."

Gregory took her hand. "It'll be over soon enough."

Pepper squeezed his hand. "At least you'll both be there. I couldn't do this alone."

"Sure you could, doll. But I for one will feel better if we outnumber that little bastard Robert DeGraaf."

The walk was an easy one, down Eighth to Fourth Avenue and then a hook onto Seventh. They found Mr. Peabody's shingle hanging over a small door a few steps past the Old House at Home tavern. It pointed up a flight of stairs. On the second floor, they found the offices of Jonathan J. Peabody, Attorney at Law. Pepper turned the knob and made a small bell chime.

Inside, the wood-paneled lobby looked like a gentleman's club with a lighted fireplace flanked by four leather armchairs. The door chimed again as Pepper closed it, and a thin man with a silver shock of hair and a goatee appeared in a doorway to a corridor on the far side of the room.

"Miss MacClair?" the man inquired.

Pepper raised her hand. "Yes, I am she. These are my . . . This is my family."

"I see," he said, without regard or interest. "If you would be so kind as to follow me."

The man led them down a passageway to a room anchored by

a large round table and a wide window that overlooked Seventh. Around the table sat Gertie Walters in a black percale shirtwaist suit and veil, Robert, and the three men she recognized from his visit to the theater.

"Good day, Miss Walters, Mr. DeGraaf," she said with a curt nod to each and gave Gregory's hand a squeeze before letting it go.

Gertie nodded.

Robert gave no reply, but leaned to his nearest colleagues and said loudly enough for everyone to hear, "I still do not see why she is here."

Mr. Peabody, who was gathering papers from his desk, answered the question. "As I said before, Mr. DeGraaf. It is a stipulation of the will."

Robert glared at her from across the room, but if he had hoped to intimidate her with that stare, it was having the opposite effect. It gave her strength. The knowledge that her presence caused him distress and discomfort had already made the trip worthwhile.

"I shall bring this meeting to an official open, on this twenty-ninth of April of the year nineteen hundred ought-seven. To begin, I state for the record that this is the last will and testament of Mr. James Perseus DeGraaf, signed on the twenty-fifth of January of the year nineteen hundred ought-six."

And after reading through the usual preamble, Mr. Peabody enumerated the provisions.

"First, I direct that all my just debts and funeral expenses be paid and discharged.

"Second, I will and bequeath to Miss Gertie Walters one thousand dollars, with a subsequent five hundred dollars a year every year for the rest of her life.

"Third, I will and bequeath to Miss Pepper MacClair, who resides within The Chance Theatre, the sum of eight hundred dollars, in repayment for a loan received from Mrs. Bessie MacClair on the fifth of September of the year nineteen hundred ought-four."

Pepper clutched at Gregory's hand. Was this true? Had Mr. DeGraaf left her an inheritance?

But Mr. Peabody was still speaking.

"Fourth, I will and bequeath to my beloved son, Robert Henry DeGraaf, all my property belonging to me at my death, both real and personal or mixed wherever situated, including bonds valued in the neighborhood of fifty thousand dollars."

"An abomination," Gertie mumbled under her breath. And something undecipherable about shame.

Robert paid no attention to the old woman. He rocked back in his chair and exhaled what seemed a long-held breath. He adjusted his black silk cravat and smiled broadly at Pepper, then pulled a cigar from his lapel. "Very good, Peabody. When—"

"Excuse me, sir," Mr. Peabody interrupted and pulled another document from the stack before him. "Your father attached a codicil to the will on the eighteenth of April of this year."

Robert pulled the cigar from his mouth and sat forward. "A what?"

"An amendment, sir. Shall I continue?"

"Yes, of course." Robert finished the lighting of his cigar and leaned back.

"The aforesaid amendment provides for the reassignment of a portion of the estate, specifically that relating to The Chance Theatre."

Pepper sat forward.

Robert frowned. "What do you mean 'reassignment'?"

Mr. Peabody responded coolly, "It shall be explained. May I continue?"

Robert answered with a curt flip of his hand. He settled back against the leather cushion and draped one leg over the other.

The man continued to read: "All parts of the last will and testament shall remain in force, with the exceptions noted forthwith: First: I will and bequeath the theater in its entirety, including its property, operations, and all associated business dealings, to Miss Pepper MacClair, current resident of the aforesaid premises."

There was a simultaneous gasp from around the table.

Mr. Peabody continued undisturbed. "Second: All just debts shall be paid in full prior to the aforesaid transfer, including all incurred wages and taxes, and shall be completed within one month of the date of this reading. And third: An endowment of ten thousand dollars shall be arranged for the theater's future operations and shall be accessible through the will's executor, Mr. Jonathan J. Peabody, to Miss MacClair alone."

"Impossible!" Robert was standing when his fist slammed upon the table. "I will not allow this."

A distinct chuckle rose from beneath Gertie's black veil.

The attorney closed the file and said to Robert, "I understand your disappointment, Mr. DeGraaf, but I assure you, these are your father's wishes."

"He wasn't in his right mind. He was sick. Perhaps she even planted this outrageous business in his mind. It will not stand."

Mr. Peabody looked dispassionate. "Then am I to understand you intend to appeal this will?" he asked.

"Yes, absolutely. And at the soonest possible moment."

"I see." The attorney opened the folder again and searched through the pages. He pulled forth another sheet. "If that is the case, there is one more stipulation your father included in his amendment. He has stated that if there is any contention from another beneficiary . . ." He glanced up over the rim of his spectacles and regarded Robert. "That would be you, sir." He then resumed reading. "If there is any contention or delay in the transfer of property to Miss MacClair, it shall alter the distribution of the estate to provide for all save Miss Walters's portion to be passed to Miss MacClair."

"You must be joking," Robert railed.

"I assure you I am not, sir." The attorney settled back in his chair and regarded Robert with weary apathy. "And I must caution you. I believe, should your lawyers look into the matter, you will find you stand to lose far more than you might gain."

"She deserves nothing."

"Your father was of a different opinion." He pulled a sealed letter from the folder and handed it across the table to Pepper. "He asked that this be given directly to you."

Pepper had been unable to say anything until now. "The Chance, the endowment, all of it, are you sure?"

"Quite." The attorney lowered his gaze. "I understand this must come as a shock. Perhaps the letter will better explain."

"Yes, let's hear it," Robert demanded.

"Miss MacClair," Mr. Peabody said, "you may consider this a private matter and perhaps now is not the time."

"Yes, thank you. But I prefer you read it. We have no secrets." She squeezed Gregory's hand again.

"As you wish," the attorney said. He unsealed the letter, cleared his throat and read:

"Miss MacClair, let me begin by admitting I have done you a disservice. I allowed you to believe my protest between you and my son was for the reason that I did not want him involved with you. That was not my concern. In fact, it was quite the opposite. I already knew he would prove less than you hoped of him. I, in my clumsy way, had hoped to protect you and it only resulted in increasing your pain. For this, I am sorry.

"But my greater transgression is this: While you may believe this inheritance is a gift, I assure you it is not. You see, your mother, may she rest in peace, was once a savior to this theater. The occasion was shortly after your first performance, and she was concerned for you, I'm afraid. You were distraught and beyond condolence, and your mother implored me never to allow you to return to the stage. She meant only to protect you from further pain. That afternoon she presented me with a sewing basket filled with what I can only assume to be her life's savings. I should have told her that first performances, as a rule, tend to turn out badly. I should have told her to keep her savings, but the truth is that she had caught me at a delicate time. The bank was threatening to call in a debt I had no means to repay. In short, I accepted her money. I offered her a stake in the theater, but she refused it. She wanted only two things from me. A promise that I provide for you. And a promise that I never speak to anyone of this arrangement. Not to you, Miss MacClair, nor to anyone. I'm ashamed now to admit I eagerly pledged both.

"I have regretted this bargain, but as long as your mother was alive, I was duty bound to uphold it. After she passed, I told Stanley to allow you to return to the stage, if that was your wish. I was also determined to give you the stake your mother had refused. It was the fair thing to do, since you have never been a burden in any way, but have always proved a benefit to this theater. I dallied on that score, however, and in hindsight, I am glad I did, for I have had a change of heart. I had always hoped that Robert would grow into a proper steward for the theater, but I now know the boy has no love for it. In you, however, I see the glimmer of what I had hoped to see in him. In you, I see a future for my Chance, a stubbornness to push through difficult times and a love for the place that may rival my own. I hope with all my heart, my dear, that you will accept it."

Pepper could hardly breathe.

She stared blankly at Mr. Peabody, then at Gregory and Em. "But what does it mean?"

Gregory appeared as unnerved as Pepper, but Em could not keep the grin off her face. "Doll, it means you're the new boss."

• • •

LATER THAT AFTERNOON, EM AND PEPPER SAT IN THE brownstone's parlor sipping tea, while Gregory went to tell whoever was left at The Chance about the change of plans. Em seemed to know that Pepper did not need rest, as she had professed to Gregory. The woman knew that something else was holding Pepper back.

"What's troubling you, doll?" she asked when he was gone.

Pepper went to the cabinet of curios. She ran her fingers over the glass. "Did you know what she had done?"

Em pulled a cigar from her pocket and chewed the end. "No, but I suspected."

The betrayal cut just as deep. "You should have told me."

"I meant to."

Her voice lacked the usual spirit. There was pain there.

"I always meant to," Em continued. "But there was always a reason not to. I suppose I was trying to protect Bessie. I didn't think it was right, what she did. I never believed it was necessary. But then, she believed all your despair stemmed from that performance. She never dreamed it could be something else."

"You did?" Pepper had believed herself so clever in masking her pain. Had Em seen through her even then?

"I could see how you looked at him. I saw you stealing away to be with him. I figured it was only a matter of time. And then, when he left so abruptly the day before you danced for the first time, yes, I suspected. But I never breathed a word to Bessie. For her sake as much as yours. She already carried so much guilt about the life she had subjected you to."

"Subjected me to?"

"That was how she saw it. She believed she failed you."

All this time, Pepper had believed she had been the failure. That she had been the disappointment. Could she have been so blind?

"After you debuted, when Bessie saw how hard it was for you, she only wanted to protect you from ever facing that again."

It made sense now. Her mother had not shipped their savings to a faraway family. She had used it to ensure Pepper's future, and had done so in a way even she could not have imagined.

There was one question left, though, and Pepper found she could not look Em in the eye when she asked it. She stared into the cabinet's glass.

"Will you go with me to her grave?"

• • •

THE FERRY RIDE WAS A CHOPPY ONE. PEPPER STOOD AT THE stern and watched as the Grand Street dock came into view. Once they disembarked, it took only minutes to hire a cab to take them inland to the New Calvary Cemetery.

Pepper was glad that Em had accompanied her. She had returned to the grave site frequently and knew the quickest path to Bessie MacClair's stone.

When they arrived, they purchased tiger lilies from a seller at the gate and made their way inside.

They passed a man with a brood of young children huddled around a fresh grave, and a woman sitting quietly beside another. Otherwise they seemed to be alone in this vast expanse of rolling hills, just them and the dead.

When they reached the spot, on a gentle slope facing west, toward her Scottish home, Pepper saw a nearly fresh bouquet already alongside the stone. Em's flowers, she knew. She set her own beside the marker.

"I'm going to take a stroll."

She knew Em wanted to give her privacy, and she appreciated it. She knew what she wanted to say, so it would not take long.

"Mother," she said, when Em was a safe distance away. "I know I should have come earlier and I'm sorry for that." Everything she wanted to say, all the pretty words she had planned so carefully dissolved into the early-afternoon sunlight. Only the lump in her throat remained. "I was wrong," she blurted. "That's what I want to say. I've been wrong about so many things, and I was mostly wrong about you. I thought you did not care, I thought I disappointed you. I'm sure I did disappoint you, but . . ."

It was impossible to keep back the tears. She swiped them away, but fresh ones replaced them just as quickly.

"Mr. DeGraaf gave me the theater today. Can you believe it? I'm going to run it. I don't know how exactly, but I want to do it. Mother, I don't think I've ever wanted anything more." She stopped and caught her breath. "Em told me something. She said it distressed you that you had raised me in the theater, that you felt I had missed something. I want you to know I do not feel that I have missed anything. In fact, it was the greatest gift you could have given me. The Chance is a wonderful place to belong. I just wanted you to know."

Pepper did not know that Em had returned and was standing behind her, silently, until she heard her voice. "I'm sure she knows, doll," Em said. "She only wanted you to be happy. It was all she ever wanted."

• • •

FOR THE REST OF THE AFTERNOON, PEPPER COULD NOT HELP but feel that the world had been wearing black and had now cast it off. As if the tethers that had pulled her down were released, and she was free. And for the first time in a long time, she was truly happy.

When Em and Pepper returned to the townhouse, Gregory was inside, waiting for them.

"Edda let me in," he said, his cap in his hand. "Everyone is awfully anxious to see you, Pepper. They're asking about you."

To Em, she said, "I should probably go. But I'll be back later, if that's all right."

"Take all the time you need. I'll be here. I'm always here, doll."

They embraced, long enough for Pepper to whisper another "Thank you," and then she and Gregory stepped out and made their way toward Broadway under the warm afternoon sun. The trees were full and green, and as they walked, Pepper noticed all the window boxes of daisies and daffodils, posies and tulips, a whole spectrum of color brightening the street.

"So much has changed," Gregory said. With his hands in his pockets, he seemed to speak to the breeze.

"It has."

"Has it changed things between us?"

She glanced up at him as they turned the corner onto Broadway and passed a newsboy hollering the headlines to passing pedestrians. In the creases around Gregory's eyes, she saw his questions. And his concerns. She pulled one of his hands from its pocket and brought it to her lips. "Not for me."

He seemed to breathe easier. "What do you intend to do about the theater?"

"That does change our plans, doesn't it?"

She had hoped to lighten the mood with the casual comment, but Gregory's jaw remained firm.

"I suppose it'll require a bit of thought," she said, more earnestly. "I don't intend to leave, though, and if it can be managed, I think I'd like to restore the old residence."

"I don't like the idea of you living down there alone."

"Good," she said, "because I was rather hoping you might like to live there, too."

At last, a hint of a smile played on his lips. "That might be arranged. After proper nuptials, of course. I would not want people getting the wrong idea about me."

She nodded. "Of course. We want to be sure that sterling reputation of yours remains intact."

"And after that?"

"Perhaps I'll get in touch with that *Variety* fellow. I believe I might have a story that could be of interest to him."

"Ziegfeld won't like the idea of competition from his own protégé."

They passed the kinetoscope parlor's window. It was locked up tight when Pepper glanced in. "I could hardly compete with Mr. Ziegfeld. I wouldn't even try. But maybe it's time to do something new. We could start slowly. Put a flicker on the bill, with a bit of music, put the players to work speaking the parts or narrating behind the screen."

"Flickers, huh?"

"Yes, flickers. You see, I might have a connection in Edison's studios. And I hear these moving pictures might not be so bad. They're not vaudeville, of course. But they may have other merits."

"So there might be room for them in the old *Stars, Marvels and Delights*?"

"Not the old show, no. But perhaps a new one."

They stopped in front of the theater. The marquee still announced *The Utterly Unauthorized and Entirely Unofficial Last Chance Show.*

She glanced up. "I suppose that will have to change."

"Of course it will. It should read *Miss MacClair Presents.*"

"That would hardly be appropriate," she scoffed. She turned to him and wrapped her arms around his neck. "Considering that with any luck I shall be Mrs. Gregory Creighton by morning."

A HISTORICAL NOTE

Did Florenz Ziegfeld, Jr., entangle himself in the business of a vaudeville venue in New York called The Chance Theatre? No. The theater, like the characters associated with it, is fictional, although it was inspired by many of the small and struggling theaters that populated the city at the turn of the last century.

That entanglement aside, I tried to preserve the details of Ziegfeld's life and work as much as possible. During the spring of 1907, when the bulk of this narrative takes place, Ziegfeld's wife, Anna Held, was starring in his hit production of *A Parisian Model* at The Broadway and he would have been making preparations for his inaugural *Follies*, which in its first outing was titled *Follies of 1907*.

And while history records no evidence of the famous impresario ever intending to debut his landmark *Follies* anywhere but the New York Theatre Roof, a venue that was renovated and renamed Jardin de Paris for the occasion, there is ample evidence to suggest Ziegfeld's relationship with the men who controlled that venue, Marc Klaw and Abraham L. Erlanger, would have been troubled. The Klaw & Erlanger partnership, and Abe Erlanger in particular, had a reputation for hostile business dealings, which earned the distrust, if not outright dislike, of colleagues and the industry at large.

Klaw and Erlanger were by no means alone in that regard.

Theater owner Benjamin F. Keith and his partner, Edward F. Albee, as well as many others, regularly engaged in ruthless tactics to achieve and maintain power in an industry that was facing increasing competition from other theaters, as well as from the burgeoning moving picture industry. Keith, Albee, and many of their peers sought to protect their interests by forming alliances that allowed them to limit the earnings of performers appearing on their stages, as well as those performers' ability to work elsewhere.

In the writing of this novel, I also took the liberty of placing pioneer moviemaker Edwin S. Porter on a Broadway sidewalk for the purpose of shooting a street scene. It might have happened, but it was far more likely he was devoting his time to the creation of story films at Edison's rooftop studio on East Twenty-first Street and to the building of the company's newer facility in the Bronx.

Finally, I would like to mention that while I invented the banquet where Erlanger and Klaw were expected to announce a partnership with their longtime rivals Jacob and Lee Shubert, such a partnership was in the works and resulted in the United States Amusement Company, a corporation dedicated to building and operating a national circuit of vaudeville theaters. That merger proved to be short-lived, however. The *New York Times* announced its dissolution on July 16, 1909.

I relied on many books, interviews and online resources to research this story, but the books listed below were among the most influential and may be of interest to readers seeking more information on vaudeville, early cinema, and New York at the turn of the last century.

No Applause—Just Throw Money: The Book That Made Vaudeville Famous (Faber & Faber, 2006), by Trav S.D.

Ziegfeld: The Man Who Invented Show Business (St. Martin's Press, 2008), by Ethan Mordden.

Rank Ladies: Gender and Cultural Hierarchy in American Vaudeville (The University of North Carolina Press, 1999), by M. Alison Kibler.

The Emergence of Cinema: The American Screen to 1907 (University of California Press, 1994), by Charles Musser.

Old New York in Early Photographs: 1853–1901 (Dover Publications, 1973), by Mary Black.

New York Life at the Turn of the Century in Photographs (Dover Publications, 1985), by Joseph Byron.

For additional background information, please visit: www.DeAnnaCameron.com or http://DeAnnaCameron.blogspot.com.